PENGUIN BOOKS

1670

EATING PEOPLE IS WRONG

MALCOLM BRADBURY

MALCOLM BRADBURY

Eating People is Wrong

*

What men or gods are these? What maidens loth?
What mad pursuit? What struggle to escape?
What pipes and timbrels? What wild ecstasy?

*

PENGUIN BOOKS

Penguin Books Ltd, Harmondsworth, Middlesex
AUSTRALIA: Penguin Books Pty Ltd, 762 Whitehorse Road,
Mitcham, Victoria

—

First published by Secker and Warburg 1959
Published in Penguin Books 1962

—

Copyright © Malcolm Bradbury, 1959

—

Made and printed in Great Britain
by C. Nicholls & Company Ltd

To my Mother and Father

With acknowledgements to
Michael Flanders and Donald Swann,
originators of the song *The Reluctant Cannibal*
from which the title of this novel
is taken.

Do I say man is not made for an active life? Far from it. But there is a great difference between other men's occupations and ours. A glance at theirs will make it clear to you. All day long they do nothing but calculate, contrive, consult how to wring profit out of foodstuffs, farms, and the like. But I entreat you to understand what the administration and nature of the world is, and what place a being endowed with reason holds in it; to consider what you are as a person, and in what your good and evil consists.

EPICTETUS

CHAPTER ONE

I

TERM had just begun. Professor Treece, head of the department of English, sat at his desk, his back to the window, with the cold, clear October light shining icily over his shoulders on to the turbulent heaps of papers upon his desk, on to the pale young faces of his three new students. As the rain rattled against the panes behind him, and the students stared speculatively out at the last leaves falling damply from the trees, Professor Treece spoke sonorously. His comments were academic and solid. To speak in this mode had meant, over the last years, a certain settling down, a certain closing in of interests, a certain assumption of weighty mannerisms. It was not that he had ever been what was called, disparagingly, in the Senior Common Room 'a bohemian', or 'a bit of a wild man'; if he had affectations, they were all permissible ones. The matter of it was really that for this appointment he was a very young man. Not too many years behind him were the wet and lonely days of post-graduate research, which persisted for him in the image of walking, with a briefcase full of books, among cold Bloomsbury houses, near the British Museum, breathing in the odour of the Underground Railway and of teashops that smelled always of weak tea. He had been born during the First World War and had, as he sometimes put it, just missed seeing the old England. Believing himself essentially hostile to the ambitious, expansive England of the years before his birth, he had in fact in full measure all the native nostalgia for it. He felt now essentially *passé*; generations, it seemed to him, don't last very long nowadays. His generation was the one between the wars; the thirties were his stamping ground, and his predominant emotion was a puzzled frustration in the face of the fact that all the passions he had held then almost but not quite fitted the situation of the present time. The middle fifties kept dissolving, curiously, under his grasp. He was constantly in speculation as to what he might really catch hold of ; life now was full of traps. Thus his political affiliation was socialist, but the socialist party never seemed to be on about the right things nowadays, and, further, it was curiously hard to determine what the right things were. The whole quality of injustice had changed now. Prime Ministers said, 'You've never had it so good'; but intellectuals, surely, had never had it so bad. Where were things? People got angry but there didn't seem to be anything to be angry about ; perhaps that was why they were angry. It was as if his motive power, his sense of identification with the advancing movement of the world, had run short. Living in the provinces intensified the feeling. New terms and new students did not depress or excite him; he was hardly conscious of the renewing of the seasons. A routine was now established; he had been at the university long enough to know what to expect, not to demand too much.

This tutorial, the first of the new academic year, had already assumed a characteristic tone of embarrassment and uncertainty. Learning lay heavily in the air like pipe-smoke. Treece leapt up jerkily from time to time to pull books suddenly from off their shelves, and it was like throwing stones into a pool; the students jumped visibly in their seats, as if they expected to be attacked. The cold light shone on the pupils of their eyes. Students (it was at Oxford and Cambridge that one called them undergraduates) were not at all cast in the heroic mould when it came to the study of literature; they plodded along the towpath like barge horses. And, for the teacher, the desire to mould the great spirit, along with the search to lead one's own life on the heroic level, was soon defeated by the pressures of a heavy routine. Thus these three sat before him, the usual unpromising examination material which three years of tuition and, more importantly, self-discipline, concentration, good influences, would bring to degree level – gauche youths, shuffling their feet, opening and shutting their new briefcases, noting down with ostentation the not-always-valuable points, turning red when spoken to, propounding the too-glib possibility ('Wouldn't you say that was because of the influence of Marlowe?'), furtively inspecting their new watches to see how much longer this was going to continue. You couldn't help wondering about their sex-life; did they like it, would they get it, what would they do with it? It was with thoughts like these that Treece gave an extra-mural gloss to the academic man. That the place of knowledge was with experience he had no doubt, and the endeavour to attain to the former when one had so little access to the latter always seemed to Treece a hopeless and foolhardy proposition.

Cumulo-nimbus stacked up outside; Treece always associated it with the provinces. Three weakly marigolds stood in a jar on his desk. Treece peered over the top of them and spoke on. He was saying nothing very interesting and no one was saying anything very interesting back. He had become disabused with his own sparks of passion. It was difficult to engage, in the issues he felt to be interesting, students who didn't even buy books, who didn't read the books they were invited to read, who had a scanty grasp of the contemporary or any other scene, who were unacquainted with the principles of logic and straight thinking. 'Mind, a wasp,' said one of them, pointing at a seedy-looking, tired wasp that was making forays at Treece from a refuge in the marigolds. It was as if their eyes sought out and fixed on objects as an antidote to Treece's abstractions; their gaze flitted emptily about the air and focused on wasps, raindrops coursing down the pane, the decorated spines of books in the bookcase. And as, with the clearer formulation in his mind of the impressions gained from passing glances, the students each began to assume their own individuality, it became obvious to Treece that two of them at least were persons for whom statements about creativity meant exactly nothing. They were youths straight from some grammar school sixth-form, rejects of Oxford, Cambridge, and the better provincial universities, whose course could be charted easily enough; one could name almost the haphazard collection of books that they would read, one could sketch out beforehand the essays they would write, indicate simply their primary values. They appeared each year, to eat for three more years in the university refectory, to join sports clubs, and attend the students' union dances held each Saturday night, sliding gracelessly through weekly waltzes and tangos, drinking down beer at the impromptu bar, tempting girls out into the grounds in order to kiss them on damp benches; to throw tomatoes at policemen on three successive rag days, to go out in three years with perhaps as many girl friends, and finally to leave with a lower second or third class degree, passing on into teaching or business seemingly untouched by what, Treece thought, the university stood for – whatever that was. Each year he wondered, is it worth it? Each year he planned to send out into the world, at last, a little group of discontented men who would share his own disgusts, his own firm assurance in the necessity for good taste, honest feeling, integrity of motive; and each year the proposition came to seem odious as he foresaw the profound weariness and depression of spirit that would overcome such people when, with too few vacancies in the faculties of universities, they would find themselves teaching in grammar schools in Liverpool or working in the advertising department of soap factories in Newcastle. The trouble with me is, Treece thought, that I'm a liberal humanist who believes in original sin. I think of man as a noble creature who has only to extend himself to the full range of his powers to be civilized and good; yet his performance by and large has been intrinsically evil and could be more so as the extension continues.

At this point Treece began, covertly, to inspect the third member of the tutorial group. He came as a slight shock of surprise. Unlike the others, he was not a youth and clearly had not come straight from school. He had an extremely large head, moulded in great pocks and cavities and formed on, it seemed, almost prehistoric, pterodactylian lines. The front of his pate was bald, but, starting in line with his ears, a great fan of unkempt black hair stood up; from out of large, eroded eye-sockets, black shining eyes fixed Treece with a wet look that besought attention and interest. 'Who?' wondered Treece, pausing in his discourse. He had forgotten the man's name and wondered whether he should, in fact, be here at all; he looked the sort of man who might have been passing the door and, seeing a tutorial about to start, had decided to participate. One could tell that he wanted to *know*. He was folded up tightly in a chair too small for him, but he held his head up high, fearless and brave, careless of the shoddy little receptacle that held him. The holes in his pullover disclosed a shirt with a pattern of heavy stripes. 'Well, now,' he kept saying judicially from time to time; occasionally he nodded his head with slow, approving motions. While he went on talking, Treece furtively consulted the pile of application forms left handy in a folder on his desk. Among the passport photographs pinned to their corners, he noticed one where the face of this disconcerting man peered fearlessly out, as if he was ready to have this one published in *Time*; the heavy light from above and the inferior photography emphasized the large bone structure of the cranium and the shape of his excessively large, wet mouth. The man's name was Louis Bates, aged twenty-six. He had, the form revealed intriguingly, formerly been a teacher in a girls' school. Then followed a gap of some time during which he had not apparently been employed, but elsewhere on the form a bit of a hint was given to the nature of this pause; his experience, he said, included six months' library work in a mental hospital. Elsewhere, Bates had written, against the place marked *Interests*, in a large, European-style hand – 'My interests are what the ultra-democrat would call "highbrow" or "long-hair".' This was a curious mixture of the promising and the absurd. Treece, possessed, paused and looked again at Bates. The moment of interest was, it appeared, all that Bates had been waiting for for the last three-quarters of an hour. 'Excuse,' he said, wetting his lips with his tongue.

Treece stopped, surprised. In a low, insistent, carefully modulated voice, Bates began to talk, taking quick advantage of the lull. 'What do you mean, precisely, by organic?' he demanded, taking up a point Treece had made a few moments before, and when Treece, a trifle disconcerted, did not answer immediately, he went on. 'Well, it's really no use our talking in the way we have been doing if the words we use mean something different to each of us ... and nothing', he added with a wet grin, 'to some of us. It's all very well using these coins, as long as we know what their value is, and agree on it. But do we?'

These near-impertinences drew looks of mingled consternation and amusement from the other two students. Treece looked a trifle uncomfortable, as if he had been invited to the wrong sort of party and had now been asked to sing. 'Yes,' he said, 'but is this let's-define-our-terms academicism really important at this early stage?'

'Well, I think it is,' said Bates, after considering this with a great appearance of sagacity.

'Do you?' said Treece. Generously, he felt, he granted the fact that Bates was simply trying to state a presence; I am here, was what this was all about, and, perhaps, I know all about logical positivism.

'Well, is this ever irrelevant? When Coleridge called any aspect of Shakespeare's work "organic", he knew what he meant, and he left enough references elsewhere to make it clear what he meant when he used the word. We don't. And in any case the word is debased currency, in my view, and has been ever since Coleridge. I mean, words are all very well, I grant you, and in the beginning was the word, which is to say that what thought is is articulation. Now it's true that a play by Shakespeare can be described as "organic", but if we consider that in, say, almost any one of the comedies, there is a large body of added matter that is, after all, apparently if not actually irrelevant to the main theme, the word doesn't mean all that much until we've narrowed it down and clarified it. What are words for? How are words true? I mean, we want to know, don't we?'

Of course Bates should have gone to Nottingham, where all the members of the English Department have read Wittgenstein, Treece thought; the truth is, Treece had to admit, that I don't want to get mixed up in this kind of thing. He said so. 'What seems of most value to us all just now is a discussion on a simple level, accepting simple meanings.'

'Well,' said Bates, 'let's see what the others think.' He looked about him. 'What do people feel?' he asked.

Immediately all was embarrassment. Feet were shuffled, faces reddened, useless notes were consulted diligently. No one spoke; then Bates, who seemed unconcerned by, or completely insensitive to, the confusion, remarked, 'Perhaps Mr Sykes will give us his opinion?' Mr Sykes desperately fastened and unfastened his briefcase. 'Mr Cocoran, then,' said Louis.

Treece heroically took command. 'The point must, I suppose, be a matter for some concern,' he said, 'but let's save it up for your literary criticism tutorials. Here it's rather a diversion than anything else.'

'Why?' asked Louis Bates.

Treece looked at him ominously.

'I mean, isn't it a matter wider than critical?'

'No,' said Treece. 'And so, I think, back to Shakespeare.'

'What happens when you cut off my head?' demanded Bates and Treece wondered for a moment if he had actually threatened this aloud. 'I'll tell you,' said Louis. 'I die.'

'I grant you,' said Treece.

'But if you merely cut off my feet,' went on Bates triumphantly, 'I live. Yet both are organic to me.'

'That's enough of that,' said Treece.

On the fringe of the hour, when the corridor outside echoed with the amplified sound of thunderous feet and barbarous whoopings, Professor Treece dismissed his tutorial. 'Good afternoon, Professor, thank you very much,' said Mr Sykes and Mr Cocoran, bumping into each other as they rose, wondering what sort of an impression they had made, and whether they had, perhaps, worn too bright a tie or shoes too fancily stitched. 'Thank you very much, Professor,' each repeated in turn, with little smiles, as they jammed side by side in the doorway.

Louis Bates, meanwhile, sat firm in his chair, openly enjoying the performance, waiting for the jerky mood of embarrassment to subside. Then when the door was closed again, when Treece had taken his place at his desk once more and looked up questioningly across his papers, Louis commenced to speak, explaining in his carefully modulated tones just why he expected special treatment. He said that he hoped that Treece would not mind his taking him to task on the matter of the word 'organic', but he believed that it lay in the true function of the university to promote that interplay of view, that discussion and dispute, that cumulative narrowing down of possibilities that led to the formation of accurate opinion. The student could be, as it were (he said), the rubbing-post for the thought of his teacher. Treece peered down at his desk and, picking up a pencil, drew great rotundities on a scrap of paper. Bates looked just the way a bassoon sounds – gruff, heavy-footed, pompous. Let this be a lesson to you (thought Treece) not to have children after you're forty; and with this came the uneasy recollection that he had only a year or so left. Him, Stuart Treece, forty! – why, he was just not built for it. Bates went on. He explained that he admired the tutorial atmosphere, though the resolute refusal of his colleagues to enrich discussion was a matter of some woe to him. He used that word – *woe* – right there in Treece's office, and Treece supposed that it was the first time the word had been used there, in the ordinary passage of conversation, in forty years; one had this perpetual whiff of the Victorian when one talked to Bates. Bates now said that Treece would appreciate that he, Bates, was somewhat different from – indeed, he said, somewhat apart from – the other students in the University and suggested that the difference was, in part, one of maturity and energy of intellect. He went on to announce that, if Treece was prepared to cooperate, he could quite easily get a first. This was, he said, not sheer bravado on his part; on the contrary, he had come to the decision on a strict and critical assessment of skills and deficiencies. He reiterated his comment about the maturity and poise of his attitudes, adding that, moreover, he knew a bit about these degree examinations and had come to the conclusion that it was little more than a question of effort. What was necessary, he said, was that Treece and he should work *together*. 'I must have someone to give my work *direction*,' he said. 'I see,' said Treece.

Bate's manner of speaking was quiet and firm and therefore somewhat impressive; Treece was affected. 'I happen to be a very good worker,' Bates went on, with what Treece could only define as a coy smile, speaking quietly in order to efface any suggestion of bravura. 'And there won't be any distractions. I'm not bothered with the social side, you see, and it's that, I think, that dissipates most people's time and effort. Much leisure is required to consolidate friendships, so I shall regard them as an indulgence to be infrequently sated. Actually, as it happens, you know, I don't exactly fit in here; I'm a lot older than the other students, and I come from a different social class, perhaps.'

'Oh, I don't know . . .' said Treece.

'Well,' said Louis brusquely, indicating that he intended to come from a different social class from the others whether Treece liked it or not. 'My father was a railwayman, and that was in the days when the railways were a form of puritanism. Hard work, honesty, thrift, clean living, self-restraint. Indulgence I'm suspicious of. I believe in application and self-training. I'm self-made. Now you have me in a nutshell.'

Treece had to grant it to Bates – self-made was exactly what he looked; he might have been the finished product of a physical do-it-yourself kit. 'Most of us are self-made,' said Treece, wondering as he said it whether this was precisely true. One of the depressing things about Bates, Treece was discovering, was a kind of hideous juxtaposition of taste and vulgarity, a native product for the self-made man. This is the way the world must end, Treece was beginning, these days, to think, in taste fragmenting and hanging on only in certain departments of the human soul. Fragmentary was clearly the right word for Bates; his spirit hung in tatters in the room before Treece, part good, part bad, and splendidly irreconcilable.

'And', Louis went on, 'I'm a poor man; I've no money to spend on amusements; it all goes on books, what there is of it. Don't misunderstand me and think I'm complaining; I'm not,' he cried, casting an intense, soulful look in Treece's direction, 'I'm merely explaining the conditions that I live under. I mean, these are my terms, and they're what I think will make me do well here. That's my aim and intention, of course; or, to put it better, that would represent a proper statement or fulfilment of myself as I judge myself to be, if you see what I mean. What I say is that there won't be anything – friendships or entertainments or affairs, you know, or anything like that – to stop me working.' He said all this very quickly, as though to gloss over its essentially confessional content and give it the aspect of objectivity. His tone was a mixture of dejection and . . . could it be pride?

Treece found himself growing nervous of an excess of self-exposure; some ingrained social *mœurs* was beginning to be offended. 'Well, it's as well to be aware of what one is about from the start,' he said dismissingly.

Bates seized on the comment as on a favour. 'Yes,' he said, 'it is, isn't it?' His assurance was far from shattered, however, and the unspoken contention that, in view of his hardy apprenticeship in a girls' school, they were equals of each other, returned into view. 'Actually,' he said, 'and I hope you can fit in on this, I don't think I'll be attending any lectures here, if you don't mind. I gather that that's an undergraduate privilege, and my reasons are very sound; my memory works visually rather than audially – you'll be familiar with the phenomenon. So of course lectures, however good they may be, don't register with me at all.'

'But it's a question of keeping up . . .' said Treece.

'Oh,' said Bates, 'I thought we'd settled that with our little treaty of cooperation.' He rose to go. 'And now,' he said, 'I've a few essays here that I've been doing which might clarify to you, if you've an odd moment, the actual nature of my powers . . .' and he added, with a smile deprecating, modest, yet with a hint of a snigger, as if he knew he was clever to put it in just this way '. . . and my deficiencies.'

When Louis Bates had gone, bowing his great head under the doorway, offering a last glimpse of trousers frayed at the bottom and of worn heels, Professor Treece felt as if he had, up to now, been living in a dream which had now exploded. He recognized Louis Bates as essentially a burden, a personal problem with whom he had to come to grips. What he saw – *had* to see – in Bates was man as essentially the buffoon, the creature who couldn't be taken seriously. He mirrored in himself all that was absurd; he postured, he strutted, he affected. Yet at the same time good sense and taste had to be granted to him. The whole problem was presented for Treece in the sheaf of essays which Treece now found himself reading. Instead of the usual freshman work, which called Pope, with error and not alas with subtlety, a Romantic, said his poetry was 'charming', and, if the author of the piece had found him, borrowed heavily from Dr Samuel Johnson on the evident supposition that Treece had not yet tapped this mine of critical opinion, Bates on Pope was not lacking in assurance. The essay was almost good enough for *Partisan Review*; if any other student had written it, Treece would have concluded that this was where he had got it from. But the Batesian mood was so firmly there that Treece had no doubts. He went on to another essay, which held that the main theme in English literature was 'the escape from reality into morality'; this, said the essay, was the reason for the contemporary decline in the novel, for the novelist of today lacked (he excepted E. M. Forster, 'our old figurehead', as he called him) the training in moral stature. Let us look to the Americans, moral pragmatists all, cried the last line of this manifesto. A third essay pleaded for a reconsideration of Shaw, because, in his work, morality ceases to be morality and becomes art. Treece, who was always hideously afraid that he was overlooking and mishandling some sort of genius, perhaps a sort that hadn't been discovered yet (genius and stupidity have so much in common that the problem bobbed up constantly), read on and grew increasingly nervous.

2

'Towns', Professor de Thule, head of the history department, used often to say (it was practically his one intellectual proposition), 'are the dynamic image of our selves as social entities'; to this Professor Treece used often wearily to reply, 'Obviously.' But what could one say of the provincial city in which the University stood? It was just bric-à-brac. Chaste up to the late eighteenth century, it had given itself to all comers during the industrial revolution. There were, indeed, parts of the town in which one felt a real sense of place; but most of the time one felt a sense of *anywhere*. Treece had amused himself over the few years he had lived there by trying, a little at a time, to unravel the little threads of puritanism, for to his London mind, provincialism and puritanism were the same thing. It was sheer Tawney; religion, and the rise of capitalism. Gradually the place for him began to emerge as an entity; he found he could say, in certain moods, in the new intellectual tradition, Why, I like it here. Though the eighteenth century was his period, and he found it attuned happily to his disposition, he found himself getting more and more a Betjemanesque *frisson* from Victoriana. As business and nonconformity boomed, the former market town had erected Victorian Gothic churches, a Victorian Gothic town hall, an Albert Hall for quiet concerts and methodist services, a temperance union hall, a mechanics institute, a prison, and a well-appointed lunatic asylum. 'Why doesn't Betjeman come and live *here*?' people asked when they saw the place. As for the University, which had still been a university college even when Treece was appointed to his chair, it was frequently mistaken for the railway station and was in fact closely modelled on St Pancras. The pile had, in fact, a curious history. When, in a riot of Victorian self-help, the town had finally decided that it wanted a university, it had provided it with all that vision, that capacity for making do, that *practicality* which had been the basis of the town's business success. Its founders had obtained its cloistered halls for next to nothing. The town lunatic asylum was proving too small to accommodate those unable to stand up to the rigours of the new world, and a larger building was planned. It was not big enough for an asylum, then; but it was big enough for a university college. So, as Treece frankly admitted, it became an asylum of another kind; great wits are thus to madness near allied. There were still bars over the windows; there was nowhere you could hang yourself. The place sat, with its red-brick spires and towers, with its Gothic slit windows and its battlements ('At least it's easily defended, if it should ever come to *that*,' said Professor de Thule practically) on Institution Road, between the reception centre and the geriatric hospital. If I retain an image of these Groves of Macadam when I am gone, thought Treece, it will be of old men in worn suits picking up cigarette ends in the forecourt. 'It's lucky we're all sophisticated,' Treece always told his visitors, 'or we shouldn't like it a bit.'

When Treece arrived at the University the next morning, the first person he saw in the main hall of the building was Louis Bates. The hall, which smelled noxiously of floor polish, was filled with 'freshers', trying to find out how to register. This was true, Treece observed, in both senses of the word: how the problem hovered in the air, do we establish terribly, terribly interesting university personalities for ourselves? '*Essen sie?*' someone asked near him, very affectedly. Most of the students were fat little girls, fresh from school and pubic-looking. Bates stood in a corner, looking like a renounced undertaker, talking to an evangelist from the Christian Union. 'I just want a straight answer, yes or no,' he was saying, 'is this a bounded, or boundless, universe?'

Treece went up to the Senior Common Room and bought himself a cup of coffee. He sat down in a chair and began to read *Encounter*, which as usual was full of articles about Japan. 'Do you know you can get twenty-five non-proprietary aspirins for fourpence at Boots'?' cried Dr Viola Masefield, who lectured in the department in Elizabethan drama, coming to the door. She delved in her shoulder bag, which was as big as a newsboy's satchel, for the little tickets that one bought coffee with. 'Isn't it a ramp?' Treece admired Viola's indignations. She was always full of protest about *ramps*, and overcharging, and overcrowding in houses, and lack of toilet facilities at the bus station: her principles were always directed against tangible objects, whereas Treece's, these days, could fix on nothing save unresolvable complexities. Viola had taken her degree at Leicester and then had come here; she didn't know anybody, and to her London was a big place where it was easy to get lost once you got away from the British Museum. Viola's reactions to problems and to people were violent and immediate, as Treece was well aware; people who met her for the first time sometimes used the word 'sophisticated' to describe her, because her manner was bright and when she smoked it was through a long jade holder, but those who knew her better were aware that this was the last word for Viola, for even simple female cunning of the type that's given to every sheltered country girl was missing in Viola's case; this itself was her charm. Treece therefore thought he should give a warning to Viola about Louis Bates, who was in one of her tutorial groups. 'Viola,' he said, 'can I have a word . . .?' 'Just a minute,' said Viola, 'I want to wee-wee'; and she was off, swinging her dirndl skirt like something that had just come off-stage from a performance of *The Bartered Bride*.

'I hope it goes well for her,' murmured the man in the arm-chair next to Treece's, looking up from the *Women's Sunday Mirror*. He was a sociologist whom Treece remembered as a post-graduate student; then he had been a slim, dark-haired, very English young man who played football for a university team and wanted an M.G. sports car. Now all that had changed; he wore green, German double-breasted raincoats (all his clothes were double-breasted; indeed, said Viola Masefield once, I think *he* must be double-breasted), carried large brief-cases made of wide-grained red leather, and cultivated a Central European accent; most of the best sociologists were, as he said, from *Mittel-Europa*.

'I'm catching up on the ephemera,' said the sociologist, whose name was Jenkins (he hated it, because it didn't end in 'heim'), noticing that Treece was looking curiously at his reading matter.

'You're lucky,' said Treece. 'It must be nice to be a sociologist and be able to read *anything*.'

'It's terrible,' said Jenkins with feeling. 'There are times when I begin to think that vot we need is a benevolent fascism. I have a television set,' he went on, leaning forward confidingly. 'I think I am perhaps the only man in this University with a television set, and I sit there all night and watch it. You know, this is the great culture-leveller; all over England people watch this stuff and go away and take the same image of the world, and themselves, and standards of value along with them. Oh, and it's terrible. All those people . . . I hope they *know* what it is they're doing. I wish I didn't have to watch it. I wish I could get away.'

'How was America?' said Treece. Jenkins had just returned from a year at the University of Chicago, or Colorado, or California (faculties of sociology in America drift about like flocks of birds; you wake up one morning and find the ones you are interested in have risen from their perches and have settled again, *en masse*, at the other side of the continent), where he had been, financed by a Rockefeller Scholarship, in order to find something out about a new discipline called Group Dynamics.

'I suppose you're glad to be back,' said Treece.

'I don't quite know,' said Jenkins. 'It's like coming back home, looking for England, and finding America again. Is it I that have changed, or is it England ? I suppose it's me; I always thought England was so much more reactionary than it is. It seems so proletarian. All the shops are chain-stores, all the local societies are ironed out; soon it won't be necessary for us to go to America. It will all be here.' Jenkins looked round furtively, as if he were saying something that shouldn't *get back*. 'Sometimes I feel like a traitor to sociology. Sometimes I want things as they were. We are making the world nice, you know,' said Jenkins, 'for all people except ourselves. Once, I can't help remembering, we used to think people like us were important. Now we're just a little group of disordered citizens with no social role in the society we live in.'

'You're the first sociologist that I've met who ever felt guilty about it,' said Treece.

'Quite,' said Jenkins. 'I begin to wonder myself – just who are we working for ? What is a university for ? I mean, should we be advancing and developing the processes of middle-class business morality ? Surely we ought to be protesting against them. All this social engineering . . . I'm not sure it's as good as I want it to be. Let me tell you about Group Dynamics; that's what I'm trying to get them to start up here, you know.'

'What is it ?' said Treece.

'It's a study of the social abrasions that are in-built into every group situation. You know how you feel uncomfortable at parties if you've forgotten to fasten your flies ? Well, that's Group Dynamics. It's a new field. At Chicago we were doing experiments to show that the physical constitution of rooms had a big effect on the people who used them. We were doing some experiments with conferences for the Pentagon. You know how at conferences it's usual to use two tables set in a

23

T shape? Well, we were able to prove that certain seats at the table were actually dead seats and that because of various factors – not being able to see the chairman's face in order to observe his reaction, and so on – the people sitting in them were virtually excluded from useful participation in the conference. A similar problem arose with the entry of people into the room; we found that some had to come in first and others last . . . well, we knew that, of course; but we found that this tended to dramatize latent status problems. That is, people uncertain about their status in relation to others present were made aware of the quandary when it came to the problem of whether to enter the room first, or in the middle, or last. So, you see, we were able to make some useful recommendations; but the feeling that's left is that if only social engineering can get around to enough things, life will be a bowl of cherries.'

Treece said: 'I hope you don't mind my asking this, but what were the recommendations you made.'

'The recommendations?' asked Jenkins. 'Well, actually what we recommended was that conferences should use a circular table, and a circular room, and a separate door in the wall for each participant. I don't know whether the Pentagon are actually using this yet, but I fancy they will.'

'I see,' said Treece. 'I see.' He turned and looked round the room, with a mystified and oddly tired eye; if all the chairs had been filled with horses, instead of with lecturers and professors taking coffee in their matitudinal quiet, it would have seemed no odder to him than the conversation from which he had just emerged, as from some long black tunnel. Are there then, he asked with a mind that seemed over the last few minutes to have grown quaintly old-fashioned, in the cast of some barbarian confronted with Athens at its heyday, are there then people who do *that* and call it thought?

3

On the previous evening, the Vice-Chancellor of the University, a stout, well-meaning man, full of *bonhomie*, was walking homewards through the darkness, wondering what *else* one had to do in order to get a knighthood, when a pane of glass shattered in the wall beside him. The Vice-Chancellor looked up, surprised, nervous, and in the broken window a frightened black face appeared. 'How do you do, sir,' said the face. 'I am in prison in the toilet.' 'Who are you?' said the Vice-Chancellor. 'Eborebelosa,' said the black face. 'Are you a student here?' 'Yes, indeed,' said Eborebelosa.

It was late at night; the Vice-Chancellor had, as he used to put it, been working late at the office (he was by training a business-man, and he always claimed that academics were woolly-minded and 'had no business methods'; he had hundreds; he had nothing but). There was no one else on the premises. The Vice-Chancellor got out his keys and went back into the darkened building. He went to the men's toilet; the porter, as his duties bade him, had locked the door. Unused to a quandary of this sort, the Vice-Chancellor did not know where to lay his hands on a suitable key (he afterwards discovered that a master key which he had in his pocket fitted this, as every other door in the University) and he set to work with a paperclip. In a few moments the door was open. Inside, Mr Eborebelosa was in one of the cubicles, seated on the bowl, his white eyes rolling with fright. 'Who is to blame for this?' 'Society,' said Mr Eborebelosa. 'Whose student are you?' asked the Vice-Chancellor, trying another tack. 'Professor Treece,' said Mr Eborebelosa. 'Then go and see him tomorrow,' said the Vice-Chancellor. The automatic flush worked, with a great rush of waters, on the urinals, and Mr Eborebelosa gave a little sob. Trapped there in the dark, among these regular regurgitations of water, he had clearly undergone a terrifying experience.

As Treece was leaving the Senior Common Room after his tête-à-tête with Jenkins, the Vice-Chancellor appeared in the doorway (with the Vice-Chancellor all doorways looked too small; he was tall as well as fat and, for him, doorways were a challenge) and told Treece this whole story . . . or almost all of it, for however could he admit to anyone that it was possible to open the locked doors of the University with a paper-clip? Moreover, that morning he had talked to the porter and had discovered that Eborebelosa spent his days closeted in the toilets; no sooner had the cleaners turned him out of one cubicle than he bobbed up in another; no sooner had he been put out of one door than he popped in by another. The toilets were checked before they were locked; but who could foresee wilful self-incarceration? 'Talk to him,' said the Vice-Chancellor. 'Find out whether he's refusing to face up to the reality of the world, or whether he's got a weak bladder.'

Treece knew Eborebelosa; he had been sent over from West Africa to be educated and groomed at the expense, he explained to Treece on the first day, of a terrorist society devoted to driving out the British. He was to study English language, sociology, economics, and chemistry, paying particular attention to the making of gunpowder and time-fuses. Since he retailed this information so openly, Treece found himself set with him in one of those hazy relationships of cultural quandary, where nothing said and nothing done seems believable because the specific cultural context for the form of behaviour, the way of speech, is lacking. Treece knew that he and Pontius Pilate were brothers under the skin; if he had lived in Jerusalem and met the Son of God he would have said, with monumental fairness, with no wish to be illiberal or to suggest that the foreigner was in any way inferior to ourselves: 'Well, perhaps he is and perhaps he isn't, but you really can't expect *me* to tell; perhaps they're all like this; I just don't know the cultural background.' He was quite prepared to help Mr Eborebelosa be a terrorist, if that really was his fulfilment, and people out there seriously felt they had to be terrorists; but surely, in any case, reason would prevail and he'd work in a post office or a government building, creating rather than destroying.

Treece returned to his office, which in the earlier dispensation had been one of the padded cells; it was splendidly warm in winter. It was not, alas, a *homely* room; the Lippo Lippi reproduction and the bundle of dirty laundry that Treece had forgotten to take home could do little to mitigate the essential starkness of the place. Presently there was a little knock at the door and, since no one responded to Treece's hail of 'Come in', he went himself to open it. Mr Eborebelosa stood there, with his eyes turned up to heaven. Treece led him to a chair and sat him down.

'Now, look, Mr Eborebelosa. Please understand, all we want to do is to help you.' He looked up; this evoked no response. 'But you'll have to tell me what is the matter, won't you, if I'm to do that?' Treece was uneasily aware that his tone was that of a man who had been reading from Dr Spock's book on baby care. At times like this he didn't like himself; there must be better *personae*, but he never found one.

'Now, tell me, why do you hide in the lavatories?' he went on. 'Well, it's silly, isn't it? You can't go on hiding in lavatories all your life, can you? How many public lavatories are there in your country?' Eborebelosa was not roused even by this sally. 'Probably not many. You'll be hard put to it, won't you? Or is it just because you're in England that you hide in public lavatories?' Eborebelosa shifted uncomfortably; and Treece suspected, with unease, that he was expecting the familiar argument about his coming over here and exploiting the advantages of the Welfare State. Treece, further, was beginning to wonder whether something unsavoury and morbid did not lie at the bottom of it all; perhaps he liked the smell, or something. 'Are you afraid of something? If so, you must tell me, and we'll put it right. Are you unhappy?'

Eborebelosa nodded his head in quick movements.

'Why?' went on Treece. 'What's troubling you?'

'I am despised by all,' he said suddenly in a deep clipped voice. People laughed at him, he said, because he was black and the other Negroes in the University did not like him because he was the son of a chief. He asked them for presents and they wouldn't bring him any.

'People don't laugh at people because they're black,' said Treece.

Mr Eborebelosa looked strangely at him and said nothing. 'We're all pleased', Treece added uncomfortably, 'that you've honoured our country by coming here.' 'I was unable to attend the university of the United States,' said Eborebelosa frankly. He went on to explain that the son of a chief was what he was, and if people didn't recognize him as that, then he was nothing.

He said he had an inferiority complex. What you have, my lad, thought Treece, is a superiority complex; for Treece began to suspect that the trouble with his visitor was that he was all demand.

'I am turned out of my house because I am a Negro,' said Mr Eborebelosa, at last beginning to feel that here was a place where his complaints had some validity. He was visibly expanding. 'You have a house?' asked Treece. 'The house the University has given me,' said Eborebelosa. 'Those are lodgings,' said Treece. 'That is not your house. What did you do there? Did you tell the landlady it was your house?' 'Yes,' said Mr Eborebelosa. 'What else did you do? Did you damage anything?' 'I have dogs to sleep in my bedroom. People also.' 'Women?' asked Treece. 'Some women; some men,' said Eborebelosa.

'You must be more *thoughtful*,' said Treece. 'We have great difficulty in finding landladies who are willing to accept Negro students as it is.'

'Aha,' cried Eborebelosa. 'You see, sir, you see. You do not accept us.'

'But don't you find us difficult to understand?' asked Treece. 'Well, we have the same difficulties in understanding you. It isn't easy for landladies. I'll have a talk with your landlady and put things right, if I can. But you must remember this. It is not your house. It belongs to her. You are her guest. You must not take people or animals into the house without asking her permission. We have different customs.'

'There is more,' said Eborebelosa. 'English women do not like me. They despise me because I am circumcised. In my country I have four wives. I do not wish to lie alone. Perhaps there are women in this University of more progressive views . . .'

'You must find that out for yourself,' said Treece. 'It's not my job to help you. The point is this. Life here may be difficult, but you can't go on retiring into lavatories indefinitely. You must come out into the real world and face these problems sensibly and maturely. These lavatories are just an adolescent escape-mechanism, like going to the pictures; they're a dream world. You must come to terms with things, and not expect too much. In your country you may be an important person, but here you can only win respect in terms of the way you behave and the kind of person you are. I want you to remember that and . . .' Treece gave a crinkly smile '. . . try and be nice to people.'

Mr Eborebelosa, his face registered, had come across this kind of advice before, and knew how to rate it. Try and be nice to people! What sort of a world was *this*? And how did one come to live in so dewy, so bright-eyed, a mood? And as for Professor Treece, who had tried to be nice to people, and was going to go on trying to be nice to people, even though all they were *was* people, and as such things tremendously difficult to be nice to – as for the good and liberal Treece, even he found himself cracking a little under the strain. The foreign students were always difficult to integrate into the group, and problems of communication loomed large; but, hoped Treece, these things would be better after the departmental reception for foreign students, which was to be held the following afternoon. It is well I am a liberal, and can love all men, thought Treece; for if I were not, I doubt if I could.

CHAPTER TWO

I

EMMA FIELDING put on a wool dress, splashed herself with perfume, and set off for the English Department reception for foreign students. She was a post-graduate student in the department, and was writing a thesis on the fish imagery in Shakespeare's tragedies; there was quite a lot of fish in Shakespeare, and there was more to it, now it was being at last exposed, than you would have thought, or even Sigmund Freud would have thought. The reason for Emma's attendance at the occasion was simple; Treece was, not surprisingly, nervous of the reception and wanted to have some *reliable* people there, and there was no one more reliable in the department than Emma. Treece had, therefore, telephoned Emma and asked 'if we might trespass on your time and good nature'. If Emma did not have too much of the first, she had an abundance of the second; and so here she was. She was twenty-six, and therefore rather older than most of her fellow-students; older you had to say, and wiser. When you saw her, the word you thought of for her was 'handsome'; she looked like the photographs you saw of Virginia Woolf, or those tall, brown-eyed fragile English beauties that fill autobiographies these days, the sort to whom it is not absurd to say, deferentially, 'Do you want to go and lie down?' for, it seems, even to be what they are is enough to make them look a little tired; life is so intense. Treece did not like beautiful women – he had suffered with them too much, in making the discovery that, in our world, to be beautiful is a way of life, which has its own customs and regulations – but he liked Emma; by not being quite beautiful she seemed to have gained everything.

The reception was being held in a large, dirty room with a splintery plank floor, decorated for the occasion with a large circle of wooden chairs and a large metal tea-urn from which Dr Viola Masefield, likewise co-opted for the occasion, was dispensing tea to a variety of nervous students of all nationalities and colours. Treece was there, trying to get everyone to sit down; no one would. 'Vot', demanded an extremely stout German student, greeting Emma with a bow as she entered, 'is your vaderland?' 'I'm English,' said Emma. 'Oho,' said the German with great cheerfulness. 'Then it is your task to entertain me. I am ready.'

'I'll bet you are,' said Emma. She went over to Dr Masefield at the tea urn: 'Is there anything I can be doing?' she asked. 'Just mingle, I think, if you would,' said Dr Masefield jovially, looking up.

'I think the English nation is much ashamed that it has imprisoned its great national bard, Oscar Vilda,' said someone at her side. It was the stout German, who knew when he was on to a good thing.

'Who?' asked Emma.

'Oscar Vilda,' said the German. 'As told in the ''Ballad of Reading Goal''.'

'Jail,' said Emma. 'Jail; not goal.'

'Write down, please,' said the German, taking a piece of paper from his overcoat pocket; Emma did as she was bid.

Professor Treece passed at a trot. 'Make them take their overcoats off,' he said. He stopped and came back, painfully aware of his task, which was a word for everyone. 'Good afternoon, Herr Schumann,' he said. 'I hope you're going to share Miss Fielding with the rest of us.' He caught Emma's eye and blushed. 'Oho, no,' said the German. 'As you say, finders, keepers. She is my *captive*.'

'Well, Miss Fielding, the long vacation appears to have invigorated you a great deal. How do you do it?' went on Treece jovially.

'I went to Italy and got drunk every day on chianti; it's very therapeutic,' said Emma.

'Italy,' said Treece, who had a far from Lawrentian vision of that country; he regarded it rather as a place where all moral law had long since been overthrown and where a degenerating race was having its last frantic fling. 'Were you all right?'

'More or less,' said Emma.

'Did you go to Rome?'

'We did,' said Emma.

'There are a great many things of architectural interest in Rome,' said Treece, 'and the railway station is one of them.'

'I have been to Rome,' said Herr Schumann. The tale he was about to divulge was, however, never told, for at that moment a sudden commotion occurred in a far corner of the room; a Negro student, in an excess of nerves, had spilled a cup of tea over a reader in economics. 'My word! Eborebelosa!' Treece said; and he hurried off.

'You are enjoying this party?' inquired the German. 'Yes,' said Emma. 'I think it is a very good party,' said the German. 'It is permitted to kiss these girls?'

'I don't think so,' said Emma. 'It's only the middle of the afternoon, isn't it?' 'You tell me when is the time,' said the German.

'I must go and talk to somebody else,' said Emma, and went over to a group of Indian students gathered in a corner. As soon as she announced her name, a sharp silence fell over the group. Their former animation turned to a comatose contemplation of each other's shoes. 'You are a tall woman,' said someone politely. Silence fell again.

' "Midwinter spring is its own season",' said one of them, a nun, suddenly. 'You know this quotation, of course, and how pertinent are those words, for now, as you see, the sun is shining.' She pointed to the window.

'It is of T. S. Eliot,' said a voice at Emma's side; it was the German, who had followed her over. ' "Lean, lean on a garden urn . . ." You know this too?'

Suddenly all the Indians began quoting Eliot. 'A hard coming we had of it,' cried one. 'There were no tigers,' intoned another contrapuntally.

'In India,' said the nun; all the others fell silent, 'the work of Mr Eliot is very much respected; he is translated; and many people have written his thesis for his doctorate on inclinations of his work.'

'In Germany too,' said Herr Schumann.

'I am a graduate, of course, though it is true I have not yet received my degree certificate, and I too hope to write a doctor's thesis on the work of your distinguished poet, though he was born in the United States of America, as I expect you know. You understand his work is open to many interpretations. I am a Christian, and his work is open to Christian interpretations.'

'Yes, so they tell me,' said Emma.

Herr Schumann turned to Emma and, with an ostentatious bow, said, 'You permit I bring you a cup of tea.' 'Yes, please,' said Emma, feeling a little tired. 'And for you also,' said the German to the nun.

'Yes, please, and it will be interesting to reflect that the leaf of the tea we are about to drink comes from my own country, and perhaps indeed has been picked by a member of my numerous family. One of the best poets of the part of India from which I come – it is in the north – is at this moment at your Oxford University writing a thesis on the Oriental imagery of the poems of T. S. Eliot, and on the influence of the *Upanishads*. He has been in correspondence with Mr Eliot himself.'

'Here is your tea,' said a voice from behind Emma.

'And he tells me,' went on the nun, 'in a letter that Mr Eliot has shown him the greatest courtesy.'

There was a violent tug at the back of Emma's dress. 'Here is your tea,' said Herr Schumann. 'Thank you,' said Emma taking it.

'You have been to Germany, then?' asked the nun of Herr Schumann. 'I am from Germany,' said Herr Schumann. 'What is your reason for coming here?' asked the nun. 'It is to learn the English language and to study the literature,' said Herr Schumann. 'Germany has many poets,' said the nun pleasantly. 'There is Goethe and Heine and Rilke, to name only a few. It is very good of you to come to England, of course, since you were fighting it only a few years ago. It is very civilized of all of us to forget this so easily. I think we are all very developed persons.'

'Yes,' said the German. 'I see you are a nun. I would very much like to be a nun. There are many advantages. Of course, one would have to be a woman.'

Emma suddenly saw once again amid the press the face of

Professor Treece, mouthing something in her direction. 'Ah, Miss Fielding,' she heard him say distantly. 'There are . . .' and at once his voice was miraculously magnified; he had somehow reached her side '. . . some people I want you to meet. Try and get them sitting down on chairs,' he added. 'Everyone's standing up, and it's making things very difficult.'

Suddenly he was high up in the air, standing on a chair. 'Hello, hello,' he shouted. 'Why doesn't everyone sit down? It's so much more comfortable.' No one did; indeed, those who were sitting down became embarrassed about it and stood up. Emma felt Treece's disgrace hardly. Like most people who speculate about the moral problems of human relationships, Treece was really much worse at them than those who are not moved to cogitate; in his care to offend no one, to be honest and true to all, he moved about in a sort of social badlands, where nothing ever really grew. Intention was all. Sympathy – for all these people, for being foreigners – lay over the gathering like a woolly blanket; and no one was enjoying it at all.

Foreign students' parties were things that, notoriously, didn't go well; with Treece, to whom disaster was the normal resolution of parties, they went, of course, disastrously. And so at this point on the present occasion there came a striking interruption; and people did not blame life, which could bring such interruptions, but Treece, for not foreseeing them. A group of Negroes, who had been chatting quietly in one corner, dressed in their native robes, had to pray to Allah – or someone like that – in ten minutes' time and wanted to know where there was a consecrated room. 'We have no consecrated rooms,' said Treece, embarrassed. *No consecrated rooms!* Here, said the world, is a man who gives a party for foreign students and fails to provide a consecrated room. One of the party offered to consecrate one; all he needed, he said, was a room; he could do the rest. 'Boiling water is necessary,' he said. Luckily, Viola Masefield had a kettleful. It was finally settled that the Senior Common Room should be consecrated; one felt that there was nowhere worthier of it.

'Oh, dear,' said Treece to Emma when they had all gone. 'One can't foresee everything, can one? What I was saying was, if I remember rightly, that ... yes, I want you to meet one of our friends from Nigeria, a Mr Eborebelosa. He's rather a difficult case, I'm afraid; he's already spilled a cup of tea over someone in the Economics Department ...'

Then, suddenly, they all streamed in again, at the trot, the whole consecrating group. There were dogs' hairs in the Senior Common Room. 'But we never have dogs in the Senior Common Room, they must be off people,' said Treece, 'since people are all we have there.'

The Negroes consulted for an anxious moment, and then resolved to do it in the grounds; and they picked up their kettle and sallied forth. The passing traveller, wending his way along Institution Road, would have been refreshed that day with a strange sight – the sight of a group of Negroes, in long robes, ceremonially pouring hot water over one another and making obeisance on the flagstones of the courtyard.

Meanwhile Treece, trying hard to salvage what he could from the wreckage of the occasion, was endeavouring to introduce Emma to Mr Eborebelosa. 'I'd like you to meet ...' he said tentatively. 'No, no,' said Mr Eborebelosa, looking down. Treece turned to Emma and explained in a low voice that Eborebelosa disliked meeting people and had been closeting himself in lavatories to avoid it. Emma, grasping the problem and sincerely wanting to do something to help Treece, approached Mr Eborebelosa again, smiling a generous smile, and his agitation grew so intense that the tea began to splash out of the cup in his hand. Emma gently took it from him, just in time, for Eborebelosa became, suddenly, loose-limbed, stepped backward a pace or two, and fell over on to his bottom. Emma took his arm and helped him to his feet. He was shivering all over. 'Socially maladept,' Treece's phrase for him, seemed a ridiculous understatement. 'How are you liking England?' asked Emma sweetly. 'Not, not,' said Mr Eborebelosa. 'But you haven't seen very much of it, have you?' she rebuked him. Eborebelosa tried to work up a scrap of indignation: 'Yes, London, Tilbury dicks,' said Mr Eborebelosa. 'Docks,' said Emma. 'Dicks,' said Eborebelosa.

'This is a good party, I think?' said a voice by her side; it was of course Herr Schumann. 'But when do we have the intoxicating liquors?'

'Leave me alone for a bit, Herr Schumann,' said Emma. 'Can't you see I'm busy with my friend Mr Eborebelosa?'

'Oh,' said Herr Schumann. 'Oho. So that is the way wind is blowing? That is what brews, I see.'

'I have friend?' said Mr Eborebelosa, beaming all at once. He capered about for a moment.

'You have no taste,' said Herr Schumann. 'I would have given you cakes, chocolates, food of all natures; you have been very unwise. I have many friends in positions of great responsibility to whom I should introduce. Beware. Life will slip you by.'

'I am son of a chief,' said Mr Eborebelosa. 'I will give you a goat.'

'In England, how shall she use a goat? In Europe there is no place for goats. We do not ride on them, we do not drink the milk; goats are defunct. We have gone past the goat. Culture has trod on.'

'Now, Herr Schumann . . .' said Emma.

'Aha, so,' said Herr Schumann. 'You are his friend, yet you allow him to think he can purchase with goats. ''I want typewriter, how many goats?'' You are poor friend, dear woman, I tell you so.'

'You would like to wear the clothes of my country,' said Eborebelosa to Emma.

'This is white woman . . .' said Herr Schumann; and then, catching a glint in Emma's eye, he stopped. 'So, what for do I beat myself to death? Women you must not trust.'

Schumann withdrew in a huff, and Emma and Eborebelosa talked pleasantly on, Emma occasionally proffering the teacup to him so that he might take a sip; soon he calmed down and was able to hold it himself. By the time everyone was ready to disperse, after a hard afternoon, Mr Eborebelosa was becoming enthusiastic about Emma's smile. ''I like this smile,' he kept saying. 'Do it more.' Emma, a thoroughly amiable personality, obliged, and Treece kept looking over at the two of them suspiciously as empty grins kept shining forth on Emma's face. Afterwards, Treece came up and congratulated her on her handling of what he called 'a difficult case'. 'I feel really sorry for him,' said Emma. It's simply impossible, of course, to respond fairly to him; there's just no common ground.' 'Oh,' said Treece sharply. 'I wouldn't have thought that was true. Indeed, you seem to have disproved it.' 'Well, it's like talking to children,' said Emma. 'You get some pleasure out of doing it, but you never really feel you're exhibiting any part of yourself; just exercising in a void, and that just isn't good enough for you yourself.' 'Oh, you expect too much from life,' said Treece, adding with a sweet smile. 'You're just like me.'

Poor, poor Treece, thought Emma; for she loved to sympathize. Poor man, he has tried to show us all that foreigners aren't funny; but they are. After all, there was one thing that every Englishman knew from his very soul, and that was that, for all experiences and all manners, in England lay the norm; England was the country that God had got to first, *properly*, and here life was taken to the point of purity, to its Platonic source, so that all ways elsewhere were underdeveloped, or impure, or overripe. Everyone in England knew this, and an occasion like the present one was not likely to prove that things had altered. I have lived in England, was the underlying statement, and I know what life is like. What you wanted to say to Treece, under such circumstances, was what Machiavelli told his prince: it is necessary for a man who wishes to maintain himself, to learn how not to be good, and when or when not to use this knowledge; here was a time when one withdrew. It was only Treece who could believe that the destiny of nations was being forged in such small and seedy rooms, with no carpet on the floor, and wooden benches for seats. As for the rest of us, we are unerringly provincial, Emma had to concede; this is just the Midlands, and we don't have to carry the burden of things like that out here.

2

Treece wished that he did not have to stare, all the time, at pretty women; sometimes it seemed to him his one overriding interest. It was not that he willed it like that; it was something that was drawn out of him, and it was in consciousness of facts such as this that he sometimes had to concede that perhaps Freud might be right, and there was a bit of the irrational in man after all. It was the following Saturday, and the occasion was a meeting of the town's Literary Society, a group of fanciful persons who met monthly to discuss the prosecution of good literature. If an atmosphere of seediness hung over the Society, it was not because of the weakness of its membership; the persons who attended were all worthy personages, not without status in the town, and not without performance; no, the trouble was that, as in all literary discussion, there comes a point where the critical has to give way to personal fondnesses, personal friendships, and this was the point at which the society had stalled. Nowadays, there, nobody said what they thought, for they knew whom they liked, and whom they loathed, and whose toes they wished to spare, and whose to stamp upon. Today, the meeting was addressed by a local writer of children's books, a stout and hearty personality whose suit looked as though it had been made from the skin of a donkey; and it was this person that Treece had come to introduce. There were people who, in such a context, could introduce, and there were those who could not; Treece was so oppressively one of those who could, none better; so he nearly always did. The room was a big one, and wintry sunlight lay in big pools on the old Victorian carpet; the audience, scattered about the room in armchairs, shimmered in the half-dark of the place; and time seemed to move indolently, slower than the tick of the clock, while the writer spoke on, talking of Piaget and infantile communication. And in the front row, eager, intense, lips halfparted as if in pleased surprise, sat Mrs Rogers, mother of three boys, wife of an accountant, a contributor of short stories to *Woman's Journal*, a delight to look upon. It was enough that she existed, felt Treece; he asked no more of her than that. Bronzed, fair, finely dressed, she came each month, and said nothing, and smiled brightly, and scattered approving interest about her; she was a motherly woman, and Treece loved motherly women. He thought of Mallarmé, who had written, surely, about *her*:

Votre très naturel et clair
Rire d'enfant qui charme l'air.

And the talk went on, and Treece thought, with a little giggle to himself, and with a sense of discovery: Why, women are much more interesting than *anything*, and I don't even know why.

The speaker stopped, and Treece thanked him, and asked for questions. 'I just want to say that I think you're a very interesting man,' said a woman from the back. Someone else then asked how many people Enid Blyton were. Mrs Rogers smiled, and said how interesting it all had been, and how all mothers were often frightened to think of the hands they left the writing of children's books in, but now that she'd seen the speaker, she would have no qualms about letting her children read his work. After this a lady at the back, with a long-drawling voice, said from beneath a large flower-pot hat: 'Well, I read one of your things, and I didn't like it.' 'Why not, madam?' said the speaker, a little put out; he was the sort of man that always called ladies 'madam', and it brought in the aroma of an *ancien régime*; one thought of Wells and Bennett and a sort of literary society which was gone – gone, no doubt, for good. 'I don't know *why*,' said the woman in the flower-pot hat. 'I just didn't like it.' Treece thanked the speaker and brought the meeting to a close. Mrs Rogers beamed sweetly at him as he did so.

It was the custom for the members of the literary society then to retire to the lounge of the Black Swan Hotel, where they took tea together. Shepherding their speaker fondly, they made their way there in cavalcade, past Dolcis and Woolworths and Sainsburys. In the lounge of the hotel were huge leather armchairs that looked like cows; you wouldn't have thought it odd if someone had come along to milk them. Here they sat and looked at each other. The lady in the flower-pot hat sat down beside Treece and sighed deeply. 'It's terrible to be abnormal,' she said, and heaved another sigh. 'Did *you* have an unhappy childhood?' 'I had an unhappy maturity,' said Treece. 'I had a frankly bloody childhood,' said the woman.

'Tell me, do you like this hair style? Be frank: I can have it done again somewhere else.'

'Darling, I was going to ask you what happened to it?' said a man in a bow-tie. 'You could have fought back. Or did they give you an anaesthetic?'

'You should have seen what he did to my dog,' said the lady. She turned again to Treece. 'I suppose you know lots of writers,' she said.

'I know some,' said Treece, 'but I think I prefer people.' This remark was not intended as a sally; Treece quite seriously divided the world into writers, who led life as a conscious effort, and people, who didn't; sometimes he preferred writers and sometimes he preferred people.

The lady in the flower-pot hat greeted this with a little giggle; then she said, 'Do you know any of the London crowd?' This was said so wistfully, with such an air of hope, that Treece was sorry to disappoint her. But really, he had to admit, he didn't.

'It's so difficult if you don't live in London,' said the lady in the flower-pot hat. 'I don't like London, but I must say I often wish I lived there. It's so hard to get published if you aren't in the swim, and can't butter up the right people. I mean, I have published, but it's twice as hard as it would be if you lived in London. People don't *ask* you for things.'

'I think it's much easier now for people from the provinces to publish than it ever was,' said Treece. 'Don't you?'

'Well, no, I don't think that,' said the woman. 'People seem to think that it was hard, once, for provincial writers to get published, but I don't think it was any harder then. I think you need to be in London more now than you did in those days. . . .'

Treece had the wit to perceive that this topic was a matter of something more than passing interest to his companion, that they had touched on the soul of something; and it was not difficult to see what it was, for Treece knew reasonably well the sort of surburban milieu in which the woman circulated; and he also knew some of her work, which was poetry of a sound and intense kind. There exists a vast sub-culture of literature in England, of writers working on a part-time basis and circulating their work in closed circles, such as this very literary society; their work is good, but little known, and is lacking simply in the intensity and originality of that of the committed artist. 'Here's the tweeny,' said the lady in the flower-pot hat; and tea was brought.

'Where's Mrs Rogers?' said Treece as he spied around the circle present and noticed the sad omission.

'She has to go home and get tea ready for her boys,' said the man in the bow-tie. 'She's a dear woman. Have you seen any of her stuff?'

'She writes as though she's just come in out of the dew,' said the lady in the flower-pot hat. 'I once went to her house and she said, "Have you seen our goblin?" and, do you know, I wasn't in the least surprised. It's the one place where you wouldn't be. The goblin turned out to be a make of vacuum-cleaner, but, you know, if it had been a real one I should have accepted it just as simply.'

There were times when Treece felt more at home in the pellucid air of the provinces than anywhere he had been in his life before; the conversation lapped on in little wavelets and the stout business-men passed and repassed outside the door and the buses screeched outside the windows. One felt cosy. England expanded and became a continent, and all that lay outside was infinitely remote; England contracted and became an islet, and all that lay inside was sound and secure. 'Sugar?' said the lady in the flower-pot hat. 'Yes?' asked Treece; he thought she was being fond, but she was simply pouring out his tea. He didn't take sugar, but the mistake was too complicated to explain. 'How many lumps?' 'One, please,' said Treece lazily; he had stretched out his legs and was now practically lying down. 'Nonsense, you can't taste one; I've given you three,' said the lady in the flower-pot hat. She handed him the cup. 'You know, you're as *lean* as a rake,' she said. 'You need fattening up. Doesn't your wife feed you?' 'I'm not married,' said Treece. 'I think that's disgusting,' said the lady in the flower-pot brightly. 'Don't you?' She turned to everyone else: 'He says he's not married.' 'Well, it's not a matter of principle,' said Treece. 'I've wanted to marry, a great many times; I always seem to be asking women to marry me. After all, there are things a wife can do that not even the best of housekeepers can manage. But they won't marry me.'

'What nonsense,' said the lady in the flower-pot. 'Let's see, who do we *know*?' '*Why* won't they marry you?' asked someone else. 'Well, I can see their point,' said Treece. 'I must be about the least desirable bachelor I've ever come across. I just don't seem to have the attributes women like in a man – a car, a television set, you know.' 'We'll find somebody,' said the lady in the flower-pot hat.

The Secretary of the Society was a stout little man named Schenk, who sold carpets. 'It's six o'clock,' he now said. 'They're open.' 'Who are?' asked the lady in the flower-pot. 'The bar is,' said Mr Schenk, who was an organizing genius; for instance, the Society always had a poetry week-end, at some country house devoted to conferences, and Schenk not only managed to get hold of the most distinguished speakers, but, simply in order to give the thing more tone, he used also to persuade the A.A. to cover three or four counties with large yellow marker signs saying POETRY CONFERENCE. The group rose and made their way into the bar, which was quaint and old-fashioned; there were post-horns on the wall, and yards of ale. Business-men chatted about wool and cotton, and county young men, in blazers and cavalry twill trousers, teased sweet girls with plummy accents and short hair. The countryside around was hunting country. They sat down in Windsor chairs and ordered. Treece now found himself next to Butterfield, the man who ran the Department of Adult Education. Butterfield, who had got the job because at the interview he claimed that he had once taught an all-in wrestler to love Shakespeare (he was, Butterfield explained afterwards, a very literate all-in wrestler), always described himself as 'a pleb'; it was his ambition to retire and keep a pub somewhere. Academic life at once charmed and bored him; he liked, as he said, to be in the vicinity of a university, but not too firmly anchored to it. He used to go over to Cheltenham most week-ends; he was having an affair with a very slick and sophisticated woman who had a hairdresser's shop. The woman had now decided that she wanted to marry Butterfield, and he was having rather a bad time; he had told the woman, falsely, that he was already married, and she now wanted to meet his wife so that they could decide between them who was to have him. 'She's here,' said Butterfield. 'She's rampaged all over the town, looking for my wife. If you should come across her, don't tell her I'm single. That would be the finish.' Butterfield, who, rumour had it, had fathered two children by his hairdresser, didn't look any too worried; he was splendidly aware of his ability to cope with the most extreme situations. 'I'm a bit of a rat, aren't I?' said Butterfield. 'Still, they say the strongest human instinct is self-preservation, and once they get the noose round your neck, you can never get it off.'

'. . . I always feel that reading does much more good to others than it does to me,' Treece found a stout elderly lady saying to him good-naturedly, as she sipped a gin and orange.

The children's novelist now leaned over. 'Do you read much children's literature, Professor?' he asked. 'I don't,' said Treece. 'I think you're ignoring, if you don't mind my saying so, a very fruitful field for study,' said the novelist. 'I'm sure you're right,' said Treece, 'but the trouble with me is that I have a sophisticated mind. Was it Chesterton who said he didn't like children because they smelled of bread and butter. I dislike them because they aren't grown up.'

'But aren't you charmed by their innocence?' asked the lady in the flower-pot hat.

'But innocence is in the eye of the beholder, isn't it?' said Treece, 'and in any case innocent is the last thing that children are. I think they're cruel and savage. If I had any children, I'd lock them up in a cage until they could prove that they were moral creatures. That's because the only interesting thing about man, to me, is that he's a moral animal; and children aren't.'

'I can see now why you aren't married,' said the lady in the flower-pot hat. 'Of course, you'd soon change your mind if you had any children.'

'Besides, children are like old people; they're culturally disconnected,' said Treece.

'You think that children should be seen and not heard then?' asked the novelist.

'I don't approve either category,' said Treece. He was growing expansive, more and more so as the day wore on; he thought the bit about not being married was funny enough, funny but true, but that all this was funnier still. However, no one seemed very amused. He realized that he was in a mood of almost manic elation and irresponsibility, and that he would have to pay for it all with a countervailing depression. 'Of course,' he said, concluding the topic, 'what you don't realize is, I'm a bastard.'

The lady in the flower-pot hat had sweet little ears, and Treece was just taking a really good look at them when Butterfield turned around to him, and said, 'Mr Schenk asked me to have a word with you about the poetry conference. He wanted to know if you'd be prepared to speak at it again this year. He wanted you to talk on poetic drama.'

'Very well,' said Treece, looking at the ears. 'I'm quite prepared to do it.'

'He also wondered if you knew of any ... well, the phrase he used was "Big Name", who'd come down and speak to them.'

'Had he anyone in mind?' asked Treece, swinging his leg idly.

'Well, he wanted Eliot, or perhaps a Sitwell.'

'We shall have to see,' said Treece.

Meanwhile, Mr Schenk had been trying to talk everyone into going to see the nude show at the variety theatre; he said that anyone who was interested in society or in our contemporary estimate of the worth of man should go. 'Yes, let's, just for fun,' said the lady in the flower-pot hat; you knew this was her phrase. One or two of the ladies said they had to go and feed people. 'You must come,' said Schenk. 'We want to watch the expression on your faces.' Butterfield was equally keen. 'It's not that I have a sociological interest,' he said. 'I just *like* nude shows.' 'This is fun,' said the woman in the flower-pot, as they drank down their glasses and off they all went. 'If only Mrs Rogers could have been here,' said Treece. They went in cavalcade through the streets to the theatre and in the interval

Treece kissed the woman in the flower-pot hat on each pretty ear, just for fun. He found he was liking the provinces, more and more; it was something *less* than London, but it was also itself.

3

Of all the problems that nibbled at Treece's mind and brought him to anxiety, there were none sharper than his worries over status. The catechism began simply: what, in this day and age, was the status of a professor in English society, and what rewards and what esteem may he expect? Secondly, and to add another dimension, what was the status of a professor *in the humanities*, in England, in this day and age? Third, what, then, was the status of a professor in the humanities *at a small university in the provinces*, in England, in the present age? It could not be denied that all the forms of social stratification, once solid, were liquefying in the torrid heat engendered by reforming zealots like himself. Treece had to admit that, if it became a choice between being respected too much and not at all, he would, in spite of his liberal pretensions, rest easier in spirit under the former régime. And, to sum the matter up, what emerged for Treece was that to be a professor, of the humanities, at a provincial university, in England, in the nineteen-fifties, was a fate whose rewards were all internal, for in the matter of social status he was small enough beer. A man who had a fondness for human manners, the local manners of circles and groups that are formed by a traditional accretion of associations, he sought to follow the given manners for himself, to live within them in no spirit of cheap emulation, but with the zest of one who believes that manners are an access to morals, and that manners pursued with passion never atrophy. Such was the passion with which Treece queried whether it was proper for him to possess, as he did, a motorized bicycle; and a somewhat seedy late Victorian house; and an account with the Post Office Savings Bank, because it was always useful to be able to go and draw out a few pounds, anywhere; and a National Health Service doctor, because you paid once to be ill, anyway, and Treece was never ill enough, in the course, it seemed, of any given year, to make those weekly payments a fair bargain in his case; and pyjamas bought at Marks and Spencers, because they seemed just as good as more distinguished garb, though perhaps less well-cut around the crotch; and paper-backed books, because you could possess more (though you had to go, always, to the library to provide references for scholarly articles from the hard-bound editions). On the other side of the coin, however, to point up that, even in the fluidity of the contemporary English social scene, not all is lost, Treece wore: an establishment shirt, made to measure for him, usually in blue or grey fine stripe, with three loose collars; a suit, also made to measure for him, from a small local tailor, with pockets at the back of the trousers, and the side, and the front (this for the wallet), and a buttonhole for the passage of a pocket watch; and braces, because one did, though belts were pleasanter. Treece's answer to the problem of what is *à propos* for the person that, in terms of social status, he supposed himself to be, was that if most of what he had was *à propos*, and a little was flagrantly not *à propos*, then society would grant his recognition of the fact that here was a problem, and that, for the future, it was an open problem. A partial immersion in professorship was really the most the world could hope for from Treece, and it accepted that.

Treece was no aesthete, no exotic; his driving forces were self-discipline and moral scruple, or so he was disposed to think. He had no time for the pleasurable, only the necessary. For instance, he spent most of his time in his office, having painful encounters with students, who wanted him to read stories they had written about sensitive youths, pining for a new world, or inquired at what sort of shop one could buy books, or wanted to know whether he collected dinner money – although he would much rather have hidden behind the door or in a book cupboard. People always thought he had been to Oxford or Cambridge, that he was that sort of man. But he had gained his wisdom at the University of London, which is a very different thing; he had gone to university not to make good contacts, or to train his palate, or refine his accent, but rather to get a good degree. He had had to give up punting, which he enjoyed, because to punt one had to punt from one end or the other, and one end was the Oxford, the other the Cambridge, end. So much of the world was like that too. The same sort of people wondered too about his regiment, which they supposed would be the Guards. In fact, during the war Treece had been a member of the London Fire Service, putting out fires with Stephen Spender. People supposed, likewise, that his family would be a sound one, his father an artist, or a bibliophile, his mother at home on a horse. In fact his father had had a wallpaper shop, and when, once, he had told his father that it was wrong that people's relationships should be those of buyers and sellers, his father had gazed at him blankly. What else could they be? Treece was never ashamed that his background was of this sort; but he was *surprised* by it; it was not what he would, if he had met himself as a stranger, have expected.

Of Treece's formative years, which were the nineteen-thirties, of those busy days when to be a liberal was to be something, and people other than liberals knew what liberals were, of this period Treece had one sharp and pointed memory, that cast itself up like a damp patch on the wall of an otherwise sturdy house, a memory of a time when late one night – indeed, at the two o'clock of one early morning – he had gone from the room he rented in Charlotte Street because he had had a row with the woman he was living with. On the night in question, Treece, then a research student with holes in his underpants and not a change of socks to call his own, was determined to leave Fay, in part because she did not like his poetry, but also because he knew that she did not trust him, since, with the cunning of females who know what faculties are of most or least worth in their prey, she had observed that he was a person without a firm, a solid centre; he was easily blown or altered. On this topic they had exchanged acrimonious words, and Treece had hurried forth into the dark street, pausing only to dress and snatch up his thesis, which reposed, well-nigh completed, at the side of the bed. Coming along the Soho street, wearing a leather jacket and a most determined visage, Treece had met a friend of his, a speedway rider of strong and engrossing character. He was a communist and, unlike Treece, took an active part in the political life. The two withdrew to an all-night café and Treece, pressed to account for his presence abroad, told him of the row with Fay; he said he was fed-up with her and didn't wish to go back. The speedway rider observed that severed links were the order of the day; he had finished his job and was going away, probably abroad; and he asked Treece to come with him. I have no money, said Treece; whereat, from all over his leather jacket, the speedway motor-cyclist produced wads of pound notes, all his savings, which he had withdrawn. But as they talked, through the night, Treece began to think about Fay again, and how warm it was in bed. Finally, uncertainly, he went back to Fay, receiving a poor welcome; she had hoped, she said, that he meant it. Some time later Treece learned that his friend had in fact been on his way to Spain, where he had fought; and later still he heard that he had died heroically holding a solitary machine-gun position which had finally been wiped out accidentally by planes on his own side. When Treece heard all this, he felt that, if only the man had said that it was to Spain that he was going, he would surely have gone; afterwards he wondered whether he would; from time to time he certainly wished that he had.

It was against this sort of background that moments like the reception for foreign students, or Treece's responses to provincial life, took their shape. Being a liberal, after all *that*, meant something special; one was a messenger from somewhere. One was, now, a humanist, neither Christian nor communist any more, but in some vague, unstable central place, a humanist, yes, but not one of those who supposes that man is good or progress attractive. One has no firm affiliations, political, religious, or moral, but lies outside it all. One sees new projects tried, new cases put, and reflects on them, distrusts them, is not surprised when they don't work, and is doubtful if they seem to. A tired sophistication runs up and down one's spine; one has seen everything tried and seen it fail. If one speaks one speaks in asides. One is at the end of the tradition of human experience, where everything has been tried and no one way shows itself as perceptibly better than another. Groping into the corners of one's benevolence, one likes this good soul, that dear woman, but despairs of the group or the race; for the mass of men there is not too much to be said or done; you can't make a silk purse out of a sow's ear. Persons tie themselves into groups, they attach to this cause and then to that and, working with these abstracts and large emotions, they rush like a flock of lemmings into the sea to drown themselves. What can one do? One gives, instead, teas for foreign students, teas which say, in effect, 'Foreigners are not funny'. And even that is hardly true. Treece wanted to hear no more of the departmental reception; far from proving that foreigners were as normal as you or me, the occasion had been a subject of public amusement and complaint ever since; a letter had appeared in the local evening paper about the religious rites that had taken place on the University's front lawn, asking if young girls were safe any more, and a Frenchman had been arrested afterwards for urinating against a tree on Institution Road. He had telephoned the Vice-Chancellor from the police station, to enlist his aid: *'C'est moi,'* his rich French voice had announced in the Vice-Chancellorial ear. *'J'ai pissé.'* Moreover, Treece's fond hope that Emma Fielding's kindness at the departmental reception would dissuade Mr Eborebelosa from hiding out in the lavatories was answered; Eborebelosa forsook the lavatories for another cause, the pursuit of Emma Fielding.

Every morning since the reception he had sought her out in the refectory, whither she retired, along with her fellow-students, for coffee and conversation, those two eighteenth-century graces, now equally ersatz in the twentieth. He would pass back and forth behind her stool, remarking finally, as he came up close, 'How do you do. You do not want me to sit here.' 'I do,' said Emma, who in this situation had little choice of words. 'Come and sit down.' Eborebelosa would rest his bottom precariously on an adjacent stool; she would introduce him to the people present; conversation would continue and Eborebelosa would sit silently, nodding his black head in a somnolent fashion, until at last he would stir from his speculations to poke Emma in the ribs and say, 'You do not want me to talk with you.' 'Yes,' she would say. 'I do. What do you want to say?' 'You do not want to hear it,' Eborebelosa would say, 'and a silence is golden.' And, eyeing each other warily, into silence they would both subside.

4

'It's an extremely difficult examination,' Ian Merrick, M.A., Lecturer in Philology, was saying to Treece when Emma Fielding entered Treece's office for her tutorial. 'My word, is it?' demanded Treece, concern bursting out on his face like spots. 'Do you think I shall pass?'

'No one ever passes first time,' said Merrick, sitting on the desk. 'The real problem is the practical part. . . .'

Treece noticed Emma standing there. 'Do sit down, Miss Fielding,' he said. 'I shan't be a minute '

'Yes,' said Merrick; 'there's no problem about the theoretical stuff, of course; that's simply a question of mugging up the notes. But when it comes to practical performance, they're very sticky.'

'Oh, my goodness,' said Treece.

'Have you got a crash helmet?' asked Merrick.

'For a motorized bicycle? Oh, really old boy. . . .'

'Well, you have to show willing. I know it looks ridiculous. I always say they should make them look like bowler hats, and then a gentleman could wear them as well.' Merrick, if he was anything, was a gentleman. He was, it always seemed to Treece, a typical Cambridge product gone to seed; he was the bright young man of fifty, handsome, fair-haired, bursting with romantic idealism, the sort that nice girls always loved, the sort that had gone off in droves to fight the First World War. There was something *passé* and Edwardian about Merrick. He was conceited, cocksure, a public school and Cambridge Adonis fascinated by what he called 'the classical way of life'. Treece privately described him as a Rupert Brooke without a Gallipoli, and this was really almost fair; he seemed as if he had outstayed his lease on the earth, and now his romanticism was turning into a kind of Housman-like light cynicism, his open and frank assurance curdling, his Grecian-god looks becoming almost grotesque with wrinkles. He reached into his waistcoat pocket and took out a gold cigarette case: 'Gasper?' he said. He would, naturally, wear a waistcoat; cigarettes he would call, of course, 'gaspers'. He smiled brilliantly at Emma and put his cigarette case before her; you felt that, like Bull-dog Drummond, he would say, 'Turkish on this side; Virginias on that.' 'I'm sorry; I should have offered them to you first,' was what he actually did say. 'You must make your presence felt, my dear.'

'To revert to this driving test . . .' said Treece.

'Well, as I say, you mustn't feel too disappointed if you don't pass first time. They throw the book at you. They failed me for not giving proper signals. I was sticking my arm out as far as the bloody thing would go. But no, they expect you to lean so damn' far out of the car that the examiner has to hold on to your feet. They just don't like passing people.'

'This is only a bicycle,' said Treece.

'It makes no odds, old boy,' said Merrick. 'They're even worse with those things. If you pass on that it means you're entitled to ride a bloody great motor cycle. That's why they're so rough. Believe me, no one passes first time. I've taken it four times with my motor-mower and I haven't passed yet.' Merrick got up off the corner of the desk and began to depart. 'Anyway, good luck,' he said. He nodded affably at Emma and went out. 'Bye-bye, old boy,' he said.

Treece, who was to take his driving test that afternoon, was already in a high state of tension; he peered through a haze of distress at Emma Fielding, sitting there in her chair, her intense black eyes fixed upon him. His stomach felt weak; he wanted to lie down. 'Pleased to be back?' he asked. 'Well, not really,' said Emma frankly.

'Well, how's the thesis coming along?'

'I'm afraid it isn't, really,' said Emma. 'I haven't been able to get anything done over the vacation. I've been away; and then coming back was so unsettling; I always get dreams of glory whenever I go abroad, and England is something of a shock when you come back to it. It's all so matter-of-fact.'

'That's the problem with vacations,' said Treece. 'It's a

good thing you're back, really. After all, the function of a vacation is regenerative, not luxurious. It's to restore our equipment so that we can live our ordinary lives the better. Do I look pale?'

'A bit,' said Emma.

'I feel queer,' said Treece: then, with a briskness he didn't feel, he added, 'Well, when are you going to let me have something written down?'

'Next time,' said Emma.

'Good,' said Treece. 'Well, come and see me when you've something on paper.' He rose, but Emma was not so easily got rid of. 'There's something I wanted to talk to you about,' said Emma. 'It's a personal matter really, and I suppose it's something I ought to clear up on my own. I mean, I suppose it's one of the risks one takes just in being a woman, and one ought to know how to cope with the situation. After all, women are always being pursued, and they ought to learn to live with it, and be pleased, not sorry.'

'What *is* it?' said Treece.

'Well,' said Emma, 'you remember that Negro student that you introduced me to at the departmental reception.'

'Mr Eborebelosa?'

'Yes,' said Emma. 'Well, I thought about this very carefully before I decided to mention it to you, but he really has gone too far.' She explained that one morning, in a pause in conversation in the refectory, Eborebelosa had announced, spluttering on the synthetic coffee, that he was in love with Emma and wanted to make her his fifth wife; he was, he said, prepared to give up entirely intimate relations with the other four; he was jaded with black girls; he wanted only Emma. He further claimed, Emma told Treece, that, because of some action which she could not identify, she was actually engaged to be married to him. 'This *is* interesting,' said Treece. 'I wonder if it was your holding his teacup for him at the reception? Isn't there something about that in *The Golden Bough*?' – and up he bobbed, to look for it on his shelves. He's so *annoying*, Emma thought. Was it worth going on? But she did. When she had told him that she could not marry him, Eborebelosa had become

indignant and, waving in the air a box which, he said, contained his grandfather's skull, which he wanted her to have, he said he was a chieftain's daughter ('Chieftain's son,' Emma had corrected him, reflecting as she did so that *this* was the sort of role she had in mind in relation to him), that she could have as many goats as she wanted, that if she wanted anyone killed she had only to say. 'You see,' said Emma, 'there simply is no common ground. And then he did this awful thing.'
'Great Scott!' said Treece, forgetting about *The Golden Bough*.

'Well, he got the idea that I was engaged to someone else, and he said he was going to kill him. He comes up to me every day, grinning like mad, asking if he's dead yet.'

'And is he?' 'Is who what?' asked Emma.

'Is this man you're engaged to dead?'

'Well, there isn't anyone. I had to invent someone.'

'You shouldn't have done that,' said Treece.

'I know,' said Emma Fielding. She looked downcast; she bent her head; and then, Treece noticed with horror, there was a bright crystal tear in each of her eyes. She hadn't meant to tell this bit, for how guilty she felt about it. Oh, she had never meant to lie; it wasn't as if it was an ordinary lie, which would have been bad enough; she was lying to a member of a race which had been lied to too much already. If he ever found out, he would surely take it as an insult to his colour, though it had been meant to spare him. But, in any case, was it, for a liberal-minded person, fair even to spare him? Would one want to spare a white person like that? Yet if one told him what one would tell a white person – 'I don't love you' – wouldn't this seem like an attack on his colour? And if he had been a white person, wouldn't one perhaps have married him?

'Oh,' she sobbed, 'it's so difficult.'

Treece, watching her body shake with sobs, got up and popped half-way round the desk; then he thought better of it, and popped back. Someone might come in and catch him at it. 'Now, now,' he said from his safe distance.

'That's not all, either,' said Emma. 'It was *you*. It's you he's sticking pins into an image of.'

'What do you mean?' demanded Treece.

'Well,' cried Emma, 'I said I was engaged to you. It had to be someone he was scared of, you see. So I thought of you.'

'Did you, by Jove?' said Treece.

'You don't understand,' said Emma accusingly. 'This is the sort of thing that only happens to women. Men don't see this dilemma. One is congenitally a woman, you know; one tries not to be, but it's a condition of one's humanity. But his being a Negro makes everything so much worse. It's not just a question of doing what a woman ought to do, is it?'

'No,' said Treece.

She blew her nose. 'Well, then,' she said. 'And that's why I came to you, because it isn't just a personal problem, and I can't handle it on my own. I mean, it is very flattering, to be admired by someone out of a different culture. But you see – if I turn away from him it won't just seem like a simple *rejection*, will it?'

Treece pondered a moment. 'Well, will it?' demanded Emma, and Treece found that her eyes, sprouting tears, were gazing accusingly at him, as if *he* were to blame, as if he were the cruel arbiter of dilemmas of this sort (which, in a sense, he had to admit, he was). 'He'll think, won't he, that I'm discriminating against him because of his colour.'

'And you aren't?' asked Treece, taking strength.

'Oh, oh, I don't *know*,' said Emma. 'But I couldn't marry him. I don't want to.'

'But you must give him a fair deal, now, mustn't you? That's all that's necessary. Have you thought it through in the way that you would have if he were a white suitor?'

'Well, how do I know, because he isn't,' said Emma. 'White suitors don't try to give you their grandfather's skull. And when one's getting married one has to take things like that into consideration. I mean, it does matter, doesn't it?'

'But have you even thought of the matter as a feasible possibility?' asked Treece. 'At least you have to do that, don't you?'

'I suppose so,' said Emma.

'I think you do,' said Treece. 'In many ways, Eborebelosa is an admirable man. His ways are not our ways, but that doesn't mean they're any worse.' Treece weighed this for a moment, and then added, scrupulously (scrupulously was his word), 'Or any better. He does have the advantage of national vigour on his side; he's close to his roots, you know. That should appeal to a woman, shouldn't it? I mean, he's extraordinarily male, vital, in a way ... well, you've read Lawrence. He deserves to be considered on his merits.'

'Yes,' said Emma. 'Yes.' A brave smile shone through the tears. Treece felt as though he had put the case rather well, had given her something to think about. That was his job.

'Are my eyes terribly red?' asked Emma.

'No,' said Treece, adding, as if he were her father, *somebody's* father, 'Sit here for a minute; and stop rubbing them.' Treece tried to think of something nice and warming to say; but he could only, really, think of one thing. This was the driving test.

'Oh, I wish I hadn't to take my driving test,' he said; somehow, after the tears, it didn't matter about telling Emma. 'I hate that machine. You know I get off it every time shaking like a leaf. It's full of vibration. It has a life of its own. I dream about it in bed at night.'

'Why not get rid of it?' said Emma.

'It's a challenge, you see. They shouldn't make people take these cruel little tests, it's so belittling.'

'Well, you do,' said Emma.

'Yes, I know, but it isn't the *same*, is it? I wasn't at all nervous when I took my PH.D. The thing with this one is that you aren't being judged on your own terms. I'm an expert in English literature, and they're going to ask me questions about street signs. It's a field outside the ones in which I have control, you see. I shall *expose* myself, I know.'

'It isn't so very hard,' said Emma.

'You've taken it, then, have you?'

'Yes,' said Emma.

'And passed?'

'Yes,' said Emma.

'Oh, well,' said Treece, 'perhaps you have a mechanical mind. What I'm getting at is how cruel life is in the spheres of it in which you aren't influential. You think you have a protected corner, and you're safe; but once you emerge from it, war is declared. You think life is ideal, so long as you can pursue it along the lines you favour; and then it suddenly comes upon you that it isn't, it's corrupt, that the area in which you are resolute, and make decisions, is so very small. And now and then life goes to work to remind you of it.'

'Yes, I know exactly what you mean,' said Emma. 'The blind, uncontrollable forces of the universe break through, suddenly, the great overpowering energies of the world. As in *Moby Dick*.'

'Quite,' said Treece. 'And the question remains: is it right to stay in the protected corner, where things are controllable, or should one venture out, and start again in a new world, where things are strenuous, and reclaim something else from the wild?'

'I don't know,' said Emma. 'How does one decide? One concludes, I suppose, that one world is worth more, I imagine, and opts for that.'

'It isn't even as simple as that,' said Treece, morosely; the discussion was affecting him profoundly; these were his corns that they were treading on. 'Because when one ceases to cultivate one's own garden, then one ceases to be influential. There's so much to lose, not in goods, but in manners, patterns of living. Outside those that one has, one is nothing – one is a buffoon. Like Mr Eborebelosa. He's not funny on his native heath – but here! No, there's nothing really you can do; for then the abrasion itself becomes a dominant condition of life, and one gives more time to it than it deserves. And one has to commit oneself to actions that perhaps are not right – or they might be right for you, but not for other people.' He stood up and walked over to the door, taking a black cycling coat from a hook on the back of it. 'It's a problem, Miss Fielding,' he said, putting on the coat. 'It's a problem.' On the hook there also hung a pair of cellophane goggles, and these he seized and pulled down over his eyes, ruffling his hair wildly as he did so.

'Well, you look your normal self now,' he said, presuming on their intimacy. His eyes crinkled into a smile behind the cellophane. 'I hope it will all come out all right,' he said, ushering her out of the door and following her down the corridor. Notices flapped on the boards like great birds as they swept past them.

'And good luck for your driving test,' said Emma.

Treece paled, but regained his composure. Students swept round them as they stood still in the middle of the corridor. 'Oh,' said Treece. 'There's something I wanted to ask you.' He began to fiddle with his clothes, right there in the middle of the corridor, in a most alarming way; is he going to do it here, in public, to compromise me? Emma wondered. But it was nothing like that at all; Treece's black motor-cycling coat was covered with great zips, which he kept undoing, thrusting his hand inside, in order to produce, after a great deal of struggle, simply a diary. 'I wonder if I could trespass on your time and good nature again,' said Treece. 'I'm giving a little tea next Friday for the first-year honours people, at four, and I wondered if you could come along.'

Both of them realized, simultaneously, that this was how it had all started last time; after playing with the thought for a moment, both politely ignored it. 'I'd be pleased to,' said Emma. 'Nothing formal, you understand,' said Treece, looking down gratefully at her through his goggles. 'It would be pleasant and I thought too that you could act as a sort of bridge between them and me.'

'I suppose I could,' said Emma, pocketing any expectations of the evening; no-man's-lands were notoriously difficult to populate. 'Well, I must be on my way,' said Treece, doing up his zippers; and with one more nod and a smile apiece, both went their ways to their respective problems.

Treece went out to his bicycle, in the middle of the back wheel of which sat a squat black engine. He climbed aboard and drove off, his L-plates fluttering in the October wind, the engine puttering down there in the wheel behind him. 'Mind,' cried a nervous old man as he whistled past. A drizzling rain was splashing coldly on his face and misting his goggles. Treece scarcely noticed, for he was still within the warmth of the little encounter. Emma Fielding was a sensitive and mature woman, careful of the feelings of others, and what he was wont

to call 'a very worthwhile person'; if anyone asked for a reference, that was what he would have said. Sensitive, intelligent,
scrupulous, liberal-minded (and pretty, too – one had better not
forget that), she was just the sort of person to marry Eborebelosa. Why, then, had she rejected him? Perhaps he was being
unfair – and then he saw that he *was*, of course. Why had he
been feeling so offended? As if it was he who had been rejected? Because it was he who had been rejected; this had been
the thought nagging at the back of his mind. His motives were
far from pure; it was his protest on behalf of the international
spirit, his cry for foreign races, that he felt had been turned
down. All that Emma was doing was conceiving the matter in
simple human terms; she was all that he thought she was;
she had simply wanted to do as little harm as possible. Like
so many liberals, he had conceived of actions in terms of ideas,
when there was nothing in the action but pure action. As soon
as he observed the treacherous nature of the moral stance he
had taken, he was bathed in apology. Of course she didn't
have to marry Eborebelosa, not if she didn't want to.

Treece found the driving test office and went in to look for
the examiner. He was a tired-looking little man with a suspicious face, and he was clutching a clipboard. 'Heyup,' he said.
'You're early.' 'I know this is just a gesture; I know you don't
pass anyone first time,' said Treece to him, politely. 'Where's
your vehicle?' asked the examiner. Treece took him outside
and showed him the bicycle. 'Right,' said the examiner. 'I want
you to go down the hill and then round the block back here,
giving the appropriate signals as you go.' Treece let in the
clutch and drove off. He turned the corner at the bottom of
the hill and ran over a policeman's foot. The policeman stopped
him and told him that the next time he saw him riding like
that he'd have him at the police station so fast his feet wouldn't
touch the ground. Treece looked back; the examiner seemed to
be out of sight. As he got into the heavy traffic of the Market
Square his nerve started to go. Then, suddenly, the clutch cable
snapped. Treece tried to get started again, nervously, for he
was at the central point of five intersecting roads, and traffic
was piling up around him. It was no use. There was only one

thing to do, and Treece did it; he lifted the bicycle up and carried it to the kerb. He looked around for the examiner, who had said he would be in the crowd. 'Are you taking my driving test?' he kept asking little men in the press. Then, to the right, he saw the clipboard. He went up to the examiner and told him what had happened. 'Did I pass?' he asked.

CHAPTER THREE

I

IT had become the custom for the professors in the departments of the Faculty of Arts and elsewhere to give those little teas, to one of which Professor Treece had invited Emma Fielding, in the interests of good conversation and invigorating contact between (as they said in the provinces) staff and students. Professor Treece had fallen in line, rather recalcitrantly, with the established custom; established customs were, after all, things one did fall in line with. He was, however, very nervous of these occasions. Treece's predecessor had been in the habit of having night-long house parties, circulating around a keg of beer which was placed in the middle of the room, and everyone (even the professor whose home, on one such occasion, had caught fire) agreed that those had been great occasions and had much advanced the quality of university life; but in those days the department was smaller, everyone knew everyone's first name, and students gladly cooperated in carrying home drunken faculty members to lay them on the doorstep at dawn. Treece now felt about his predecessor much as he felt about what Adam did to Eve: he could have forgiven him, if it hadn't been for the precedent he'd set.

Treece's real problem was that, while the other professors were equipped with wives, he was not; and wives, in particular circumstances like these, turned out to be a positive advantage, for wives poured out tea and sustained a level of polite conversation. Treece's own ventures in this spirit had always taken on a strange tone and had not remained unvisited by disaster of one kind or another. On the last occasion, for instance, the year before, Treece had been inveigled into disclosing an interest in bell-ringing, and had actually been persuaded into giving a performance of 'Mary had a Little Lamb' on a peal of handbells which he did not feel he had yet lived down.

It was a cold November day when Louis Bates, in his long overcoat and his mittens, arrived at the door of Treece's house an hour early. The pavements glittered with frost, a yellow haze hung in the air, and the gardens of nearby houses were an expanse of naked, hard brown soil. Treece was one of those persons who go through life endeavouring not to accumulate possessions, because possessions are ties, and Treece wanted to be tied to nothing, because possessions define character, and Treece did not want his character defined. Treece had moved all his possessions into his unfurnished house and it still looked like an unfurnished house, waiting to be rented, in a none too distinguished part of town. He had a housekeeper, who came in from time to time, when the spirit moved her; she talked and worked, and then she talked and rested, and then she just talked. Dust blew about the landings in great puff-balls, but Treece was grateful to her for coming in, because he had learned what Mrs Watson thought about birth control; and he learned that if you bought blancmange you only had to add milk to it, and it was very filling; and he learned that if you bought nylon shirts, you could wash them out yourself at night and hang them over the bath, and they would be ready for wear next morning; and he learned that you can get quite good biscuits at Woolworths; and sometimes he felt that, if Mrs Watson won the pools, and he lost his job, he could have made Mrs Watson a very good housekeeper. When Louis Bates rang the bell, Mrs Watson was having the afternoon off, helping someone to have a baby, and Treece went to the door himself, expecting to find the laundryman. He was straightway presented with a major social quandary: could one fairly ask the too-early guest to wander about the cold winter streets and return in an hour, when the sandwiches would be made and the preparations completed, the old pair of working trousers and the frilly apron replaced by a suit – or must one invite him in and perhaps even entertain him? Louis, on the other hand, had no such social doubts, and politely and firmly indicated what he considered appropriate:

'I'm afraid I'm a little early,' he said, 'but that's because I didn't want to be late. I have no sense of time.'

'I think we said four o'clock, didn't we?' asked Treece, opening the door no wider. 'It's now not quite three.'

'I know,' said Louis, and at this point it dawned on Treece that Louis actually intended to stay, for some abstruse purpose.

'None of your colleagues has arrived yet,' Treece said.

The remark did not perturb Louis at all. '*Après moi, le déluge,*' he said.

Treece saw that he had no alternative and gave way, and Louis stepped confidently into the hall, unbuttoning his coat and looking with interest about him at the decoration. 'I thought we might have a little chat about how I was getting on, you know,' said Louis.

'I think we might try and preserve this as a social occasion,' said Treece; then he had some doubts about this remark, which he feared might give Louis a false impression of his progress, and he added, 'Though I don't think Dr Carfax, who'll be here tonight, incidentally, would mind if I told you that he was remarking only the other day what a bright lad you were in all the work you'd done for him.'

Louis disclosed embarrassed delight and promptly became entangled in his coat. 'Yes, I thought I'd done a few good things for him,' he said. 'Let me take that for you,' said Treece, rescuing Louis from his remarkably long overcoat, which he had somehow contrived to wind about him like a shroud. He took the coat into the closet. It was really the first time he had been confronted by Louis Bates; and confrontation was exactly what it was, for the full impact of Louis Bates, person, was for good or ill stamped upon his mind at this moment. He was still annoyed with Louis for his too early arrival (even if Louis was a genius, which he hadn't yet conceded, he didn't expect him to take eccentricity to the point of downright inconvenience; and supposing he wasn't?), and he was suddenly reminded of something that had been said in the Senior Common Room over coffee on that occasion earlier in the week when Adrian Carfax had remarked, 'Bates is a bright lad.' Everyone who knew Louis appeared to agree with this except Dr Viola Masefield, who had Louis for tutorials, and who had remarked, 'But what about him as a person?' Treece had been inclined to be amused by this example of the faculty which women seemed to have for reducing abstract issues into personal terms, in the manner of one of his girl students who had once said she held a low critical opinion of Donne's poetry because she 'didn't think she would like him as a person, really'. 'I suspect', Treece had remarked, 'that his personal qualities are underestimated here by his fellow students, largely because they aren't used to his kind.' Treece wondered as he said this whether he really believed it; it had not occurred to him before, and he was a little surprised to find himself coming so strongly out in Louis's support. 'He's brighter than the others and much more widely read,' said Viola, 'but there's nothing special about that.' 'Well,' said Carfax, laughing, 'that remark wouldn't be an unjust epitaph for anyone in this room' – and he gestured at the solemn conclave of professors and lecturers, each sipping coffee from behind a copy of the *Manchester Guardian* or the *British Journal of Sociology* – 'and it would certainly bear the stamp of the age.' 'Spengler would like that,' said someone. Viola Masefield became somewhat heated at this point, and began to flick the ash of her cigarette about violently; it wasn't funny: 'But he seems to think that it entitles him to special attention, and I don't see why it should.' Again someone laughed, but Carfax, as if suddenly recognizing the truth of the observation, and its special aptness, said, 'Yes, I suppose that's true' – and he went on to tell how, the previous day, while in the middle of a lecture on Chaucer, he had been seized by a fit of coughing, and in the pause before he recovered his place there had come from the back row of the lecture-room the sound of Louis's voice, low, insistent, concerned, saying, 'You ought to take more care of yourself; it might turn to something. I always take rose-hip syrup.' After they had laughed at this story, Viola said, 'Yes, that's just the sort of thing he would do.' 'Oh, come now, Viola,' Treece had said, for the remark sounded malicious; 'his keenness seems as good a reason as any for giving him the attention he wants. Intelligence is a good thing to discriminate on behalf of, surely.' 'I don't mind giving it,' Viola said firmly, 'but I don't think he should expect it. He sees himself as quite naturally privileged.' 'But why not?

Where can he, if not here? He comes from a background where intelligence isn't an advantage, but a curse; he's fought to get here, where he thinks it's respected; and then we're as bad as everyone else.' Treece had been left uneasy by the whole matter. He was always somewhat awed by that tendency of people, of women in particular, to come to immediate personal judgements on acquaintances, to like or dislike them intensely from the moment of encounter. Love at first sight, with its emphasis on the physical aspect of personality, its concern for appearance, was something that Treece did not believe in for other people. They might do it but they were wrong. He objected strongly to other people's idylls; if they weren't going to live properly, if they were going to make a joke of the whole human business, well, he had no time for them; he expected a thoughtful apprehension of all men by all men. It worried him that he very rarely got it. He himself was perfectly responsive to all influences, and took experience as it came, registering it, analysing it, but not coming to immediate decisive judgements on it; after all, experience was what it was, and it came out of the void. You didn't make up your mind about it like *that*. Thus while he had a favourable or an unfavourable impression of people, Treece never supposed that the fact that he did not get on with them, or that they did not appear to like him, was to be traced to anything but a deficiency in himself; his soul was not, alas, wide enough to encompass the whole world, but at least he *wished* that it was. With Treece you felt that the world was his fault; by existing himself, he *made* it, and he wanted to apologize for it, as he was sure God would want to if he were here.

Thus Treece had not given any assent to Viola's opinion (in any case, as she sat there, with flushed face, she seemed to know that her arguments were bad ones; if only she had found the right words, and then everyone would have seen what it was she was putting her finger on) because he considered that it was based on purely personal reasons – which was true. The personal reason was that Louis had announced widely to unimpressed colleagues that he was madly in love with Dr Viola Masefield, and in tutorials he would sit, wet lips shining, eyes firmly fixed on the low necklines of Viola's dresses. Viola had had to stop wearing sweaters and low necklines, a matter of pain to her, because she still had a husband to catch. Moreover, Louis would call on her at all times for her help, this ever since the second day of term, on the slightest of pretexts, observing her every movement – the way she stretched up for books off the shelves; the sight of her legs as she emerged from behind her desk – 'with eyes popping out', as Dr Viola put it in complaining to her dear friend, Tanya. On one occasion he had actually telephoned her, late at night, at Tanya's house, where she had a flat (bringing her downstairs three flights in her nightdress to the telephone), to ask whether she objected to a mixed metaphor in an essay on the historical background to Restoration drama which he was writing for her – so long as he knew it was mixed.

But *naturally privileged*! The phrase stuck, and although Treece went on to say then, as he had to, 'I feel compelled to pooh-pooh this, Viola, you know,' it formulated something recognizable in Louis's behaviour. Treece now realized that his impression of Bates had in fact been coloured by Viola's, and by Louis's behaviour now, which seemed to bear out what she said. Treece realized with shame just how hard he had been on Viola's viewpoint up until now, when he was actually sharing the experiences that formed it; how easy it is to say that others are glib! Damn, thought Treece, as he reflected just how unprepared he was to deal with a guest; Louis had caught him with his small-talk unprepared, his sandwiches unmade, his fire unstoked. One doesn't allow social solecisms, because manners are made for easy living; they are a species of kindness; it is not the Emily Post in one that is affronted, but the moral core. Why had Bates done it? Perhaps, Treece thought, as he padded back in his old slippers to the hall, it was a self-centred insensitivity to the responses of the world about him; or perhaps it was a sense of inferiority which manifested itself in poses of excessive assurance. Oh, I can say this, Treece thought, I can be liberal spirited about the whole thing; but it doesn't make me *like* it. Out in the hall Louis stood, looking ungainly and forlorn, slapping the pockets of his rather shabby suit and pulling down his shirt-sleeves at the wrist. Treece shunted him into the drawing-room, which had been filled for the occasion with a miscellany of chairs brought from all parts of the house, from other houses, from (it seemed), the scrap-yard.

'You must excuse me if I leave you here, but I haven't finished getting things ready yet, and I have to change,' said Treece. Louis appeared at first hurt, and then baffled, by this news. He was well aware that if he was left alone in an empty room he would quickly be nibbled at by misfortune; he would pull over a bookcase while trying to take out a book, or be discovered by an unwarned housekeeper and accused of burglary. He knew himself and he knew his gods; he knew the rotation of his misfortunes. 'This is a nice room,' he said quick-wittedly.

Treece looked around, surprised; it had not changed, it was as it was, and that was patently the last thing that could be said of it. If he was the sort of person who *liked* nice rooms, he was damned if this was the sort of room he would be living in. 'Oh, I don't think so,' said Treece. This bewildered Louis, who wondered why, if it was not, Treece had got mixed up with it. He had not yet associated the philosophy of *Live as I say, not as I do* with Treece. However, he hastily tried another tack.

'Is there anything I can be doing?' he suggested. 'I'm afraid there isn't,' said Treece, nervous of Louis's desire to please. He made hastily for the door and Louis planned an even more desperate move. 'Do you think I could have a bath?' he cried.

But Treece had gone. He had withdrawn to the kitchen and, up to his elbows in pastry (Mrs Watson had taught him how to make cakes), was wondering what Louis was doing and what would have happened to the room when he got back. In fact, Louis passed through all the stages of privation in a strange house – he examined the ornaments on the mantel, looked at the pictures on the walls, noticed the books in the bookcase and read the spicier pages of the medical directory, peered at his teeth in the mirror, made sure his fly buttons were fastened – and he was cutting his hair at the back with a pair of scissors found in an open drawer of the bureau when Treece returned, nearly an hour later, to start the fire. 'I ought to have done this before I came,' said Louis Bates.

And now the other guests began to arrive, chilled by the frost, noses watering, to find Louis, ensconced before the fire, his hair cut at one side, acknowledging his introduction to his colleagues, whom he knew well, but to whom Treece introduced him none the less, with a gracious 'How do you do?' The group accumulated, sitting in a quiet half-circle about the barren room, discussing the weather and how the house must be filled with sun during the summer. 'What a lovely fire!' exclaimed a very young-seeming girl. As people began to point out to one another, it was an odd house; Treece looked as though he had been billeted here; he probably slept on straw. 'I wonder whether it looks any different when it's empty,' whispered someone.

A drawing by Picasso of a dove of peace was pinned roughly up over the mantlepiece. 'I say,' said a knowing girl, coming into the room, 'isn't that a Peter Scott?' A girl who was always having her bottom pinched had it pinched in one corner; she let out a cry and Treece looked round nervously. 'Wind,' said the girl unsteadily. It was a usual enough group of people, for those who were in it, and everyone knew how everyone else could be expected to behave. Louis Bates, from his chair, was wondering how many women in the room were virgins, and he determined to ask before the night was out. Treece, coming again into the room, heard someone say: '... I suppose he remembers the war.'

The evening promptly started, when it did start, on an unfortunate note when Professor Treece, steering the tea-trolley into the room, took the corner too wide and drove it hard against the doorpost. People jumped up and exclaimed in fright. 'It's all right,' cried someone heroically; cakes and sandwiches hailed about the room; cups flew into the air and smashed hard on to the floor. 'All's well,' cried Treece so genially that it seemed as if he had done it on purpose. Students gathered round and salvaged the debris, wiping buns clean on skirts and trousers. 'Never mind, never mind,' said Treece. 'Let it stop until Monday.'

'Didn't I see you at the theatre last Saturday night?' said a student with a beard in a very sly manner. Treece noticed some of the female students looking at him curiously. He remembered the nudes. He said something noncommittal. The doorbell rang.

It was Emma Fielding, breathless from her bicycle ride. Treece greeted her warmly. 'Come inside, Miss Fielding; how nice,' he cried, taking her coat as though his life up to that time had been empty without it. He ushered her into the hall, where a Utrillo reproduction hung precariously. 'Isn't Utrillo delightful?' said Emma pleasantly. 'It's exciting, isn't it?' said Treece; he had, Emma noticed, a fondness for using oddly exaggerated words to define things, as if the ordinary commerce of language was just not quite enough for him. 'But,' he added, 'I sometimes wonder if Utrillo is appropriate to a hall.'

It was just a simple conversational gambit of mine, thought Emma, but if he really wants to make something out of it – well, let him; it's his party. He probably wanted to make it appear as if he had *thought* about the way the place was decorated.

'Oh, I think so,' said Emma.

'He always goes well with the smell of a river, or the sea, doesn't he?'

Grasping at a straw, Emma said, 'But the whiteness of your hall brings out his blues so splendidly.' Things were getting rather strained; even Treece was beginning to realize that this was the phoneyest kind of conversation you could get.

Sounds of something not unlike riot now came from behind the door of the drawing-room, and this recalled Treece to his responsibilities. 'Look, Miss Fielding,' he said rapidly. 'I'd be glad if you could act informally as a kind of hostess. My housekeeper's gone home, and things aren't going very well. I upset a tea-trolley and there's a man called Bates in there who's been very difficult. Everyone seems terrified of him and I'm afraid he's going to get up and start cutting his own hair.' Gently, gently, Emma wanted to say; you poor, poor thing. Under which king, Bezonian? was clearly the gist of his little speech; are you with them, or with me?

'Yes, of course I will,' said Emma.

Treece beamed and pulled the creases out of the arms of his suit. 'This is one of the occasions when bachelorhood proves a disadvantage,' he said gratefully and took her arm so affectionately that she presumed he had thought of another. Was he going to haul her off upstairs, leaving first-year honours to riot among the cakes below while he satisfied his passion? Was it worth the loss of a master's degree to resist? Did she want to go, anyway? Questions flurried in Emma's head and it was with the greatest surprise that she found herself not in bed, but in the drawing-room, being introduced to people she already knew. Earlier arrivals now sat silently about the fringe of the room, appraising the wallpaper and looking around for a dog to pat. The man who was causing all the trouble was evident enough; he was a tall, ghoulish man, who could be seen bobbing up and down, smiling a great wet smile, interrupting people's conversation and repeatedly proffering his chair to people who would not have dared to take it from him. Treece introduced her to Bates, and he gave her a very studious looking over, finally reaching down for her hand, shaking it firmly for several moments, and at last replacing it back at her side, where it had come from. 'Where would you like to sit?' he asked. 'I'll sit on the floor,' said Emma. Bates now felt compelled to make the supreme sacrifice: 'Have my chair,' he cried. Emma refused, and relief and offence mingled in his face.

Treece went to the door to let in Adrian Carfax and Ian Merrick, and riot broke out again. Emma felt like a spy. Someone was twanging the elastic in the brassière of a girl with a very full figure, who obviously liked it.

'Men are such prancing, leering goats,' said a prim young girl, very stiffly, to no one in particular.

'I broke my teeth on one of those cakes,' said a girl with a lisp. 'Do you think I could thue?'

'I wonder why the prof. doesn't marry?' said a girl in spectacles.

'If only', said the man with the beard; his name was Hopgood, 'to get this place dusted.'

'No, I mean, seriously, Larry, why?'

'Why don't you sleep?' a man was meanwhile asking a girl with a fringe. 'What do you worry about?'

'I just don't know,' said the girl. 'For one thing, I worry about being worried.'

'Just look at you now; you're all tense,' said the young man. 'Relax a minute, relax. Forget about things. There, isn't that better?'

'No,' said the girl.

'You don't want to sleep, that's what it is,' said the man. 'You think there's something about not sleeping. You think it makes you more sensitive.'

'How silly you are,' said the girl spitefully.

'Perhaps we could be reading poems aloud,' said Bates.

'Well, now, everyone's here, I think,' said Treece coming back into the room. He consulted a list which he took from his pocket. 'Yes; that's right. So shall we sit down and talk communally?' Treece had planned out a norm for the evening, to which he insisted it conform, so everyone took his place in a half-circle about the fire, and talked communally, while Treece, conscious of his role as host, tried assiduously to mix everyone's taste, now being highbrow, now lowbrow, now being *piano*, now *fortissimo*, all the time advancing prepared topics – the cinema, the cost of toothpaste, the fun of making one's own lampshades. He was editing the occasion; perhaps it's going to be on television, said someone.

'What a lovely fire,' said the girl who had said it once before.

'Do you like fires, Miss Winterbottom?' asked someone politely. The student with the beard was furtively hooting with laughter. Conversation in the half-circle of guests, who were all now clasping large paper serviettes, was fitful. The sandwiches and cakes, which had clearly been made by a none-too-competent confectioner some days before, were passed round. 'Do eat some more cakes,' cried Treece heartily. 'You seem eager to get rid of them,' remarked Carfax pleasantly; as soon as he had bitten into one of the confections he realized the error of his comment, which would, he knew only too well, be retailed around the whole department next day.

'This is one of the occasions when one could do with being married,' said Treece with a bright smile to one of the girls, the enthusiastic Miss Winterbottom. 'Can I help?' asked Miss Winterbottom. The man with the beard burst into fresh laughter. 'I mean, like getting something from the kitchen,' went on Miss Winterbottom, blushing to a full shade of red. 'Next time you must let me lend you my wife,' said Carfax amiably. All were amused, on the politest level. 'Like the Eskimos do,' muttered the man with the beard. 'What's that?' asked Treece pleasantly; there were no secrets here. A girl in glasses with immense, brightly coloured rims kicked the man's ankle to indicate that his remark lacked taste. This spurred him to further efforts and he embarked on a premeditated routine.

'Is it true, Professor Treece, that you're interested in hand-bell ringing?' he asked with an assumed nonchalance that reminded the girl in glasses how sweet she found him.

'It was an interest of mine, Hopgood; you're perfectly right,' said Treece, going a little red. 'But there are richer pastimes.' This was what Hopgood thought a typical 'Treece' remark and he smiled inside his beard and looked about him as if for approbation.

'Aren't bus-fares terribly expensive?' asked the girl in spectacles, smiling maternally at Treece.

'Transport', said Treece, seizing this kindly opening, 'must be something of an item to those people who live in lodgings a long way out.' Due consideration was given to this proposition; assent followed.

'Like me,' said Louis, as if to give the remark direction. 'It's rather hard, you know, for me to decide whether it's cheaper to travel on buses or whether to walk and have my shoes repaired more often.' Louis spoke so slowly and deliberately that his quandary took on the guise of a metaphysical problem set before learned arbiters. 'I was hoping to buy some new pyjamas this winter, but I see I shall have to make do with the others.'

All present appeared to sympathize silently with Louis's dilemma, save for the hardy Hopgood, who was busy scraping out his fingernails with a penknife and looking for someone to exchange grins with. All at once Treece stood up and took a silver cigarette box, bearing his initials, from the mantelpiece, offering it about the room. Most people present confessed that they did not smoke, and Miss Winterbottom invoked a moral issue by stating that her parents would be ashamed of her had she accepted. 'They fur the lungs,' said Louis. 'Nonsense,' said Carfax genially. Only he and Emma Fielding took cigarettes. 'I have my pipe,' said Mr Lee, patting his pocket. 'I have my beard,' said Mr Hopgood in his turn. The point of this recondite jest was missed, or ignored, by everyone save Dr Carfax, who laughed affably.

'It seems to me that the young people of today haven't any wish to appear sophisticated,' said Merrick, somewhat bitingly. 'Undergrads aren't what they were.'

'This isn't Cambridge, you know,' Carfax told Merrick, who did know, knew it bitterly.

'I just don't think our families would like it,' said Miss Winterbottom.

'But don't you ever feel the least desire to shock your parents, to break away from their values and begin to establish a code of your own? Surely part of the task of the young intellectual is to revalue traditions and values and assess their validity for his own generation.'

'Oh no, Mr Merrick,' said Miss Winterbottom. 'Oh, we're not intellectuals,' said someone else. 'I don't know what my father would think if he heard you'd been telling us that sort of thing,' said Miss Winterbottom further. Again Mr Hopgood laughed; he was sophisticated enough to be having a lovely time.

'What Miss Winterbottom wishes to say,' intoned the deep voice of Louis Bates, 'and would tell you, I think, if she were more articulate, is that we aren't young intellectuals. What have we to do with thinking? These are the fifties, not the twenties. We're even sophisticated about being sophisticated. We're out-and-out relativists; we can't believe that *anyone's* right; their rectitude turns to ashes in our hands. And what good is it being an intellectual? This is the time of the common man. You miss everything if you are an intellectual. All you can say, if you are one, is that if we had been invited to the party we should have made it a different kind of do. The pattern of things doesn't come from us and we wish to be as little a part of it as possible. I think that's what Miss Winterbottom was trying to say, isn't it?'

'No,' said Miss Winterbottom.

There followed a long pause, while everyone looked into his teacup and tried to think of something to say. Louis wondered if he could ask about the virgins now. 'I like your curtains,' offered Miss Winterbottom, 'or have I said that?' The pause was resumed, while everyone pretended to listen to the sound of cars passing along the main road outside. 'How is the thesis going, Miss Fielding?' said Dr Carfax at last.

'I'm just reaching the stage where you feel that it will take you at least a hundred years to finish writing it.'

'What's your thesis on?' said Miss Winterbottom politely.

'It's a study of the fish imagery in Shakespeare's tragedies,' said Emma with a smile. People began to warm again after the shock of Louis's diatribe.

Meanwhile, Louis had been gazing interestedly around the assembled company, wondering what they were thinking of him. Opposite him he noticed Emma Fielding. She offered, he noticed, a warmth of feature that was conspicuously lacking in the other students; her comments up to now had been pointed and intelligent, such as they were; and she was not affected noticeably by the common unease. The process by which she ate a cake, nibbling it with white, straight teeth, somehow held him fascinated; it was as if he had never seen anyone do it before. 'Do you mind if I change places with someone?' he said and, looking at the girl to the right of Emma, added, 'You, for instance?' The exchange was effected and Louis, to his great delight, found himself beside his quarry. 'Hello,' he said.

A student who was doing very badly, and thought that Treece had taken a dislike to him, decided to make his mark. 'I don't believe Eliot's poetry means anything at all. I think everyone's taken in by it. I'll bet he doesn't know what it means himself.'

'Well, Cocoran has taken only one term to see through our professional charlatanism,' said Merrick, satirically. 'Well,' said Carfax more generously, 'as one who has marked finals papers, I wouldn't say that was completely false.'

'What do you think of Eliot, then, Bates?' asked Treece. Louis had been peering inquisitively at Emma's white arms, and now he looked up questioningly. 'I never read any,' said Bates. Cocoran wished he had said that. 'Through lack of time or inclination?' asked Treece. 'As a matter of principle,' said Louis impressively. 'Anyone who has any pretensions to writing poetry, however modest, is better away from him at present, in my view. I read him once, and, as you know, his idiom is pervasive. I simply want to avoid it.'

'You have literary aspirations?' asked Treece pleasantly. 'I've had a few poems published in a tiny literary magazine,' explained Louis. 'They didn't pay me much for them, of course.' Actually they had not paid him anything, but at least he had *published*.

'I'm always interested to come upon signs of literary activity among my people,' said Treece. 'Do any of you others do anything in that line?' No one responded. 'No,' went on Treece, with a little sigh. 'I suppose not. Of course when I was up at University, everyone seemed to have a novel or a sheaf of poems tucked away somewhere. It was that sort of time, of course – Auden at Oxford, Empson and Isherwood at Cambridge; there were so many *enfants terribles* that it was almost fashionable not to be writing anything. I suppose that kind of thing wasn't so bad really. You don't find it so much in the provincial universities, of course; people aren't so concerned to make an impression, I suppose, and they come here to work and get a job, not have a good time or enrich their souls too much.'

It was the little sigh, so evocative of vanished glories, that amused Hopgood, to whom the present had a stamina that no other time could ever have had; people, he felt, were sensible, knew where they were going, wanted to get there safe and sound. He said so.

'Well,' said Louis, in defiance of all, 'I think I'm enriching my soul.'

Merrick looked at him in amusement. 'The trouble is, isn't it, Stuart,' he said, 'that people like that very rarely come to very much in the end? Auden and Isherwood are the ones who did, but think of all those others.'

'Oh, that's almost inevitable, isn't it?' answered Treece. 'There's always a certain amount of wastage of this sort. The question really is, are universities the best places for geniuses to prosper? I'm not sure they are. I know they gain some kind of stimulus and training. But then they miss in experience – and so they either overreach themselves, or they write one of these satirical novels about university life that people keep writing. I hope no one's writing one of those about us, is he?'

'No one, surely, would set out to be a social outcast,' said the girl in spectacles, with a laugh. 'Oh, I don't know,' said Merrick. 'There are many who like it.' 'Besides,' said the girl, 'we don't do funny things.'

Louis felt extremely rebuffed. 'I think I'm not without wider experience, in so far as what you say applies to me; not that I want to be hypersensitive about all this. Besides, I spent several years in a girls' school.'

'And then they spotted you?' asked Hopgood.

'No,' said Merrick. 'You won't be without experience, then.'

But Emma Fielding thought these remarks rather unkind; she began to feel about Louis that he was not as black as he was painted. Treece's nervousness of him seemed to be highly exaggerated; but since he expected her to shepherd Louis, and control his extravagances, she determined to do so – but now for his own sake. 'I think it's wonderful to be able to write,' she said, and Louis, turning amid the laughter, found her pretty face bent in his direction, intense, serious, her dark eyes clouded with thought, her dark, wispy hair falling over her brow, her white teeth shining. 'You know, what amazes me about writing is this,' said Emma, 'what an amazing organization of all corners of the spirit goes on, if you see what I mean, to concentrate on what's being written. When it's good, I mean.'

'Well, yes,' said Louis speculatively; women, he thought, said things like this, of course – it was part of their congenital course towards maternity, their natural proclivity towards the mystic. Yet as a remark it was more than kind; Louis was at least not too pedestrian to see that. He looked at her and grew warm. What if he surrendered to mad passion and kissed the inside of her elbow there, in front of Treece and Merrick, Carfax and the prim virgins of the department? Would he be sent down? Would he be regarded as a lovable literary eccentric? Would his marks in terminal examinations have gone up or down? And if he could have no more kissed her arm than have thrown cakes at Professor Treece, yet it was still the fact that this fresh, vigorous, youthful passion had grown where there was none before. He leaned close to Emma's ear and murmured, gently, confidingly, 'I like you.'

'Well, now,' said Professor Treece all at once; a plate from his lap tumbled to the floor as he rose and was picked up by some student attentive to his chances in examinations, 'I expect you'll all want to be getting back.' Treece wanted to have a bath and cut his toe-nails. Most people took his point. 'I suppose we'd better,' said someone, glossing over what Treece had not even bothered to conceal. 'Is that the time?' proffered someone else; and they all began to troop, in little bands, into the hall, carefully avoiding the debris of the accident with the tea-trolley. Only Louis lingered; he wanted to talk about literature. 'Talking of creation ...' he began; his voice echoed in an empty room. He rose and went across to the doorway, where in frantic haste everyone was busy with the process of departure. Coats and hats were put on at speed; dishevelled people burst at trotting pace out of the door, uttering terse farewells.

'Such a pleasant evening,' said Miss Winterbottom to Louis. 'I don't know how he can *endure* on his own like this, do you? What he needs is a nice wife.' 'Isn't he a lovely man?' remarked the girl in spectacles, while Louis held her handbag as hastily she powdered her nose. 'I wonder if he realizes how devastating that sort of embarrassed look of his can be?' 'I wonder,' murmured Louis.

Then Treece was among them once again, ten coats over his arm. 'Does anyone want to use a cloakroom?' he asked politely. 'What for?' murmured Hopgood to Louis. 'No, thank you,' said someone who obviously did.

Treece was looking for Emma. We all of us have small secrets that we would not wish to have charted up against us in any history of our days, and Treece's was that, when Emma had told him that, in her crisis with Eborebelosa, she had named him as her suitor, named him surely with consideration, he had felt enormously pleased. It was not a passing gesture; it counted for something, but what? Treece had, of course, absolved Emma from any responsibility concerning Eborebelosa; in fact, when he had returned home, chastened after the driving test, he had written at once to tell her so; and she had written back, telling him that she had already absolved herself, and that, while she still suspected her reasons, each human being had to live a liveable way of life, a *modus vivendi*, and life with Eborebelosa as his fifth wife was certainly, for her, not that. Treece now wanted to see her and tell her that he thought this reasonable and right. But already she had gone.

Louis permitted himself to leave last. 'Thank you very much, professor,' he said, hovering in the hope of some final blessing. 'Good night, Bates,' said Treece; bath and not benediction was what was in *his* mind. 'A most pleasant evening,' went on Louis tentatively; the girl in spectacles pulled warningly at his coat. 'Don't slip in the drive,' said Treece. 'It's turned rather icy.' Aware of strong pressures against him, Louis gave ground. His purpose changed; now what he wanted was to find Emma Fielding. She seemed to have disappeared completely. 'Oo, I'm cold,' said Miss Winterbottom pleasantly. 'I can't talk to you now,' said Louis.

Hopgood was saying: 'I was sitting next to Carfax. His stomach never stopped rumbling all the time we were there.' 'His wife doesn't feed him properly,' said Miss Winterbottom. 'It was like a ball rolling very slowly down a bagatelle board until it reached the bottom,' said Hopgood. 'Then it would somehow go back to the top again.'

They emerged into the road and then Louis saw Emma, in the distance, riding away on her bicycle. 'Lend me your bike,' he said to Cocoran. 'No,' said Cocoran. 'I don't lend it.' 'You're so naïve,' said Louis spitefully, and he set off hastily down the road in pursuit of the red tail light. In another moment it was gone from view. 'Ah,' sighed Louis, and he turned his footsteps homeward. As he walked, frost biting his ears and fingers, the collar of his long overcoat turned up, he devoted himself to reflection on the events of the evening. For the most part, the people he met had been passers-by; that is, he did not see them as a source of profound sympathies, or in any context wider than the immediately social. To experience people in the context of their full humanity, their whole width of being, was a rare and moving experience; none the less, he had experienced it, and with no less a quantity than Emma Fielding. Parading on through the streets of the municipality, he shortly came to the house at which he lodged. The household – a Mr and Mrs Hopewell, and dog – were sitting in the lounge in silence, contemplating the crumbs of their existence with an admirable solidity. Louis went into the kitchen and made himself a cup of the malty night beverage he always took before retiring. A man has to coddle himself when there is none to do it for him. Then he went upstairs, opened the door of his room, put on the light, shut the window firmly and drew the curtains, for he did not like draughts, took off his overcoat and placed it on the bed as an extra blanket, for he did not like cold, stored away in a drawer two lumps of sugar he had captured at Treece's, went to the bathroom, sat on the toilet, used it and flushed it, washed, cleaned his teeth, and squeezed out a facial blemish, returned to his bedroom, shutting and bolting the door, stripped off his clothes to the top layer of wool underwear, put on his pyjamas, which were rather tatty, sat on the bed and scratched his athlete's foot, and climbed into bed. As he lay there in the darkness, shivering with cold, he thought to himself, I am a lover. He tasted the role for a moment or two; it wasn't all it was said to be. He was not a ladies' man; indeed, he was not anyone's man. But passion visited him from time to time, as it does do most of us, and he had a disposition which laid him open to falling in love quite frequently with persons whom he had never seen before and was not likely to see again. He was not even sure, at times, that success in love was what he wanted; that took you on to the next stage, and this was the one he liked. But now (his face beamed in the darkness) there was Emma. Quite, quite different. Did he want her? Yes he did. Did he love her? Yes yes yes. Did she like him? He rather fancied that she did. He would write to her, or seek her out, tomorrow. And he fell asleep in the warmth of two delightful thoughts: 'I am in love with Emma' and 'Won't she be pleased when I tell her.'

3

A day or two later Treece took his driving test again. It was the same examiner and, Treece felt, rather a strange relationship was growing up between them; it was as if both of them realized that they would both be at this little job for a long time, and had better face up to the fact. 'I like your tie,' said the examiner when Treece turned up again. It was a frosty day and Treece's ears were cold. He slapped them a few times. 'I feel nervous again,' he said. 'If it hadn't been for all that twisting last time, the clutch cable wouldn't have snapped. Look, I've got it again.' He held out his hands, which were vibrating hysterically. 'Now, now, take it easy,' said the examiner. 'I'm not going to chop off your head, you know.' They went out into the road. The bicycle stood there, seedier-looking than ever. 'I want you to go up the hill on this,' said the examiner, 'and come down towards here, making the appropriate signals as you go. We'll try the emergency stop; I'll step into the road and you stop as you would if I was an ordinary road user.'

Treece adjusted his goggles and climbed aboard. Up to the top of the hill he went, signalling with his arms for the most trivial reasons; around he turned, and down he came. Suddenly, out from behind a car, a figure stepped. Treece squeezed the brakes, the bicycle skidded, and then he hit him. His clipboard and hat hurled into the air. It was the examiner.

He'd spoiled his suit, but otherwise he was all right – right enough to go on with the test. Treece had a graze down his nose, but that was nothing. Afterwards, when it was all over, Treece asked: 'Did I pass?' 'Knocks me arse over tip, and then wants to know if he's passed,' said the examiner laughing delightedly. He was getting really fond of Treece. 'Let me know how much it costs to have that suit cleaned,' said Treece. 'See you again,' said the examiner. 'Yes,' said Treece. 'See you again.'

Solace was what Treece wanted at this point; and solace he was offered, for as he chugged off down the High Street who should he see, gazing into the window of an antique shop, but Emma Fielding. He pulled into the kerb and uttered her name. She turned and, on seeing that it was he, came over to his side. 'What have you done to your nose?' she said. 'I've been taking my driving test,' said Treece, taking out his hand-kerchief and wiping the graze. 'Did you pass?' asked Emma. 'I didn't,' said Treece, 'and if the truth is to be expressed I never shall. That is what I have to understand and come to terms with.'

'I'm sorry,' said Emma.

'I wondered if I could trespass on your time and good nature,' said Treece. 'I was just going to have some tea. Will you join me?'

'I have to get some vegetables,' said Emma. 'They sell them off cheap in the evening, and prudence is a virtue that my mother taught me.'

'What were you looking at so concernedly in that window?' asked Treece.

'There's a harmonium in there that I'm very fond of,' said Emma.

'You are fond of music,' said Treece politely, wheeling his bicycle through the streets, 'or just of musical instruments?'

'Both,' said Emma. In fact for her, the harmonium brought back the recollection of a happy period in her youth, when her mother had played at the harmonium on quiet evenings, and she and her sisters had sung. The pursuit had a quaint and foreign flavour about it. What perhaps struck home sharpest was the name of this instrument, which expressed precisely that quality, of harmony, which Emma sought from life. Life as she now led it was perpetually restless, searching, inharmonious; nothing was resolved and there were no firm rocks to settle on. To go home – that was Emma's one desire, but there was no home. It had broken up long ago.

The housewifely aspect of marketing was not lost on Professor Treece, who was interested in the flavours of separate sorts of experience. To pass among the wooden stalls of the market, lighted with heavy yellow-hazed lamps, while the evening airs of the town gathered round its grey buildings in a twilight mist, was a pleasant sensation. It may be, said Treece, that one feels much like this when one is married; he was thinking, specifically, of the heavy bag of potatoes which he was carrying; it was a cosy kind of experience. Things like this had not, for Treece, lost their cultural novelty. Presently they retired to the Kardomah Café and, on the first floor, found a table overlooking the square. It was filled with housewives and clergymen, biting delicately on crumpets.

'I always have tea in town on Mondays,' said Treece, as they sat down, 'because I teach an evening class at the Adult Education Centre here.'

'Do you enjoy teaching adults?' asked Emma.

'Sometimes I think I prefer them to university students; they know what you mean when you talk about life.'

'Do you like talking about life?' asked Emma.

'It's the only way I can get my own back on it,' said Treece. 'And after all its behaviour is scandalous enough. I'm glad I saw you, because I've been wanting to talk to you,' said Treece. 'I wanted to ask you what happened about Mr Eborebelosa. I felt I . . . well, stepped wrong over that.'

'Well, the position now is really rather more complicated,' said Emma with a smile, 'because now someone else wants me to marry *him*, and I don't want to, so I begin to feel that if I ought to marry Mr Eborebelosa then probably I ought to marry him too. With Mr Eborebelosa it's his colour, and with this other one it's his class, that come into the picture. As he told me in a letter, with class you need a lot of goodwill.' Emma was referring to the fact that she had received two letters from Louis Bates, in which he had confessed his mad passion and sought to drag her some way towards the altar. These letters had been so pompous and ill-considered in tone, and so un-related to effective action, that it was impossible for Emma to think of them without either annoyance or amusement. 'Per-haps', said Emma, being a little over-bold, 'the best thing to do would be to decide which one I like least – and then marry him.' Treece peered about him, as if he could see words written on the air, and he looked severely at them; it was not at all funny. Obviously what people had to do in this sort of situation was to summon up all their reserves of goodwill and honest feeling, and get this thing sorted out.

'You know,' Emma said, 'I did go over the whole thing very carefully and seriously. You must do me the justice to think that I try to do the right and honest thing.'

'But I do think that, Miss Fielding,' said Treece, with a pleasant, approving smile. 'I respect your choices.'

'This really upsets me, to be honest,' said Emma. 'Am I some sort of Belle Dame Sans Merci, who tempts people into love without having the least capacity to respond with any? Of course, everyone thinks his behaviour has been sound and honest, and if people only wouldn't be so blind, they'd see it's absolutely right that you should have committed the murder, or stolen the money, or performed the adultery. But I don't think I'm deceiving myself like that, Professor Treece; I honestly don't.'

'And I don't either,' said Professor Treece.

Emma looked out of the window, feeling shaken and dis-turbed. Outside the dusk was creeping up between the market stalls, and it was beginning to rain. The winter weather was really coming; afternoon rain dripped off the roofs, blustery winds buffeted the black, leafless trees, and people went by in their raincoats, looking enclosed and self-contained.

Treece scratched his ear uneasily. 'I want to tell you', he said, 'that I felt I'd misled you in my little conversation, last time we talked. I suppose you're right in accusing me of under-estimating your integrity.'

'Well, I didn't really do that,' said Emma, 'but, you know, I'm twenty-six. It's a terribly old age. I can't afford to make any more mistakes. I try to be fair to people and things, but I want to be fair to myself as well.'

'Yes, I know,' said Treece, 'and I ... well, I apologize.'

'Well, what is it, then?' said a brisk voice; it was the waitress. Treece's head bobbed up. 'What will you have?' he said to Emma. 'Just tea and toast,' said Emma. But Treece was obviously going to take the amount she ate as an index of the degree to which she accepted his apology; he pressed her to more and more.

'The trouble is', said Emma, when the waitress had gone, 'that with one's behaviour one doesn't know what to believe.' Believe, believe, who said believe? Treece's eyes seemed to say; here in my universe there is someone who talks of believing!

'Do you believe?' asked Treece.

'No; I don't really believe; I just do things,' said Emma. It was only men, Emma considered, who believed in things; women recognized that being a woman was way of life enough.

'Do you believe?' asked Emma.

'I believe, I suppose, in my way; I believe in scrupulousness in the face of action. You know, I've spent all my life trying to understand the relationship of action and consequences. I wonder if I shall ever learn – I find myself singularly obtuse. But the two seem in such different spheres – actions are in time and consequences are in suspension.'

'I know what you mean, and in a way I'd say the same,' said Emma. 'But at the same time you aren't really saying anything, are you? Not about the world. I mean, where do you take your values from, and how does this apply to other people?'

'But it doesn't,' said Treece, 'and it isn't a valuable position. You mistake me if you think I'm trying to elevate it into a public philosophy. All I'm saying is that I don't believe in public philosophies, that I want to live according to my own lights, and that I don't want to change anyone else.'

'But you did, with me,' said Emma.

'That's true,' said Treece, 'and I've repented. But ... if people can believe in God, so much the better; they have a code they can, and ought to, live by.'

'But you cultivate your own garden?'

'My *avant*-garden,' said Treece.

'And how do you determine what's scrupulous?'

'The same way as you do,' said Treece. 'I try to examine what lies before me in all its complexity and to bring to bear on it all the moral resources at my disposal. That is what life is, as far as I'm concerned.'

'But there are three obvious objections to that, aren't there?' said Emma cruelly. 'One is that your process inhibits action; that is you weigh intellectually, instead of being a moral being and acting and letting your morality come out in your action. And then one can scrupulously rob or murder or commit perversion. And it offers nothing for other people.'

'I am a teacher,' said Treece, 'and I talk about life, as I told you. And, moreover, I think there are certain moral passions common to all men.'

'The trouble with me is I just enjoy more and more things,' said Emma. 'First I just liked milk; then I learned to like tea and coffee; and then cocoa and lemonade; and then port and sherry; and then gin and whisky. Soon I shall like everything.'

'You must hurry up,' said Treece.

'What I begin to suspect about life is that anything in it is pleasure if you can only simply adjust, in some ways, to the terms of what's offered. If anyone has a pure and honest self, that stays meticulously clean on the sidelines, I have; but it's a fight to remain like that.'

'Well, this *has* been interesting,' said Treece. 'I don't know about you, but I've enjoyed this. There's something about tea-shops,' Treece added. 'I can take teashops in the same way that people take tranquillizers.'

'Yes, I've enjoyed it too,' said Emma. 'You must let me repay this invitation. Why don't you have tea next Monday with me at the flat.'

'Splendid,' said Treece. He half-rose and gave an expansive gesture with his hand, which overturned the teapot, pouring its contents neatly into Emma's lap. 'Damnation,' said Emma, getting up suddenly. 'I'm terribly sorry,' said Treece. He kneeled down in front of her and tried to eliminate the large stain with a discarded teacake. Emma pushed his hand away with an angry gesture. A waitress came with a cloth. Emma looked at his face and said: 'It will wash out.' 'I'll buy you another dress,' said Treece. 'Certainly not,' said Emma. Treece got out his diary and made a note: 'That's one suit and one dress today,' he said plaintively. 'Sometimes I wish I could just go away and start again in another town.'

Emma asked for her coat and he brought it. 'It doesn't show under the coat; that's one consolation,' he said. 'I don't need consoling,' said Emma. 'It was an accident.' 'No,' said Treece. 'Oh, really,' said Emma. 'Must you make a crisis out of it?' The waitress brought their change and they left. Outside the evening was cold and wet, and Treece was terrified that he had given her pneumonia; it was a poor way to start a friendship. Tea dripped steadily from the hem of her dress to the pavement; sadly he rubbed it in with his foot. 'You ought to take that dress off,' he said. 'Here?' said Emma sharply. 'No, not here,' said Treece. 'I'm going home to change,' said Emma; she was annoyed with his officiousness, for all she wanted was for him to look after her, neither humbly nor apologetically, but sensibly; it wasn't a crisis for him; he should be thinking of her. 'Has it gone right through?' he asked. 'Yes, it has,' said Emma. 'And can I still come to tea next Monday?' he added as she turned to go. 'I suppose so,' said Emma.

CHAPTER FOUR

I

DR VIOLA MASEFIELD'S flat was not a place where you simply lived; you *proved* something. It was a showpiece of the unendurably modern – when you saw the modern like that, it looked so dated that you couldn't believe it. When you went there, you always discussed things as they discuss things in *Vogue*: What does one do with dustbins to make them look interesting? What goes with *shishkehbab*? How often do you water succulents? How high up do you put your bosom this month? Which is the best make of motor-scooter? What do you do with a mobile when it isn't? What is the best way of renovating old skis? Reading articles called 'Are you an understanding wife? – test yourself' and 'Have a goat's-milk bath this week', Viola felt at home in the world. She seemed to have boy friends because they could make bookcases, or transplant cacti, or cook *wiener schnitzel*; at least there was always one there doing it, whenever you went, and they really were boy friends, like the ones in the women's magazines. Meantime, Tanya would be standing by, with a quiet, a knowing smile on her European face. There is such a thing as a European face, which seems to say, 'I have lived where you never could have survived'; Tanya had one. She was a lecturer in Slavonic languages at the University, and owned the house; she had taken Viola under her wing. Herself of Russian stock, she had come to England before, during, after the war – it was impossible to say – after knowing God knows what horrors and savagery. What she had learned could not be effaced from her; she could look at Machiavelli or La Rouchefoucauld and find them innocent. To treat her as a person, to offer her civilized manners, took on with her almost the quality of an insult: only young people and innocent countries could afford to play about like this. The proximity of Viola's English, fresh-cheeked innocence and Tanya's experience was a mystery. It was commonly rumoured that Tanya was Lesbian, but Viola denied it, said there was nothing, that Tanya liked her to have men friends, and one was left not knowing whether Viola was less innocent or Tanya more innocent than each seemed.

Viola had only one popular gramophone record, Trenet singing *'Les Enfants S'Ennuyent Le Dimanche'*, and at tonight's party she had played it six times already. She played it at parties as a joke (though it was really Tanya's joke) and now she, and everyone present, was ready to break it. The party was having its peculiar difficulties. The ale-cup, as she kept telling people, tasted like wee-wee. Viola was a simple yet intelligent woman, and she had friends who were simple and friends who were intelligent; she was always introducing the ones to the others and discovering that they didn't like each other; she herself couldn't tell which were which. The Nicholsons, the people who had Tanya's bottom flat, were freethinking and open-minded; they both invariably wore pink shirts. They made dandelion wine and loved to give it to people; they took the *New Statesman* and felt that it was getting very conservative nowadays; they went to the cinema on Sunday evenings, not because they liked the cinema (they hated it; it was too mechanical), but because they felt that someone ought to go to preserve the right of Sunday cinema-going for those who did not realize the powerful forces at work against it; they walked two or three times a year along disused footpaths to preserve them as a right of way for those who did not realize, etc.; they made their own shoes; they prayed, as someone once cleverly said of them, to To Whom It May Concern. If William Morris had still been alive, he would have had all his time cut out trying to keep them out of his house; they would have been more William Morris than William Morris; he would have died of shame in the realization that he had not been enough himself. They baked their own bread and wove their own curtains, and it tasted as though they wove their own bread and looked as though they baked their own curtains. Their friends brought them home-produced honey (they introduced Viola to these friends and Viola said, 'You made it? You have your own bee?'), and whatever they ate, they ate because it was good for them. Viola, who had dietetic interests, followed their cuisine with fascination; they practically lived on wheat germ. Now, at the party, the Nicholsons were going about, trying to like everyone, as they always did, and were finding it terribly hard. Tanya they looked on with a specially kindly eye, because she must have suffered; and Tanya, who had, and was as hard as nails about it, hated their inquisitive guts, as she put it – her English was not quite perfect, but it was idiomatic. They also looked benevolently on a morose, barrel-chested artist named Herman, and the woman he was living with. What made them stand out of the ordinary run was that this woman, who was thirty-five at least, ten years older than Herman, went out on the streets in order to earn enough to keep them both alive. 'He doesn't respect her for it, in fact he despises her, but that's because he despises anyone who earns money, and he treats her badly. But she loves him and she won't leave him; so she sells herself. I think she's a saint,' Viola was saying. Unfortunately she chose to say this to one of her *other* sort of friends, an elderly librarian named Miss Enid, who was known to all present as quite an exponent of the harp; and she, as anyone but Viola would have expected she would, set to to dispute this. 'Viola dear, if she walks the street, how can you call her that?' 'But she's giving herself because of something she believes in, his work, and because she loves him,' said Viola. 'She's spending herself.'

'But why, Viola dear, do you call that saintly? I know I'm an old-fashioned thing; but you know a lot of saints got their promotion, so to speak, because of their chastity. You talk as if she's doing something very moral; I can't see how she is even by your standards.'

' "Even by your standards" isn't very kind,' said Viola, 'but it is moral, in the sense that she's living life worthily.'

'I suppose sex has just ceased to be a moral issue,' said the librarian.

'No,' said Viola, shocked. 'Oh, no. It's just a different morality. I think sex is full of moral problems; luckily, I like moral problems, and I think that's the difference. People are prepared to have moral problems nowadays, instead of shying away from the places where they come up.'

'I insist,' said the librarian. 'You *aren't* moral about personal behaviour. Look at this situation. This woman, you see, could so easily do some other work and keep him. But if she worked in Woolworths you wouldn't call her a saint would you? You're just being terribly romantic.'

'I'm *not* romantic,' cried Viola indignantly, smarting under this insult. Dr Adrian Carfax happened at that moment to be passing by, and Viola seized his arm violently. 'Adrian, I'm not romantic, am I?' 'How should I know that?' asked Carfax, surprised. 'I'm a married man.' 'I mean in *spirit*,' said Viola. 'Who was it who said at a public lecture that if the nineteenth century did not exist, it would not have been necessary to invent it?' 'I shouldn't bring *that* up,' said Carfax, who was a Swinburne man, one of the very few of them left.

'You don't understand me,' said Miss Enid forgivingly.

'Excuse me, Viola, but now you're here, may I carry you off,' said Carfax, giving Viola a significant look.

'Wherever you like, dear,' said Viola.

'Just a minute,' said Carfax. They withdrew to a cranny beside the fireplace and Carfax said: 'Are we going to talk to Treece tonight about you know what?'

'Yes; when he gets here,' said Viola. 'It gets worse.'

'Faculty politics?' inquired a passer-by perceptively.

'Illicit passion,' said Viola with a laugh. She turned back to Carfax. 'But we mustn't press him too hard. You know what Stuart's like.'

'He means well, you know, Viola,' said Carfax, who prized loyalty. 'Oh, I know,' said Viola, 'he couldn't mean anything else if he tried. Don't misunderstand me, Adrian; I *like* Stuart.' Children sometimes say, I *like* you, and you feel honoured that, when they have so much to choose from, when they live in such a thoroughly amiable world, they should bother to pick you distinctly out, to like; Viola's comment, Carfax felt, had a lot of this intonation; he wished that he could tempt her to say the same thing about him. How nice of her, in her headlong rush through life, that she should stop and like someone! Love, these days, is so firmly *in* that liking has quite gone out; and here was Viola doing it.

Time passed; beer was drunk; the evening wore on and finally Stuart arrived. He was covered in snow and had virtually to be carried to the fireplace and stripped of his outer clothing. 'Oh, what a night,' he said. 'I've had such a rumpus at my evening class. Keats, Keats, Keats,' he said spitefully. 'I don't care if I never see another keat again.' He looked up at Viola; she looked charming, with her hair done in what Treece always called her lunatic fringe, and with a low-cut dress that ought to have been more tight-fitting; it would have made a baby cry. Some of the younger sporters in the room kept placing things she wanted to pick up low down and just out of reach; and Viola, delightfully herself, had no idea why. 'Did you bring a book to read?' asked Viola, when Treece had had time to thaw a little. This was a reference to the fact that, at parties, Treece had a habit of reading in a corner, with his back to the assembled company; there was a famous occasion when, at a faculty dinner, he got through *A Farewell to Arms.*

'I have just the thing to warm you up,' said Viola. 'Vodka. You drink it all down at one go.'

'Did you know that vodka is made from potatoes?' said Treece when she brought it.

'Oh damn,' said Viola. 'And I've been boiling mine.'

The drink warmed him and he smiled benevolently at Viola. Then he noticed that she had someone with her. It was Carfax. 'We want to talk to you, Stuart,' said Viola. 'Oh,' said Treece suspiciously; they looked as though they were going to steal his trousers.

'It's about Louis Bates,' said Carfax.

'He's not here, is he?' cried Treece.

'No; of course not,' said Viola.

Treece realized that one of the symptoms of paranoia was the feeling that one was constantly pursued, and he tried to control himself; but, damn it all, he *was* constantly pursued, wasn't he? 'I've had enough trouble from *that* source for one evening,' said Treece. 'Must we talk about him?'

'I don't know whether you've had any work from him lately?' asked Carfax. Treece hadn't, of course, but he wasn't going to tell Carfax that. 'Why?' he asked.

'What do you think of it?' asked Carfax, swaying judiciously back and forth on the balls of his feet.

'Why?' demanded Treece.

'Now please tell us,' said Viola, 'because it's a matter of some importance.'

'Well now,' said Treece. 'It was passable.'

'Was it?' demanded Carfax. 'Well, that's more than I can say for the work I've been getting.' Carfax sat down and began to puff militarily at his pipe; Carfax had been an officer in the First World War and always stood very stiffly, talked jovially but with a somewhat officers-to-men attitude, and had a precise sense of discipline which, if violated by anyone, stirred in him violent indignations. He was in this mood now. Treece had once heard him, in an argument with a student about some critical point of view, say, in reply to the student's tentative 'Well, I think . . .' 'You're not here to think'; and then he remembered that he was in a university, not the Army, and to think was just what the student was here for; he had apologized handsomely and genially. About Carfax not all has been told. He was also Uncle Adrian in the schools broadcasts put out by a commercial television station in the afternoons; his bluff avuncular figure, smoking a pipe, could be seen, once a week, talking heartily about Shakespeare and what folk were like in them days; his producer had urged on him a quaint West-Country accent for these occasions, and he was now known in the University as the poor man's Bernard Miles.

'I haven't been able to persuade him to do any work for me at all,' said Viola, 'so I can't even offer a judgement. But it seems to me that if he doesn't intend to get anything out of this place then he'd better get out and make room for someone who does.'

Treece realized that Carfax and Viola had already met on this point, and reached agreement, and without disclosing the fact that he had himself, earlier that evening, been proposing to himself some action of this sort, he tempted Carfax and Viola to a firmer stand. 'It's true he's guilty of a high degree of irresponsibility,' he said.

'He told me in the middle of one of my lectures that I ought to take rose-hip syrup,' said Carfax, furnishing what seemed to him incontrovertible proof.

'And the way he looks at me sometimes,' said Viola with an embarrassed laugh.

'What does he do?' said Treece interestedly.

'Nothing,' said Viola. 'He just looks.'

'Well, I found him cutting his hair in my drawing-room the other afternoon before the departmental tea-party.'

'Fantastic,' said Viola.

'Well, there's only one way to talk of someone whose values are as remote from life and independent as his are, isn't there?'

'What do you mean?' said Viola.

'You mean he's mad,' said Treece.

'He wouldn't be the first person of that sort to be found in a university. I always thought my tutor was; he'd change over from one set of false teeth to another in the middle of a lecture.'

'Well,' said Viola. 'Then we ought to get him out of here as soon as possible, to somewhere where he can be looked after.'

'No,' said Treece; 'we can't do that.'

'What do you mean?' said Carfax. 'I thought you were agreeing with us?'

Treece turned to Viola. 'What Carfax means, when he says Bates is mad, is that he's psychotic, that he suffers from schizophrenia, and is subject to delusion about his status in the world. And I suppose it's true that his character does lie within that pattern of derangement. But if he is like that, that puts our whole problem on another dimension.'

'What do you mean?' demanded Carfax. Treece's change in spirit was too much for a simple Army man; Treece's own image of Louis had seldom changed, and in this new perspective Bates's faults seemed eminently permissible; they were pathological lesions and excusable on that count. His virtues, on the other hand, became his own. 'You can't punish a man for his nonconformity, after all. We can punish him for his lack of quality or for his failure to obey the rules. But it isn't that at all; he doesn't lack quality, I feel convinced. He simply has qualities of a different kind. We have to keep him. Where else can a man of his kind go if not into a university?'

'Into a mental hospital,' said Viola.

'But do you know what mental hospitals are like? Do you suppose he's a severe case? It seems to me more than likely that a mental hospital would send him over the edge.'

'But he might do someone harm,' said Viola.

'Nonsense, Viola; he's not psychopathic. It isn't that kind of derangement at all, as far as I see it. Madness, genius, originality – it's all the same thing; it's a breaking of our normal value structure and the substitution of another one. In a sense we all do this. He's simply an original; he's no more wild than that. His delusions don't prevent him from living in the ordinary, everyday world; he isn't that severely impaired. No, better throw out all the other students than throw out the one man we can help, the one honest man.'

'Why honest? Are you sure you don't just like the idea of having a madman of your own, Stuart? I'm sorry, but I really mean this, Stuart,' said Viola, 'because in some ways I think you're a sort of moral cheat. You always espouse the right cause; look how well you show up in relation to us in this. You do the proper moral thing, as it appears under the gaze of the *New Statesman* or whatever the proper moral agencies are these days. But after you've done that you've still left everything in the air. Your soul rests easy, but nothing's solved.'

'So I ought to avoid the moral satisfaction I get from taking this viewpoint by letting Bates go into a mental hospital? This is what you're saying, isn't it?'

'No, I'm not,' said Viola. 'All I'm saying is that discussion doesn't *always* end when your conscience is salved. Life for you is a play with a message. You should stop worrying about your conscience so much. It doesn't worry about you, you know.'

'And where does that get us?' asked Treece.

'There are practical problems to face as well, Stuart, and

the question is, what should we do if we keep him? Give him a B.A. honours degree in schizophrenia?'

'It isn't *funny*,' said Treece.

'No, I know it's not; but you see what I mean. We aren't here to provide a haven for the ill-adjusted. He just doesn't respond to the terms on which we have him here. The question isn't whether we should give him a home for a while; it's whether he's a suitable student to take an honours course in English.'

'I disagree then,' said Treece. 'I think a university is more than that. You know what the world is like now.' The world, in Treece's view, was an ominous organization; he had been fighting it for years now. The world was a cheap commercial project, run by profiteers, which disseminated bad taste, poor values, shoddy goods, and cowboy films on television among a society held up to permanent ransom by these active rogues. Against this in his vision he was inclined to set the academic world, which seemed to him, though decreasingly so, the one stronghold of values, the one centre from which the world was resisted. He was as upset as the most devout of monks when people he knew 'got mixed up in the world'; that was the end of *their* capacity for effective living. 'Great *Scott*!' he said. 'We of all people shouldn't be asking what use a man is to the firm.'

'That is *not* the point,' said Viola.

'Have you talked to this man Bates?' asked Carfax. 'Have you taken any personal cognizance of him?'

'Yes; I have taken personal cognizance of him, on a large number of occasions,' said Treece. 'In fact, half my days seem to be spent in taking personal cognizance of Louis Bates.'

'Then you must realize that he's egocentric to the most extravagant degree. He's irrepressible, he's a personal problem. He devotes himself ceaselessly to trying to win attention and sympathy.'

'I often think', Treece said rather smugly, 'that it's equally true to say that genius is an infinite capacity for faking pains. But we should still foster it, however much of an embarrassment it may be to us.'

'All right,' said Carfax. 'Louis Bates is a wild, untutored genius. In my humble opinion, he should stay untutored. I don't want other people's humanity tied round my neck. We all have our own troubles, you know – we have our own pains and separations and our own last breath s. We can't carry everyone else. Our lives are too little.'

'I think that's a shameful plea,' said Treece. 'I really do. Truly, what do we live for?' He became excited; vodka splashed in his glass; professors nibbling cheese straws peered over the tops of them to see what was happening. 'Caring is our role,' cried Treece. 'We're not secular people. We have no business to accept life as trivial.'

'Please, Stuart,' said Viola, disturbed. 'Please.'

'I don't mean to let him go,' said Treece, sitting back on his tuffet extravagantly. 'He needs looking after.'

'Take it easy, Stuart,' said Viola. 'You're wasting adrenalin.' It took several minutes more for Carfax and Viola to soothe Treece back to his normal level of complacency; and still they all stared at each other as if each had been the victim of a great betrayal.

2

There are parties where everyone comes to like all the others present, and parties where hate burgeons and what is left at the end of the evening is a deep estrangement from the human race. This was the latter kind of party. All about people were reflecting how alone they were and how little their friends mattered to them. Viola's punch was steaming away like a geyser on the sideboard. The people who before ten o'clock had been standing were now sitting; those who had been sitting before were now lying. 'This', Tanya murmured to Treece, 'is a party at which everyone almost imperceptibly moves nearer to the floor.' 'Where they belong,' said Treece sadly. Across the room the kittenish wife of a lecturer in sociology was tearing up into little pieces someone else's plastic mackintosh. 'I thing it's obscene,' she said. 'Ah, poor child,' said Tanya. 'You see at one glance how *that* mind works.' A young lecturer in economics, trying to be amusing, knocked off his cigarette ash down the front of Viola's dress. The record-player was now playing Mozart.

'When I hear Mozart,' said Tanya, 'I could nearly cry. It is my world as it used to be. You do not know what it is when civilization comes to an end. If I could show you the old Salzburg, the old Budapest. You do not know what it is you are selling for dollars and cents. And I can't tell you. Think of a world in which Mozart, whom we know has existed, could not. You see this loss I am speaking of? Of course, you are not a patriot; it does not do nowadays.'

'I am in some ways,' said Treece.

'Yes, in some enlightened way. You are 55 per cent British, and 45 per cent Terylene, eh? I wasn't a patriot until it had all gone; then I would have sold my soul to buy it back.'

'I'm watching you, Stuart,' said Viola as she passed by.

'Ah, Stuart is helping me to regain my lost innocence,' cried Tanya, laughing.

'He looked as though he was making it even more remote,' said Viola.

'No; Stuart is a little boy; if you could take out his soul and look at it, it would be the soul of a boy. To him I am like an old witch in a wood.' Treece began to look hurt. 'Ah, look. He is offended; he thinks I am unkind. Ah, Stuart, do what you want; you will never go to hell.'

'I'm annoyed with Stuart,' said Viola.

'Leave him alone,' said Tanya. 'You will make him cry. He is not as hard as you.'

Treece said nothing. He was furious. He got up and went over to the bookcase. 'The tips of your ears have gone red, Stuart,' said Tanya behind him. He took out a copy of *Essays in Criticism* and began to read. People grew annoyed with him. He grew annoyed at himself. He grew even more annoyed with Viola, who ought to have known better, and was after all his friend.

Viola meanwhile went into the kitchen, feeling somewhat upset herself; she had been rather naughty. But, after all, the whole Louis business still rankled. Carfax came in to ask if he could be doing anything, and Viola, giving him a bottle of red wine to open, said that she was far from being appeased, and that she didn't think she could take another tutorial with Louis, because he made her self-conscious about her legs. 'I'm sure he doesn't mean to stare at your legs, Viola,' said Carfax, somewhat embarrassed, as he was with all modern women. 'Perhaps he's just thinking.'

'Oh, he's thinking, all right,' said Viola with a short nervous laugh. 'What worries me is, what is he thinking?'

'Quite,' said Carfax. 'But we both know that this isn't material for complaint.'

'Well, I think it is, if he's mad. . . .'

'He's not mad,' said Carfax. 'We pushed too hard.'

'Well, I just don't feel safe with him,' said Viola, 'and I don't find his eccentricities in the least lovable. You know my trouble? I'm a normal, healthy woman; that's what's wrong with me.'

'Viola dear, are you trampling your own grapes?' cried a member of the Economics Department, entering the kitchen with an empty glass.

'We're not having this party in the kitchen,' said Viola. 'Now both of you back in there.'

'You know, you're absolutely wonderful when you're angry,' said the economist, a stout. sleek young man named Marshall who had been for two years at Harvard and now behaved as though he had actually invented it. 'Come and talk to me, pet.' 'All right,' said Viola. 'Why don't you show me your bedroom?' said the economist. 'Because I'm supposed to be entertaining my guests,' said Viola. 'All of them?' said the economist. 'Then start with me.'

They went through into the living-room, and Marshall began to throw peanuts at Professor Treece, who was sitting on a tuffet reading through the whole run of *Essays in Criticism* and probably annotating the margins; he looked as though he was in there sheltering from the rain.

Viola went across to him and said, 'Put down that silly magazine and talk to me.' 'What about?' asked Treece peering suspiciously with one eye over the top of the review. 'Anything you like,' said Viola. 'Honestly, Stuart, you are awful.

This is the last bloody party I invite you to. You just sit there and *read*.'

'I can't do anything right for you tonight,' said Treece.

'You're annoyed,' said Viola.

'No,' said Treece. Then he added cleverly, 'Of course, I wouldn't tell you if I were.'

'You're annoyed with me. Well, I'm sorry, Stuart, whatever it is.'

'You make me feel as though I've punched your mother or something.'

'I'm sorry, Stuart. I really am,' said Viola. 'I'm very fond of you. You mustn't confuse me with Tanya. She doesn't like you because she thinks I do. Now, come along, get off that tuffet and talk, join in the chit-chat.' 'I was just wondering: did I switch off the petrol on my bike?' 'I never heard anyone in the world fuss so much as you,' said Viola, dragging him into the middle of the room. 'Now, say something.'

'Has everyone', asked Treece, timidly, of the gathering, 'sent off his Christmas cards?' 'Good,' whispered Viola. 'I've already sent off about two hundred because Adrian won't do a thing about them,' said Mrs Carfax. 'He claims to be a writer; I say he should write all the letters and cards. After all, I *am* practically illiterate. He only married me because I was that, and he wanted someone to get away to from his students.'

'No one knows why I married you, least of all me,' said Carfax heartily, 'and I don't claim to be a writer. I claim to be a scholar. Who'd dare claim to be a writer in an English provincial university, except Kingsley Amis?'

'Why on earth not?' demanded Treece.

'Because there's no room for dilletantism of that sort. A provincial university is just a modern version of the workhouse. We're trainers of the aspiring bourgeoisie.'

'But why are we teaching in a university in the first place? Goodness knows it's not for the money. It isn't because we want to teach, or because, simply, we love scholarship. Isn't it because we want to live in a world of circulating ideas and critical valuations? Isn't it because we love independence and freedom of thought? Or am I being naïve?'

'In a way, Stuart, I really think you are,' said Viola.

'Well, I don't,' said Treece. 'If our function isn't to talk about what is good when the rest of the world is talking about what is profitable, what *can* we do?'

Lionel Marshall interposed, 'You seem to think that the function of the university is to give a training in taste and improve the standards by which people live. But to what effect? How would this serve them, as far as their social function is concerned?'

'They would act as a group of protestants when people tried to lower standards and mortgage the values of our civilization; you must admit there is always that risk.'

'Yes, there is, but what is going to happen to this group of malcontents?'

'They would form a pressure group on behalf of the survival of serious values.'

'Yes,' said Marshall; 'but you simply develop a group of disordered citizens with no social role in the society they live in.'

'But they do have a social role; every society needs its intelligentsia.'

'No; I disagree,' said Marshall; 'especially when by that you mean an intelligentsia that is preserving the values of aristocratic as against popular taste. I think the function of the intelligentsia is changing.'

'What you mean then is that it's ceasing to be an intelligentsia,' said Treece.

'No,' said Marshall. 'Simply that it's ceasing to be a liberal one; intelligentsias are by no means always liberal in outlook.'

'Oh, not all this again,' said Viola, laughing. 'But you have to admit it, Stuart. We are parasites on the big world; we can't exist without its approval; we happen to be luxuries they can afford, and if things get hard they'll push us overboard.'

'In any case,' said Marshall, 'it's necessary to accept the fact that university graduates must go into business and industry. Some can stay outside, a lucky few like ourselves; and we can *afford* to know better than everyone else. We don't have to face the moral problems of living with it.'

'But even those who can't be independent can at least perceive what is wrong, if they are shown.'

'Well, aren't you just saying it's better to be neurotic, sensitive, and miserable than unimaginative, adjusted, and content? Is it really better?'

'It's my belief that it is better. That's why I'm what I am,' said Treece. 'What concerns me is that the quality of life and the standards that people live by seem to me to be getting worse, and we're not doing anything about it.'

'You're still saying that the function of a university is to make people discontented, which is an anarchistic position to take up.'

'In any case, Stuart,' said Viola, 'I truly distrust these abstracts; I don't want to talk about *culture* or *civilization*. I'd rather have some working man reading *Reveille* and sopping his pint than any of these middle-class, cultivated people, who take their library list down every Monday morning and do eurythmics and support causes.'

'Well, that's where we differ,' said Treece. 'It seems to me that the radical middle classes in England are the salt of the earth. Practically everything that we value seems to me to have been won by their efforts.'

'Viola seems very temperamental tonight,' said Miss Enid. 'I'm sure she doesn't mean all those things.'

'I do,' said Viola. 'People don't say things they don't mean. I know I'm only a woman....'

'The point of all this display', said Lionel Marshall mischievously, 'is that she's in love with one of her students, named Louis Bates.'

'I'm not. I'm not. I hate him,' said Viola, and, in tears, she swept out of the room.

3

Some parties improve in the absence of their hostess, but this one did not. The most interesting people left, and the least interesting took advantage of the permissive atmosphere. Was it all his fault? Treece wondered. At least an apology seemed necessary. He looked in the kitchen. She was not there. He tried the next room, which was her bedroom, and found her standing there alone, looking out into the darkness. She turned and, seeing him, said, 'I want to talk to you, Stuart. Shut the door.' He did, and she crossed the room until she stood in front of him.

'I'm annoyed with you,' she said.

Her aggression made him uneasy. 'Why?' he demanded.

'Oh, you *know* why. This Louis Bates thing. All I want to say to you is, Professor Treece, he upsets me, and I think you ought to give him another tutor. I can't go on with him. I am *not* in love with him. That's ridiculous.'

'You might be without knowing . . .' said Treece.

'Honestly, how could I be? He gives me the shivers. He's sexually unpleasant, Stuart. I call him The Solitary Raper. He's like a walking phallic symbol.'

'Well, you don't have to look at him, Viola, do you, if you don't want to? And you must give him a fair trial.'

'I've no intention of giving him any trial at all,' said Viola.

'Women are so cruel,' said Treece. 'Think how he must feel.'

'Women *have* to be abominably cruel, Stuart,' said Viola. 'You know nothing about it. They're pursued with offers. Look, Stuart. It's the hardest thing in life for a woman to face, but she has to do it; she has to hurt, hurt, hurt people all the time. She can't afford to feel sorry for them. I feel sorry for lots of men. I feel sorry for you.'

'For me?' said Treece.

'Yes, of course. I suppose all women do,' said Viola. 'You're a dedicated man; that makes me admire you. But your life is arid, and you know it, and you go about with that little-boy-lost look on your face as if you want to turn at last to someone, but dare not for fear of being accused of being unprofessional.'

'Oh, but . . .' said Treece.

'Well, perhaps that's unfair. Whenever I look at you I think of Simone Weil's definition of the religious man – "Morality will not let him breathe." But the trouble with your morality is that it won't let other people breathe either! You're fair in a way I can never be. You're a very honest man;

you weigh up and judge and speculate and criticize. You're an insult to us all!'

'It's hard to see yourself from that far away,' said Treece slowly. 'One can always satisfy oneself, I suppose; it's other people one can't satisfy. One thinks one's way of life is sound and then comes an external vision to say: you are a fake, you are nothing, you're animal and must die, and no one will know you were ever there. It's an intimation of the whole absurdity of what you are and do. It's the worst kind of despair.'

'I know, pet, I know.' Viola put her hands on his forearms and looked up at him with clear grey eyes. 'You're a funny person. You live so tensely, don't you?' Even as Treece perceived that this was a different Viola, simply a woman, who could end suffering, he was kissing her. He fumbled ineffectually with the front of her dress. 'There's a zip at the back,' said Viola. 'You're supposed to find that out for yourself; but it's an expensive dress.' She slipped out of the dress.

'I say, that's a nice brassière,' said Treece, very impressed. 'It's broderie anglaise,' said Viola, flattered. She slipped out of the brassière.

'I was so dulled, so stupid, I needed this so much,' said Treece.

'Yes, Stuart, I know.'

'You're so good to me,' said Treece. 'Do you like me?'

'Of course I do,' said Viola, 'or I wouldn't be here now. Why are you so humble? You don't trust anyone, do you? You're afraid that secretly they don't really respect Professor Treece as he ought to be respected.'

'Stop it,' said Treece. 'There are no Professor Treeces here.'

Viola giggled. 'It was Tanya, you know . . .' she said.

'Tanya, I know what?'

'Tanya who said I ought to do this.'

'She did? Why?' said Treece, rolling over.

'Well, I'm such a mess about this. She said I ought to, and that you . . . She takes a great interest in me.'

'Are you and she lovers?' asked Treece.

'No; she's never done *anything* to me,' said Viola. 'It's just one of these stories that people put about, people who gossip like me. She has affairs with men; she's having one with Herman. I don't think she enjoys them, but she has them.'

'Do you enjoy them?'

'I enjoy this. Do you like me?'

'Very much,' said Treece. All the same, somehow, his excitement began to diminish. He felt slightly disturbed by all this; it reminded him that it was she, with him, who was involved. All at once the room began to boom with moral reverberations. Notions of responsibility spilled lazily about his head as he lay there on the bed.

'That bloody coffee,' said Viola. 'I put some on. Fasten me up at the back, my baby.' My baby, Treece noted in astonishment; there it was again, as always. Treece was the sort of man that people always wanted to mother, or father: indeed, as someone had once said of him in the old bohemian days in London: 'Some men go around leaving illegitimate children; Stuart leaves illegitimate parents.' Treece had never exactly wished this, but it was a concomitant of his character. 'I wish you could stay, but all these people ... Can you come back?' Here, Treece saw, was a future, a complex of consequences; and it meant, too, problems of discipline within the faculty; after all, what he had done for her he ought to do for every member of the department. So now, as he repeatedly kissed her on the end of the nose as she put on her dress, he was stomaching a desire to hurry from the room, leap aboard his motorized bicycle, drive madly to somewhere safe – for this, which had once been safety, was now safety no more. He had to make the point to her; it was only fair. She was sweet, she was gentle, she was good. When she had first been appointed, she had looked like a damp, frail figure rescued from a shipwreck, needing a protector. It was an illusion; at the interview Treece had observed that Viola had a strong line in articulation, an assurance of opinion, which had earned her the appointment. But ever since then Treece had really responded to the other side of Viola, the frightened girl; he hardly granted that she was a woman, a modern woman with opinions that ran counter to his own, that she was of a generation that he felt he didn't even understand, the fifties, the Willoughby lot. When he thought of this he trembled; but he had to make his position plain. 'This doesn't mean I agree with your opinions,' he said. They went into the kitchen. 'Don't worry,' said Viola rather grimly. 'Intellectually, you're in the clear.'

CHAPTER FIVE

I

PEOPLE who think that architecture is a facet of the soul, and are concerned about what sort of house they dwell in (they have to be people with money to believe this) all, nowadays, either live in Georgian houses, or want to, or would want to if it were not so inconvenient. The house in which Emma Fielding lived was, as all her visitors squealed, a collectors' piece. It was Georgian, civilized, spacious, and dense; corridors gave on to charming rooms and staircases. It was such a good example that people had already formed an organization to protest against its demolition; no one had tried to demolish it yet, but if you are interested in houses, you know what the world is like; and it is not like you. The fact was, however, that Emma had chosen the house not because *it* was a collectors' piece, but because the people who owned it, the Bishops, were; Emma collected people. When, a little time ago, a song came out called 'Eating People is Wrong', Emma felt a twinge of conscience: she agreed with the proposition, but was not sure that she exactly lived up to it. When she had first gone to the house to see the room, she had been greeted by Mrs Bishop, frail, white-haired, with a deaf-aid. The flat consisted of a bedroom and a living-room, and a peculiar stunted sofa.

'That's rather nice,' said Emma, pointing to the sofa.

'Yes, dear,' said Mrs Bishop. 'It's a chaise short.'

'Do you get the sun in here?'

'No, dear; it's the wrong side of the house for the sun,' said Mrs Bishop. 'Still, it's an ill wind, you know, and there is one compensation: it's on the right side of the house for the shade. You look thin, don't you, dear? What have you been worrying about?'

'Nothing,' said Emma.

'Nonsense. I can tell you're a worrier. You're worried about not being married.'

'You're quite wrong,' said Emma.

'Of course you are. All girls do. You aren't married, are you?'

'No,' said Emma.

'Well, then, that's what it is.'

'I don't want to marry; I'm not equipped to marry,' protested Emma.

'Don't be silly,' said Mrs Bishop. 'Everybody's equipped to marry. It's very simple equipment.'

'I mean I'm simply not ready to settle down. I have so much to do first.'

'Well,' said Mrs Bishop, 'if you're going to be like that. We don't allow animals or children, dear. . . .'

'I must be careful not to have any,' said Emma.

'I used to be a big friend of Marie Stopes,' said Mrs Bishop. 'And you'll be surprised how useful it's come in since. And no musical instruments or firearms; and I don't know what you use, but don't block the toilet with sanitary napkins, will you?'

'No,' said Emma.

'I know these rules seem terrible, but one has to have them; and don't get the wrong impression – there are lots of things you *can* do, if you just think about it,' said Mrs Bishop. 'Well, I'll tell my husband we're having you. He thinks a lot of what I say. In fact, he thinks more of it than I do.'

One got through life, Emma believed, by convincing oneself that each stage was a *temporary* condition, a momentary expedient, accepted half-heartedly and just for the time being. Compromise was shocking, but she was always doing it; and there were unexpected rewards. This time, in order to have the Bishops, one went without the harmonium. Secret harmonium playing would be quickly detected; and there was nowhere to hide it; the wardrobe, though large for a wardrobe (you could probably have hidden another wardrobe in it), was small for even the most self-effacing harmonium. Whatever her happier qualities, moreover, Mrs Bishop proved to be a practised investigator. She had a metaphysical sense of evil operating in the world around her, even in her own house, and she was perpetually on a look-out for the world's corruption (Is it you? Is it you? she seemed to ask as she peered around her, wondering if her tenants were really married, whether her neighbours were pickpockets or prostitutes), not because she condemned it, but because she was interested in it. What worried her was not the actual sin, which she encouraged, but the failure to repent afterwards. She was a true provincial Nonconformist; when you looked at her the word Nonconformity took on shape. She belonged to one of those small vestigial Christian sects that meet in rooms over teashops. 'We had some lovely sins today, dear,' she would cry, knocking on Emma's door on Sunday evening, fresh from church in her fur coat and fox fur, a frail figure, yet (as Emma came to realize) as strong as a horse, in character and physical endurance. The church she attended made a practice of public confession, so that, as Mrs Bishop explained, you not only had the pleasure of *doing* the sin, but the second, more sophisticated, pleasure of talking about it afterwards. As the weeks went on, the confessions got more lurid; competition grew up as to who could commit adultery the most times in one week. 'Thirteen times,' said Mrs Bishop one week. 'You wouldn't think anybody had it in them, would you?' 'Perhaps he was lying in order to have something to confess next week,' suggested Emma. It was Emma's view that it was more Christian not to sin at all than to sin and repent, but Mrs Bishop speedily disabused her on that score. 'Who did they kill the fatted calf for, the prodigal son or the other?' she demanded. Emma was reminded of a remark made to her by Herr Schumann, the German student, who had said once, meeting her at coffee, 'I like the English. They have the most rigid code of immorality in the world.'

The house itself was a citadel of the old guard – frondy, ornate, bubbling with flowers. Pianola rolls filled a cupboard on the stairs, the faded titles recalling romantic operas. In the lavatory there was a large wooden chest, and when it was opened (it was unlocked) it revealed to Emma a collection of Edwardian hats, with great brims, and ostrich plumes; when she was using the toilet Emma would sit there and try them on. The Edwardian period was their period; if only there hadn't been that war, what wonders, said Mrs Bishop, would have happened. 'People like us would have come to our own, you know, if the

Hun hadn't . . . You know, it's terrible when your generation isn't the one that's on top any more. Perhaps it's wrong to make a virtue out of the age one lived in, just because one did live in it; it's such an unfashionable age just now, too. But it was a more civilized age than this one; it was so much more peaceable. '

'But wasn't it very vulgar?' asked Emma.

'I don't think so. I detest vulgarity; I won't have it in my house; and people then were very conscious of what vulgarity was. If you were not a gentleman, it was no use being anything.'

'It seems to me it's vulgar to call things vulgar in that way.'

'Oh, well, I liked it, but then I'm naïve,' said Mrs Bishop. 'I heard a famous writer on the radio say how awful it must be for intelligent young men now that they can't have servants, because now they have to do all the things they shouldn't have to waste time doing. I understand that; I don't suppose anyone much younger than me *can*, any more.'

'No, not really,' said Emma.'

'Things seem to me rather awful now, and all those foreigners seem to do what they like with us, and people don't know their places any more. I went into the Post Office this morning and they were so rude to me because I was slow. I told them: I said, "If you don't want my business, I'll give it to another firm." But', concluded Mrs Bishop forlornly, 'there isn't any other firm, is there?'

The simple truth was that Mrs Bishop and her husband – he was 'Rotary', a business-man, and no one knew exactly what he did (Emma asked him once, and he said that his business was not her business) – had strayed into Emma's world out of another one, inconceivably remote, positively unreal, so unreal that Emma could scarcely believe in it. Emma Fielding was, as she phrased it, 'upstart middle class', but until she went to the Bishops she did not really know what middle class meant. When Emma went into other people's rooms, she found herself straightening cushions, wiping dust off ornaments with her sleeve, and if she was not shocked by people who passed the salt from hand to hand without putting it down, she noticed and thought that her mother would have been shocked; this was her vestigial middle-classness, which, like her vestigial Christianity, seemed to her a poor, shady, furtive thing. But to the Bishops, who believed in Keeping Yourself to Yourself, Having Nice Things, Getting On In the World, Keeping Decent, Settling Down, Having a Bit of Property Behind You, Emma was close to communism. Emma had inherited a tradition of snobbery, but had spent the last ten years of her life trying either to eliminate it or to make it intellectually respectable; with the Bishops it was there, plain and overt. Emma did not see why women should want exact equality with men, for, after all, they had their own things in the world, but Mrs Bishop . . . well, Mrs Bishop said: 'I don't think women are intelligent enough to have the vote, do you? At least, not until after the change of life.' If she had not met the Bishops, thought Emma, she would not have known what the old world was; as it was, she knew, and wondered. The Bishops talked of the town they lived in, and it was another town; they talked of the time when the poachers used to go out into the country in the evening, on the tram, and return with their rabbits and pheasants just when the policemen were changing over shifts. They could remember the policemen going round the streets with a handbarrow and piling the drunks that lay in the streets on to it to take them to the station. They had friends who came round in the evenings and sang; and after they had finished their piece, Mrs Bishop would clap her hands and cry, 'Voix d'ange!' Donkey-carts and flower shows and conservatories and bicycle trips to the sea figured in their conversation. They thought the Conservative Party would have Britain back on the Gold Standard by 1960. Emma looked at them, and gasped; and wondered, if the world is what I think it is, how have you lived, how have you carried on?

2

One damp, rainy day Emma returned home from feeding some pigeons to find poor Mrs Bishop in a state of considerable upset. 'There's been a nasty man here this afternoon,' said Mrs Bishop, 'and he's up in your room and he won't come out. I don't know what he's doing. I've been standing on the stairs shouting "Fire!" but even that doesn't seem to worry him.'

'Now, don't worry so much, Mrs Bishop,' said Emma, not a little worried herself. 'Did he say who he was?'

'Well, he said he was a friend of yours, but he didn't look like it to me, and I've never seen him here before,' said Mrs Bishop. 'He was tall and frightening and very ugly and his coat collar was turned up, and he had a foreign black beret on. There were great big drops of rain dripping off his ears. Then when I opened the door a crack, he pushed it wide open and stepped inside and said if he stood out there in the rain another minute he'd get pneumonia, and he wanted to dry off, and he asked for you then. So I said you were out and he said he'd go up to your room and wait and dry his clothes.'

Emma rushed upstairs. 'Mind,' cried Mrs Bishop. 'He might be naked.' She threw open the door and there, in front of the gas fire, a plaid rug round his shoulders, sat Louis Bates. 'What do you think you've been doing?' demanded Emma. Louis, who had come expressly to seduce her, was a little taken aback. Looking at it from his point of view, you could understand his disappointment; it was not a promising beginning.

For weeks now Louis had cavorted with love. Day after day he had searched the University for another glimpse of Emma – peering into lecture-rooms, scouting systematically along corridors, hovering outside the women's lavatories at strategic times. He had written her letters. He had stopped working. It had disorganized his life. He could live with it no longer; he had to act. When he looked into the mirror each morning, as he shaved around the contours of each cheek, he had been braving himself up to all this: he half expected to find, one morning, a different face there, the face of Louis the lover, Louis the seducer, the fresh, cherubic face of a young man with sparkling eyes and shining teeth. Alas, it was always the same face, long and gaunt, that met his look; and it wasn't fair, for this was a new Louis, an extravagant, passionate Louis, doing new things, thinking new thoughts. Each morning he gazed at the solemn, hollow face that peered back at him from the mirror, smiled at it, teased and tempted it, said to it, 'Emma, Emma, Emma.' But it didn't seem to get the point at all. And now that she was sitting before him, not a fiction, but a real creature, the more desirable, but the less accessible, his daring faltered. How did one do it? Would she mind if he leapt up and heaved her into the bedroom, stripping off her clothes as they went? Yet he could live with it no longer; he had come to a kind of desperation, and had, somehow, to act.

'I had to see you,' he said. 'I can't live without you.'

Emma went to the door and shouted downstairs: 'It's all right, Mrs Bishop, it's someone I know.' Then she returned to Louis. 'You frightened Mrs Bishop out of her wits: did you know?'

'Why?' demanded Louis. 'I didn't do anything.'

'Coming storming into the house like that, and waiting in my room when I'm not here. You simply *don't do* things like that.'

'Why simply don't you?' demanded Louis satirically. 'I was soaking wet. I have a weak chest. And I had to see you. I can't go on like this. I can't work. I can't eat. I think about you all the time.'

'I can't think why,' said Emma. 'You hardly know me; it's silly.' She went over to the window and looked out; the weather that day had become wilder and more blustery; rain bounced in the streets and dripped from the eaves of houses; bedraggled dogs sat in doorways.

'I've changed completely. I'm a new person,' said Louis. 'I'm tired, now, of staying indoors and contemplating my navel. I want to get out ...'

'And contemplate other people's?' asked Emma.

'Yes, then,' said Louis. 'Look. Don't I matter to you?'

'It's very flattering, of course, and I'm grateful.'

'Look. I'm a human being, you know,' said Louis. 'I need love like everyone else. You're involved in this; you can't just throw the issue aside. What are you going to do about it?'

'Let's have some tea,' said Emma.

'Look. This has to be taken seriously,' said Louis. 'I don't think people know how to take things seriously any more. The world is a great big joke; they want a laugh, a bit of amusement, and not to worry about anything. But *you* aren't like that.'

'How do you know?' asked Emma.

'I do know. And nor am I. I can offer you something. I'm old enough and responsible enough to marry; I'm not an ordinary undergraduate, playing at affection.'

'Please don't,' said Emma.

'I don't think you realize my ... well, *feelings* about this. Emma ...'

'No,' said Emma. 'Don't say any more.'

'But I'm sure we could make each other very happy,' said Louis despairingly. The phrase rendered itself ridiculous in the air, for this was surely what Louis did not have the gift of. 'I often think about marriage,' he went on, looking at the door to the bedroom.

'Do you?'

'Of course, most men have married by the time they have reached my age. I'm not a young man any more. But my background is rather different from most. I'm working class, you see; it's more difficult for me. A man needs to be understood.'

'So does a woman,' said Emma.

'Oh yes; I know,' said Louis. 'In a different way, though. But what I mean is, in my class, things are not the same. People don't *recognize* each other in the same way. That's why working-class novels don't quite come off, because the novel is so often about one person's sense of another, the recognition of their entity, but where I come from we don't exist like that. But a man like myself, with a reasonable amount of intelligence, because I really do have that ...'

'I know,' said Emma.

'Well, a man of that sort needs an intelligent wife. He needs to flourish as an individual, if you see what I mean. Not to be subjected. He needs really to be the intellectually dominant party in the relationship. He needs the wife to understand and agree with his allegiances. And there's something else.'

'Do you take sugar?' asked Emma.

'Two spoonfuls. My health isn't good. I have a weak chest. I need a lot of looking after. You see, I'm frank. And an intelligent woman doesn't have a lot of time for that. Sometimes I think I'm like William Blake. . . .'

'Yes, I expect you do,' said Emma.

'And that I'd like to marry an ignorant but good woman who'd know how to look after me, and who, perhaps, would agree with my opinions simply because they're mine, and would enjoy making love in the garden. What do you think?'

'What about love?' asked Emma. 'Does that enter into your scheme of things?'

'Well, yes,' said Louis. 'Love is a problem, but one often loves the sort of person one wishes to. It's a problem, but I think I've solved it.' He nodded solemnly at her, and his meaning was unmistakable; all Louis's meanings were.

She looked at him, and wondered why he revolted her so much. She had to admit that it just wasn't fair. But there were, it seemed, some people to whom one never could be fair, whom one could never take seriously, however generous one wished to be. Because of some grotesqueness, or a simple lack of charm, one didn't allow them the dues that one granted to people one knew. She had to recognize that Louis had such a place in her scheme, and that she did not know how to handle him. Now, as he became supplicant, a sort of horror fell upon her. He said that there were problems, but that they could be solved. Life was not simple and it was folly to expect that of it. She was of another status and another class. She would want to eat in expensive places and he wouldn't. She would want their children to go to public school and he would not. But with goodwill this could be solved. 'I'm like the poet Keats,' he added. 'I am certain of nothing but of the holiness of the Heart's affections. The Heart's affections – that's what I believe in.' That is all I am certain of, thought Emma, but between what you mean by those affections and what I do there is all the difference in the world, and try to solve that one by goodwill! To you it is a poultice for your chest, for me it is the most intense of frictions, consuming and purifying and changing. The heart did not make one happy – one registered the beat of one's living on it, happiness and sadness, pain and desire. How could he say they were alike? They were at opposite poles of the world. As she watched his lips moving, close to her, there seemed an immensity of distance between them, as though he stood at the far end of some long but distorted perspective.

'I have never felt like this before,' Louis pressed on. 'Passion has happened to me before; I'm a man, after all. But generally I preferred to ignore it, to get on with my work.' This was true enough; it had always seemed to Louis that a fundamental desire to take postal courses was being sublimated by other people into sexual activity; that he was at the root of things. All this was, in a sense, something of a come-down. He *could* have remained independent; he wouldn't have lost his vote, food would still be served him, there was no real excommunication. But he had decided that this was not enough, that he had to *act*, get mixed up in the world. 'I'm of this world; I *feel*, you know,' he cried. 'Up to the time I met you I had an unrealized sense of isolation, one that I only perceived at parties or in theatres. It hadn't mattered. But then I saw you, at the Prof.'s party, and I said, "There, that's the one; get *involved*. Life is spending itself in events, not withdrawing from them." It was such a change I promised myself, such a change. This will make you normal, I said.'

'Oh, Louis,' said Emma.

'I don't claim to be handsome or charming. I expect you like that sort of thing. But I have other virtues. I'm not in the pattern of modern romantic love; but nor are you. You feel beyond the ordinary – you're like me.'

'Not very,' said Emma. 'Not much like you.'

Louis leapt to his feet, pushed beyond endurance. 'Emma, we're both adult men and women,' he said.

'I know that,' said Emma.

'Don't you ever think about sex?'

'Yes,' said Emma. 'I like it as a system.'

'Emma,' cried Louis, gulping with terror, at the apogee of his courting play, 'let's go and drink this tea in the bedroom.'

'What for?' said Emma.

'My God! Women!' said Louis; sometimes the opposite sex were just too opposite for him. He went over to the bedroom door and went in. Panties and nightdresses lay in exotic array about the room; family photographs stood on the dressing table; on one wall hung some postcard reproductions of classical statuary; on another a sign, stolen from some public place. It said, 'Please Adjust Your Dress Before Leaving'. What's he doing? wondered Emma. His head popped suddenly round the jamb and, with infinite cunning in his voice, he said, 'Come in here.'

'No,' said Emma.

'Come on,' said Louis. 'Come in here.'

'You come in here,' said Emma, 'and finish your tea.'

'Please come,' said Louis. There was no reply. He popped his head back into the bedroom again. His voice came again, apparently talking to itself: 'Goodness, it's lovely in here,' it said. There was a pause. Then he said: 'I'll throw the alarm clock out of the window if she doesn't come in here.'

'You'll pay for it if you do,' said Emma warmly.

'Damn, damn, damn,' shouted Louis apoplectically. He came out of the bedroom furiously. 'What's wrong with me? I'm the plaything of the gods. The buffoon, the whipping-boy, the scapegoat.'

'Sit down, Louis,' said Emma.

'At least, spare me one little kiss,' said Louis, in desperation.

'No,' cried Emma. He looked at her and she was sobbing. Little tears coursed down her cheeks. 'Go away, Louis, please.'

'Why am I the one who goes unloved?' demanded Louis. 'What's wrong with me? Don't you like my face? Or is it my class? Isn't that good enough for you?'

'Louis, don't,' cried Emma. 'I hold nothing against you.'

'I know I'm not very good with women; I'm no Don Juan. My intentions were honourable; I'm not doing this for *fun*, you know.' No, fun was the last thing it was. Love, for Louis, was a serious matter. It was big business. He could imagine no more delightful prospect than that of being seen talking intimately to Emma, walking with her in the street, helping her off with her coat, being leaned on by her as she tipped stones out of her shoes. He could see her in these simple images – cooking at his stove, darning his socks, making their bed, dandling their children, nursing his influenza, knitting his sweaters. And it was images of the same sort that filled Emma's mind – the prospect of darning his seedy socks, washing his great socks, ministering to his weak chest, producing his snotty brats – and assured her that there was no hope of their intimacy.

'Stop talking about it, Louis,' she said.

'Can I still hope? Have I offended you too much?'

He had, but Emma could not say so; he would take it as a slight to his face, to his class, to his lack of normality. 'I'm not offended,' said Emma.

'And I can hope?'

'I don't know,' said Emma.

'You don't see how much I need you.'

'All right then, Louis, but please go.'

He picked up his damp coat, heaved his black beret on to his head, and she saw him to the door. As she went downstairs with him she wondered how she could have let all this happen. She wasn't a hard person, making quick dismissals of unwanted people. She placed the highest regard on personal relationships: what else, in this day and age, did one have? But Louis was hardly normal, hardly real. With his great, balding head and cadaverous body, his shabby, shapeless clothes and that immensely long, unbelted raincoat that hung down close to his feet, those large, knuckled, simian arms that dangled from sleeves always too short, he looked an absurdity; in him there was something of the butt. How could one offer him anything but pity?

Meanwhile, Louis walked home under the damp trees, perversely trying to catch pneumonia, bursting with chagrin, and asking himself furiously why everything good that he touched snapped in his clumsy paws. Why isn't my life like other people's? he wondered. What do I *do wrong*? Why are some singled out for special misfortune, congenitally condemned to writing to Anne Temple or Dorothy Dix, and being advised to join a tennis club or learn one topic of conversation really well? Louis tried to think of some stratagem by which he might restore himself to favour, a neat little social subtlety that might make up for the solecisms. But subtleties! – he was about as subtle as the smell of bad drains. And then he thought of something; he thought in fact of someone, and that was Mirabelle Warren.

3

There are people to whom life seems so simple, and so *pleasantly* simple, that when you look at them you wonder, 'Well, look, perhaps I just haven't thought this through far enough – I, and Shakespeare, and the rest of us.' Mirabelle Warren, the girl who had lisped about the cakes at Professor Treece's departmental party, was just such a person. If someone said to her, in passing, 'Life is not a bowl of cherries,' she would doubtless have protested, mystified, 'But it is, of *course* it is.' For her zephyrs blew softly, rivers ran sweetly, the sun shone daily. If Pippa had gone past her, singing, 'God's in His heaven, all's right with the world,' Mirabelle would have looked at her curiously, as she did at cynical people, and said, 'Well of course He is; you don't have to tell me *that*.' In her scheme of things, everyone at this lovely university nursed secret passions for everyone else, and was afraid to *speak forth*; but she wasn't; speaking forth was her forte. Affection swarmed like bees in everyone's heart, and the world was one great big party. Parties were her dedication; she was a sort of intellectual Elsa Maxwell. 'You're not enjoying this party as much as you ought,' she once told Louis, when she found him standing uncooperatively by a wall. If she was mystified by Louis, he was even more mystified by her. How could she possibly see life as so chummy an affair, when people were immense and solitary and one held them in fear and awe, as a sensitive child holds adults, when punished for misdemeanours he cannot understand and praised for goodness he cannot identify. Mirabelle seemed to have a compulsive liking for people.

Mirabelle was now planning her Christmas party. To be invited to her parties, it was said, you had to be one of the best people or, if you couldn't be quite said to be that, then fit to mix with those who were. Louis was now generally ranked as neither. The impact that his austere and donnish appearance had made on some was diminishing under his poor social performance, his strange pretensions and manners, and his habit of inviting himself to occasions to which he had not been invited. At the last party of Mirabelle's, he had insisted that people play 'Sardines' and when unwillingly they did he had locked himself in the lavatory so thoroughly with an hysterical girl from the S.C.M. that the door had to be taken off at the hinges. Louis did not care whether he went or not, in the ordinary way; but now he did, because he wanted to appear publicly in the role of Emma's escort; he was the one who went round with her, if anyone did.

When therefore he went into the University the next day he sought out Mirabelle Warren. The sign of Louis Bates, breathing heavily, approaching to detain one in conversation, was enough to send terror into the hearts of the virgins of the University; and Mirabelle Warren was the apotheosis of them. She popped into the library; a girl was pretty safe in a library. Louis followed and found her at a caryl in the reading-room, amid the dense religious silence, where she was back at work on her essay on subdued homosexuality in George Meredith. 'Hello,' he said, in that sibilant scholastic whisper, so much more irritating to those nearby than a conversation through megaphones, which is always adopted by those who chatter in libraries.

'Oh, hello, you,' said Mirabelle Warren.

'I came', said Louis cunningly, 'to see if I could bring someone to your Christmas party.' This was cunning because, while Mirabelle's irritation at Louis's inviting himself could easily make her say a firm no, her curiosity about who he was going to bring was stronger and she said a firm yes. 'Who's the lucky girl?' she asked, bursting with interest

'Well, actually,' said Louis modestly, 'it's Emma Fielding.'

'Louis, I do believe you're in love,' said Mirabelle with a great squeal of delight. Her words resounded and boomed through the stacks of books and people at the far end of the room looked up as the words rocked in their ears, and, thinking they were being addressed, began to form a reply. There was a pause; then a steady hissing, the native call of the disturbed library worker, arose. Poor Louis! What could he do? – for he was left with only one course. Everyone had heard the question and, if he was to go through with this, everyone must hear the answer. In a loud carefully enunciated affirmative syllable he broke the news to all. Furtive giggles sounded among the stacks.

'You must be careful, you know,' said Mirabelle, full of advice, 'she's not *our* sort, at all. She's clever with men, I imagine. She always seems cold to me. I think women should be warm.'

'So do I,' said Louis.

'Attention please; no talking,' a large middle-aged Central European woman who was writing a thesis in sociology announced in imperious tones.

'Well don't forget to bring a bottle,' said Mirabelle. 'It's a bottle party. Don't you just love them? It mixes the drinks before you even start.'

'There iss no talking in this rum,' came the loud, uninhibited tones of *Mittel-Europa*.

'Thank you so much,' said Louis.

'Hist!' cried the sociologist; and Louis left. He made his way to the telephone booth in the Union Building. It was engaged, but he tapped on the glass and the couple inside stopped kissing and emerged. Louis hated the telephone; people always seemed so unreal and disembodied; it was like being in touch with the spirit world and one forgot what one wanted to say. He lifted the receiver and chirped into it, 'Hello, hello. Who's there?' No one was. Someone waiting outside the booth to use it pulled the door open: it was the Central European sociologist. She gave him a sour look. 'I always get behind people like you with the telephone.' she said. 'I am a foreigner, but even *I* know this: you must dial.' He read the instructions, looked up Emma's number, and dialled it. It was access to a new mechanical world; numbers were whirling, sorting themselves out, making contact. Suddenly out of the dark world sounded the voice of Mrs Bishop, magnified and altered.

'Wait while I fix my deaf-aid up. I have to switch it on and put it next to the thing. I hope I'm talking in the right end. Now then, can you hear me? Can I hear you?'

Louis talked. 'Hello there,' cried Mrs Bishop.

'Press button A,' said the Central European sociologist.

'Hello, Mrs Bishop. May I speak to Miss Fielding?'

'I'm afraid she's engaged,' said Mrs Bishop.

Louis decided that he couldn't possibly go through all this again. 'Is she in the toilet?' he demanded.

'Certainly not,' said Mrs Bishop, as if nothing like that ever happened in her house.

'You see, it's urgent,' said Louis.

'Wait a minute,' said Mrs Bishop. The minute extended itself into several minutes. Outside the booth the Central European was salivating heavily. She stepped towards him as if she was going to ask why he wasn't talking, whether he just liked to hear it buzz. He started to speak rapidly into the mouthpiece. 'I come from haunts of coot and hern, I make a sudden sally, and sparkle out among the fern, to bicker down the valley,' he said.

'Do you?' said Emma Fielding.

'Oh, hello,' said Louis. 'It's lovely to hear your voice.'

'It's lovely to hear yours, except that I'm stark naked and dripping with water. I'm having a bath. Who is it?'

'I'll crawl down the wire,' said Louis, excited by this image. 'It's Louis Bates.'

'You just stay where you are,' said Emma. 'Well, what is it, before I catch my death of cold?'

'We've been invited to a party,' said Louis.

'We have?'

'Yes, you and I.'

'But I hate parties.'

'So do I,' said Louis.

'Then we won't go, will we?' said Emma.

'But we ought to go. Its Christmas.'

'What, again?' said Emma.

'Yes,' said Louis. 'Look, you must come. I've been to all kinds of trouble to get us invited; Mirabelle didn't want me to come, because I cheated at "Murder" last time, I think.'

'What did you do?'

'I committed suicide,' said Louis. 'You see, it's not that I want to go; I don't; I wanted to take you.'

'Look, Louis, I'm shivering; if I get any colder they'll have to wheel me off on a barrow. Let's leave it for now.'

'Say you'll come, then.'

'Oh, all right.'

'I'll pick you up, then.'

'No, there's no need. . . . '

'That's how it's done,' said Louis firmly. Emma said good-bye and rang off and it wasn't until Louis had come out of the booth and past the steaming sociologist that it occurred to him that he did not know, and therefore had not told Emma, on which night the party was to take place. He hastened back to the library to find Mirabelle and repair the omission.

4

A stout woman in her corsets ran across the dress-shop. 'Whoops!' she said when she saw Treece. Treece, who did not like dress shops, picked up his parcel and hurriedly found the exit. It was the following Monday and Treece was on his way to Emma's. Complex motives had filtered through his mind and brought him to this spot. After Viola's party, Treece had felt himself to be a little committed to Viola, or Dr Masefield, as he now preferred to call her. The fact that he felt committed made him determined not to be. No one owned him (except perhaps his motorized bicycle, whose subject he felt himself to be). A visit to Emma was the answer. Then again on the last occasion they had met he had spilled tea on Emma and she probably regretted her open invitation. She would not wish him to come after that solecism. But she might respect him more if he did. Lastly he wanted to honour his promise to buy a new dress.

He arrived at Emma's and rang the doorbell. No one came. Within a piano rang out loudly. He rang again and then he tried the door. It was unlocked, so he entered. In the room directly facing him, a strange vignette met his eye. An elderly lady was lying full-length on the floor, reading *The Times*. Behind her an elderly gentleman sat at a pianola, treadling it furiously to keep it working. The machine was grinding out the inevitable Chopin waltz. Treece picked up the hammer to the dinner gong and rang it loudly. No one heard. Then, all at once, the old lady looked up and saw him. 'He's back, he's back,' she cried, jumping to her feet and snatching up a statue of a whistling boy.

Emma was up in her room, filing her nails, chewing biscuits, twanging the straps of her brassière and betraying all the symptoms of intellectual toil when she heard someone downstairs calling her name. She stepped out on to the landing to see Mrs Bishop poised to strike down her thesis supervisor. 'Wrong one,' she shouted frantically. 'It's my professor of English.' 'Switch on, switch on,' shouted Mr Bishop, dancing up and down beside his wife, 'Miss Fielding says this is her professor.' Immediately Mrs Bishop was all smiles. The Bishops were very deferential to education. 'I thought you were someone else,' she said. 'Oh, it must be wonderful to be educated. What does it feel like?'

'It's like having an operation,' said Treece. 'You don't know you've had it until long after it's over'

'Come upstairs,' said Emma.

'No, no; it's not every day you get the chance to get to the bottom of a professor,' said Mrs Bishop. 'What class do you belong to? I'm always interested in people. Most of my friends seem to prefer animals, but I stick by people. Do you read at all?'

'Yes,' said Treece; 'often.'

'I used to, but nowadays all the novels you seem to get are about what's wrong with other novels. It's a vicious circle. I'd like to break in, but I can't. Too old, you know.'

'Oh no,' said Treece soothingly.

'I am too old, damn it,' said Mrs Bishop. 'It's the only satisfaction I get. Those shoes look to me as though they could do with a good clean, professor, but it's none of my business.'

'This is a lovely house, Mrs Bishop,' said Treece, looking around the long, high room with its white panelling and high Georgian windows. 'I suppose it gets rather cold in the winter.'

'Yes; it's charming, isn't it? And when it gets cold we

just throw another servant on the fire. He, he,' said Mrs Bishop. 'I'm being naughty now; I love it.'

'Come in, now, dear, and finish reading *The Times*,' said Mr Bishop tactfully.

'We're top people, you know, professor,' said Mrs Bishop. She added to her husband, as he led her away, 'He doesn't talk much for a professor, does he?'

'Surprised to see me?' asked Treece. Emma was; she had no stockings on; dirty dishes sat in the chairs.

'I've brought you a little present,' said Treece. He handed it over and prowled around the flat inquisitively. 'Are you alone or do you share?' he asked, opening the broom closet and looking in.

'Alone,' said Emma. 'I say, this is lovely.' She pulled out the dress and put it in front of her. 'But you shouldn't have done it. I told you, didn't I?'

'I know, but I wanted to,' said Treece.

'I'll go and try it on and you can see how it looks,' said Emma.

'Lovely,' said Treece.

'You'll find something to read in the bookcase,' said Emma, and went into the bedroom. She could hear Treece prowling noisily about in the other room.

'This is fantastic,' said Emma, coming out again with the dress on. 'How did you do it? It fits perfectly.'

'Well, I just went in the shop and asked for a dress for a girl that came up to here.' He put his hand to the end of his nose.

'But the bust size and everything's right!'

'Well, I looked at all the assistants until I saw one with a bust like yours. I'm glad it suits you so well.'

'I didn't know you'd observed me so carefully,' said Emma.

'Oh, I like looking at women,' said Treece. 'How's Mr Eborebelosa?'

'I haven't seen him for ages,' said Emma.

'That was all rather a mess, wasn't it?' asked Treece with a smile. 'I'm afraid people like us are too reasonable to be true. Personal relationships, civilized human contacts – how splendid it all sounds, doesn't it, like some intellectual Fabian club, you know, full of goodwill and rather spinsterly. Poor Mr Eborebelosa! What does he want to get mixed up with people like us for? We're much too dried-up for him. I suppose it's something that cultural boundaries conceal.'

If Treece hadn't been smiling at her so sweetly she would have supposed he was insulting her: that was what it *sounded* like. 'You mean that if I had been interested in him the advantage might have been for *me*, not him?' asked Emma interestedly.

'Possibly,' said Treece. 'It's a funny age, isn't it? There are so many literatures, so many religions, so many cultures, so many philosophies, one doesn't know where to turn. Do you remember the thirties?'

'I'm not *that* old,' said Emma. 'I remember the forties, after the war. There were lots of grants for everybody and people used to sew leather patches on the elbows of perfectly new Harris tweed sports jackets.'

'I *am* that old,' said Treece. 'My goodness me, talking to you, I feel it. But the thing about the thirties was you knew you were a socialist – there was nothing else to be – and there were all these socialist clubs, with people doing things about human quandaries. There were quandaries too. I think that really, however pessimistic we were about the state of the world, we had a kind of Rousseauesque belief in the perfectibility of man. It's such a paradoxical belief, of course; the evidence of ordinary experience is against it, and as Rousseau himself admitted, wickedness is a source of considerable embarrassment. But we did think there was something to be done about the social order; that the human condition could be mended; that there was so much further to go. Now one doesn't. Do you have any hope for the future?'

'No,' said Emma. 'I don't.'

'And I don't, none at all. If I see the future as anything other than an explosion, then I think of it as the present, only worse. But in those days ... take adult education. In those days it seemed really important work. One was evolving the new man. If you had in your class one of those old-style working-class intellectuals who started in the mines and finished in

Parliament, you felt really a part of the world's process. One was of the English scene. Now the classes are for middle-class ladies whose families are grown up, and there they come, a little lost, improving themselves and using the place as a kind of knitting bee. Don't misunderstand me, I'm not contemptuous. ...'

'No, I know,' said Emma; Treece was never contemptuous of anything.

'But their prejudices are formed, and one teaches them nothing except facts. Not how to improve the world. All this is why someone like Louis Bates interests me. You know him, don't you?'

'Yes; he's Eborebelosa all over again,' said Emma.

'He's told you, has he? I knew, you know. And really, when one thinks of him, one can't help feeling sorry for him. Are you going to marry him? All he needs is some simple human understanding.'

'No, damn it ... excuse me, Professor Treece, but I am not. It's the other thing all over again. It's exactly the same dilemma.'

'Well, not quite, is it?' said Treece. 'I mean, Bates is a marginal man like ourselves. Admittedly he has more vigour ...'

'You're very cruel to us both, you know,' said Emma. 'You seem to despair of us.' What made Emma uneasy was that he did define her own doubts; she was the sort of person, she feared, to whom nothing happened, who set no worlds on fire and who, because there were so many identities to choose from, had none at all. Treece's plain assumption that she, along with him, was not in the ripeness-is-all faction, not among the livers and doers, disturbed her. How did he know?

'Ah, we poor Platonists, this just isn't our world,' said Treece. 'Well, let's have some tea.'

Emma had a small gas ring in one corner of the room. She went and put on the kettle. Treece had a picture of Emma's life here, that of a quiet, intellectual soul working studiously amid the fuss and furore of this slightly depressed area, over which train-smoke billowed and fog collected.

'So', said Treece, 'you think that Mr Bates is a Yahoo?'

Downstairs the front door bell rang and rang again, soulfully, yearningly, passionately.

'I didn't say that,' said Emma.

'Oh,' said Treece. Heavy footsteps sounded on the stairs.

'You are strange, you know,' said Emma, looking up from her sandwich-making. 'You seem almost as though you're trying to marry me off. First it was the other one; then you produce this one. Really, you know, I want to marry someone who's good for me. You seem to think that I'm in heaven and all I need do is pull other people over the threshold. Believe me, I'm outside and I'm looking for someone to pull me in. I'm not a human sacrifice.'

'I know,' said Treece, adding speculatively, 'I understand all that, but what worries me is, if you don't marry him, nobody will. No one will ever recognize him....'

He flung open the door, the subject under discussion, and they recognized him quickly enough. 'Ah, Mr Treece,' he shouted. 'Who invited you here?'

'Be careful, Bates,' said Treece, standing up and looking dreadfully alarmed.

'I've caught you, haven't I?' cried Louis. 'Wait until everyone hears about this.'

'Louis,' said Emma, 'Professor Treece happens to be my invited guest. You aren't. I asked him to tea. He brought me this dress.'

'Take it off, this instant,' cried Louis.

'Don't be ridiculous,' said Emma.

'I think I'd better go,' said Treece.

'I agree,' said Louis.

'You stay where you are,' cried Emma. 'You're not leaving this room until Louis has learned to behave himself.'

'I'll pull his ears off,' said Louis.

'It's Louis who has to leave,' said Emma. 'You're my guest. I didn't invite him.'

'Why are you lying?' shouted Louis. 'You did. I'm taking you to Mirabelle's party tonight. You'd forgotten, hadn't you?'

'You didn't even say when it was,' said Emma. 'In any case, if it's tonight, I can't go.'

'You have to go,' said Louis. 'I've bought a bottle of wine.'

'Drink it yourself,' said Emma.

'I can't afford to buy wine to drink myself,' said Louis. He looked spitefully, meanly, nastily at Treece, and only succeeded in presenting himself as infinitely ridiculous and pathetic. The only person who could take him seriously, even in a crisis of this sort, was Louis Bates himself, but his offering in that direction practically made up for everyone else's. You could not be too angry with him; after all he was a sensitive and intelligent creature, in his own way, and situations always turned sour on him. 'You can't win against competition like *that*, can you?' he said, looking at Treece.

'I'm not competition like that,' said Treece. 'You have much more right to Miss Fielding than I do, and . . .'

'He certainly does not,' said Emma indignantly.

'Look, let's sit down; this is getting like a Restoration comedy,' said Treece. They poised themselves on the edge of chairs.

'Is it still raining?' asked Treece.

'Yes,' said Louis curtly.

This concession to social law having been made, Treece rose from his chair. 'Well, I don't want to trespass on your evening, Miss Fielding. Many thanks for the pleasant tea.'

'You haven't had any yet,' said Emma, 'and you came to trespass and trespass you shall.'

'I thought you wished to go to a party?'

'I should never forgive myself if I allowed people to come in and break up a tea-party in this way. We're civilized people, aren't we? At least, I know I am. I'm not going to the party.'

'You mustn't let me stop you,' said Treece.

Louis took out a bottle of wine from his pocket and waved it about. 'We've got to go,' he said.

'Well,' said Emma graciously, 'if we go, Professor Treece comes as well.'

'Oh, I can't go,' said Treece. 'I should ruin the occasion.'

'And think how I should look, bringing him,' said Louis.

'I absolutely insist,' said Emma implacably.

'Oh, all right, then,' said Louis.

'You must tell me what you think of these cakes, Professor Treece,' said Emma.

'They're very nice,' said Louis.

'I'm not really interested in your valuation,' said Emma. 'Who established you as a judge of cakes? Now, Professor Treece, what are they like?'

'They're very nice,' said Treece.

'Good. I shall go there again,' said Emma.

'I should,' said Louis.

'People are always trying to interfere in one's business, have you noticed?' said Emma to Treece. 'As if one can't do one's shopping on one's own.'

'Look, really, I ought to . . .' said Treece.

'You're not going. I shan't let you,' said Emma, conscious that she had never behaved as badly as this in her life before, and enjoying every minute of it. 'Your evening's already booked.'

'Why don't you leave him alone?' said Louis.

'If he goes, so do you,' said Emma. 'Well, since you're so conversational now, Mr Bates, tell me what you really think of this dress?'

'I think it's terrible,' said Louis frankly, 'and it amazes me that you accept gifts like that. You're a cruel woman. Don't you think so, Professor Treece?'

'Oh, that's hardly fair, is it?' cried Treece.

'I'm surprised at you too,' said Bates. 'I told you that this was the one I was after.'

'But this was simply a friendly visit. . . .'

'I'm not naïve, you know,' said Bates. 'I worked in a paperbag factory once. I know what friendly visits are.'

'You have a horrible mind,' said Emma Fielding.

5

Treece knew that it was very naughty of him to go to Mirabelle's party. But then the mood of the evening seemed permissive: Louis had been naughty and threatened to pull Treece's ears off; Emma had been naughty and had practically pinned him down in his chair so that he shouldn't escape, at the same time teasing Louis Bates to fury; the conventional moulds seemed well and truly broken, and the trouble with feeling in this spirit is that the rest of the world, not sharing the initiatory experience, looks on in amazement. Moreover, all his life Treece had been doing things that he did not exactly want to do, journeying off on holidays he had no intention of taking, watching plays he did not wish to see, playing sports he detested, simply because someone had gone to the trouble to persuade him, simply because he felt they *cared*, simply ... well, simply because he could not say *no*. He always thought what a hard time of it he would have had if he had been a woman; he would have been pregnant all the time. In addition to the fact that he lacked the positive sense of what his life ought to be doing at that moment, he possessed, equally, a simple faith in the unexpected – in the capacity of Fate for coming up with something new and interesting. He liked being nudged around.

It was thus that he found himself trudging through the hard rain on the way to Mirabelle's party, with Emma and Louis at his either side.

It was impossible to miss Mirabelle's house, once you got within half a mile of it. It glowed with light, roared with noise, and as they grew nearer they could see people in the garden outside, being sick into the bushes. They rang the bell and Mirabelle opened the door. 'We brought a friend,' said Louis. 'It's Professor Treece, actually.'

'Oooo,' said Mirabelle. You could see she thought this a brilliant touch.

'They pressed me,' said Treece. 'I mustn't stay. . . .'

'Oh yes, you must; come and see how the other half lives.' 'Other half of what?' asked Treece. They stepped into the hall. 'Throw your coats on the floor,' said Mirabelle; and then, after a moment of reflection, she added to Treece: 'I could hang yours up, sir.' 'No,' said Treece, tossing his coat on to the pile on the floor with the best of them.

'What do you think of my kissing bunch?' said Mirabelle, gesturing to the decoration of hoops, hung with holly and mistletoe, that hung around the hall light. The mention of kissing roused Louis from his self-engrossment; he looked at Emma; all that was needed was a slight, accurate push that took her sideways and under the hoops and, simultaneously, a lunge forward with his lips, carefully aimed. It was too complicated and he rejected the idea.

'Let me show you the way to the bog, if you get taken short,' said Mirabelle. 'It's the door at the top of the stairs where that man's lying.' She led them down the hall. 'Did you bring a bottle?' asked Mirabelle. 'Someone brought a bottle and asked us to fill it.'

'It's British Wine Port Type,' said Louis, unwrapping his gift. 'I got something that everyone was sure to like.'

They emerged into the living-room, which was filled with people, all packed together so tightly that if someone's nose itched he had to go outside to scratch it. A large ivy plant, in a bowl, was clinging to the wall; a number of people were clinging to the ivy plant. People sat on chairs, on cushions on the floor, on bookcases. A young serious-looking girl was sitting on the floor in the corner, smoking a large briar pipe and reading the index to the Talmud. A group of deep-chested young men in the corner were singing a song called 'The Bastard King of England'. In a row on the settee sat three German students, clearly perplexed by the whole business: 'Is this a typical English party, please?' they kept asking people. Treece withdrew with his back to the wall and surveyed the throng. Suddenly he felt a sharp pain in his leg; he looked down; a stoutish, beaming girl had pulled up his trousers and was biting him familiarly in the calf. She looked up at him and giggled. 'Your eyes are like peascods,' she said.

'Take no notice,' said another amiable girl. 'She's been doing that to all the men.'

'I find it quite painful,' said Treece.

'What she wants is kissing,' said the girl. 'She associates biting with erotic experience, and when her control is lessened she expresses herself sexually on these lines. You should hold her down and kiss her. I'll hold her if you like.'

'Not me,' said Treece. 'Let one of the others do it.'

Mirabelle came over to them with some drinks. 'Do you want to go upstairs, Emma?' she asked. 'Yes, please,' said Emma. 'I'll come too,' said Louis, not wanting to be left alone. 'You can't go where she's going,' said Mirabelle. She turned to Treece. 'I hope you don't mind if we sort of pretend you aren't here,' she said. 'I mean, if we don't let it inhibit us. People shouldn't be inhibited at parties, I always think. And if you feel uninhibited at all, *do* join in.'

'Thank you,' said Treece.

'We shan't hold it against you,' said Mirabelle. 'What can I get you to drink?'

'What do you have?'

'Well, most of us are drinking rum and ginger and paprika while it holds out, because someone said it was an aphrodisiac. I don't suppose it is *really*. Still you can hope. You know that bit in *Macbeth* about drink increasing the desire but diminishing the performance. Come on, try it.'

'Me?' cried Treece.

'Yes, it'll be interesting to see what happens, won't it?'

'I'd prefer whisky if you have it,' said Treece.

She turned to Louis again. He stood dejectedly against the wall. 'I'll bash you if you don't smile,' she said. 'Aren't you enjoying yourself?' 'I always enjoy *myself*,' said Louis. 'But I'm not so sure I enjoy other people.'

'Louis, you're so immature,' said Mirabelle. 'Have a cigarette.'

'I don't smoke,' said Louis.

'Well, try then. It's a social accomplishment.'

'Very well,' said Louis. He took one.

'Now,' said Mirabelle, giving him a light. 'Suck in.'

'Oo,' said Louis. 'You've burned all the hairs on the inside of my nose.'

'Well, suck in, stupid. Don't blow out.'

'I think I'm going to faint,' said Louis.

'You make such a fuss about things,' said Mirabelle.

'I just don't know how people can smoke,' said Louis. He waved his hand extravagantly, passing the cigarette over a bowl of punch, which promptly caught fire, burning with a tall blue flame. A number of young men came and put water on it and someone fetched his fire-extinguisher from his car and put it out. Little was said. Across the room the deep-chested young men were singing 'Oh, Sir Jasper, do not touch me'.

Treece was tired of waiting for his drink. He picked up a chianti bottle and began to pour one out, only to find that the bottle was a table lamp with the shade knocked off. He put it back where it came from. More and more people kept swarming into the room; a man who could actually pronounce the name of Faulkner's county kept pronouncing it. Treece set out to look for a full bottle of something. Two people lay on the settee as he passed, kissing violently, yet holding out with meticulous care their glasses and cigarettes in each outflung hand. The girl recognized Treece. 'Professor Treece, honey. Professor Treece,' she said.

'Good evening, Miss Weston,' said Treece.

'We're neither of us enjoying this, you understand,' said Miss Weston. 'We're both engaged to other people.'

'Splendid,' said Treece.

'No, don't go, Professor Treece, honey,' said the girl. 'Come and hold my other hand, you great big pornographic bear you.'

Treece disengaged himself from the encounter and went on towards the drinks. The three Germans stood in a cluster by the wall, chatting with puzzled expressions among themselves. 'This is a typical English party, yes?' asked one of them.

'Of a kind,' said Treece.

'Of which social class, sir?'

'The thing to do is to look at the bottles,' said Treece. 'Bottles are great class-indicators. If more whisky has gone than gin, I should say upper middle.'

Over at the table beside the class-indicators a serious literary conversation was taking place, Treece found. 'How is your novel?' cried a brittle, cultured voice. 'My novel, did you say, or my navel?' replied someone. 'Your novel, old boy,' said the brittle voice. 'Well they're both suffering from lack of contemplation,' said the second voice. This was Walter Oliver, the literary *enfant terrible* of the University, who had once told Treece in a tutorial: 'The intellectual society in this

University is me.' He nodded amiably at Treece. 'My trouble is that I only write seventh chapters,' said Oliver. 'I have dozens of those. If only I could meet up with a few other fellows who write first chapters. ...' 'You should send them to some of these American phoney *avant-garde* magazines. They specialize in printing seventh chapters. Just write a little introduction saying that the rest of it was stolen by the priesthood.' Thoroughly embroiled in the literary world (he had been kicked in the groin by a drunken Lallans poet at the Edinburgh Festival), Oliver was the kingpin around which university literary life circulated. He was the Editor of the university literary magazine (people kept complaining that it was in the hands of a clique. 'Who are you calling a clique?' demanded Oliver) and chairman of the University Literary Society; he was a kind of provincial Ken Tynan. His patronage was positively feudal in character; to be taken up by Oliver (Louis Bates had been taken up by Oliver) was to become his tool. For instance, Bates, who had no powers of extended creation, had been inveigled into starting a novel, so that he could put Oliver into it. 'I'm watching you,' said Oliver as the novel progressed. 'He keeps getting me into little attics with girls and I roll their skirts up and then, for God's sake, somehow I can't bring myself to do anything. I shall sue him.'

'Good evening,' said Oliver. 'Big wheels here tonight, eh? Spy from the Conservative Party?'

'I got here by accident,' said Treece.

'Your mummy should have been more careful,' said Oliver. 'Give me a cigarette, will you?'

Treece produced his packet and Oliver took five. 'I'll give you these back some day,' he said.

'I didn't know you were writing a novel?' said Treece.

'Well, somebody had to. Nothing was being done. It's a good one too. You want to keep in with me; I'm on the way up. Man told me the other day I was a great man. It's true. And the cock crew three times. The trouble is if you don't write these poor-young-bugger novels no one will look at you. I'm an old-fashioned moonlight-on-the-water-and-meanwhile-in-my-lady's-boudoir man myself. I got arrested at the Ronald

Firbank stage. I'm the missing link in the evolution of the twentieth-century novel. Besides, I'm too busy to waste my time writing. I just talk about it.' It was indeed surprising that Oliver had reached such a position of literary eminence without actually having produced one piece of written work that anyone had read. He simply talked about books that no one had read.

'You don't know who'd put up a bit a money for an interesting commercial speculation?' he asked.

'I don't think I do,' said Treece. 'What is it?'

'Well, I was thinking of starting a correspondence course for people who are socially mobile. It's called Room-At-The-Top, Limited. It's to enable people to fit easily into any socket in the social scale – what shoes to wear, what books to read, whether to be sado-masochistic or anal-erotic, whether to know what words like that *mean*. Things to say for all occasions at different class levels. How to have opinions if you're a Man in the Street in a television interview – this sort of thing.'

'I don't know who'd help, I'm afraid.'

'Might interest the Sociology Department,' said Oliver. 'They could probably get a Rockefeller Grant.'

'I doubt it,' said Treece. 'Well, I'm pleased someone here is writing a novel. . . .'

'You know,' said Oliver, 'if you're interested in the provincial literary scene, I can smuggle you into a local literary cabal of some passing interest. They meet at the Mandolin every week.'

'Where's the Mandolin?'

'It's the espresso bar. It works without steam. You ought to come.'

'I'd like to, actually,' said Treece.

'Good, I'll let you know then,' said Oliver. He smiled pleasantly, shut his eyes, and slid slowly down the wall, in a stupor.

'Leave him,' said Mirabelle, passing by. Across the room someone had splashed gin all down the wall. In the corner Louis Bates, who had been nervously dismantling and reassembling his fountain-pen, was rejoined by Emma.

'Where have you been, if it isn't a rude question?' he demanded, surly at her long neglect of him.

'I've been in the lavatory, if it isn't a rude answer,' said Emma.

'You were a long time,' said Louis.

'I'm not going to have you timing me every time I go to the lavatory,' said Emma.

'You know I came here to be with you. It certainly wasn't for the party. You don't care anything for me, though; you make that quite apparent.'

'You shouldn't take yourself so seriously,' said Emma. 'I'd hate you to think I was cruel, but really you behave absurdly'

'Good evening, you remember me? I was with you before at a party,' said the stout German student, Herr Schumann. 'You like this party?'

'Yes,' said Emma. 'Do you?'

'It was my hope that some discussion of literary subjects would take place, but it does not matter. We are all happy, I think.'

'I'm not,' said Louis Bates.

'You don't find it difficult to understand what people are saying?' asked Emma.

'Oh no, I understand very well. I think parties are alike in all countries. In my country we have bathing parties, where all go naked into the water. I am very fond of such parties. Perhaps we all might make one day a bathing party. Also in Germany there are parties of homosexuals, which no doubt there are here also. *Coelum non animum mutant qui trans mare currunt.* You speak Latin, I think.'

'I understand,' said Emma.

'I like parties. However, in England it is not often I am to parties.'

'No?'

'The evenings I am so busy.'

'What do you do in the evenings?'

'The evening,' said the German, 'I sit babies.'

'It's a pity you didn't sit some tonight,' said Louis.

'I bring you a drink?' said the German. Emma asked for a gin and lime and Herr Schumann departed.

'How could you be so awful?' said Emma. 'How do you think he feels now?'

'How do you think I feel now?' demanded Louis. 'I didn't come hobing dat ve should dalk about liderature. I came to talk to you. I don't understand this. Have I got something my best friends won't tell me about? Why is everything I do wrong? Why am I everybody's whipping-boy? What is it about me that makes eggs addle when I cook them, cars go wrong when I get in them?'

Now the German was back.

'You are hot?' he asked of Emma, inclining from the waist. 'Will you come with me into the garden for fresh air?'

'Am I invisible?' demanded Louis. 'Can't you see me here? She's with me.' The German looked at him and departed.

'I'm going to talk to someone else', said Emma, 'since you find it so difficult to behave like a civilized person.'

'No, don't leave me,' said Louis, grasping her by the arm. 'Let *go*,' said Emma, prising his fingers from her.

'Damn,' said Louis furiously. 'You said damn,' said a voice at his side; it was the girl who had been smoking the pipe and reading the Talmud. She wore black woollen stockings and a folk-weave skirt. Louis decided to make Emma jealous, and he sought something to say to the girl. He remembered Dale Carnegie and asked about her hobbies. 'I collect conches,' said the girl, puffing on her pipe. 'Can anyone do it?' asked Louis seriously, 'or do you have to be childish?'

Meanwhile Emma had slipped away, out into the garden, which smelled freshly of the recent rain. In the darkness she saw someone coming towards her. It was Walter Oliver. Without speaking he put his arms around her and began to kiss her. He smelled of sick. She pushed his arms away and freed herself. 'Why not?' said Oliver. 'It's only little old me.' 'No,' said Emma. 'Sex rules the world, you know,' said Oliver. He put his arms around her again and at this moment Louis, who had been looking everywhere for Emma, stumbled upon them. He looked at them in horror. 'I just came for some fresh air,' he said. 'The fresh air's over there,' said Oliver.

Treece nodded pleasantly to Louis as he went back inside. 'All right?' he asked. 'Not feeling sick?'

'No, thank you,' he said. When Emma came in a moment or two later, a few spots of rain beaded in her hair, she found Louis waiting for her in the kitchen.

'What are you up to?' he demanded. 'Is it just everybody except me?'

'You know it's not,' said Emma, starting to cry a little. She felt hideously ashamed of herself.

'He's only playing with you, Emma; I'm not. I'm serious. ... What is it about me?'

'Oh, please don't keep on,' said Emma.

'No; I want to know. This is important to me. I have all the big virtues, don't I? Aren't I honest, fair, reasonable? I know I lack the small virtues, charm, good manners, pretty speeches. But are those all that count with you?'

'Oh, I hope not,' cried Emma. 'The trouble is one does like charming people better than good people. It's a hideous truth; it's a moral corruption. But it's so. Look, Louis, I'm like most women; I have my limitations. I'm just practical. I'm damned if I'm going to live in some mean little house all my life. If you marry me, you do it to make me happy, to take me away from the things that depress me, not to make life harder to bear. I don't want marriage to be the end of my life, but the beginning. Marriage isn't suicide, you know. I know it can destroy, but not me, please. I have immortal longings, I suppose. So you see.'

'I see,' said Louis. 'People like me don't matter, because we don't say things out of a handsome enough face or with a charming enough voice. Have you ever thought that your distrust of me might come from a deficiency in you?'

'Yes, I have,' said Emma, 'but it doesn't do you any good to point it out.'

'You don't know what you do to me. You show everyone I'm unlovable. People would like me more if you could love me.'

'This conversation's getting us nowhere,' said Emma.

'Won't you give me one little kiss?'

'No,' said Emma. 'No.'

'You kissed him.'

'I'm sorry, Louis, no.'

Watching him go off in his dejection, she felt herself suffused with pain; yet as he went, his shoulders exaggeratedly drooped, there was an air of falsity about his actions which lay behind all he did. He didn't really know what was happening to him. Even so, Emma had to feel ashamed; she had dismissed him far too easily, had as good as said that he didn't count for much. Wanting to live her life with point and relevance, she found herself looking for meanings under stones; she saw what she had done as an ethical decision. She had rejected a great deal that was worthy under the personal detestation that she confessed she felt for Bates. By being such an awful person, he had driven her to something for which she could not now forgive herself. Back in the living-room there was hardly anyone left. All the bottles were empty save one – the British Wine Port Type that Louis had brought.

CHAPTER SIX

I

IT was the last tutorial of the Michaelmas term, and Professor Treece sat at his desk, his back to the window, while the dull December light shone on to the pile of examination scripts upon his desk, on to the faces of his three students. Two of them were, he knew, pondering on the quality of their amorous performance for the Christmas Ball, which was to be held in the Town Hall that night, an end-of-term festivity before everyone left for home on the morrow. The third student, Louis Bates, lacked the general excitement. Wedged there tightly in his chair, he looked a pathetic figure, and Treece felt a sense of guilt as he looked at him. The performance of that do-it-yourself intellectual in terminal examinations had been shocking; there were good reasons for sending him down, and the attack had been strongly renewed by the anti-Bates faction at a faculty meeting, where Carfax, careful not to make the same mistake twice, had claimed that Bates had deliberately and while of sound mind abrogated his responsibilities as a student and should be asked to leave. Invited to contribute essays on literary subjects to his tutors for evaluation, he had refused; the fact was, simply, that. Treece had, it must be said, been tempted; Bates didn't now seem to fit so well into the category which Treece had designated for him, that of the working-class intellectual rising in the world through his own efforts, aided by the tutelage of liberal-minded teachers. Yet in a sense he was this. For it wasn't necessary that he should be pleasing, or grateful, or even liberal like his teacher. One doesn't have to stamp the new generation with one's own concerns and attributes. One has simply to give it the means to emerge in its own shape.

What made Treece so uncomfortable was that he was talking at this moment about Shelley. He remembered the nasty little mistake that Oxford had made in expelling *him*. He read out to his tutorial group Shelley's indictment of Oxford: 'Oxonian society was insipid to me, uncongenial with my habits of thinking. I could not descend to common life; the sublime interest of poetry, lofty and exalted achievements, the proselytism of the world, the equalization of its inhabitants, were to be the soul of my soul.' Treece read, and watched Louis's eyes light up. To think that Louis might be put in a position to say the same about their own University was too, too much. Shelley had been an oddity, just like Bates; and at school and university they had called him what Carfax, what they all, had called Bates – mad. Treece knew now that this word should never have been used of Bates. It was strange how unseriously serious men could use serious words. Shelley used to send out offensive atheistic letters to divines, over a false name; to blow up fences with gunpowder; to ask mothers carrying babes in arms, 'Will your baby tell us anything about pre-existence, madam?' All right, thought Treece, so he was interested in dianeics? Shelley, it was said, had his tutor 'in great perplexity'; and Treece had to admit that when they wrote up Bates they could use the same phrase of him.

He looked over at this erratic, easily despised, and pitiable figure, unstable, yes, but honest, pure, and concerned for human values, sitting there in his chair, scratching the end of his nose with a long, nobbly forefinger. He made a lousy symbol, if it was a symbol you wanted, Treece told himself; but then people always did make poor symbols, even in his view. Treece had to recognize an uneasiness here; Louis was brilliant, did not crave the cheaper kinds of success, had worked hard for what he had, which was little enough. Yet what mystified Treece, who really only needed to look at his own case for illumination, was that someone could be so clever at his subject and so unclever at living. Louis's brilliance was a narrow strip of cultivated ground; the ordinary experience of the world, however, was, to him, untilled ground, something that he had just not bothered to go to work on. And because of this, Treece further perceived, there was – you had in all honesty to recognize this, as Emma already had recognized it – something faintly ridiculous about Louis. Other people knew this; it was, indeed, all they did know about him. Louis's manners were as strange as Eborebelosa's; he came out of as foreign a culture. Treece could not help but think of a story which Walter Oliver had told him about Bates, and the story was this:

In the early days of his attendance at the University, Louis had sent to Oliver, as Editor of the student literary magazine, a sheaf of poems for him to consider for publication. A few days later, Louis received a note from Oliver, saying, 'I think we're on to something,' and asking Louis to go and see him in his lodgings. When Louis arrived, Oliver, who was sitting on the bed clad in a pair of Y-front undershorts, stringing a cello and eating cheese, greeted him with great warmth, offering him cheese and making him sit down. He produced the poems (which had, Louis noticed, been heavily overdrawn with sketches of girls) and, 'You know, dumbo, you've got something here,' said Oliver, in a voice that seemed to Louis to mingle distrust and pride – distrust, doubtless, at what Louis had got and pride at his having been able to spot it, whatever it was. Once you got Oliver's patronage, you did not get rid of it easily. A few days later Oliver returned the call, to tell Louis that he had decided to publish his poems. Louis was clearly loath to let him in; he disliked having visitors. The room was redolent with the rich, plummy smell of sweat-filled socks; it smelled, said Oliver, when he told this story, as he so often did, like the women's changing-room at Holloway Prison. Oliver had thrown open the window, and Louis protested, saying that he was medically excused from having the window open in the winter, or taking baths, because of his weak chest. 'Look, amigo,' said Oliver, who had little time for this sort of thing, 'these poems are good, but you smell like a goat. I'll make a bargain with you. I'll publish these poems if you'll have a bath.' 'Do you want to kill me?' cried Louis. 'It's for the sake of art,' said Oliver implacably. Louis, though he had not let Oliver in until his privates were covered over with water, had at least taken the bath, there and then; and the poem had been published in the University literary magazine, to universal apathy.

Treece looked at Bates and thought of this tale, which Oliver had put into wide circulation. Bates was seedy, frowsy; he wore ugly and ungainly clothes; he spoke with long sheep-like North-Country a's (and had, thought Treece, who loved this sort of joke, a long, sheep-like North-Country arse); he did, to some extent, smell. The perception of this ridiculousness came to Treece as a kind of insight. He was immediately aware of the need to protect Louis from odious people who thought like himself. It was not, therefore, abruptly, but with a sympathetic mien, that Treece addressed Louis thus at the end of the tutorial :

'I have your examination papers here, Bates, and they were not, to be honest, very satisfactory.'

Louis had been sat sullenly waiting for this. 'I didn't think they would be,' he said.

'Now you understand there's nothing personal in this if I say I'm disappointed. We like you as a person ...' this touch was a bit overwarm, Treece knew, but how could this be done otherwise? '... but academically your work has been falling off, and if it continues like this I'm afraid I can't hold out any hope that you'll get even a poor degree.' Bates looked very chastened. 'Now, what's wrong? Do you feel you can do better than this? Is this a fair sample of your work?'

'You know it's not,' said Louis. The remark sounded like an impertinence, but then so many of Louis's remarks did.

'Then what went wrong?' demand Treece sharply. 'Are you short of money? Are you unhappy in your lodgings?'

'It's *her*, you know,' said Louis. The two other students present exchanged a look and giggled audibly. 'You know I'm in love. I told you.'

'That has nothing to do with me,' said Treece, brusque because Louis should have had more sense than to embarrass him; that surely was not too much to expect. ''The simple question is: do you *intend* to improve, or am I to recommend that you be asked to make way for someone who *will* work?'

'I've had enough of her,' said Louis. 'If that's love I prefer not to be in it. Everything will be all right next term.' He sat unmoved while Cocoran dissolved into uncontrollable laughter.

'Don't be childish, Cocoran,' said Treece. 'I don't know that you have anything to delight in; your marks weren't much better. I suppose we have that luxurious blonde to thank for that?'

'I suppose so, sir,' said Cocoran.

'Well, I'm not going to keep either of you here simply so that your sex life can bear fruit. I should probably be doing the fair sex a good turn if I brought both your stays here to an end.'

'You don't need to worry about them any more,' said Louis. 'I shall start work again tonight.'

2

The note said:

I want to apologize to you for the way I treated you the other night. I was so rude and I don't know what possessed me. Please don't misunderstand me, Louis; I still think, equally firmly, that we're completely unsuited to each other, and that to take things any further would be a mistake, but I am ashamed of the way in which I tried to tell you this.

> *Emma Fielding*

Louis had returned home hideously chastened, and full of determination to get down to some good hard work. Everything, he felt, had gone wrong, and he had only succeeded in getting himself detested in all the departments where he hoped to have himself acclaimed. To offer to pull the ears off the Head of the Department was no way to get a first; and he had likewise proved a failure in the world of human love. He had treated himself suicidally, he felt. Admittedly what had happened was in part an indictment of the University itself, and those who attended it; it offered neither the liberality nor the respect for wild genius that he had expected to find there. His function here was negative – he might as well have taken his degree by correspondence course. He decided to detach himself; after all, life cannot be simply spending oneself in events, or who would praise the celibate, the ascetic, and the saint? Emma and the Emma values were a scented delusion.

But tonight she would be at the Christmas Ball. Who with?

Oliver? Treece? She would be telling people about him, and how glad she was to be rid of him. She'd be having a wonderful time, and here he was moping in his bedroom. And, after all, the note was in part a retraction. She was sorry. He would go and let her tell him so.

At the Town Hall the Christmas Ball was well under way. Upstairs, perhaps, in the darkened room, affairs of high civic importance were being wrangled by councillors and aldermen, late at their duties; down below in the ballroom, let out by the night for a not intolerable sum, all was abandon. Big brass ashtrays like spittoons stood about the floor in large numbers. An air of rather frowsy jollity depended from the paper streamers. It cost Louis sixpence to put his coat in the cloakroom, a sum he did not willingly disemburse; he wished he had not worn it, though the night was cool, it being early December. As people had to get drunk before eleven o'clock, when the bar closed (or else smuggle in their own liquor), they had set to work early. Emma was not to be seen in the press. Louis, with some wit, looked into the bar, and observed there an august party: the stout Vice-Chancellor, full of bonhomie, a scattering of professors, Dr Masefield, Merrick, and, at the end of the row, Treece. They were having their photograph taken, a distinguished group. 'Grin, gentlemen, grin,' ordered the Vice-Chancellor. 'No need to look miserable. The next round's my privilege.' Treece, affecting a nervous smile, was clearly ill at ease. 'Further forward, you, please,' said the photographer. Treece moved forward. 'Now back; no, *back*, I said, a bit more.' Treece tripped over his feet and looked ungainly. 'Smiles all round,' said the photographer, and there was a great, explosive flash. Amused by this little comedy, Louis withdrew and walked along the outer fringe of the dance floor towards the stage. He suddenly saw Emma, sitting in a blue basket chair, her feet thrust out, drinking lemonade through a straw and talking with a girl named Anne Grant, a creature with a very short haircut and a sharp, pixie-like face. 'If he's as bad as that, why does he *show* himself to people?' Anne was saying.

'Who?' asked Louis, coming up. Emma turned round, and flushed, and said that she thought Louis did not like dances;

and Louis flushed, and said that he didn't, and asked her to dance, simply in order to separate her from Anne Grant. 'I don't dance very well,' he said when they got on to the floor. 'I can only go straight; I don't know how to do the corners.'

'Well, we can stop and come back when we get to the end of the High Street,' said Emma.

'What's this one?' said Louis.

'A waltz,' said Emma.

'That's in threes, isn't it?' asked Louis, dancing on his own for a moment, to get the beat, 'Right, come on, quick. No, we've missed it. Try again ... *now!*' And off they went into the throng, dancing straight across the room, banging up against the wall, stopping, starting again. Louis pulled Emma closely to him until he was practically inside her dress. 'So *this* is dancing,' he said. 'I like it.' They moved up under the dais, beneath the band. 'I'm sorry about the other night,' said Louis. 'So am I,' said Emma, saying what he hoped she would say. 'I've regretted it very much, as I told you in that note.' 'Thank you for that,' said Louis. 'I know I seemed cruel; I haven't been able to forget it. But I was right, wasn't I, now honestly?' 'Why were you?' asked Louis. 'It's so hard for a woman, Louis,' said Emma. 'I like men and want them as my friends, but they always want to make love or something. I don't want to hurt them, but I don't want to hurt myself. Love is some- thing other. I doubt if I'm capable of it. Sometimes I want to try it, but I suppose I'm too afraid.' They hit up suddenly against the wall, turned round, set off again.

'I'm a mess,' said Emma. 'You're better away from me. I'm just terrified of the whole business, I suppose.'

'You're like a child of eighteen,' said Louis. 'You have to come to terms with the world. You can't go on like some young virgin who can ignore all men until at last her prince comes and the air trembles, and trumpets sound, and you know this must be love. It's not like that. People like you ought to live in a different world; you're a menace to the rest of us, when we run up against you, because we count for nothing with you. We're so plebeian about love, aren't we?'

'I suppose you're trying to find out whether I'm a virgin,'

said Emma. 'Well, I don't go talking about my sex life to all and sundry.'

'I am not all and sundry. I'm *me*,' cried Louis exasperated. 'What does one have to do to get to know you, to come into your world? Have a blood-test? I don't mind. Just set me an examination and I'll take it.'

'There isn't any examination,' said Emma. 'You have to take me as I am. I don't want to do anything unless I'm really in love, and I'm not with you, and that's it.'

'In any case,' said Louis cunningly, 'I don't think you are a virgin. I think you just think like one. When you get to my age, you don't meet virgins any more.'

'Really, you have a terrible cheek,' said Emma.

'What about you?' demanded Louis. 'You adopt this terrible feminine hauteur, so that it's simply impossible to get near to you, and you won't respond emotionally to anything or anyone. I know I'm as bad, but it's you we're trying to sort out. If you don't touch up against people, you are nothing; you never define yourself, you never exist.'

'That's a terrible thing to say,' said Emma.

'It's a terrible thing to be,' said Louis. 'But the trouble is, I am too.'

They hit up against another couple. All about them, in the wide, darkened area of the dance hall, couples were disclosing their Christmas plans to interested playmates: this one was off delivering letters for the Post Office; that one ski-ing down wet snow-slopes in Austria. He would go off home, that awful place; and Emma would be gone, for five cruel weeks, an insurmountable interval in which people are forgotten, personal impacts elided from the memory, to her family's metropolitan urbanities. Resentment arose. All the time, around him, intellectuals moaned of the breakdown of working-class culture, that vigorous healthy life, bellies close to the soil, that they believed themselves cruelly severed from; as for Louis, he was in the damn thing, and all he wanted was to get out. If one married on one's level, one was tied. But an intelligent and sophisticated wife (an Emma) could give every entry that was needed by a man of talents into finer society, could tell him what clothes to buy, what to do about one's dandruff, what courses to order in restaurants, how one wine tasted differently from another, what ties to wear with what suit.

'Are you going away for Christmas?' he asked Emma.

'I'm going home,' said Emma. 'What about you?'

'I don't know yet,' said Louis. 'Where's your home?'

'Oh, no,' said Emma. 'I'm not telling you. You're quite capable of just arriving . . .'

'Who me?' cried Louis, aghast, though the comment was true enough. 'Well, I hope you'll think about me.'

'Why should I?' said Emma.

'Because I love you,' said Louis. For a moment Emma strove with herself to face this fact and respond to it, but she couldn't; all there was was pity, and a scrap of distaste.

All at once they were among the band; Louis, lost in amorous transports, had failed to watch where they were going and now the musicians were scattering as the pair of them flailed mercilessly around, knocking over music-stands. 'Oh,' said Emma, detaching herself and hurrying to the side. Louis stood firm in the middle of the disaster, apologizing sweetly. By the time he had pushed his way through to the side there was nothing to be seen of Emma. He went and looked into the bar. She was not there, but, leaning against a doorpost, talking to a pretty girl in a very short dress, with her mouth touched up with black lipstick, was Walter Oliver.

'Have you seen Emma Fielding?' he asked Oliver.

'Come and watch me do a seduction,' said Oliver. 'This girl has put herself in severe moral danger, and I'm it. Come on, amigo. Tell her what a fine fellow I am.'

'Yes, he is,' said Louis feebly.

'Good God! Not like that,' said Oliver. 'I want her virtue, not her vote. Try some of that old moonlight on the water stuff, or a bit of crap about Ceres and the essential fertility of the world. Come on, man, boost me.'

'I think he's horrible,' said the girl, turning her black-painted pout to Louis.

'Luckily for you, I am,' said Oliver. 'O.K., amigo, slope off now and I'll get on with my idyll.'

'I'm looking for my partner,' said Louis.

'Try the river,' said Oliver.

Treece came by at this moment, on his way back from the dance floor; his tie had come untied and he looked dismally unhappy. He had been doing the Gay Gordons with Viola. Viola was a little tight, and had refused to walk up and down at the bit where you walk up and down; she just wanted to spin round all the time. Finally, she had fallen down and had had to be taken to the sidelines to recover. Treece had never really wanted to come to the ball in the first place. It was the Vice-Chancellor, who spent the weeks before these student occasions in indefatigable effort, gathering up members of the faculty to go along in order, as he liked to express it, 'to put up a bit of a show', who had tempted him here. The Vice-Chancellor, like all vice-chancellors, had clear ideas of what a university should look like, and taste like; vice-chancellors all share in common a Platonic ideal for a university. For one thing, it should be *big*. People should be coming to look at it all the time. There should be a special place for parking Rolls-Royces. There should be big sports grounds, a science building designed by Basil Spence, and more and more students coming every year. There should be new faculties – of Business Administration, of Aeronautical Engineering, of Sanitation, of Social Dancing. Vice-chancellors want big universities and a great many faculties; professors want small universities and only the liberal arts and pure sciences. Vice-chancellors always seem to win. Seeing Treece now, he left the local dignitaries whom he was buttering up at the bar, took Treece familiarly by the arm, and said jovially : 'I think the little lady here has set her heart on you, my boy,' pointing to Viola, who was approaching. 'Oh, Viola, nice dress; didn't get that out here in the provinces, I'll be bound. Changed your hair, too ? Like it, Viola, like it.'

'Thank you kindly,' said Viola in a quaint voice. She turned to Treece and murmured, 'Christ, can't we get out of here ?'

'Not yet,' said Treece.

'Come and meet the Lord-Lieutenant of the County,' said the Vice-Chancellor. 'Very interested in boys' clubs. Think he thinks this is one.'

They went over and met the Lord-Lieutenant, who asked Treece if he rowed. They met the Lord Mayor, who asked Treece if he was active in politics. Town and gown rarely met, and when they did both were embarrassed. Treece now asked the Lord Mayor if *he* rowed, and whether he had time to read very much. Finally, conscious of having done good, they retired, Viola and Treece, to the bar for a quick drink. It was really the first time he had spoken to Viola since her party. 'Stuart, you're getting fat, you know,' said Viola. He speculated about this strange remark for a moment and then recognized it for what it was, the comment of an eccentric old spinster. He looked at Viola in surprise, and noticed, for the first time, the little lines around her eyes.

They took their drinks and sat down. 'You and me last night!' said Viola, raising her glass.

'It wasn't last night,' said Treece.

'Well, whenever it was then,' said Viola.

For a moment nothing was said. Then Viola said: 'Take that squishy-looking cigarette out of your mouth, Stuart, and talk to me properly. Don't you want to talk to me?'

'Yes, of course,' said Treece. 'What shall we talk about?'

'I've *missed* you,' said Viola.

'Have you?' said Treece. He wondered what she'd do for herself, and suddenly felt sorry for her future. She had had her hair cut in a new way that made her ears stick out – it was called the *gamin* look – and it made women look like little boys. He found her appearance affected and annoying, and he didn't like to see her drunk.

'Poor old Stuart,' said Viola; 'you get such a frightened look when you think you're committed to something; but don't worry, you aren't. I just take a friendly interest in you, though.'

'I know,' said Treece, 'and I'm glad you do.'

'But you do like me, don't you?'

'Yes, of course I do. I'm your friend.'

'Yes, but who isn't – at least, on *your* side.'

'Well, I know, but you mean a lot to me, Viola,' said Treece, 'and I wasn't just mafeking about that time.'

'However,' said Viola, 'it's stupid to talk about situations of this sort, because when you've mulled over them they always seem less satisfactory than they are. Everything has proved that, if you're careful, actions don't have consequences. If you changed my life because of meeting me it would wound me. I'd rather change my life to please you, because at least you would have to take the responsibility, and I've got nothing to lose. But what can you make of people who don't make actions of their thoughts? They're nothing; they're impotent, they're invisible. We're invisible, Stuart; we try to live our lives as though they don't count, as though they go unnoticed.'

'Yes, that's true,' said Treece.

'Of course, it doesn't worry me,' said Viola, 'but you have to know it, don't you?' She looked pointedly into her empty glass.

'Another?' said Treece.

'Please,' said Viola. 'Oh, I want to ask you something. Did you send the ghoul down?'

'No,' said Treece.

'And then you say you're my friend. I *knew* you wouldn't. I forecast this to myself.'

'It simply wasn't necessary,' said Treece. 'He's going to start work again.'

'I see,' said Viola. 'He's over there by the door now, smelling girl's ears when they go past. You know, you can't go on like this. You're a mess, Stuart. Oh, don't look like that. I don't mean any harm, but nothing's getting anywhere. This department has settled down into staid middle age. So have you. So will I, if I don't squeal a little occasionally. You'll come up to my bedroom every Bank Holiday Monday and the students will persuade you to ring your handbells every departmental tea-party and you'll charm all the little girls straight from school for ever and ever, amen. And there we are. What are you doing for Christmas?'

'Conference at Oxford,' said Treece.

'Oh yes; you told me,' said Viola. 'Look, Stuart, I'm feeling randy. Come outside and give me a kiss. See me home. You know what all this has been about.'

'Viola, you're a little tight, and we've got to stay here and be sociable.'

'Just because I fell down and bruised my butt doesn't mean I'm tight, my pet,' said Viola. 'I'm going to have another drink.'

'I'll join you,' said Merrick. 'Hello, Viola. Nice dress, and a new haircut! You do us proud. Fascinating glimpses of lovely white buz. I see in *Vogue* that the last cry is to have the hair done *en bouffon*.'

'It wouldn't suit me; my face is too round,' said Viola.

'Nonsense,' said Merrick. 'It's not too round, is it, Treece?'

'Drink, Merrick?' asked Treece.

'I'll have Dubonnet,' said Merrick.

At the bar, Treece, congenitally a person who is always served last, found himself in the centre of a violent contest for attention, for it was now closing time. Beside him was Oliver, the sort of person, it was apparent, who was always served first. 'Observing all the local idylls?' asked Oliver. 'All this lotus-eating. Came for a bit of lotus-eating myself, actually. Did you see that girl I was with? The one in blue? Never saw her before tonight in my life. Bet I get there, though. Here, serve this man next, barman. He's a professor. Make way for the prof., please. Make way for the prof. New rule: professors served first.'

'Thank you, Oliver,' said Treece. 'Let me get yours.'

'Ta, then,' said Oliver. 'That's a gin and lime and a Guinness.' Treece got the drinks and turned.

'By the way,' said Oliver. 'Don't forget next term, I'm going to show you the local *vie littéraire*, the British beats.'

'Are they interesting?' asked Treece, picking up one of the drinks from the tray and drinking it. Treece found himself speculating about his relations with Oliver (of course Treece found himself speculating about his relations with anyone, for the mysteries of human contact were, to him, so profound, that he wondered how he ever *did* it, how he went out and had relations at all). The way in which he was affected by Oliver was in the splendid freedom of Oliver's existence; the barriers, the bolts and bars, that one discerned on every side, were invisible to Oliver. He was not awed by professors or barmen or moral codes or any of the things that limited, for Treece, free access to the world. He patted him on the shoulder in a very amiable sort of way, and drank the last drink off the tray. He then went back to the table and Merrick said: 'Viola went off outside with someone from French. Have a tiggy?'

'Thank you,' said Treece, rather relieved about losing Viola. It was a Turkish tiggy. What had happened with Viola that evening seemed to Treece rather disastrous, and it was this curiosity of his strained relationship with Viola that was to act as a solvent in a situation that was to develop later in the evening.

'Do you like this tie?' asked Merrick. Treece looked him up and down. Merrick always looked as though he had just that moment dismounted from a horse: his clothes were always cavalrytwill-y, trousers with sixteen-inch cuffs, the standard wear (at this time) of the Guardsmen/Stockbroker/Underwriter smart set, though already the teddy boys were being imitative and spoiling things. You could always tell that Merrick went off to Cambridge or London for his clothes – 'even for his socks and pants', Viola once avowed. Whenever Treece talked to Merrick, he was reminded of that Poet Laureate who confessed that his idea of Heaven was to sit in a garden and to receive constant telegrams announcing alternately a British victory by sea and a British victory by land. Merrick was so Establishment that it just was not true; he was one of the Old Boy system who had somehow just not known quite enough Old Boys to get a Cambridge fellowship, or into the Diplomatic, and so he had missed the gunboat and was left, continually mystified, among people that no one really mixed with at all.

'It's a very nice tie,' said Treece.

'It's a mistress tie,' said Merrick. 'Why is it that one's mistresses always gives one ties?'

'I don't know,' said Treece, who didn't. Merrick was, in his romantic way, a sort of professional co-respondent; he was in bed so often that the wonder was that he didn't have bed-sores. From behind, someone tapped him on the shoulder. It was Oliver. 'Do you happen to have any contraceptives on you?' he asked confidentially.

Merrick promptly opened up his wallet and went carefully through it. 'Should be able to oblige, old boy,' he said.

'Good,' said Oliver. 'Always wanted to do it outside, you know, ever since I read *Sons and Lovers*.'

'No, sorry, old boy. I'm out,' said Merrick. 'I didn't think I'd be coming tonight.'

Treece took out his wallet and looked in it; if he hadn't been drunk he would have been shocked, and if he hadn't been drunk he wouldn't have tried to pretend he had any, when he most certainly hadn't.

'Don't let me take your last,' said Oliver.

'Sorry, I haven't,' said Treece, slapping his wallet to.

'Just have to risk it,' said Oliver, departing.

'I say,' said Merrick. 'I thought you brought me a drink?'

'I must have drunk it myself,' said Treece.

'Well, that's a bit thick, old chap. The bar's closed now.'

'Sorry,' said Treece.

'Never mind. I say, absolutely ducky pianist, isn't he? Have you seen the local jazz band? You should. All trad. stuff, of course, and straight off the records. But then there is no English culture left, is there?'

Viola now came back into the bar with the fat little lecturer from French. 'How about a round on the Ford Foundation?' she cried to the man from French, who had a grant from that institution. 'The bar's closed,' said Treece. 'Nonsense,' said Viola. 'Don't you be so easily put off.'

The French lecturer went over to the bar.

'Soon they'll be having all these research foundations in England too,' said Treece, 'as part of the conspicuous consumption of industry. It seems the next stage in the democratic process. You've got the Nuffield Foundation; next it will be the Marks and Spencer's Foundation, the Chappie Dog Food Foundation, the C. and A. Modes Foundation. . . .'

'The Strodex Foundation Foundation,' said Viola; she was really very drunk. They were all really very drunk. Looking around, Treece felt upset nearly to tears by the sort of wanness of the milieu, by the Violas and the Merricks, by everything.

He wondered if he was going to be ill. The sensation of

being in the world, in this spot, suffused about him in a dull wash, and all at once he thought of a sentence out of Thomas Mann, and he thought of himself reading the sentence, as he did when he talked on D. H. Lawrence, to bored students in a lecture-room. The sentence was this: 'In an age that offers no satisfying answer to the eternal question of "Why? To what end?", a man who is capable of achievement over and above the expected and average modicum must be equipped either with a moral remoteness and single-mindedness which is rare indeed and of heroic mould, or else with an exceptionally robust vitality.' Perhaps there were some people like that; but here there were, really, no heroes and no vital men, and one simply filled in time.

This was no thought to be bringing to realization amid the entertainments of an evening like this, Treece told himself. 'I feel sick,' said a girl behind him. 'Try and hold it till we get outside,' said her escort. At the bar the lecturer in French was in the middle of a fracas with the barman, who was washing up the dirty glasses. At this moment Treece noticed Emma Fielding coming into the bar, and he felt relieved of his disgust. He went over to her; she looked over her shoulder. 'Good evening,' he said. 'Are you having a good time?'

'Well, I don't really like these hops very much, but I'm certainly having a time. One sees life.'

'Are you alone?' asked Treece.

'I came with a friend, but she got picked up.'

'Oh, dear.'

'No; she was pleased.'

'I mean for you.'

'I thought you'd gone looking for him, or the other one,' said a loud whisper from Emma's other side. It was Louis Bates.

'Good evening, Miss Fielding,' said Viola, returning to the group. 'I like your dress. Good evening, Mr Bates,' she added, observing this unwelcome figure in the group. 'Mr Bates, Mr Bates, what does that word remind me of?'

'Don't be naughty,' said Treece in Viola's ear; he had an instinct for these things, and knew that Viola was determined to be very brilliant at Louis's expense. This opening sally had already gone down very well, and Viola was ready for more.

'You know, Miss Fielding, I've often thought : you would be pretty if you stood up straight. Your eyes are lovely. You really don't make the most of yourself. You don't rate yourself high enough. You go about with quite the wrong sort of people. You're a mature woman; you need a more adult society; you'd flourish in it.'

'Well thank you,' said Emma, taken aback.

'You must come to one of my parties,' said Viola. 'They're rather fun. Even Stuart likes them, and that is something of a commendation, isn't it, Stuart darling ?'

'I suppose it is,' said Treece.

'I worked this afternoon,' whispered a dull voice in Treece's ear. 'Oh, you might as well enjoy tonight, Bates,' said Treece generously. 'I don't want you to think ...' murmured Louis.

'I didn't know you two were so intimate,' said Viola, inter-rupting. 'Tell me, how's the flageolet, Mr Bates ? Mr Bates once told me that he has a flageolet, and goes down by the canal and plays Benjamin Britten-y tunes beginning with "Heigh-ho". Wasn't that what you told me ?'

'Something like that,' said Bates.

'And the embroidery . . . it was you who did embroidery ?' went on Viola.

'Oh, no,' said Bates.

'Or am I confusing you with Ivy Compton-Burnett ?' asked Viola. 'Tell me, Mr Bates, how is your chest ? Don't show it to me; just tell me.'

'It's a bit nasty,' said Bates.

'I'm sure it is,' said Viola. 'Mr Bates hasn't been well since I've known him. Were your parents old when they had you ?'

'Yes; they were,' said Bates.

'You can always tell,' said Viola. 'Well, let that be a lesson to us. . . .' This was a reference to one of Treece's own jokes, which he had shared with Viola; and the reference involved him and made him feel very guilty. Viola had said too much, and he tried to tempt her away.

'Stuart is afraid, Mr Bates, that I find you too attractive,' said Viola. 'He is really very protective towards you. You must be grateful to him.'

'I am, very,' said Louis.

'I shouldn't have thought you were a dancing man,' continued Viola. Louis by now had realized that he hadn't a chance of coming out of this alive; you knew he had said his prayers and left his flageolet to his next of kin. Nor was there any stopping Viola. (She turned to Treece and murmured: 'Have you ever seen this man's birth certificate? I swear one of his parents was a rhinoceros.') The hunt was on, and every one knew it. 'Grey suit and everything,' went on Viola. 'It might be worth investing in a new tie, though?' 'I haven't much money, you know,' said Louis with a touch of defiance. Viola had known he would say this, even down to the defiance, and she went on: 'Well perhaps we could have a whip-round for a tie for him, Stuart?' Stuart, on whom the fact that this was as much at his expense as Louis's was not lost – and this precluded his intervention – said: 'You mustn't say that, Viola.'

'You see how concerned he is for your feelings?' said Viola. 'Much more concerned than you are, I'm sure; he imagines that you're ultra-sensitive. I keep telling him, I keep saying, "Mr Bates isn't sensitive at all, you do him an injustice." You've been through the mill, as they say, haven't you? Didn't you once teach in a convent, or something?'

'It was at a girls' school, yes,' said Louis. 'I did have to work to get here, you see. Lawrence used to work in a factory that made artificial limbs, you know; I worked in a school. For the same sort of reasons, I believe.'

'You feel an *esprit de corps* with Lawrence, then?' said Viola. 'Do I mean *esprit de corps*?'

'That's when you have a body of men,' said the Ford Foundation lecturer.

'Well, put Lawrence and Mr Bates together, and it seems like a body of men. I saw you in town the other day, Mr Bates, but I don't think you saw me.'

'Did you?' asked Louis.

'Yes; you were waiting for a bus. You fell backwards over a

wall into someone's garden. I felt quite concerned for you. You weren't hurt?'

'No,' said Louis. 'I'm very clumsy like that.'

'What time is it, Stuart?'

'Nearly midnight,' said Treece.

'Time for bed,' said Viola.

'I'll telephone for a taxi,' said the Ford Foundation man.

'No, let's ask Bates to do it for us,' said Viola. 'You'll do that, won't you? Wait a minute. You haven't any money; you'll need some pennies. Here we are. One, two, three ... it is threepence, isn't it?'

'No, fourpence,' said Louis.

'Oh yes,' said Viola, who knew. 'Give Louis a penny, Stuart.'

Everyone dispersed to collect their coats. Treece and Emma both had one like thought in their minds: it was not to go home with the person who seemed intent on taking them. Treece knew that he could not face Viola in this mood, and to stay the night with her in this spirit would be, for him, masochism. He therefore detained Emma and said: 'Do you have someone to see you home, Miss Fielding?' Emma, likewise, felt an immense relief at this offer, and took advantage of it at once; she could not face the thought of having to fight off Louis at her door.

Viola came back and said: 'You're seeing me home, Stuart, aren't you?'

'I'm sorry, Viola, but I'm already seeing someone home. Miss Fielding has no one with her, so I said I'd see her safely back.'

'I'll go and get my things,' said Emma.

Louis reappeared and conducted a short, whispered conversation with Emma, to one side; he emerged from it looking furious.

'I wanted you to take me,' said Viola to Treece.

'I'm sorry,' said Treece.

'You'd better be,' said Viola. 'You realize you've cut out your protégé Mr Bates?'

Treece went into the foyer to wait for Emma. She came down the stairs and he went to meet her. They took a final look into the hall and saw Viola exchanging some last gibes with Bates, while the Ford Foundation lecturer looked on proprietorially. 'This tune they're playing is the one Carey Willoughby's novel is named after,' said Emma.

'Oh, what is it?'

'It's called "Baby, It's Cold Outside". It's a very appropriate title.'

'For tonight, you mean? I think it's rather warm.'

'No,' said Emma. 'For his novel. It's about this young man, who is an outsider, excluded from the ordinary life of the world because he isn't in the class system, and in the business world, and doesn't share the common values. . . .'

'Please,' said Treece. 'I'd rather not hear about it. Modern novels depress me so much.'

'Yes, I suppose they might,' said Emma.

'What's this tune about, then?' asked Treece. 'Is that a modern tune too?'

'Oh, no. I don't think these things filter down into popular culture that quickly,' said Emma. 'And it's quite an old tune. It's a sort of duet, you see. He's asking her to stay the night, because it's cold outside. She's saying she must go. I think it ends with his proposing, so that she can stay inside in the warmth for good.' She laughed with a long husky ripple of laughter. Laughter always affected Treece, strangely, because it betrayed a kind of possession of the world that he lacked. Looking now at the bright line of her teeth and the intimate cavern of her mouth, he found himself encompassed by a warmth and delight. This impression went with what she was saying, and suddenly the licence of the evening conveyed itself to him and he felt a real growth of affection. He looked at her and said, 'Shall I get a taxi?'

Something of his point conveyed itself to Emma; she paused, as if surprised, and then responded, a little uncertainly, as if she felt she had detected something that might not be there.

'No, look, if it isn't cold outside, shall we walk? It isn't far. Actually, you don't have to take me at all; I simply had to get away from Louis Bates. And I owe you an apology for dragging you off to that terrible party the other night; you can't have enjoyed it a bit.'

'Please don't worry about that.'

'But I shouldn't be dragging you into the mess I make of things. I do, you know. I'm the untidiest woman – emotionally, I mean – that I know. And then Louis threatening to pull your ears off.' She laughed again, a furry, animal laugh, and Treece joined in. 'It was funny, after all, and he didn't mean it. It's a bit of phatic communion that he's picked up. All Louis's conversation is phatic communion. In conversation he never says anything. He thinks that conversation is a very imperfect form of communication, you know. It's true, isn't it?'

'Yes, it is,' said Treece, amused.

'He didn't mean any harm. You won't hold it against him, will you? I've been wanting to ask you this. He doesn't mean any harm; that's what makes it so hard; if only he *did*. If only you knew that he was out for trouble. But he isn't. He almost seems as if he wants to be hurt, or blamed, or disliked. He invites it. And yet I feel so sorry for him; when Dr Masefield behaved as she did, and made him get their taxi, for instance.'

'She was playing him off against me, because she thinks I permit him too much,' said Treece.

'Yes, and it was sexual as well, wasn't it?' asked Emma. 'You don't mind my saying that, but it was so obvious, to a woman at least. The trouble is that he is the sort of person, too, that you do play off. I've done it, without wanting to. Someone once said about him to me, ''That young man is the sort of person everyone wants to use.'' There are people like that, that you use but don't want.'

'Viola was a bitch,' said Treece. 'Honestly, you know, women!'

'It amuses me, you know, the way you seem to see women. You think of them as sort of loose-fitting men. I mean, you don't realize that we're made different because we are different, or the other way round.'

'I was always grateful for that,' said Treece. They were outside now, in the park : the Town Hall was very happily situated.

Whenever there was a dance one had practically to queue up for the use of the benches. Every bush rustled and swayed.

A light wind was blowing, catching at the hem of Emma's dress and coat; noise came in ebbs and bursts from the dance. The night was clear, bright, filled with stars. The sky was lit up from beneath, just above the rooftops, by the glow of the street-lamps, a translucent blue that shaded off into colours, darker and richer and then finally matured into a black flecked with little stars, burning deep and white and remote. The great bare trees arched over them; it was the beginning of winter, when everything began to be crisp and hard. They could see across the town; great patterns of light were set out in the blackness of the facing hillside, great whorls and curves described by the street-lamps and rows of houses. A furnace glowed red in the dip. Suddenly – it was midnight – whole series of the street-lamps would be extinguished, as the day's life officially ended, and the intensity of the blackness increased. 'It's an *immense* sort of night, isn't it?' said Emma. 'One sometimes has this feeling.' 'Are you cold?' asked Treece solicitously. 'No, not at *all*,' said Emma. 'Miss Fielding ... may I kiss you?' asked Treece. Emma considered for a moment: 'Yes. I'd like you to,' she said cogitatively. They stopped under a tree.

'One shouldn't do that with a student,' said Treece after a moment. 'I'm happy that you did,' said Emma; 'and it puts you in no sort of difficulties with me. You owe me no favours. I admire you because you're so honest; it's something I wish I was, more, and you are.'

'You know, if anything, it's the reverse that's true. I'm really an old puritan. To me you are a good woman. You're not the sort of woman who needs constant entertaining, perpetual juggling tricks and sleight of hand. For you I don't have to stand on my head. You look at everything with a clear and civilized eye, as if it were all in a contest and you were judging; and so few women can do that. Think what love would be from a person like that. You're a fine and virtuous woman.'

'*No*,' cried Emma; there were tears in her eyes. 'No, I'm not. Don't say that. I'm not virtuous, not sexually or in any other way. Only children can be virtuous. It's all right when you aren't out in the big, wide world. But I'm not the sort of woman you think I am. There's nothing about me, Professor Treece.'

'Yes, Emma, there is. Look, I'm always making you cry.'

'No, no. One needs money, one's allotment of friends and possessions, confidence and charm, before one can practise virtue. You need to be free of the world. You need an access to a richer culture. But there are no rich cultures left, are there? It's a seedy world.'

'I'm sorry to have upset you so much,' said Treece. 'Look, we're here at your door. Can I see you tomorrow?'

'No; I'm going home tomorrow,' said Emma quietly.

'Oh, yes; it's the end of term. I'd forgotten,' said Treece, and he looked disappointed, and deeply intense, as if he were trying to communicate some truth to her which words did not express; and Emma reacted suddenly. 'You could come up, if you really and absolutely certainly wanted,' she said.

Treece looked at her. 'I really and absolutely certainly do want to. But are you sure?' he asked. 'Yes, very,' said Emma, 'but you must take your shoes off, because I'm not allowed to take anyone in after eleven.'

He took his shoes off. Emma unlocked the door; she was shivering. The truth of it was that it was really a very cold night, no matter how they denied it. But it was warm indoors. They went inside, out of the cold, and crept up the stairs.

CHAPTER SEVEN

I

COMING back to University for the new term was, to Emma, for the first time an enjoyable experience. It was Emma's theory that the only time one ever acted – that is, acted so fully and positively that one's character was altered or developed – was in moments of diminished responsibility, or under special duress: in liquor, when one was tired, or ill, or at war, indeed at any time when one was rid of that murderous, inhibiting, civilized pause that always came before the fact of action. Looking back on that night of the Christmas Ball, when Stuart saw her home, and then stayed, she would have said that she was drunk; but it wasn't true. There was simply a willing suspension of disbelief in things, a lifting of control. She couldn't go on as she had been doing; that was clear enough; there was no real solution. Something had to come from outside. The great pleasure came from not withholding any more; it is sometimes harder to withhold love than to give it; but it is only by this kind of violence to oneself that one does come to the final acceptance. There is a point at which one sits back and sees what happens. The answer to the prevailing question – can one lead a good life in this world, without retiring too much outside it? – had come haphazardly, but it had come; being rich, private, and apart from things, in an ideal state of innocence – all this sensation of herself was gone from Emma. And from here on she began to form a character for herself, she began to bathe herself in the world. This was Mrs Bishop's own thought, of course; her concern with sin was not that it should not exist, but that people should know it for sin, and being upper middle class and civilized and believing Emma to be much the same, but apostate, she had no qualms when she began to suspect that an affair had grown up between Emma and her professor. In fact she was rather pleased, because there was so clearly nothing vulgar about it. For Emma too the rewards seemed greater than what was lost, for there was at last a sense of identity. She had never before felt pretty; 'I may not be as pretty as Mona Lisa, but I bet I can spit farther than she could,' she once protested wryly; now she felt as pretty. Her mother's contention – 'No one will ever marry you, my girl, you can't *do* anything' – no longer hurt her, and now, when her mother asked her on her arrival home, 'When are you going to settle down and do something?' she thought to herself for the first time that she had settled down and done it. 'You're a splendid woman, Emma; other women always want praising and flattering and amusing; but you're content.' A splendid woman, a good woman.

But the life one leads cuts out all the lives one might have led; one is never a virgin twice; events engrave themselves. Life is a unity to the soul. We meet events half-way; they are part of us, and we part of them; and nothing is incidental. Ahead comes the point where all events exist at once, and no new ones are in sight, the point on the edge of death, which is a reckoning point. It is the motion towards this that one tries to halt by crying, 'Do you love me? Respect me? Will you always remember me?'

These were the sentiments that filled Emma's mind when she returned for the beginning of term. If she did not see him again, this would be enough; but she hoped that she would. He had not written to her; there had been an ordinary, noncommittal Christmas card. But as soon as she arrived and was carrying her suitcase upstairs, Mrs Bishop came out of her room with a smile, and said that Treece had telephoned, and had asked her to call him back. That evening he came and stayed. They were in a poor state for receiving visitors when there came a knock on the door and 'Miss Fielding!' cried Mrs Bishop's voice. Emma hastily buttoned up her blouse and pushed some underclothing under a chair. 'Miss Fielding!' 'Oh, come in,' said Emma. 'I just wanted a word with the Professor,' said Mrs Bishop. 'Professor, I bought your book today and I want you to sign it. I feel you should. There ought to be some of these about in the world when you've gone, you know.' She proffered the Housman book. 'I'm not very proud of it,' said Treece.

'Oh, really,' said Mrs Bishop, noticing with interest that Miss Fielding had removed, or had had removed, her brassière. 'You must be. To have published a *book*. It must be so pleasant to be so fecund.' He signed it and away she went; they returned to the bedroom.

This in a sense set the seal of Mrs Bishop's approbation, and he began to come to the flat quite regularly through the cold weeks of February and March. The curious gap of five weeks after their first night together had excited his curiosity about her, and he began the new term with the sense of missing her deeply. Indeed, their first meeting after the vacation had been almost a disappointment, for she was simply a person, with freckles on her face, a few hairs on her top lip, and disappointing too was the satisfaction she was able to give him. As he lay on the bed, later, listening to the running flush of water that preceded her return, his attention was drawn to himself, and to his commitment; he feared that he was allowing himself to be possessed. It seemed to him that he had not been the prime mover in the affair; she gave ground only when she wished, with him following, having no choice, possessing nothing and simply being possessed. And then, with the scrupulous fairness with which he ordered everything, he thought of those long five weeks when he found himself looking for her in places that she could not possibly be, in restaurants and cinemas and trains, sometimes thinking that he had seen her, or sometimes noticing some action that reminded him, in some other person, different except for a smile or a haircut, of her. He knew that he always expected too much and would never be satisfied in this human world; the simple truth was that he would never do better, and his dissatisfaction was painful to him, for it was there in all things and so disorientated him in the world that he wondered if it were psychotic.

Whenever he came, he always began by walking slowly round the room, inspecting its contents, reading the titles of books, as if he had never seen them before, or was trying to reconstruct some experience. She always felt uneasy at this: 'Sit down and talk to me!' she would say, and he would sit down in the armchair near the gasfire, and in conversation they would do the same thing, walking around each other, starting again. Only then, when he had smoked several cigarettes and they had talked for a while in a distant, untrusting way, would she come and sit on the floor beside him and take his hand, saying, 'Well, how are you?' Then, laying her head upon his lap, she'd throw her arms around him, crying, 'Oh, oh, why don't you trust me more?' 'What is it, dearest?' Treece would say; she did not answer. He never quite knew, and he was somehow reassured by these dull cries, this unspoken hint of her need for him; it stirred him each time. He'd put his arm round her shoulder and tilt her head up to kiss her. Then her hand would come round his waist, pull up his jacket and shirt, and run over the warm flesh at the small of his back. Meanwhile, he sat stiffly, while she lay twisted on the floor close to him, her hands running over him. Status-wise, it seemed like sacrilege, but what was so peculiar about Stuart was that he had no status, or could not accept the terms of the one he had. If his helplessness was attractive, for she perceived him to be helpless, it was also not good enough; you couldn't go on like this, you had to reclaim some pieces of the world for yourself. Why didn't he learn to cook properly? – at least, that was one way of subduing the objects of the world about him, and objects were an image of the soul. In his view, man had simply no territory to walk on and call his own; there was nothing reclaimed from the jungle.

He was always passive, not easy to excite, and she began to feel that she was artless. She was afraid that he was tired of her, or self-conscious and ashamed, and she blamed herself; she wanted to do what he liked and when he liked. At the same time she knew she was up against something harder and more difficult than this, up against some quality in himself which he only half perceived. Afterwards when he went he seemed to hurry away, as if he carried some positive burden of guilt. 'What is it?' she asked. He never really knew; in part it was disappointment, part a desire to escape, part a sense of human mortality. Perhaps too (he began to suspect) he was overtired, or ill, or out of stamina, for the whole world seemed colourless, and not simply times like these.

There were other things that pained Emma. One was that their relationship had simply no cultural life; it existed only in her room and not in the world outside. It had no social quality or face except there, it had no places, no public images. Viola Masefield had begun to invite her to parties, and she had met Tanya, whom she liked; sometimes Treece was at these parties, sometimes not, but there was never anything to show that they were anything other than teacher and student. Viola thought that she was the girl friend of Louis Bates; indeed, she began to observe in Viola a kind of possessive curiosity about the matter.

'Don't you think it's time you let this Louis Bates business drop?' demanded Viola one evening.

'Why?' demanded Emma in reply.

'Well, you're only wasting your time and his. You can't marry him, can you?'

'No,' said Emma honestly.

'Then why don't you tell him so?'

'But *why* can't I marry him? That's the problem. I don't even know.'

'Oh really, Emma,' said Viola. 'You aren't fascinated by his charm, are you?'

'He doesn't have any,' said Emma.

'It isn't his appearance?'

'No.'

'Quite. I think he ought to have an X certificate.'

'But that's not fair; that's not a reason.'

'I know; you must have the *reason*. Honestly, Emma.'

'But I must.'

'Well, then, surely it's that he's too wrapped up in himself. He just doesn't understand people; therefore he offers them nothing. Emma, you're stupid about this, you know. You have this saint complex. You always want to help lame dogs over stiles. You should keep away from people like that. They drag you down. You have to stay away from people who can't give you anything, or otherwise you destroy your own potential. It sounds cruel, but it's a truth of existence that everyone accepts.'

'Is it?' said Emma miserably.

'Yes, it is,' said Viola firmly. 'Think about it. Surely, vitality of personal relationships is *all*; it's all there is. Life is catalysed by knowing interesting people. That's where the vivid moments come from. And there just isn't time for bores and fools.'

'And Louis is one of those?'

'Louis is a fool. I don't just mean that he does silly things. There's something entire and complete about his foolishness. He renders things absurd by doing them. He renders you absurd by your interest in him.'

'But isn't it just because we can't take his seriousness seriously? There's surely nothing wrong in being serious.'

'That just isn't the issue, though,' said Viola. 'I have nothing against seriousness, or *naïveté*, or adolescent romanticism, all of which things Bates has. He thinks he's a latterday Rimbaud, his soul an open sore, and all he wants is a nice, soulful woman to kiss the wound and make it well. For Christ's sake, what year is it? He carries his soul around in a paper bag as if he'd just bought it at Marks and Spencer's; but you can't live like that now. A lot of water has flowed under Robert Bridges since then. I once made the mistake of talking in front of him about William Blake and his wife, reading *Paradise Lost* naked at the bottom of their garden; and, my God, you could see he was thinking: when can we go and do it?'

'But I mean, what about Rimbaud and Blake – do you call them fools as well?'

'No, I don't,' said Viola. 'It's a question of modes of the mind that are fitting. Theirs was an age of the heroic, and ours is an ironic mode. Rare spirits just aren't our cup of tea, in spite of D. H. Lawrence. Louis is one of these people who want to live *so* intensely. They want an orgasm every time it rains. Well, really, how would you like to make love with someone who kept twittering about his pure mystic nodality and wanted to stick flowers in your navel?'

'I think you know him a lot better than I thought you did,' said Emma, 'but even so, he has nobody. We all think like that. We make a victim of him. You may find this stupid but I respect him.'

'Yes, so do I, in a perverse sort of way,' said Viola. 'I'm full of good things to say about him, though you wouldn't believe it; he's sensitive, intelligent, intense, rare ... but once you've said all this, you have to add one more thing, always, and that is to say, he's a fool.'

'Well, he needs a friend,' said Emma. 'I just don't want the sexual bit, though; if it weren't for that, I could be his friend.'

'You can't just be friends with a man and stop at that,' said Viola. 'There are other emotions involved, always. Friendship between men and women is the stage before courtship; either you go on or you let it drop. When people get to know you they feel deeply about you.'

'But why do they feel sexual love?'

'Perhaps people are simply lacking in imagination nowadays,' said Viola. 'I don't know; I think it's a very good way of getting to know people.'

'You see, I need men friends, because men are so much more intelligent than women, with ideas I mean, and I respect that. I liked Mr Eborebelosa; he was gentle and warm. I even like Louis Bates. So ... why is one able to hurt people one likes, so callously?'

'It's one of the privileges of being a woman,' said Viola. 'One of the very few.' 'But I don't want it, I don't want that kind of power over people,' said Emma. 'It makes me feel like some Belle Dame Sans Merci, who takes love without giving it.'

'Well, you don't have to listen to me,' said Viola. 'You're an intelligent woman. And I have no special dispensation on insights.'

And this was the extra dimension of her affair with Stuart, for a guilt about Bates, about Eborebelosa, pervaded all they did. Both knew it. The image of Louis, standing helpless under Viola's onslaught at the ball, truly at a loss for once and speechless under its violence, was the last sight she had of him for some time. He was, Stuart told her, working very hard, and doing well. All there was beside was a queer, pathetic letter that she could not answer:

Dearest Miss Fielding — I am writing this note as you obviously don't want to see me. Of course there is no reason why you should. I am not suggesting you are cruel, because you probably don't realize what sort of person I am, and the effect this has on me. Women do not like a man who is direct with them, I know, but often they blind themselves by romantic ideals to what is important. However. When we parted last term, I went off with a tear in my eye, unable to stop thinking of you. I tried to do some Beowulf, all through Christmas, but it was not any use. My tears were not because you had hurt me, but because I had meant all I said and could not really do without you, and I would have to. It is a stupid phrase of course because one can do without, but there seems no pleasure in going on, for you see when one has thought all one's life that there is no one of one's sort, and then there is and that person does not find one her sort as well, that is awful. What is love? Who knows? But whatever it is I have got it. Let us say that one likes some people more than others, perhaps because of some generosity in their view of man, some sensation that in them life is well lived, and one likes the aspects of oneself they bring out. Let us call all this, and the associated comfort and pleasure, love. For this is what I feel.

Will you ever soften? Will you ever let me take you out for a little visit to the cinema, or perhaps you would come up to my room and I will entertain you there. There is not much in the way of cocoa, cakes, etc., but we can talk there and not be disturbed. I would like to talk to you, seriously.

Your friend,

Louis Bates.

It was silly, of course, yet there, amid the stupidities, were such generous compliments and warm appraisals. 'Some generosity in their view of man, some sensation that in them life is well lived' — what greater human testimonial could there be in the world than that? If he only *knew* how awful she was. Yet she had done enough to prove it, to him more than anyone. And a sense of an enormous betrayal came over her as she thought of this phrase, which was her aim and yet showed up,

169

at its cruellest point, her failure. She didn't show the letter to Stuart but somehow he was still there, between them, and they both knew it. On him their guilts focused, and with him their civilized pretensions – one hoped it was not true, one feared that it was – fell down.

2

Who was it that always tore pages out of *Essays in Criticism*? Professor Treece, penetrating into the Senior Common Room for tea, had found the new copy, mutilated as usual. He picked it up and shook it, scarcely able to believe his eyes; the world, he felt, was tumbling to pieces about him; people – people he *knew*, people he took coffee with, even – were chipping steadily away at its hard, round moral core. Consider the circumstances: the Senior Common Room, entered only by persons of faculty rank; a serious intellectual review, of interest only to highly educated specialists. He was surrounded, it was clear enough, by intellectual crooks and vagabonds, people cultivated enough to teach in a university and read this, yet boorish enough to tear it up before anyone else had read it. *That* was the thing; the wooden horse was inside their gates; the enemies were within the town he had thought so well protected. Who was it? Any of these somnolent figures, sipping lethargically on their tea, could be the one. The soft, refined, civilized atmosphere of the Common Room suddenly curdled; he looked again at the copy of 'Bateson's little effort', as he was wont to call it, as if he could not believe the mutilation there. Moral decline drifted everywhere around him in the air, like the stench of drains. One could only – the fact had to be faced – suspect a *conspiracy*, an overall challenge to the moral universe. There was no other way to perceive it.

'Conspiracy!' This was the first thought that had come into Treece's mind when he learned that the University literary society had invited Carey Willoughby, the novelist and critic and ... well, there was so much; he did everything ... to lecture to it. Treece had been sitting in his room at the University that morning, under the most normal of circumstances, spraying his bookshelves with insecticide, when there had been a knock at the door and the head of Louis Bates had appeared round the jamb. Treece asked him to sit down, and he advanced into the room and did so genteelly. There was a pleased smile on his face. 'I wondered whether you had a spare bedroom,' he said.

'Did you?' asked Treece.

'Mr Willoughby, the novelist, you know, is coming to lecture to us, and he said that you were a friend of his and would probably put him up.'

'I've never met the man in my life,' said Treece.

'But that's not what he said in his letter,' said Bates.

'Then it's his word against mine, isn't it?' said Treece rather angrily.

'You see, frankly, we can't afford to pay his hotel bill,' said Bates, 'because we've got so many other speakers coming this season. There's Eliot coming, and Harold Nicolson, and I don't suppose he'll be satisfied with steak and chips and a bottle of Bass.' Louis Bates was now Chairman of the student literary society, and he was really making a rather good job of it. He had been proposed by Oliver, and since he was Oliver's candidate he had gone unopposed, for Oliver had no small influence. Apart from one or two unfortunate incidents – a refusal to present a bunch of chysanthemums to a lady novelist who attacked Shelley, and a fondness for dismissing the rest of his Committee and running things solo – Bates' régime was passing off very impressively. As Treece had grudgingly to admit to himself, Bates had been clever in obtaining Willoughby, who was fashionable and was on television more often than not.

'Very well,' said Treece, unwillingly. 'For one night?'

'Well, three, actually,' said Bates. 'Mr Schenk and Mr Butterfield have got him as a speaker at the Poetry Week-end.'

'He's going to be there too?' cried Treece.

Treece's qualms were fully justified. As he had told Bates, he did not know Willoughby personally, though he had heard a great deal about him through the inter-university grapevine; but the process clearly operated in reverse, for the whole point was, to be blunt, that Willoughby, who obviously employed a large body of spies engaged in collecting stories and anecdotes for him to put in his books, had written up a long tale about Treece. He was in there.

After Bates had gone, Treece had gone storming down to see Viola Masefield, who was Treece's consultant on the younger generation. 'Do you know this man Carey Willoughby is coming here?' he demanded.

'That bastard?' said Viola. 'How nice.'

'I suppose he's rather a bright man, but he seems to me unnecessarily malicious. I read his novels.'

'I thought you didn't read modern novels,' said Viola. 'You should; I'm glad to see we're converting you.'

'You are not converting me,' cried Treece furiously. 'All the modern novel seems to have discovered since Lawrence is that there are some people in England who change their shirts every day. I knew that already. I don't need to read modern novels.'

'But you should,' said Viola.

'Why?' cried Treece. 'I read this one because someone said I was in it. And I *am*. Do you realize that the story about the professor who left the script of one of his articles among some student essays, and another tutor gave it C minus, is about *me*? Someone must have told this man. Even down to the bit about, "This is good lower second stuff." It was B minus actually. That makes it worse.'

'Poet's licence,' said Viola.

'What sort of man can he be? He makes one feel thoroughly unsafe.'

'Oh Stuart, don't fuss so,' said Viola maternally. 'You play right into Carey's hands if you let him know that you think he's betrayed you. He'd like you to think that.'

'He'd *what*?' shouted Treece. 'You know, I just don't understand you people. I don't understand how he thinks. I don't understand how you think. I believe you told him that story.'

'I did, actually,' said Viola.

'He's staying at my *house*,' cried Treece. 'I suppose he's only coming because he's short of ideas. Why else should he come to a place like this?'

'Perhaps to see me,' said Viola.

'Well, if I were you, I'd be careful,' said Treece.

172

'You're a fine one to talk,' said Viola.

Treece blushed and fired his parting shot: 'Have you seen his title?' he cried. 'What's that supposed to be? "Contemporary Poetics: Adumbration and Exegesis." Why doesn't he just call it "Modern Verse"?'

Treece left and went up to the Common Room, feeling that if he had learned anything about the younger generation, it was not what he wanted to know. Viola had betrayed him, and Willoughby had done his best; and now someone had been at work on *Essays in Criticism* and stabbed him in the back there too. The ordinary laws of sound human contact were slipping; and the people who were selling out were those within the citadel – one's own friends, people one invited to one's home, people who did not destroy aimlessly but with a philosophy of life that comprehended destruction. To Treece, the existence of people, of liberal intellectuals, like himself was infinitely precarious, infinitely unsure, and infinitely precious. The kind of intellectual purity he stood for was a tender blossom that had little or no chance in the bitter winds of the world. Sometimes you could do no more than thank God that there were people such as he was, thought Treece in no spirit of self-congratulation; he simply meant it. But those who live by the liberalism shall perish by the liberalism. Their own lack of intransigence, their inevitable effeteness, betrayed them. Already liberal intellects like his own found themselves on the periphery. The end was coming, as people like him had less and less of a social function, and were driven out into an effete and separate world of their own, to the far edge of alienation. It was on communication that they depended, and the channels were being closed from the other side; and in the tearing up of *Essays in Criticism* Treece saw the end of the liberal tradition.

He looked about him, and observed that his neighbour in the next armchair was the sociologist Jenkins. He could, he reflected, have lighted on no better person to explain the changing scene to him; Jenkins was supremely *au fait* with the contemporary world. It was said that Jenkins was so conscious of being in the fifties that, if you asked him what

day it was, he would answer: 'Oh, it's the nineteen-fifties.'
He was working, he had told Treece a few days before, on
discontent, because there was a big market in discontent things
just now.

'It's a mad, crazy world we live in,' he observed to him.
Jenkins nodded sagely. 'It's a bear-garden,' he said.

'I suppose one is old', said Treece, 'when one's surprised
at the manifestations of disorder. One comes to the point when
one doesn't want anything else to change, however hard one
has fought for change in one's youth.'

'Ah,' said Jenkins, shaking a roguish finger in a very Con-
tinental way, 'you want to have your cake and eat it. Why not,
of course? It's an absurd proverb. I always have *my* cake and
eat it. It's the only wise thing to do.' He ate several creamy
pastries with great rapidity. 'You expect too much,' he said
finally, sucking his fingers.

'I always did,' said Treece sadly, sinking lower in his chair.
Whenever Treece talked to sociologists, and he made a habit
of doing so, since he liked having himself explained to himself,
from all facets, he always felt in touch with the world of the
inevitable, with the great sweeping processes of history. And
whenever sociologists talked to Treece (and they made a habit
of doing that, because he *listened*; the sort of people Jenkins
respected most were those of whom he could say: 'So I put a
logical argument to him and in the end he actually admitted
he was wrong. "You're right, Jenkins," he had to confess.
"You've convinced me." ') they felt in touch with those
strange, unorganized minds that thought they were independent, and could do as they liked, and knew not they were
creatures of circumstance.

'And this education we're giving them is the tool of destruction, of course; that's what makes it so painful. We're showing
them how to accomplish the ritual murder of ourselves. That's
what hard-bitten Tories like yourself find so hard to bear.'

'Tories?' cried Treece. 'I'm a sort of Labour man.'

'Ah, but what sort?' asked Jenkins. 'The socialist millennium
has come at last, and how you hate it. You wish you could
send it back and ask for another. The working man has really

let you down. You thought he wanted a sturdy, working-class culture, weaving baskets and singing folk-songs. And all he wants is *The Lone Ranger*.'

'I suppose I'm becoming the most fantastic old reactionary,' said Treece, aghast at himself. He did, indeed, believe in privilege. Just as he often liked charming people better than good ones, pretty women better than plain ones, he preferred the intelligent to the fools and wanted them to triumph. And this in turn led him to believe in a kind of inverted privilege; he let himself be charmed by the pathos of the undeserving. There was no answer to the fact that the privileged had the assurance, the persuasive manner, the true gift of tongues; and so one righted the balance by being more than fair to the underprivileged, the Eborebelosas, the Louis Bates.

'Not really,' said Jenkins. 'Indeed, you're too tolerant. We allow anything, any change, everything except perhaps bad writing. One develops scruples and respect for others to the point at which action for us becomes impossible. And hence standards become obscured. It's a state of chassis,' he said, stuffing some papers into his briefcase. 'A state of chassis.' He stood up, a dapper little man, looking like a commercial traveller trying to sell his intellectual wares. 'Do you dance?' he asked.

'Pardon?' asked Treece.

'I wondered if you danced. I have to go and do some field work at the Palais.'

'*Quel palais?*' demanded Treece, amazed.

'Not Versailles,' said Jenkins. 'The Palais de Danse. Have you been down there to the rock-and-roll sessions? I go down almost every night.'

'How interesting,' said Treece politely.

'Yes,' said Jenkins. 'I'm getting quite good at it now.'

'I must be the only person in town who has never been to the Palais,' said Treece reflectively. 'On Saturday nights I seemed to have stayed at home doing my homework until I was about twenty-four. I never seem to have had a culture at all, like Richard Hoggart and all the others. I just stayed at home and *worked*. And when my father used to draw on the cultural stockpile of the working classes, I just wasn't there. I was up in my bedroom, working.'

'Well, then, come along with me,' said Jenkins. 'See how the other half lives. More than half, actually. Have a little sociological beano. As you said – with sociology one can do anything and call it work.' He fingered the buttons on his button-down shirt. He was the only man in the University with buttons on his shirt – it was the full extent of his Americanization.

Treece reflected for a moment; it seemed fully justifiable on academic grounds. 'Very well,' he said.

'Good man,' said Jenkins. 'I'll see you in the snug of the *Falcon* at seven. Wear something comfortable.' He opened a small tin, taken from his pocket, and put a throat pastille in his mouth. 'Pastille?' he asked politely.

'No, thank you,' said Treece.

'Sometimes I think I talk *too much*,' he said. 'It's compulsive, of course, this pressing urge to interpret one's surroundings publicly. Sometimes I wish I were a little kitten, starry-eyed and sweetly mystified by the oddities of this world. You know what I mean? Don't tell Kahnweiler this' (Kahnweiler was the head of the Department of Psychology). 'Don't tell anyone.' And he disappeared through the door.

3

'I feel *so* tired,' said Treece. 'So terribly, terribly, terribly tired.'

'Didn't you find it interesting?'

'Terribly interesting. Terribly, terribly, terribly interesting,' said Treece. 'But really, don't you think, isn't that enough discontent for one night. I don't think I could drink another drop.'

They had spent a long, long evening looking for discontent. They went first to the Palais. The Palais proved to be terribly respectable. Tea and soda-fountains. No Negroes. The men had all shined up their shoes, and the girls stood at the side holding on to their handbags as if they were, somehow, a physical representation of the virtue they looked determined not to relinquish. They had then gone to a low wine lodge, a great

Victorian hall with a central counter, sawdust on the floor, large mirrors of etched glass, a small trio (small, that is, in stature) playing teashop music ('Pale Hands I Loved Beside the Shalimar'), led by an old, old woman with pink hair. The people all seemed misshapen and ugly, sad victims of the impact of the Industrial Revolution. Prostitutes, old and haggard, plied their trade. Treece had been impressed by this one, but Jenkins had not. He had seen most of these people before. 'They're nearly all sociologists,' he said.

They had next gone on to a homosexual bar, the men's bar in a large hotel, where the barman held your hand as he gave you change, and kept trying on a pair of earrings while he was waiting to give service. Treece liked this one, too.

They had then tried an upper-class cocktail lounge where girls in fur coats sat and drank whisky and ginger. This one Treece didn't like, so they had gone out and on to another place that was full of old people talking about illness. They had only half a pint this time. After that, if Treece remembered rightly, they had gone on to one or two public houses, of different sorts, until at last time had been called. Jenkins had grown increasingly more depressed as the evening wore on, and he explained that what upset him so much was the sort of people that sociologists had to be *objective about*. He detested so many of them. He also detested, he explained, most of his fellow sociologists, who were still living spiritually at the L.S.E. of Harold Laski, and sneered at him whenever he wore a suit or drank wine out of the right glasses. He was also concerned about a tattooing survey that the department had undertaken. 'It's quite a large-scale project; we have a psychologist who's working on the reasons that people have for getting themselves tattooed, and then a statistical sociologist who's working out incidence among class and age groups, and incidence of tattooing among the population as a whole. Then we have an aesthetician, who's considering the tattoo as a form of popular art ... like the street ballad. The thing is that I committed myself rather rashly to the suggestion that, as a very high proportion of people in hospital seem to be tattooed, there may be some correlation between tattooing and certain forms of illness. I wanted to have a doctor in the survey. It was then observed that a large percentage of the people in hospital are working class, and that tattooing incidence is highest among that class. I could have cried.'

Treece was feeling distraught, because he had, this evening, done something very naughty; he had had an appointment with Emma, to spend the evening with her, and he had deliberately failed to go. He really did not quite know why; but the opportunity to come out with Jenkins had been seized on quite wilfully; and now he thought of her, waiting, and felt himself a rogue and a cheat. 'I'm a mess,' he said, as they walked down the street among the little knots of people from newly-closed public houses. 'I'm a terrible, terrible mess. The world is too much with us.'

'You mustn't be maudlin,' said Jenkins, reasonably (considering his own condition).

'I suffer from this shameful and useless boredom, this complete exhaustion of personality. How can I explain it to you? I do bad things. I lack the energy to carry through any process I conceive. And when I look at all the people in the modern world, and at the way things are moving ... then I trust nothing. I simply have no trust or repose anywhere. All is change for the worse.'

'Well, that's the lot of people like us. We abstract ourselves from the sphere of national effectiveness. We're too busy taking notes to do anything. It's a national as well as a personal trait now. And the fault lies precisely in the things we value most. You aren't likely to become a Catholic or a communist, and nor am I. . . .'

'God, no,' said Treece.

'Quite,' said Jenkins. 'God, no; and Lenin, no. You prefer a good honest Western *doubt* – with all the personal ineffectiveness and depression that that entails. You presumably think that your position is actually superior. . . .'

'I think it's terribly terribly superior,' said Treece. 'I can see the attractions of either of those disciplines; they're very obvious. But I think anguished and independent and critical doubt is really more fruitful for the soul.'

'Then you must expect to be depressed,' said Jenkins.

'I know,' said Treece, 'but I've always hoped not to be.'

'I'm sorry if I appeared rude,' said Jenkins.

'Not at all,' said Treece.

'Let's go to the Mandolin,' said Jenkins.

'I thought everything was closed.'

'This isn't a pub; it's an espresso bar. It catches all the trade after the pubs close. Once this city used to close down after ten-thirty. Now the espresso bars have added another dimension to provincial time.'

They passed down a side-street, and then a side-street off a side-street, until they were in the factory quarter. Huge buildings stood up silently on either side. 'What are these places?' asked Treece.

'Warehouses,' said Jenkins.

Treece thought he said whorehouses, and looked at them with interest. They didn't look like his idea of a cathouse at all. However, it was probably different once you got inside. Suddenly they pulled up short and mounted a dingy wooden stairway, which gave access to a room that appeared to be in complete darkness. 'Are you sure it's a brothel?' asked Treece. 'It's an espresso bar,' said Jenkins. Treece's eyes, now growing used to the semi-darkness, began to register the scene, and he observed that, sitting at low, oddly-shaped – one might say accidentally shaped – tables, were people. They seemed to be an indiscriminate collection. There were people from the University, in great knitted red sweaters. There were also a number of what Jenkins called 'teds'. All were young. There were girls in duffel coats with black eyelids, protesting, just for the evening. There were exhausted-looking youths in reefer jackets, carrying double basses, with their hair planed down to a thin, grass-like covering on top. They were all sipping frothy coffee in glass cups no bigger than eye-baths. The waitresses were slinky and delectable. Outside, in a little courtyard on the roof, in the rain, a small group of musicians were playing on home-made guitars. Jenkins explained that if Treece was interested in the breakdown of class boundaries the guitarist in the group was actually the Earl of . . . (he named a prominent scion of the English nobility) and the group was called the *Honi Soit Qui Mal Y Pense* Skiffle Group. 'It would be,' said Treece.

A pervasive atmosphere of *chic* filled the place. Exotic greenery slouched about the walls, decked with a casual guitar, as if Segovia had only just that moment left; the furniture was ever so very contemporary, for people with no leg below the knee-joint and a short sharp spike for a bottom. The décor mingled styles indiscriminately, and Treece felt in a cultural fog. There was a Spanish mural, an Indian statue, Caribbean vegetation, an Italian coffee machine, American music. A notice on the wall said: 'Calling all toreadors.' There was a sort of overall grotto effect; Jenkins claimed that when it opened the proprietor, a Pole named Stanislaus, had, in an excess of enthusiasm, planned to have it flooded to a depth of one foot, and issue people with waders, but had reluctantly abandoned the idea when he realized that you couldn't do that on the second floor. But if the décor and comparative licence carried one into another world (if only, Treece thought, there had been windows, so that one could make sure the real world was still there) the clientele was very English. 'It's like being on the Continong, except you can get a decent cup of tea,' said Jenkins. 'The English heaven.' Within the room, amours and intellectual discussion equally ran their fervent courses. In the corners couples embraced and fondled, stopping just short of actual fulfilment; at a centre table someone was declaring, 'Well, you can't make value-judgements about value-judgements, can you?'

'What mystifies me', said Jenkins in a whisper, 'is where they dug all these people up from. They weren't about before this place started; and you never see them in the streets. They must come in through the drains.'

'They're very new to me,' said Treece, a naïve Dante being shown through Hell by this strangest of Vergils. 'Is it always like this?' The skiffle group were now at work on a number, pertinently called, 'I was a Big Man Yesterday, but Oh You Ought to See Me Now'.

'Listen, They're playing our tune,' said Jenkins. He went on in an excited sociologist's whisper, 'A year ago, two years ago, this seemed like just an ordinary, dull provincial city, with housewives shopping at Dolcis and having coffee in the Kardomah, and going home to their suburb to count the change. You know. But now ... now it seems *full* of all sorts of bohemians, political insurgents, masochists, lesbians, men who think they're Jesus Christ, men who sleep on the radiators in the Public Library. And do you know what's done it? Italian coffee.'

Behind them the coffee machine kept giving out large, sighing hisses, like a railway engine discharging. It was a plaintive sound. 'It works without steam,' said Jenkins. 'Oh, if only I did.'

'Why is this special?' demanded Treece. 'Why is it necessary to correct the universal misconception that it works with steam?'

'Oh, don't be like that,' said Jenkins.

The espresso machine, all gilt and fancy lights, with a huge gold eagle on the top, was about the size and shape of a coffin; it was being operated – one might even say played – by a Sikh dressed in his native garb. '*Cappucino?*' asked a husky, alluring female voice, high above them. Treece looked up and perceived a very tall and extremely handsome girl, wearing a low-cut sweater and a tiny little apron like a fig-leaf, giving them a well-dentifriced smile. '*Cappucino?*' she asked again. Treece felt highly flattered that this should have happened to him. He didn't intend to let the language barrier be an obstacle to *this*. '*Non capisco,*' he said (he'd handled this sort of problem before). '*Lo scrivere.*' 'She wants to know if you want black or white coffee,' said Jenkins. 'Tell her white,' said Treece, beaming and nodding at the girl. 'Two whites,' said Jenkins. 'Thank you, sir,' said the girl. 'She spoke English all the time,' said Treece indignantly. She arrived back a moment later, bearing the coffee in tiny perspex cups. 'Two shillings, please,' she said. 'It's terribly expensive, isn't it?' Treece said when she had gone. 'Do they sprinkle gold dust on it?' 'You aren't paying for the coffee,' said Jenkins. 'You're paying for the atmosphere, the sniff you got at her Chanel Number Five. You pay to look down the fronts of their dresses. They always have such nice waitresses.'

'But can people really afford a shilling for a cup of coffee?' asked Treece.

'Well, look,' said Jenkins, and gestured around. It was true that the place was so packed that, had the people been animals, it would have been banned by the R.S.P.C.A. 'It's the new idle rich, you see, the young.'

'I see,' said Treece. 'Are you supposed to lift the cup from down there with your feet?'

'The waitresses are *aristos*. They only go out with top people, the mews cottage boys. You have to own a horse to get off with them. It's a special kind of girl, you see. They bat their long, silky legs at you, but if their sex dropped off and you handed it back to them they wouldn't know what it was. You get my point. They've never really looked down in all their lives; they know someone's going to open all the doors, move all the stones out of their path, get the car waiting. This too makes the angry young men even angrier. They hate to see the sort of rats that get girls like this. They want them themselves. But if they get saddled with one, all hell breaks loose.' Jenkins thought all this very funny and laughed loudly. He sang: 'So I took her into bed and I covered up her head, just to shield her from the doggy, doggy few.'

It was a long time since Treece had been so conscious of the English class system. He had supposed it had been quite subverted by the new post-war system of rewards; but it certainly didn't confuse Jenkins. 'Don't you ever feel doubtful of your categories?' he asked Jenkins suspiciously.

'Well, I'm speaking *ex cathedra*, of course,' said Jenkins, wiping milky froth from his lips, 'and I wouldn't want you to quote me, but it does bear some relation to reality, don't you think?'

'What else have I missed?' asked Treece belligerently.

'Middle-class youth reacting against the cultural barrenness of the suburbs. Coming to the town to seek a cultural centre....'

Across the room Treece suddenly noticed Walter Oliver, sitting in the midst of a rather strange and tattered group of apparent bohemians. 'That's the Gang,' said Jenkins. 'All pseudo-writers, pseudo-painters, pseudo-philosophers, who take over all the paraphernalia of bohemianism, but rarely actually *produce* anything. What I admire is their dedication. They really mean to do something. But those who do always seem to break away.'

Oliver saw him and waved a hand. 'Got any cigarettes?' he shouted.

'Shall we join them?' said Treece.

'All right,' said Jenkins. 'But do you know what a steamer is?'

'No,' said Treece.

'Well, you're one,' said Jenkins. 'You know how steamers come into port, and are unloaded, and then sail off again. This is one of the ways that these people live. They unload you and you sail off. Be careful.'

'Ah, you finally came,' said Oliver when they had crossed to the other table. 'Good evening, Herr Jenkins.' He looked back at Treece and said: 'If you've got some cigarettes, I've got some matches.' Treece produced a packet of cigarettes and Oliver took it and handed it round the group. 'That's what's known as buying in,' said Oliver.

'How's your novel?' asked Treece.

'I'm stuck,' said Oliver. 'I'd just finished the dedication and then I didn't seem to know what to say next.'

'Oh, dear,' said Treece.

'Oh, it's much better to be writing a novel than to have finished one.'

'I had hopes of you, Oliver.'

'Oh no, I'm finished, written out,' said Oliver urbanely. 'I'm so finished it just isn't true. I'm one of the *derrière garde*. It's a new twist. Hey, I thought of something interesting the other day. Do you realize that the title *The Holy Bible* is probably out of copyright?'

'Well?' said Jenkins.

'Well, you could probably use it again for something else,' said Oliver. He belched. Oliver had spitting friends, belching friends, and farting friends; that is, he rated people by how natural he was prepared to be in their presence. It was very hard to get to be one of Oliver's farting friends. He didn't take easily to people. He had no time for people who seemed to him to be fribbles. He demanded the strictest standards of conduct. He had really warmed to Treece and Jenkins.

'You should see Louis Bates's novel,' said he to Treece.

'Is it good, then?'

'It's ... well-typed,' said Oliver. 'And it's got *me* in it.' 'You recommend it, then?' asked Treece. 'It's one of these knee-stroking novels,' said Oliver. 'What are they?' asked Treece. 'Oh you know, all pale young working-class men, reading Shelley to one another and saying, "Art thou pale for weariness?" and girls who softly stroke their own knees and say, "You know, you're a very strange person." '

'What do you think of Bates?' asked Treece.

'I think he's good,' said Oliver. 'Of course, he's a fool.'

At Treece's other side sat a man who wore on his upper half only a dirty vest, buttoned up to the neck. He now put on sun glasses. 'Can't bear the light,' he said in Treece's ear. 'Have to stay in all day and sleep. Then they come and fetch me and bring me out at night. Want to buy a cello?'

'No; I don't play,' said Treece.

'I'd come round and play it for you then,' said the man. 'You buy it and I'll come every night and play it. Where do you live?'

'I'm not telling you,' said Treece wisely.

The man reached out and took up a cello case and, opening it, he twanged the instrument. 'Just listen at that tone,' he said proudly. 'Terrible, i'n' it?' 'Put it away,' said another man. 'Bloody thing, who'd be stupid enough to buy a thing like that?'

'This fella here,' said the man with the cello gesturing towards Treece. 'Wouldn't you?'

'No. I don't want it,' said Treece.

'You lay off him,' said Oliver roughly. 'He's my friend.' He turned to Treece and said: 'Don't you buy anything off them, anything, no matter how good it looks.'

'Friend of yours, then?' said the man with the 'cello, pointing to Oliver.

'A student of mine,' said Treece.

'Him a student?' asked the man. 'I thought he was a racing-car driver.'

'He may be as well,' said Treece.

'You a teacher? What do you teach?'

'English,' said Treece.

'Good,' said the man, who, Treece, saw more clearly, was only about twenty-three or twenty-four. 'Will you read some poems of mine? You won't understand them, but you might be able to get them published. Here, buy me a cup of coffee, will you?' He called over the waitress. 'Two cups of froth, please, Rita?'

'Have you got any money?' asked Rita.

'He has,' said the man, and, turning to Treece again, he asked politely: 'Read much?'

'Yes; it's my job,' said Treece.

'You see this belt,' said Walter Oliver on the other side of him, opening his jacket and taking off a leather belt. 'It was made by the Prince of Wales's bootmaker. Of course, the day we're all waiting for is the one when the Prince of Wales claims his boots are made by Walter Oliver's belt-maker.'

'Is there a Prince of Wales?' demanded Jenkins. Nobody knew. 'That's an interesting index of our sense of democratic responsibility,' said Jenkins brightly. People were now beginning to wonder whether Treece and Jenkins were not completely insufferable.

'I'm an anti-monarchist,' said the man next to Treece showily. 'Why?' demanded Treece. 'Well,' said the man, 'it's such a waste of money.' 'If they substituted anything else, it would be equally expensive,' said Treece. 'Well, perhaps I'm a monarchist after all,' said the man. 'It doesn't matter to me.'

'I can forgive the monarchy everything except Annigoni,' said a man who painted: you could tell he did; the paint was all over his clothes.

'Of course, monarchy gives cachet to the class system and the nobility,' said Jenkins.

'But can one be more democratic than we are?' asked Oliver.

'America is,' said Jenkins. 'America is constantly in flux, and laid open to alteration. We really aren't. Of course, in time we will be, because we're only too likely to reproduce America's experiences, thirty years later.' Most of those present were communists, and they took this rather hard, hearing America praised. To some it was the first time it had happened. They responded violently and pointed out that at least England had the Welfare State. But, as Jenkins pointed out, they themselves were waifs from the Welfare State; they refused to have their names written down, and didn't pay Health Insurance, and the Army somehow never got to know of their existence. 'That's the trouble with the Welfare State,' said the man next to Treece. 'They want everyone in. Of course, you can stay out if you're clever. But one of the great injustices of our time is this: supposing you're married, and you want to leave your wife, like I did, and disappear. Now you'd think in any sensibly run society a man could do that. But you try it and see what happens. It's impossible to change your bloody name any more. If you get stuck and have to work, you need a bloody card from your last employer. The income tax is after you. That's what started me off like this. I was quite willing to work then. I hadn't discovered my genius. But my point is this: tramps are necessary. Avenues of escape are essential. So why doesn't the Welfare State pay tramps to go on being tramps, instead of trying to find 'em work? What's all this about work? People don't realize how important tramps are. They challenge the assumption that you've got to be housed and proper-tied and well-dressed to live in the modern world. I could be like that if I wanted. I was the best pork-butcher in Ilkeston. I outclassed everybody. But I don't choose. This is what I chose, the hard way. I read Nietzsche and Schopenhauer and I realized I was something more than a butcher. I saw the light. Let me tell you my story. I think it's without exception the most beautiful story I've ever heard....'

But Oliver interrupted. 'Isn't it strange', he said, 'how working-class intellectuals thrive on Nietzsche? They all do. It's the power complex. They're all supermen. They all think they're Jesus Christ risen again. They all want to change the world.

Sometimes I just want to run away and keep bees. I get tired of the manifold voices of truth buzzing in my ears. . . .'

'There's only one way to shut that fellow up,' said the cellist, spiteful because of the interruption, 'and that's tell him he looks ill.' He addressed himself to Oliver: 'Do you feel all right?' he asked him. 'Your face has gone yellow.'

'My God!' said Oliver.

'Much remains to be told,' went on the cellist, turning back to Treece. 'I realized, as I said, that I was a genius. It explains so much. Why did people despise me? Why was I so alone? Actually I wasn't actually alone. I was living with this Negress, a huge creature she was, with breasts so high up she could rest her chin between them, but spiritually I was alone, and un-understood. I read Henry Miller. I saw that I was a rebel. Of course, rebels are never loved. You've heard of Rimbaud, Baudelaire. I was of that ilk. However, as it happened, it isn't love us rebels want; it's money. There should be a levy for rebels and poets. Every time those people sit down in their cosy airmchairs at the telly they should be made to drop a shilling in a box for rebels.'

Treece sat there, with his washed hair and thin fingers, and asked himself: What can you do? The coffee machine hissed savagely at him. He wanted to escape from the place. He felt like a useless butterfly. The ground began to open beneath his feet; he found himself dispossessed, as if he were alone in a big city, circulating among hostile formations of passers-by. He wanted to see Emma. Dejection seeped like sludge into his spirits as the cellist went on uttering his history into his ear. The crowds in the coffee bar seemed all at once to be the busy world about him, the people who were *in* on things, the people with jobs, the people with a sense of mission. Their lives were full of matter; they were in the class system; they were social functionaries. He alone did not feel a part of Jenkins's schemes and overall patterns; he was an alien in the universe; while everyone else's blazer and moustache were class symbols, it seemed to him that his hat was just a hat, his suit an ordinary unsocial suit and his tie an innocent, uncommitted tie. He felt alone, he felt as if he had no tenure in the world, as if every moment came to him, alone of men, unexpectedly. He felt that he wanted not just to be with Emma, but more : to be involved with her, to be in love with her, to be a social group of two. And he suddenly wished that Emma was here, to be turned to.

He decided to go. Jenkins seemed happy enough in this company, and so Treece went alone. He walked down to the market-place to get a taxi. A crowd was gathered there, among the deserted stalls; a fight was going on. Several teddy boys had set upon a man who was on the ground at the centre of the milling group. The assailants jostled their way through the crowd and trotted off down a side-street. A moment later, as if at a signal, two policemen appeared and scattered the crowd. 'Always too late, aren't you?' cried a little man. 'Always stay out of the way until it's over. That's the cops every time.' 'I'll have you inside if you don't watch it,' said the policeman. He advanced towards Treece. The victim was being helped to his feet, and Treece saw, with a sudden shock of shame – as if his own shame for not intervening weren't enough – that the face was black, and belonged to Mr Eborebelosa. His hands were cut with knife wounds and he had a pain in his shoulder. He saw Treece with surprise. The attack had been a motiveless one, by youths out nigger-hunting, and he couldn't quite understand what had happened to him. Treece took him up to the hospital in a taxi and then, when his broken collarbone had been set, took him to his home. He said little. It seemed useless to apologize; yet he knew he could, had he dared, have intervened,.and he did not know how to forgive himself. 'Thank you, sir,' said Eborebelosa, back at his digs. 'Thank you,' said Treece.

CHAPTER EIGHT

I

As Treece had had grudgingly to admit, Louis Bates had been very enterprising in engaging the services of Carey Willoughby as his speaker, and on the afternoon of the lecture everyone had been telling him so. All day he was to be seen, for once, in the centre of an admiring host; by four o'clock he was as dizzy as a sick bee on a surfeit of praise, and his sense of participation in the events about him was noticeably diminished. One of these events was that already a crowd some seventy strong, and including the Vice-Chancellor and his wife, the town clerk and the manager of the local dance-hall, Mr Schenk and Mr Butterfield, were packed in a large lecture-room on hard wooden benches; and Willoughby was half an hour overdue.

'I hope he really is coming,' said Butterfield, who, since Willoughby was speaking for the Poetry Week-end he had arranged with Mr Schenk, had a vested interest in the occasion, and was frightened of what Bates was going to pull out of the bag next.

'Someone *has* gone down to the station to meet him?' asked Professor de Thule, of History, sneaking out of his own department.

'Well,' said Bates, bright as a pin. 'Well . . .' – and in spite of a barrage of subtle prevarication on his part, it became apparent to all present that this courtesy had, somehow, been completely overlooked. All depended on Bates; he had dismissed the rest of the Committee of the society for all except trivial purposes; Bates worked alone. But that capacity for bold strokes which had characterized his reign had not deserted him; he produced his masterpiece: he was going, he said, to telephone the station and broadcast a message for Mr Willoughby on the loudspeakers: *Come on up.* This, it seemed to Treece, waiting disturbedly in the main hall with the academic contingent, while draughts blew up the legs of their trousers and skirts, was a typical Bates extravagance, but there was no help for it; every time Bates popped into the lecture-room with new reassurances, laughter and the singing of an old University song, 'Why are we waiting?' greeted his entrance and exit, and people were beginning to leave, unmelted by his honeyed persuasions. By now he was known to his audience as a supreme buffoon, and his ears had turned the colour of terra-cotta. Happy for Louis had this stratagem worked. But, alas, when he emerged from the telephone booth five minutes later, even his superb aplomb was somewhat dishevelled. 'I can't get through,' he said with a catch in his voice. 'I keep getting the station and then when I try to tell them what I want they ring off.' A little tear grew in the corner of his eye and he added pettishly: 'I'm going to call the telephone exchange and ask them to exchange this telephone.'

'Did you press button A?' asked de Thule brutally.

'No,' said Bates. 'Anyway, I've run out of pennies.' He started to explain that he was working class, unlike everyone else, and not used to telephones, but Treece cut him short. 'I think you'd better hurry down to the station in a taxi and meet him.' It was but the work of another ten minutes to put Bates in a taxi and send him down to the station to salvage what he could from the debris. As his taxi swung out of the drive, with Bates gesticulating out of the rear window, a second taxi swung in and pulled up in front of the steps to disgorge what was obviously a Bright Young Man, with a Marlon Brando haircut, Army-surplus trousers, and a suède zipper jacket, carrying a khaki haversack from which protruded a bottle of milk. 'Do you mind if I change my socks?' he asked. It was, of course, Willoughby.

'I'm Treece, head of the English Department,' said Treece stepping forward.

'Pay for the taxi, will you, there's a good chap?' said Willoughby. The cavalcade passed through the entrance hall and on up to the Senior Common Room, where all the assistant lecturers were gathered, doing funny walks and pulling faces in the hope of being put into a Willoughby novel. 'Treece, Treece, Treece,' said Willoughby. 'The Housman Treece?' 'Yes; that's my book,' said Treece. 'I tell my students not to read it,' said Willoughby.

'Here we are,' said Treece. Willoughby sat down in an arm-chair and peeled off his shoes, then his socks; one seedy foot appeared, and then the other. 'Well, you're a rum lot,' he said. 'I sat down at the station on my fanny for half an hour.' 'There was a misunderstanding,' said Treece. 'Seems like it,' said Willoughby.

The cavalcade stood to one side, whispering. 'But he's *awful*,' said the wife of the Vice-Chancellor, 'and I've arranged to have him for dinner. I can't cancel it now. Can I? Can I?' She looked at his bare feet with distaste.

'Excuse the tootsies,' said Willoughby. 'Doctor's orders, this.' He reached in his haversack and produced a clean pair of socks, which he donned. The Vice-Chancellor's wife watched all this in horrified fascination; you felt that she had not really seen feet before, or if she had seen them, she had not thought about them; she was thinking now.

'I just want to make a call,' said Willoughby, and he disappeared into the toilet. They could hear him whistling gaily within.

'Is he a friend of yours?' demanded the Vice-Chancellor's wife.

'I've never met him before,' said Treece.

'Does he always take his shoes off?' demanded someone else.

'This is as strange to me as it is to you,' said Treece, disclaiming the whole thing entirely.

Perhaps, he thought generously, it was fame that had made Willoughby like this; and really this was true. You not only had to be someone, these days, but to look as if you *were* someone; otherwise the gossip columnists were simply not interested. Willoughby was really rather mystified by the whole business of his success; people said he was an angry young man, though he was not conscious of it – he had thought himself a perfectly detached observer of the modern scene. They compared him with people he scarcely knew, like Amis and Wain, and called him a movement. Actually he felt as doubtless Amis felt, and Wain, that he had got on to it all first, and the others were just taking advantage. He did not know what to make of it all. He had noticed that great artists usually had a great deal of *panache* and manner, and he went in for manner, but sometimes it was this sort of manner and sometimes that. This time he was the Marlon Brando type, with his hair slicked down and the cares of the world upon his sullen shoulders. He was the victim of misfortunes, the charming buffoon, the delightful incompetent who forgot what he wanted to say in lectures and seduced his women students, who beneath his expansive exterior was nigh to tears. There was one thing he could not understand about his literary fame; and that was this: he had observed that artists – there were so many ex-amples one could name, Brecht, Picasso, so many more – had a special dispensation where women were concerned. They could ill-treat and deceive and betray them, and subject them to every kind of indignity, and they, in their dozens, loved it, and him. Willoughby ill-treated and deceived and was cruel to his women, in their twos or threes, and subjected them to every kind of indignity, and they hated it, and him. There comes a point in a relationship, he had noticed, where a woman can no longer do without a man, whatever he is; yet there was never any point in *his* relationships where a woman could not do without him. He therefore saw himself as a literary waif, cut off from all the advantages that his role should rightfully bring.

'Are we ready?' he asked, emerging from the men's room. The whisperers separated hastily. They all trooped through into the lecture room. From Willoughby's haversack there peeped still the bottle of milk. He sat down at the desk and thrust his legs out; there followed an uncomfortable pause in which a restive audience, already offended by the fact that the lecture was starting half an hour late, began to shuffle its feet in a very hostile way, until someone suddenly realized that Bates, who was, of course, to introduce the speaker, was still down at the station. 'You'd better do it,' said Professor de Thule to Treece. Treece got up and advanced to the podium. He summoned up a few hasty words. 'Ladies and gentlemen,' he said, 'we're delighted to have with us Mr Carey Willoughby, who needs no introduction from me. He is one of the so-called novelists of the new movement. . . . I mean, one of the novelists of the so-called new movement. . . .' Loud guffaws burst from the student body, interrupting the rest of the statement. The so-called novelist played to the gallery: 'You see, they're all agin me,' he said. Treece concluded in hot embarrassment: '. . . So, then, here is the author of the best-selling novel, *Baby, It's Cold Outside* – he uttered these absurd words with distaste – 'Mr Carey Willoughby.' Willoughby rose from his lolling position and went over to the lectern. He removed the top of it and leaned over familiarly, so that the whole of the top half of his body lay across the table. 'I didn't prepare anything for this little do', he said lazily, 'because I've talked to poetry societies before, and I've usually found that the last thing in the world they're interested in is poetry. I mean, they may be interested in reading their own poetry, which isn't what I mean by being interested in poetry, or they may have come to meet someone else's wife, or have someone to listen to while they're knitting. So I mean, if there's anyone who doesn't want to hear this, just shout out. I mean, we'll do what you want to do. I could tell jokes or something.' Nobody answered. 'Well, come on,' said Willoughby. 'Is there anyone really interested in poetry?' Hands went up all over the place. 'He's right out of panto-mime, isn't he?' murmured Mavis de Thule, wife of the Pro-fessor of History, rather amused by all this rhetorical trickery.

'All of you?' cried Willoughby. 'My God! Well, let me ask you this, then – *why?*'

No one answered.

'Well, come on, then, why?'

'Because it's *delightful*,' a brave fat girl in the front row finally said.

'Brother, oh, brother,' said Willoughby, for this was just what he wanted. 'You aren't interested in poetry at all, believe me. You people are all alike. Sometimes I could just sit down and weep. You want poetry to entertain you – it's escapism, it's like television and you don't even need an aerial. There are people, all over England, people like me, sweating our guts out to write poetry that really means something, that's the crystal-lization of our hard-won experience, and it's like talking to the floor. How many people here like *modern* poetry? How many people here suspect that it's a clever trick, or find it too obscure to be pleasing, or think things have gone downhill since the Victorians?' There was a general murmur of assent from many of the townees, who had come in for the occasion. 'I thought so,' cried Willoughby. 'Of course, the truth is that if you don't like modern poetry you don't like poetry in any real sense at all, because poetry is an exploration of the human spirit of a given time. This is about you, and if you don't like modern poetry, let me add, you don't like yourself. It's hard work. So what? We aren't doing it to amuse, you know. The poet is exploring *your* universe. Ezra Pound once said that the artist is the antennae of the race, though the bullet-headed many will never learn to trust their great artists. I quote from memory.'

Treece leaned across to de Thule and commented: 'I'll bet he always does.'

'But do you trust your artists?' cried Willoughby.

An old lady in front of Treece turned and beckoned to him. 'He's such fun, isn't he?' she murmured. 'Yes, isn't he?' said Treece.

'Not that it's trust he wants. He just wants a modicum of attention; he wants people to read his verse, not for its charm, but for its tidings. The simple fact is, of course, that the world doesn't like poets. They're dirty, they cause trouble, they're bad house guests, they cheat, they lie, they fornicate. They question the values people live by. They challenge your view of the world, and that's the supreme insult. They don't even like you. And you return the hate in full measure, because they've gone beyond the order and respectability of your lives and found the principle of disorder there. Chaos looms up. So you make them pay. That's what poetry is, but you wouldn't know it, because it's obscured by all the culture phoneys, the week-end reviewers, the advertising agency intellectuals, the teachers of English . . .' here Treece winced '. . . who look in poetry for everything except what is so completely *there*.'

Willoughby went on like this for a while, waving his hands loosely and explaining that every poem is a mature human experience, an attack upon the indifference of matter, and the reason that in the beginning was the word was that the word was of matter yet more than it (or something like that). He kept saying, as he talked about poetry, that he was not going to talk about poetry. Then in the end he appeared to realize that he would have to, because people don't put up with being insulted for ever, even if they like it at first. So he picked up his Army haversack and, still pretending that he had not prepared a thing, he said: 'Well, let's see what we have here.' He put in an inquisitive hand and removed the milk bottle (he explained that he was tubercular and had to drink a pint of milk every day) and three pairs of discarded socks (he explained that he was gastric and had to change his socks regularly – perhaps these two illnesses are cited against the wrong precautions, but then he had them, and in some ways they were, one felt, him), and he got a sheaf of papers, which turned out to be poems – his poems. To Treece, who pursued literature intently, seeking to distil from it deeper and more searching explorations of the human fabric, and to preserve at all costs the purity and integrity of thought and art, Willoughby's rancour was quite out of key. Willoughby's poems were full of ambiguities; you listened to them in the way that you listened to low music-hall comedians, knowing that what they said on the face of things wasn't the joke at all, and that, moreover, the joke lay in the disparity between what was said and what was meant. In other words, Willoughby's poems were a thing you had to be in on; some of the audience were in, and some were out. Willoughby saw this, and berated the audience again for a few minutes. Then he asked for questions.

STUDENT: I wanted to ask you, because I see that some of the other people in this new movement . . .

WILLOUGHBY: There is no movement.

STUDENT: But I thought . . .

WILLOUGHBY: Sorry, no movement. All made up by the Literary Editor of the *Spectator*.

STUDENT: Well, what I wondered was this: some of the other poets in . . . I mean, that have been associated with you have come out on record as being of the opinion that Dylan Thomas's reputation is excess. . . .

WILLOUGHBY: That phoney! Any more questions?

MAVIS DE THULE: Well, Mr Willoughby, I'm sure we've all of us read all the things you've written with great interest and pleasure, poems as well as novels, and I suppose we ought to take what you've said *cum grano*.

WILLOUGHBY: *Cum* what?

MAVIS DE THULE: *Grano*. Latin. But what I felt I had to ask you after hearing your most fascinating comments was, what public do you have in mind when you write? Other poets?

WILLOUGHBY: That's a fair question, lady, and I'd say: about three other people who've gone to the trouble to ask themselves what it is I'm trying to do.

MAVIS DE THULE: What are their names?

At this point Treece saw the need to intervene. 'I'm sure Mr Willoughby's speaking metaphorically,' he said, and Willoughby nodded cheerfully, 'so now I'd like to wind up this I feel unforgettable occasion. Before I do, though, there's one question of my own that I'd like to put to Mr Willoughby, and that is: tell us, do you write more than you read or read more than you write?'

Treece knew that this was rather naughty, and it sounded ruder than he had even intended; but then Treece was not himself, for he had the wit to realize that, with his little *faux pas* in introducing Willoughby, he had committed himself irretrievably to being of the new movement himself – he was certain to be in Willoughby's next novel. The question, at any rate, struck home; Willoughby blushed like a student called to account by his tutor, and he passed the remark off by playing to the audience. 'Believe me,' he said. 'You have no friends in *this game*. In this game you just have to have merit. And I never did have much of that.' The meeting closed amidst widespread hilarity.

Willoughby was, in a sense, *right*, of course; someone should have warned him that the Vice-Chancellor was to invite him to dinner. But really he did not seem too much put out that he was the only person present in Army-surplus khaki trousers. 'At least,' said the Vice-Chancellor, in a frantic attempt to put him at his ease, 'at least, my friend, you have a pocket at the knee.' Willoughby (who was thinking that if ever they decided to make a film of the life of G. K. Chesterton, *here* was the man for the part) really did not need putting at his ease; he was at it already. Indeed, he commanded the whole conversation throughout dinner; it was his views on the fetid quality of Shelley and Byron, his view on the modern decline of letters (he had written two well-known novels, and the royalties were scarcely enough, as he put it, to keep him in condoms), his views on the need for a national theatre (preferably in some place that challenged the hegemony of London, like Nottingham or Derby or Stoke), his views on this, on that, that dominated the meal. If there were views to be had on anything, he had them. He was at an advantage, of course, in the fact that he took none of the main courses. He was the only one present, he averred, as he took the five or six tablets that formed his meal, who would, barring accidents, live to be one hundred and twenty.

'I'm a layman, of course, Willoughby,' said the Vice-Chancellor weightily, 'but tell me something, will you, that our literary friends here' – he beamed wholesomely at Viola Masefield and Treece, who were also present and were drinking Blue Label Bass because the staff was tacitly expected to leave the hock for visitors – 'will doubtless think I ought to know already. But even a Vice-Chancellor can't know everything about all his subjects, or we shouldn't need to employ these chaps to do a bit of teaching for us. The question is, just what the hell are your books *about*?'

'Life and how it's lived,' said Willoughby, taking Dr Masefield's hand and holding it under the table, 'and, by implication, how it ought to be lived, and why it can't be lived properly any more.'

'You people are slippery fishes,' said the Vice-Chancellor. 'You have a faculty for defining the simplest in terms of the grandiose, so that a poor devil like me can't understand it. You're all the same. Well, a plague on your abstractions. Facts, my friend, facts.' He poured himself more wine. 'Answer me this, then: why don't your novels have proper endings, why aren't they resolved, why don't people die or live happily ever after?'

There are times when we see our friends plunging headlong into disaster, and there is nothing we can do about it, except accept the fact that it is probably we who will suffer more than them; they will never know about it. So it was with Treece now. There was no way of intervening to make this little speech sound more subtle than the simple, naïve thing that it actually was. Treece shut his eyes and withdrew from the conversation.

'You can get that sort of book at the Public Library,' began Willoughby.

'I can get any sort of book at the Public Library. I know the Librarian,' said the Vice-Chancellor, who liked it to be known that he knew everyone and could get anything done. 'What I want to know is why yours aren't like that?'

'Because I'm not trying to butter up my public,' said Willoughby. 'With my sort of book there's no resolution, because there's no solution. The problems aren't answered in the end, because there is no answer. They're problems that are handed on to the reader, not solved for him so that he can go away thinking he lives in a beautiful world. It's not a beautiful world.'

'Why not?' demanded the Vice-Chancellor's wife stoutly.

'But look, why do that?' asked the Vice-Chancellor. 'That's like saying, "I've got stomach ache. You should have it too." '

'It's meant to be,' said Willoughby. 'What you're trying to say is, "Sit down. You're rocking the boat." Look, here's the artist, dissatisfied and stringy, sitting on the outside of everything, watching the world going on like some spawning slum.

Here's the boys with the big fat fannies slapping everyone on the back and saying, "You've never had it so good." What can the poor old novelist do? He's not after more wages or more fun or more programmes on the telly. All he wants is to change the world. Things seem to get worse. What else is there but anger and frustration? He can't work for a new world, because what it calls progress he calls decline. He just sits on his arse too, like everyone else, but it's a thin angry arse and he doesn't sit so comfortably.'

Treece took a nervous look at the Vice-Chancellor, from his hue as furiously angry as any modern young man. He did have a fat fanny, and he was really an Edwardian, and he believed that if it hadn't been talked about at the Café Royal, it wasn't really life. What he couldn't understand was this: in his youth he had had opinions, and been regarded as liberal, almost a Bolshie (he had supported women's suffrage and once had chained himself to the railings outside the Houses of Parliament; it had been a Sunday – he was busy every other day – and an old-fashioned English Sunday at that, with simply no one around; no one tried to arrest him, or ask him what he was doing; what people passed him took no notice, as all decent English people do when something queer is going on; in the evening he got very hungry, and his tummy, which was a big one even then, for people ate more in those days, rumbled dreadfully, so he got out the key from where it was hidden in the lining of his jacket, and unchained himself, and went away). Now he had opinions, and he was regarded as a Tory; and what mystified him was, they were exactly the *same opinions*, so how do you account for that?

'Are you married, Mr Willoughby?' asked the wife of the Vice-Chancellor. She had not understood a word of all that had been said, but she had cottoned on to one thing, as women do, and this was that Willoughby was playing footsie under the table with Viola Masefield.

'I don't suppose he believes in it,' said the Vice-Chancellor in disgruntled tones.

'Well, why buy the cow', asked Willoughby reasonably, 'when you can steal milk through the fence?'

'I suppose Mr Willoughby is what they call an angry young man, is he? He seems to talk so loudly,' whispered the Vice-Chancellor's wife to Treece, whom she was rather inclined to blame for all this. 'Angry?' said Treece. 'He's livid.'

'Ah well, the young, you know, the young,' murmured the Vice-Chancellor's wife. 'Quite,' said Treece. 'Still, I must say I'm rather glad I'm not the head of his department.'

'Academic people chatter so,' said the Vice-Chancellor's wife. 'They're so articulate that one wonders simply how they do it. One wouldn't mind, one rather likes it, since one doesn't have to talk oneself; but one rather wishes one could *lie down*, just now and then.'

3

Treece had invited a few people back, that evening, to meet Willoughby, and when they returned, after nine, from dinner at the Vice-Chancellor's, there they all were, on his doorstep, shivering and rubbing up against one another to keep warm.

They entered in a group and, Treece observed with alarm, Willoughby at once and without invitation disappeared upstairs. Who would follow? wondered Treece. Willoughby had been behaving quite oddly in the car coming back; there was a crowd, and someone had to sit on someone's knee, and of course Viola sat on Willoughby's. Then somehow, from under Viola, Willoughby had managed to produce a hip-flask and 'Anyone care for a snort to wash his mouth out, after *that*?' he asked. He then went on to tell stories about what a poor teacher he was, always forgetting to bring books into class and failing to mark essays and dropping off to sleep in tutorials. 'Have you ever thought of taking up writing full-time?' asked Treece, again rather naughtily, since he was patently seeing the matter more from teaching's point of view, than from writing's. 'Where would he get his material?' asked Viola with a laugh; it wasn't, however, the sort of thing that Treece could laugh at. Being transmitted into art was not, he was sure, his function in life.

Viola set to work and made some hot cocoa, to thaw out Treece's guests, and they all forgathered in the drawing-room, expectantly waiting, positively poised ready for, the return of Carey Willoughby. They all had questions. Jenkins had expressly asked to come, in order to see an angry young man in, as he put it, the flesh, and observe his social motivations; it wasn't a chance that came up every day. Oliver was there, because he knew Willoughby; they had once met in the office of the Literary Editor of the *Spectator*, as they picked books from the shelves for review: somehow Oliver never seemed to have got any of his reviews, though he was always writing them, actually into print. Tanya was there, because Viola had invited her. Professor de Thule and his wife, Mavis, were there, and Mavis was already waxing garrulous. Treece, listening with half an ear and watching the stairs for the famed descent, reflected with growing horror how defenceless these people all would prove when faced with Willoughby, always supposing he came down and joined them. He took Viola aside, and asked: 'Do you suppose he's gone to sleep up there?'

At this moment the telephone rang. 'It's me, Bates,' said a voice when Treece picked up the receiver. 'I've searched the station from end to end and he simply isn't here.' 'Of course he isn't,' said Treece. 'He's here.' 'When's he going to talk?' asked Bates. 'He already has,' said Treece. 'All right, was it?' asked Louis. 'A virtuoso performance.' replied Treece. 'Who introduced him?' 'I did,' said Treece.

'Well, I'd like to meet him,' said Bates.

'Well,' said Treece, 'I don't know. . . .' The truth was that Treece simply did not feel like handling Bates at this hour and in this context.

'I invited him, after all,' said Bates.

'Very well,' said Treece. 'Come up.'

Treece put down the receiver wearily, and returned to the drawing-room to see whether Willoughby had reappeared. He had not. 'It's marvellous what a bassoon can do for a sick man,' a lecturer from the Music Department, who had a theory that music could cure physical illness, was saying. 'And those little red Chinese hats, weren't they charming; I just love Disney,' uttered the high virginal voice of Mavis de Thule.

Willoughby now put in his appearance, and all conversation

stopped short, as people observed a phenomenon which, while not much in itself, was clearly made of the stuff of drama. Stuart Treece was standing by the fireplace, looking towards the doorway, and Willoughby stood framed in the entrance where all could see him. His head was bent and he was staring down at his feet. Nor was he the only one; Professor Treece, equally, was staring, with rapt attention, at the feet of Mr Willoughby, of the new movement. People all looked at the feet; there was little apparent in them that deserved close study. They looked back at Treece. For a moment more he appeared speechless; then under the force of some powerful emotion, which he was clearly trying to control, he asked: 'Aren't those *my* shoes and socks, Mr Willoughby?'

'Yes,' agreed Willoughby.

'Did you take them?'

'Well, how else would they get down there?' asked Willoughby reasonably. 'I found them in a drawer upstairs. My feet were wet. My shoes let water in. They're no good. I've put them in the furnace.'

'And your socks too?'

'And my socks too,' agreed Willoughby. 'Why, for goodness sake, you don't *mind*, do you? What is man in this world for, if not to help his fellows?'

'My name's Mavis de Thule,' said Mavis quick-wittedly; she had been brought up on the importance of social tact, which was probably why her husband had got his chair. 'We haven't met yet.'

'Hullo,' said Willoughby.

'Tell me, Mr Willoughby,' said Mavis, tapping him on the chest with a forefinger; Willoughby looked at the finger with fascination, as if he was considering biting it. 'I mean, I've always wondered, where do novelists get their ideas *from*? What sets things in motion, you know?'

'Fruit-salts,' said Willoughby.

'Oh, don't be like that with *me*,' said Mavis winsomely. 'I really want to know. I mean, it must be awfully exciting to conceive a book that you know is a masterpiece.' This was rather clever for Mavis, and it even worked.

'You never know that,' said Willoughby, 'and really you never know where the idea actually came from, or how much of it you actually had when you started to write. It's like conceiving a baby; babies really start when the woman first drops her glove.'

'My God! We must be careful,' said Tanya, who was standing by. 'So that is how babies start.'

'You write because you're a writer,' went on Willoughby, at the same time taking a surreptitious look at Tanya, and being impressed; 'what you write about is incidental, just simply what your world happens to be. I write about universities because I work in a university and I can collect the stuff....'

'What's this I hear about your novels being *romans à clef?*' interposed Professor de Thule.

'Oh, everyone thinks he can identify people in these books. He can't of course. I'm not a fool. I like to keep my friends. I can't afford to lose any more friends. A man needs friends. It's simply that my novels are about people who exist in such multiplication in our world.'

'Oh, I hope you won't put *us* in, then,' said Mavis.

'What Mrs de Thule means', interposed Tanya, 'is that she hopes you will put us in.'

'Now would I tell you?' asked Willoughby, feeling warmed by all this attention. The group grew larger.

'Oh, dear,' said Mavis, laughing appreciatively. 'You know, people, we shall all be in a best-seller and the whole world will laugh at us.'

'Ah, a sad fate,' said Tanya ironically.

'Not the whole world,' said Willoughby. 'Have you ever considered what a lousy proportion of the public ever actually *read* my books? And of that small proportion, what a small proportion actually buy them? Have you read any of mine?'

'Both,' said Mavis promptly. 'And I thought they were awfully good.'

'And did you buy them or get them from a library?'

'We have a very good library in town, so there was no need to buy them.'

'No need?' cried Willoughby. 'If you liked them, why not

reward me, make sure I write another one? You talk about being in my next one. What next one? I work at a full-time job like you. . . .'

'Yes, Willoughby, where do you find the time?' asked de Thule.

'I *make* it,' said Willoughby. 'I work hard. If everyone in this room bought at full price a copy of my novels, and everyone else in every room that contains so-called intelligent people, who could claim to be interested in this sort of thing, I could write full-time.'

'Would you say, then,' asked Jenkins, 'that this was broadly why you are angry? Let me put it another way: do you find that the material rewards and status claims available to writers seem to you inferior, and a source of frustration therefore? Actually I'm just testing out a little theory. . . .'

The doorbell rang. It was Louis Bates. Treece went to let him in, and introduced him to Willoughby. 'I've been looking for you,' said Bates. 'I've been looking for *you*,' said Willoughby; Louis looked very pleased. 'You owe me two quid.'

'What for?' asked Bates.

'You don't think I'm going to pay my own train fare for the privilege of talking to you boys, do you?' asked Willoughby.

'This place', remarked Mavis, 'is turning into a bourse.'

Willoughby overheard this remark and turned to face Mavis. 'You people,' said he, 'you don't know what it is to have money matter to you, because you have it. I used to go into cafés, once, and have a meal and then walk out without paying, because if I hadn't done that I would have starved. There was one thing you could always do, if you were really bad; there was a photographer who took special pictures for homosexuals, and he'd help you if you'd oblige. But that sort of question doesn't occur to you at all. Does it ever occur to you that your comparative civilization, if that's what it is, is a condition of your freedom from financial embarrassment?'

'I think this point is clear to us all, dear Mr Willoughby,' said Tanya. 'But because we do not want for money is no reason that we should be ashamed of our civilization. I happen to think it important that we have it. But then, you see, I lived somewhere where it would have mattered had there been more civilization and less people who thought as you do.'

'I agree with him,' said Louis Bates, and he turned to Willoughby. 'That's why you can't have the train fare. The society will see to that. Do you know how much I have left, after paying for a taxi down to the station to meet you, when you weren't even there? Eightpence.'

'Hell,' said Willoughby, and it was clear that he was touched, unbelievable as it seemed to all about. 'Forget about the train fare. You get it from the society and keep it. I know how poor some of you boys are. Anyway, it didn't cost me anything. I came on a platform ticket.'

People were beginning to feel that it was time that Louis was weaned away from the guest of honour, and Professor de Thule popped up at Bates's elbow. 'Do you have any other speakers lined up as delightful as our guest of this evening?' he asked. 'I'll be with you in a minute,' said Bates. 'I just want to ask him to look at some poems of mine.' He did, and Willoughby looked, and he surveyed Bates, up and down, and said that he would show them to an editor. Bates looked very pleased and asked Willoughby why he didn't get out of universities, among all these effete liberals, these jolly groves of *academe*, and into real life. 'The danger of too much criticism really is, isn't it, that it tends to destroy creative activity altogether in the critic, by making him too self-conscious about his task? Whereas I write a shocking poem and think a lot of it at the time, and keep on doing that until I turn out something better.'

Mavis de Thule set to work on Willoughby. 'Isn't this a splendid sideboard?' she said. 'You don't have to say that to me,' replied Willoughby. 'I don't live here – it's just so much firewood to me.' He turned back to Louis Bates.

In a corner, Stuart Treece was talking to Oliver about his friends of a few evenings before. 'How did you meet these people?' he asked.

'Well, what we do, people like us, is, when we see someone who looks interesting, we go up to them and say, "You look interesting; what do you do?" You see, I'm interested in people of that sort. I suppose it all started with the milk-bar habit. I used to go into milk-bars, and one day I got talking to a group of three or four people, who just talked. What I mean is, if there was any subject that came up, they knew something about it. They read all the time. They knew something about everything. It wasn't particularly good talk, but it was exciting. And then there was another thing about these people that fascinated me even more. They didn't work. I couldn't understand this. I couldn't see how people managed without working; I'd never really known anyone who had. But it's all quite simple really: how it's done. You simply don't work. And everything follows from that.'

'What struck me about them, really,' said Treece, 'was their cruelty. They seemed so careless of people.'

'To you they would seem that. They're many of them self-destructive, and, like most self-destructive people, they see to it that their fate is shared; they destroy other people. But then they're so creative as well, creative of ideas, I mean. I've known running conversations that have gone on for months, every night from eight till four the next morning, about the relation between the finite and the infinite, or about Schopenhauer or Nietzsche. A lot of them became interested in German philosophy during the war, because, of course, none of them was in the Army, because they got out by taking a hundred aspirins or affecting to be homosexuals. They weren't identified with the war effort, so they went the other way. A lot of them really wept, this is true, when Il Duce was hanged. What surprises me is how underground this strain of thinking, which is all perfectly connected and rather widespread, or was, manages to be. In America it would have all been written up a thousand times. Here there's just Colin Wilson, Stuart Holroyd ... that's the kind of preoccupation.'

'Bates is like this, isn't he?'

'Yes, of course,' said Oliver, 'except that one of the conditions of this life is a certain kind of failure; whereas Bates is just a bit successful.'

Across the room Willoughby, going to refill his glass, claimed that he had trodden on Mavis de Thule's foot and wanted to apologize. 'It wasn't my foot,' said Mavis sweetly. 'Of course it was your foot,' said Willoughby. 'I trod on your foot and I want to apologize and by God I'm going to apologize.' Mavis de Thule looked frightened. 'Perhaps it was Dr Jenkins's here's foot,' she suggested. 'No,' said Willoughby, 'it was your foot. Why lie about it?' Elsewhere in the room Bates was suggesting to Viola Masefield that they all have a play reading.

'What was the name of the chick with the big behind who sat on my knee in the car?' asked Willoughby, coming up to Treece.

'Who do you mean?' cried Treece.

'The girl that teaches in your department,' said Willoughby.

'That was Dr Masefield,' said Treece. 'She's our seventeenth-century man.'

'I liked her,' said Willoughby.

'She has amazing critical acumen,' said Treece. 'An intellect at once malely strong and femalely sensitive, if you follow me.'

'I'm just an old-fashioned kiss, touch, and smell man, myself,' said Willoughby. 'But thanks.'

He went off and talked to Viola, who was taking round drinks on a tray. After this he disappeared altogether. At one point he was noticed in the garden by Mavis de Thule, who threw up the window and cried chattily, 'Why, what are you doing out *there*, Mr Willoughby?' 'Having a piss,' said Willoughby, as chattily.

Treece now found himself detained by Tanya. 'Aren't you going to talk to me, Stuart?' she asked. 'Have we offended you? You don't come so often now.'

'No, Tanya, you're too sensitive,' Treece replied; he could say this because it so patently was not true.

'Viola is worried about you, Stuart,' said Tanya. 'She is very fond of you. She worries because she thinks you don't eat enough; she says you are looking ill. I tell her, if he is not sensible enough to put food in his stomach, then he doesn't deserve to be well. You *do* look ill, Stuart.'

'I feel a bit odd,' said Treece.

'You know, Stuart, you are a naughty boy. I am very concerned for Viola, and I don't want her hurt. She told me what had happened before. I told her she was stupid. I said, Stuart is a man who has no emotions whatsoever. All he will want now, after this, is to escape. He fears he is caught in something. He feels ashamed of himself. He doesn't like women; all that is a nuisance to him. He is more than any the sort you should stay away from. I know this seems cruel to you, Stuart, but there are other people to be thought of. I am not blaming you. But I tell you, I don't want any hurt to come to Viola. She is not as sophisticated, you know, as she seems. I understand your sort too well.'

'Isn't that a bit hard on me, Tanya?' asked Treece.

'Ask yourself that,' said Tanya. 'I am concerned with the other one.'

Willoughby, when last seen, had been talking to Jenkins about jazz. Now he was nowhere to be seen, and Treece, who was afraid he was probably writing up all the guests in a note-book somewhere, went off to look for him. It was not, however, a notebook he was engrossed with, but Dr Masefield; he was kissing her at the back of the cloak cupboard. 'Excuse me,' said Treece, 'but Professor and Mrs de Thule are leaving and wish to make their *adieux*.'

'Good,' said Willoughby. 'Now let's go out and find some jazz.'

'I don't think there is any,' said Treece shirtily.

'There is,' said Willoughby. 'This fellow Jenkins is taking us.'

'Bye-bye, Mr Willoughby, bye-bye,' cried Mavis de Thule, sticking her head into the cupboard.

'Bye-bye, ducky,' said Willoughby.

4

The following morning Treece rose at seven and stoked the boiler, so that Willoughby could have a bath. As they had been retiring for bed at three o'clock that early morning, Treece had asked Willoughby: 'Would you like your bath now or in the morning? I ask because if you have it in the morning, it means I shall have to get up at seven and stoke the boiler.' Willoughby did not even have to think about the answer to this one: 'I'll have it in the morning,' he said. Treece then went back to bed, and read for an hour; then he got up again and went along to Willoughby's room to rouse him. He entered the room in some trepidation, for angry young men seemed to have some special kind of short shrift with guest rooms, which obviously symbolized something odious about hospitality; in one novel he had read the hero had burned the linen with cigarettes, and in another he had taken down all the pictures and untacked the carpet and taken that up, and probably (Treece's recollection of the novel was imperfect) he had put them all in a pile and set fire to them. The room, however, seemed intact, and the only eccentricity apparent was that Willoughby was not in it at all. He had, Treece discovered on going downstairs again, spent the night on the sofa in the drawing-room, because he slept better on couches, and in his clothes.

'You can have your bath now,' said Treece pleasantly. 'Thank you,' said Willoughby, equally pleasant. 'But do I have to take a bath? I mean, you're not going to make me go through with this, are you?' 'Not if you don't wish to,' said Treece. 'That's entirely your affair.' 'Oh, you protocol boys,' said Willoughby. 'I know that phrase. It means: if you're going to persist in being a boor and a ruffian and an outcast, then I'm not going to blame you; but you realize that we all disapprove. Look, I don't *need* a bath yet.' 'What would you like for your breakfast?' asked Treece patiently, for it was too early in the morning even to bother about all this. 'Bacon and egg? If you'll tell me now, I'll go and cook it and you can lie in for a little longer.' 'Thank you. Bacon and egg then,' said Willoughby, equally patiently. Treece went and cooked the breakfast and returned to find Willoughby fast asleep, too deeply gone to be roused even. He went back to the kitchen and ate his breakfast. At one o'clock Willoughby was still asleep. He shook him hard, and woke him, and reminded him that they were due to leave at two for the Poetry Week-end. Merrick was taking them, and Viola, down in his car, a little red sports model that Merrick ran on his private income.

Willoughby sat up, and flattened his hair down with his hand, and there he was, ready. He went upstairs and presently Treece could hear him shouting down: 'How modest can you *get* ? Do you know there isn't a mirror in this house that comes down below the waist? That's why you never say anything. You're wondering all the time whether your bloody flies are fastened.'

Presently he came downstairs drying his hands on his handkerchief. Treece had intended that they go out for lunch, but Willoughby bridled and insisted on cooking a meal. He said a man should be able to cook for himself, and be self-contained. He went and looked over the food that there was in. 'Honestly, you live like some old spinster,' he said. 'All that front, and then at home you don't eat anything. You're what I call flabby genteel.'

It was a poor meal. And there was flour all over the drawing-room, from Willoughby's cake-making, and fat all over the kitchen wall. As they ate Willoughby took tablets and reflected on what he called 'the protocol boys', who, he said, 'made him want to puke.' 'All these bastions of tired morality; all these little books on Housman. Some day the big bang's going to come, and you'll all wonder what hit you. But you'll just look at one another and say nothing, because it sounds rather like the toilet flushing and no one mentions that. You know, I'd like to go back to the Vice-Chancellor's house and stick my head though the window and shout: "Life is *not* a bowl of cherries." Just that.'

'You mustn't identify me with him,' said Treece. 'His and mine are different worlds. We really have very little in common.'

'One always dockets old people together, I suppose,' said Willoughby. 'They're all one generation to me, I'm afraid. You know these old dons at Cambridge who sit over the port and say to one another: "Yes, there was someone once, wasn't there...." This sums up my seniors, and it's another way of life, these civilized old gentlemen amateurs, full of charm and kindness, so frighteningly pathetic, saying that literary criticism is horrid and offensive and still, now, talking about *Principia Ethica*. I wouldn't do there, you know. All sherries taste the same to me; they're all like cold tea. I only know two kinds of cheeses, mouse-trap and blue. I think it would be terrible to have to live in Sicily. I've never read Sainte-Beuve. I don't think that by not having a servant to do all those things of life that don't really matter I've lost everything. Nor do I think that by not being able to go to those old country house weekends of the early years of the century I missed the most brilliant and civilized gatherings of persons that ever existed. I know this shows on me. I'm not civilized, I'm no gentleman, I don't know a great many languages and I'm not erudite in any field, I respect that old sort of scholarship and love of learning, but it's no good to me. You see, that's how we're different.'

'Not so very different,' said Treece. But Willoughby did not hear this, for Merrick's horn sounded in the driveway. Viola was already in the car and Willoughby sat beside her. 'What are you talking about this afternoon, Carey?' she asked. 'God knows,' said Willoughby, settling in the car and putting one arm around Viola. 'Don't tell Him. Tell us,' said Viola reprovingly. 'Oh,' said Willoughby carelessly. 'I'll think of *something*.' 'Charming man,' said Viola, looking over at Treece; and she winked.

Merrick, sitting behind the driving wheel with his county cap on, looked a real *rat*. Viola once pointed out a profound truth about Merrick, and that was that all his friends had inflatable life-jackets. It could rain for forty days and forty nights and you wouldn't catch *them* bending. All they needed, as Viola pointed out, was *bullet-proof* inflatable life-jackets and they needn't have a care; all eventualities were catered for. Actually, of course, they had their life-jackets because to a man they all of them had dinghies, and went sailing at week-ends; but it was somehow appropriate that these people, the self-engrossed middle classes (the other side of the coin from the civilized liberal middle class that Treece saw as the salt of the earth), should be so guarded. However, the amusing truth about Merrick was that he was, in fact, vaguely communist. He was a walking personification of Jenkins's dictum that you could, always, have your cake and eat it. He was the enlightened landowner breeding lamp-posts so that the mob would have something to hang him on. And, as Treece expected, and feared, he did not make exactly a good impression on Willoughby.

It was a bright, sunny afternoon as they drove on through the Midland countryside, splashing through the water-splashes, roaring through the villages. All over England, in just such large country houses, once the homes of the nobility, as they were going to, associations of computing-machine operators and folk-dance societies hold week-end conferences, playing parlour games in the evenings and having practical jokes with lavatory paper in the dormitories. Mr Schenk, with his extraordinary organizational talent, had once again persuaded the A.A. to make large yellow signs, saying POETRY CONFERENCE, which they bracketed up all over the Midland counties. Unfortunately, on the same day, there was also a POULTRY CONFERENCE, and this was signposted too, and many an ardent poetry-reader that day ended up at the wrong house, amid clucking birds, while dung-covered farmers kept arriving at the poetry conference and slapping their leggings with riding crops.

At the entrance to the hall, Schenk and Butterfield were waiting to greet them, looking rather frightened as they weighed up Willoughby and wondered whether today was going to be better, or worse, than yesterday. Willoughby removed his arm from around Viola's neck and got out of the car. Willoughby was speaking that afternoon, and Treece the following morning, while the afternoon was given over to a Brains Trust which included on the platform Willoughby, Merrick, Viola, and Treece again.

At three o'clock Willoughby's lecture began. He commenced by standing up and asking if anyone had a copy of the collected verse of Wallace Stevens. No one had; the first blood was to Willoughby. He went on to announce that his subject for the afternoon was: were artists, and particularly poets, insane? There was a splutter of applause from the audience, who were all poets, and would have hated it if people had not thought they were insane; that is, *they* knew they weren't, but they liked for the common man to think that they were. Willoughby then began to talk about Philoctetes, a social discard, marooned on a desert island because he had been so socially dissolvent as to have a wound in his foot that stenched abominably. He was marooned by his fellow Greeks on the way to the Trojan War, and ten years later they found that they needed Philoctetes' magic bow, given him by Hercules, in order to finish off the war. Willoughby was clearly talking about his own symbolic foot (he said the wounded foot was a castration symbol, and that Henry James had a bad leg, an important fact to remember when you read his work; but Willoughby did not look very castrated to Treece), and he told how crafty old Ulysses, a great businessman, had come to the island and tried to bargain with Philoctetes for the bow. Treece knew that Willoughby was getting all this from a book by Edmund Wilson, and he hoped that Willoughby was at least going to credit his sources (the first thing Treece had been told in the academic world, as a simple freshman, had been: a gentleman always credits his sources). Finally, said Willoughby, Ulysses had had to accept the wound with the bow, the wound as a condition of the bow, for the thing that made Philoctetes abhorrent and separate from other men also made him powerful. . . .

'Why?' demanded a woman with a flower-pot hat – the woman with the flower-pot hat, in fact. 'Why does the bow go with the wound? Why didn't Ulysses wait until he was asleep, and take the bow, and leave him on the island?'

Willoughby stepped back as if struck; now they had upset him, you could tell. 'This is the last time I do you an analogy,' he said bitterly.

'Well, it's right, isn't it?' cried the bronzed Woman's Journal woman, stirring Treece's soul by her very presence and action.

'What a low-down lot you are,' said Willoughby. 'But of course, that's what people would do these days. Do do. Who'd be an artist these days? You're like a pack of vultures. Have you ever seen it when a poet dies? It's like a night of long knives. He wasn't a good man, he was rude, he was promiscuous. . . .'

This was all just his kind of thing. The audience, pleased that he was insulting them again, just like yesterday, nodded in agreement. They were all in fact civilized, human, goodhearted people who, had Philoctetes come to them with a bad foot, would have bathed it, and not even *mentioned* that it smelled, and put him in their car and driven him down to Dr Scholl's shop, and paid for the treatment. If only, you felt of them, Van Gogh had been alive, so that they could have sewn his ear back on.

It was a hot day; flies buzzed in the air. Treece coddled his knees in his arms and smiled at the members of his poetry class who were there and who noticed him. He waved cheerily to Emma, who was present and sitting on the other side of the room. A few people in the audience were peering out rather uncomfortably through the windows at the parkland beyond. Willoughby was not having this: 'Listen,' he cried and the errant heads swung back. Willoughby was making so much noise now that gardeners were peering curiously in at him through the long Georgian windows. Treece's mind began to drift away into more glorious spheres; there was no place for militancy in his view of literature. For Treece literature's function lay here: as a humanist he pursued the record of experience as he pursued experience itself, seeking to distil from it more searching exploration of the human fabric, to chart new worlds in the universe in which human sensations are played out; he looked searchingly into the ocean to see what sort of channel was made by the human passage across the world. All that Willoughby said of literature was not of *his* literature at all. But in feeling the challenge, he also felt the failure. He had not learned very much. His passage had left nothing. He had never really come to grips with the world, after all. And now it was getting rather too late.

Willoughby was closing, now, still talking of how the world paid out its maladapted ones, for the fact was, he said, that society regarded cultural things not as living appurtenances of its world, but as dead things, museum pieces, and it would rather have the work of a dead artist than a living one; people paid a king's ransom to buy pictures by painters who had been left starving by their contemporaries. His point was that the world was mad, and the artist sane; but all madmen think this, and likewise all artists. He read from a letter of Van Gogh's, when he had nothing and expected nothing. Nothing was, he said, what he got. Van Gogh *was* mad, yet everyone who looked hard into his pictures found in them the most painful kind of sanity. The words of the letter ran: 'How can I be of use in the world? Cannot I serve some purpose and be of any good? How can I learn more and study profoundly certain subjects? You see, that is what preoccupies me constantly, and I find myself imprisoned by poverty, excluded from entering on certain work, and certain necessary things are out of my reach. That is one reason for not being without melancholy, and then one feels an emptiness where there might be friendship and deep and profound affections, and one feels a hideous discouragement gnawing at one's very moral energy, and fate seems to block up all the instincts of affection, and a flood of disgust rises to choke one. And one cries out: "How long, my God?"' And yes, cried Treece within himself, how long? Life was a dry and cruel estate without love, without thought of the future, without care and responsibility.

And he looked across at Louis Bates, who, along with several other students, was present just for the afternoon, and he thought of Willoughby's cry that the artist's madness was grown out of the most painful kind of sanity. Bates did not look harrowed; he approved of what was said, as his applause showed, as if he actually knew that what had been said would vindicate him. He realized that Bates had seen something in the discourse other than what he had seen; that what lay before *his* eyes was of the romantic figure of the poet, Shelley-like ... no, Christ-like. This was not what Willoughby meant, Treece felt sure; he was talking of the lot of the plain and ordinary man who carries the burden of being an artist, not of the great soul and the huge spirit.

Butterfield rose and asked for questions. A lady from the poetry society thanked Willoughby for the good advice about being a poet. What she wanted to know was, did he think there were enough openings for poets to publish nowadays, what with *John o' London's* ending and all? This was how all poetry society meetings ended, in Treece's experience. Willoughby asked the audience if they were not living in a fool's paradise. There were, he said, more poets actually writing poetry than there were reading it. He asked why they didn't just give up and go home. With this thought, they all dispersed for their tea.

Treece retired to his room after tea in some upset. He felt himself assailed by a violent unrest, a positive physical discomfort, a sense of loss, though he could not say what was lost or whence the feeling came. It was a sense of having uprooted himself and cut himself off from any vigorous way of life, this, and an oppressive loneliness. He realized that the last few days and weeks had passed in a kind of arduous, strained state, in a painful intensity; he could scarcely remember what he had done over these weeks. He felt challenged; he needed somewhere to turn, someone to love. He crossed over to the mirror and looked at himself, and was impressed by some change in his appearance: his face seemed strained, his eyes puffed, and his hair drier and rougher than usual; there were rather a lot of white hairs. He was sure he was ill, and that the illness, if not physical, was then mental. For weeks he had been threatened with a kind of paranoic depression, in which the universe seemed to him unerringly hostile and all persons appeared creatures fully separate from himself yet in communion with each other; they were *there* and here, alone and unwanted in their counsels, was he. Events conspired with persons to belittle him. He thought of the previous evening, when he had been the odd man out, sitting with his back to the others and sneering up his sleeve at the jazz-lovers. He thought of his hideous sense of incapacity on the evening when Eborebelosa had been attacked. How unlike people seemed to him, how great the immense human estrangement, how little they shared any common ground, how momentary and evanescent their contacts as they passed and repassed each other. And how he wanted to see that his fate was shared. Treece was sufficiently under control to see that this sense of intense dislocation was not a normal condition of his human relationships, but an exaggerated form; his depression was, he felt, psychotic. The prevailing sense of a conspiracy, which disturbed him most, the feeling that fate and persons were organized together to achieve his personal downfall, that everything was working actively and deliberately against him, was paranoic; he knew it was and yet, he found himself insisting, wasn't it true, wasn't it true?

In the evening there was a poetry reading; then they played parlour games, in one of which Treece found himself, for no good reason that he could recall, wrapped from head to foot in toilet paper and swaddled like a mummy, and then released again. He endured all this in a decidedly grudging spirit and wished that, like Butterfield and Willoughby, he had had the good sense to sneak off to the nearest inn when the poetry reading ended. Finally, he managed to get a moment alone with Emma. He took her outside, and they walked down to the pub. It was a warm night. He said: 'Will you come up to my room tonight?' 'Oh Stuart, how can I?' cried Emma. 'It's terribly risky. Someone will see me.' 'Of course they won't,' said Treece. 'They're all very tired. They'll sleep like logs. And you can say you're going to the toilet. You're in a single room, aren't you?' 'Yes,' said Emma. 'Well, I'll come there then, if you won't come to me,' he said. 'It's very important, you see. I want to talk to you.' 'Very well,' said Emma. 'I'll come to yours.'

It was after one when she came. Treece lay fully dressed on the bed smoking, eaten by his ungovernable depression. 'I know this was foolhardy,' he said when she was there, 'and it was hard for you. I'm sorry. But I just had to see you, Emma. I want to marry you.'

'Why, Stuart,' cried Emma surprised. 'Whatever put *that* idea into your head?'

'I don't know. Willoughby, I suppose. You know, I never really thought that new men could happen to me. I always felt that mine was the last generation. But it's not, is it? I'm middle-aged, and set in my ways. I'm nearly forty. I can't even cook myself a proper meal. And Willoughby can, and he's in his twenties. I feel so painfully lonely. I suppose I always wanted to settled down, but just never knew how you did it. I've never possessed anything. Every stage of my life up to now has seemed a temporary arrangement, that didn't warrant purchasing or possessing, but hiring and borrowing. Not to have *love* – that's the most terrible thing. Not to be loved by *anyone*, or to have any love of your own and spend it in the world. I mean, the love we give to women is part of the force of passion we have for the world. Don't you think?'

'Yes, I do,' said Emma. She sat silently for a moment on the bed.

'Well?' said Treece.

'Well, what?'

'Will you marry me?'

'Stuart, I'm very flattered, but I can't,' said Emma. 'You don't want to marry *me*; you just want to marry. I'm a perfectionist. I can't make do with that.'

'But, Emma . . .'

'Please, Stuart, it isn't any use,' said Emma. 'You mean a very great deal to me. I admire you in the way you like to be admired and I pity you in the way you like to be pitied. I don't mean that cruelly; this is what we share. But you don't even like me, Stuart, not *me*.'

'Of course I do. I find that quite absurd,' said Treece.

'I know you do, because you don't understand it, but it's true. Do you know, you've never talked to me. You've never told me a thing that you think or feel. I don't know you any better than I did that evening at the Christmas Ball. Why do you keep yourself so apart? Why don't you trust people? What's this great sacrifice you make when you consent to be with me? We went down to the pub this evening and what did you do? You didn't ask me what I wanted; you just bought me gin and tonic because I always drink gin and tonic.'

'What did you want?'

'Gin and tonic,' said Emma, 'but I also wanted something else; I wanted to be asked. And then, we have never had one scrap of life together outside my bedroom. There are no cultural experiences we can remember about *this*. We've never existed together. And something else, Stuart, have you ever thought how insulting it might be to me that you can't wait to get out of the door when you've been to see me. You see, your feelings must seem to you so much rarer and richer than anyone else's. I feel too, you see; we all feel.'

'I don't know why I was like that,' said Treece. 'It bothered me. It wasn't quite of my volition. I just felt I must get away. I felt that if I didn't something fatal would happen.'

'Yes, it might; I would have asked you what you were thinking; I would have wanted to *talk*. You know you *never* enjoyed it, you never enjoyed me. You never *do* anything. You always look as though you pretend you're not here. You never look at me. You've never planned one event for us. You've never had anything laid on. What there was to be done, I did. You had to have everything suggested to you. A woman needs more than that. She needs to feel safe with a man. Do you know what sticks with me most? You've only, *ever*, used my Christian name once, before tonight, when we've been together. I thought you'd forgotten it, and were afraid to ask me. I've only once existed as a person to you. That was once, in the Town Hall gardens, when you first asked to kiss me. I said there was nothing special about me and you said: "Emma, there is." I think you meant it, but whatever it was you saw in me, you've forgotten it.'

'Believe me, that's just not true,' said Treece.

'Oh, I don't know, Stuart; perhaps it's not, but it's too late now.'

'You're so unfair,' cried Treece, 'because it simply hasn't been like that. Why, I *need* you. I can't live without you.'

'I know you need me, Stuart,' said Emma, 'and that's why I stay with you, because you'd be so lost without me. I enjoyed feeding you. I'm always pleased to see you eating, and being looked after. You need me more than anyone I ever met; you *need*, just into the void. I truly wish I could say that that were enough. But the simple and honest and open truth is that for me it isn't.'

'I suppose everything you say about me is the truth,' said Treece slowly. 'I'm simply parasitic on other people and compelled to be so by a force I can't even explain, a lack of responsibility to other people and an inability to form proper relationships. And it's so cruel, because responsibility and relationships are the things I believe in so deeply; they are all there is. I've always believed, you know, in my own goodness, and thought I could never do anything wrong in the things of love. Yet it seems to me that I have.'

'I'm sorry, Stuart,' said Emma. 'I didn't ever mean to say this. I thought things would work themselves out and you'd find someone who could really give you what you wanted and whom you might even love. But I couldn't help thinking it. It's different for a woman. Suppose I were pregnant? Then what? What would you do then?'

'Are you?' cried Treece. 'Is *that* it?'

'No, I'm not,' said Emma.

'I believe I wish you were,' said Treece. 'This *is* a great reversal.'

'Oh, that's cruel, isn't it?' said Emma. 'You hope that in order to bind me to you when I don't want to be bound.'

'It's not really that,' said Treece. 'Pregnancy is such a great lesson in the laws of cause and effect; it's a lesson one needs to learn. That's why women see things so differently.'

'I think that's rather horrible,' said Emma. 'Who bears the lesson?'

'I didn't mean that,' said Treece. He took her hand. She gave no response. He said: 'Emma darling, I think you are the one person in the world that I *trust*. I do mean it. I don't feel a wild sort of love, I admit. But I want to be with you, and have you there.'

'You'll find someone,' said Emma.

'I don't want someone. I want you,' said Treece. 'You see, there were all those other things that we couldn't forget. Louis Bates and Eborebelosa. . . .'

'Why don't you forget about those two? You can't do everyone's living for them,' said Emma. 'Really, Stuart, you're hopeless.'

There was, suddenly, a knock at the door. Treece could not stir. 'Let me in, Stuart honey,' said a voice; it was Viola Masefield's. Treece sat still in an access of bewilderment. 'Open the door, Stuart,' said Viola; 'it's cold out here. It's I, it's Viola.'

'Will you open it,' asked Emma, 'or shall I?'

'Believe me,' said Treece desperately. 'This wasn't arranged.'

Emma said nothing and opened the door.

'I see,' said Viola.

It was all too much for Treece.

'My fault,' said Viola, and turned to go. 'I know where I'm not wanted. Maybe I'm stupid or unfair, though, Stuart, but it was too much for me to expect you to tell me? Don't you think you're rather a mess? The thing is, Stuart will accept anything. He's a sort of dustbin of experiences, aren't you, Stuart?'

'I thought you were rather keen on our friend Willoughby,' said Treece desperately.

'Any woman can do what she likes with Stuart,' said Viola contemptuously to Emma. 'Anyone can. She has only to be cruel to him and he thinks she doesn't like him. She has only to tempt him and he'll fall. He's one of those people who ponder all the time about human relationships, and then leave the others to act. He simply responds to whatever's tossed in his path. You can play with him so easily. But there's nothing to bite on; when you seek more, there's nothing there ... nothing there at all.'

To Treece it was the situation, rather than this statement, that made all this almost more than he could bear. As he contemplated the situation he recoiled from the horror of it; it expressed itself to him in these terms, and when they had both gone, and he was left alone, he found the pain of it all suffused him so much that he could have cried.

5

On the Monday, Treece went down to the railway station to see Carey Willoughby off. They got on the bus and went upstairs. Willoughby had begged from Treece half a bottle of milk, which he had stuck in his haversack, and somehow the top had become detached, for the liquid slopped out and flowed in a white stream along the aisle and down the stairs. 'What's going on up there?' shouted the conductor. But this did not upset Willoughby.

They stopped off at a bookshop to get something for

Willoughby to read in the train. They saw copies of Willoughby's novels, which had very contemporary book-jackets with the letterpress in a *mélange* of type faces and sizes, so that it looked as though the designer had been practising for writing anonymous letters. 'If you'll buy them,' said Willoughby, 'I'll write in them; it might be a sound financial investment for you.' Treece said he had little money with him. 'You remember that scene in Sartre's *Age of Reason*?' asked Willoughby, putting down his raincoat and picking it up again with two volumes of the Scott-Montcrieff translation of Proust inside. 'What scene is that?' asked Treece, watching this aghast. 'Never mind,' said Willoughby. Now there were only six of the twelve blue volumes left on the counter. Now four. Now ... but one of the set was missing. This did not faze Willoughby; he asked the assistant about it. It was found elsewhere and Willoughby waited until she had gone and then stole that too. 'Culture should be freely accessible to all,' he said.

'I've often thought that my scruples about stealing books were the only thing that stood in the way of my being a really great scholar,' said Treece, trying to pass the matter off.

'It's quite simple,' said Willoughby. 'Look, fold up your raincoat like this . . .'

'Oh, no, really,' said Treece.

'Here, which Lawrence haven't you got?'

'*Etruscan Places*,' said Treece uncertainly.

'Right,' said Willoughby, and he went and did it with *Etruscan Places*. 'Now you try.'

'It's not a question of *how* to do it,' said Treece. 'I could find a *way*. It's a question of why – of finding a philosophical framework to put it into. At least you've achieved that, but I haven't, you see.'

'Really, you thirties men, you're all puff,' said Willoughby. 'Leavis was right; you're all arrested at the undergraduate stage.' Luckily, his books began to slip and they had to go out.

At the station Treece bought a platform ticket to accompany Willoughby on the platform; Willoughby bought one too. He got in a first-class carriage and sat down. 'Might as well be hung for a sheep as a lamb,' he said. He handed Treece his *Etruscan Places*. 'Thank you,' said Treece. 'For your next birthday,' said Willoughby.

The train began to move. 'Hey,' said Willoughby out of the window. 'What was the name of that chick with the big behind?'

'Do you mean Viola? Viola Masefield?'

'Give her my love, tell her I'm mad about her,' said Willoughby. 'And ... Oh!' he shouted as the train gathered speed and Treece trotted along beside, 'don't expect a nice, middle-class, bread-and-butter note, you know, because you won't get one.'

Treece walked slowly back down the platform. He felt terribly, terribly old, and quaintly set in his ways. He was of the old guard now. His visions, which he had cherished so sturdily, believing them absolutes, were going out now. Somehow his time had slipped by and they had gone beyond him, the new men; though whether things were better he doubted, though he tried hard to be fair. He went home, wrapped up *Etruscan Places*, and posted it, anonymously, back to the bookseller. He thought about the Proust, too, and looked up the value in a bookseller's catalogue and posted that too, in coin of the realm; it hadn't been his fault, but he was a liberal and had to carry other people's burdens if they hadn't got the capacity to carry them for themselves. If it didn't disturb Willoughby's conscience, then that was not Treece's affair; but he had been there and he had to square it.

CHAPTER NINE

I

A FEW weeks later a distinguished event took place in the world of letters; for the poems of Louis Bates that Carey Willoughby had taken off with him were published in a leading literary magazine. Emma Fielding had not spoken to Louis Bates for months, but when she read the poems she saw that they were, in a curiously detached and self-analytical way, *good*, and she determined to tell him so. She saw him next on the occasion of the Departmental Trip to the Stratford Memorial Theatre at Stratford-on-Avon, for each year in the late spring a block of seats was booked, and a coach hired, and the larger part of the department transported itself to Stratford for the afternoon and evening. Louis, who was liable to stomach disorders, arrived at the coach early in order to capture the most medically advantageous seat. It was a cool, clear morning, with spring much in the air. The coach filled up with students, in their summery clothes, carrying picnic baskets. It was as if they had all come out of hibernation newly; this was the sort of thing that charmed Louis, and he took off his long brown overcoat and tossed it gaily on the rack. Presently he noticed Emma getting on to the coach, her clothes pleasant, but not too elegant, her eyes dark but tired-looking, for she always seemed to be in a state of some nervous tension. She came up the coach and noticed him. 'Congratulations on your poems,' she said warmly. 'They were *good*.' 'Oh, I don't know,' said Louis, who did, and he added smartly. 'This seat *is* vacant.' She sat down and they began to talk, he telling her about how difficult it was to get clothes that really fitted him, how buses always made him sick, how hard it was to be of the poetic temperament. He had a kind of self-consciousness, it seemed to Emma, that made his conversation highly unnatural, as if he sought affection from every heterosexual discussion.

The coach moved off and away through the spring landscape.

In the front four seats, reserved for the members of the faculty, she could see Stuart's sleek head and, next to him, Merrick, while in front of them sat Viola and Dr Carfax. She felt painfully sorry for Treece. She had not seen him since the evening at the week-end conference; she was not sure whether, really, she had wanted to end it all so sharply, but it really had to happen.

It was one of those fresh days of spring when the thin sun lights up the dulled grasses and brittle hedges, bringing out birds and the early buds. 'It is most certainly a *smashing* day,' said a Pakistani student across the aisle from Emma. 'Yes,' said Emma. 'And I am much relishing the thought of seeing the work of Shakespeare. People find it odd that I, as a Pakistani, should study English. They ask: "Do you not think you are out of touch with the cultural tradition concomitant to this study?" I always reply: "That is a very interesting question, but you forget one thing: I am a human being, or if I am not, then I understand them. That is all that is necessary." You remember the tale of Nero, who built an immense palace, with gold and jewels and perfume always in the air. He said: "Now at last I can live like a human being." That is a very interesting story about human beings. Yet for him to live as a human being, many other persons were prevented from living as human beings, the people he taxed and made to work. So, then, I deduce, to live as a human being is to live as a god; therefore we must live as something less than human beings. Human beings are very rare things, therefore; most of us are just people. I am just people. But I understand human beings.'

'That's very good,' said Emma.

The bus stopped, for it was intended that the journey should include visits to churches of some interest. The dedicated ones examined the church fabric while a recalcitrant few examined the fabric of the public house. Some of these grew a trifle merry as the day wore on. Meanwhile, at each church Merrick would mount into the pulpit and give an account of the history of the building. As some of his audience grew more jovial his temper grew shorter. 'Damnation,' he cried at last. 'Don't you know how to behave in the House of God!'

They arrived at last at Charlecote, where they were to visit the house and where Merrick wanted to demonstrate an interesting rare stile. 'Here's something,' he said from the front of the coach. 'This uncommon stile. I think there are only about five of them in the country. It looks like part of the fence, yet it collapses at a touch to let the passer by through. Would you mind demonstrating it for us, Stuart?'

'Very well,' said Treece. He climbed down into the road. 'Now see if you can find it,' cried Merrick. Treece bumbled along the lane, but no stile could he see. Merrick got down and showed him. He returned to the coach and said that he was going to ask Treece to demonstrate how the stile worked. 'Push down,' cried he. Treece, taking his cue, heaved sturdily upwards. It wouldn't come. 'Push *down*,' cried Merrick again. Up, up, up Treece tugged. Finally, Merrick got down and showed him. Treece looked so miserable that Emma's conscience overflowed.

Now the flotilla proceeded along the long driveway into Charlecote. It was a high and civilized scene, with the house standing square at the end of the lane of trees and the deer and sheep grazing under the foliage, in the faint spring shadows. Here one could live like a human being. But to do so one must cut oneself apart from the rest, and be the one and only human being for miles around. The choice between the two ways of being a human being seemed to Emma to be the great dilemma. The parkland and the grazing cattle were a fundamental part of one's Englishness. It was the highest civilization of a liberal and refined race that was commemorated in this parkland and this house and this tamed countryside. There were two ways of being civilized: *that* way, which the world no longer permitted, and the way that one hoped would emerge when a whole race shared the benefits that once went only to a special few. For *this* way, someone had to suffer; a whipping boy had to be found. Humanity is hung around everyone's neck, but we seek ourselves to live in a kind of moral and human suspension; we appoint other people to be the victims. One never quite comes to care entirely for others, for they haven't *you* inside them, and *you* are a special case.

Emma, as the guide showed them about the house, felt a weight of blame, a kind of universal guilt for all the things ever been and ever done. She looked out over the landscape, by Capability Brown, and felt full of the pain of living when all that this stood for was simply a little corner in her very English soul.

2

What can one do, in a place as extravagantly English as Stratford, but take tea and then go on the river? This was what Emma had resolved to do. However, descending in the bright sun of the coach park, she found Louis at her ear; he was determined not to lose her now. He asked her what she was going to do, and she told him. 'Let me take you to tea,' he said, 'if I've got enough money.' He emptied out his pockets. 'I think so, if we don't have anything cooked,' he said. Louis tried to tempt her into a milk-bar, but she refused and said she was quite prepared to pay for herself; but she wanted to go somewhere more ... Elizabethan. They did, and Louis banged his head on a low beam; he really was a modern man, and Elizabethan houses were built for rather smaller people.

They ordered tea and cakes, and Louis began to giggle. 'What was wrong with Prof. Treece this afternoon?' he asked. ' "Pull it down," Merrick kept shouting, and there was Treece heaving upwards for all he was worth.'

'It wasn't all that funny,' said Emma. Louis looked up from his meringues – he had eaten five already – and saw her eyes, serious and intense, clouded with an abstracted and myopic look. But really, she thought, it *was* rather funny, Treece standing there, as if comprehension had drained from his finger-ends, heaving wildly upwards on the crossbar. She laughed and Louis, pleased, laughed too.

'It is funny, isn't it?' he said. Her ears, he noticed, were perfectly formed, small, neat, *powerful* ears.

'Do you know what we could do? We could go on the river,' said Emma. There were freckles on her cheek, warm, friendly, fragrant freckles.

'Is there time before the play?' asked Louis. Her face was lightly tanned, a vital, pregnant colour.

'Oh, two hours, more,' said Emma. She was not, then, exactly beautiful, but sweetly formed, and with faint defects, the freckles, the myopic eyes, which brought her nearer to him, so that contact seemed less impossible as one realized that one's own dental troubles, one's own impurities of the bloodstream, were shared by her too. But not to start that again. Ah, thought Louis, but there is nothing in the world a woman loves more than to sit with a man at a table for two and pour out his tea for him, while over the shining silverware they talk *intimately* and with a mutual fond respect; it is for them, felt Louis, one of the things of love. On this highly-charged reflection he picked up his bill and rose. Emma was a minx. She tortured him and made him perpetually miserable. A terribly refined relationship existed between them. This was the sort of thing that happened to persons of this sort, sensitives, who fought the world and always, in the end, let it win, because there was a lot more taste to defeat than to victory. Louis had been fighting reality for twenty-five years; now, by God, he thought he'd beaten it.

Emma slipped some money into his hand, and he paid the bill importantly. They went down towards the river, and Louis held Emma's arm, and carried her basket, and explained in her ear how he was adapting Andalusian guitar music for the flageolet, simply a matter, he said, of converting what is essentially a twang into a reedy sound, and how he wished he had his flageolet today so that they could have gone gaily downstream playing Handel's Royal Water Music. At the boathouse, the attendant said that the river was too full for punting, and so Louis chose a canoe, a mistake on his part, he realized at once, for if punts are amorous, canoes are chaste, and all he would get for his hour was a view of Emma's back. 'Can you swim?' asked the boatman. 'What now, in my clothes?' asked Louis. 'If you fall in,' said the boatman. 'N ...' said Louis and then felt a warning kick on his ankle from Emma. 'Yes,' he said. Louis clambered down into the canoe and then reached up to hand her into the craft, her body, standing above him, dress flat across her thighs at a level with his face, affording a sensation worth all Shakespeare's problem plays put together. The boatman handed down the paddles to them and with jerky strokes the boat rode gently out into the centre of the river. Ahead the full, still water slid greenly over the weir. 'Go the other way, Louis,' said Emma. 'There are swans up there,' said Louis nervously.

He turned the boat round and they moved back towards the theatre and under the bridge, where the swans gathered round them. 'You know what to do if they attack us, don't you,' said Louis heroically. 'Lie down flat.' As this might be mistaken, he added, 'Inside the boat.'

But they reached the backwaters of the river without mishap. Louis's paddle dipped and drove them forward in a series of uneven lunges; Emma's hand dangled over the gunwale into the chilly water, and she watched it stream away with flashes of silver from between her fingers. A few cows stood mournfully up to their knees in the river, and a water-rat swam from bank to bank, advancing in scarcely perceptible movement, with only its snout and bright eyes visible above the stream. 'Look!' said Emma. But Louis neither heard nor saw. He was exerting all his energies to pushing the boat onward, for they had only an hour and he wanted to get as far as possible in the time. Moreover, he was frustrated. He had his chance and could not use it, didn't know *how* to use it.

A faint mist hung in the air as the evening came up, and it beaded on the tender twigs of the trees and occasionally plopped in a depressed way on Louis's balding pate and he canoed wildly on, morose with passion. Cowardice was nibbling at his ankles; he wanted to forget the whole thing. He wished he was a man of action; he wished he could do things. I suppose, he thought, Hamlet was just like me. Of course, in a way, Hamlet *was* a man of action – look how he was always killing people. Not that Louis wanted to do this; he simply felt uncertain about what he wanted to do. Consider marriage, which was not, he felt, the happy end of an affair, but the sad beginning of a sentence; wasn't love better as a *condition*, a sweaty Turkish bath of feeling, than a chain of events that end in

229

bathos. No divine applause seemed to greet his excursions into the field of passion; in fact he knew by now that what the fates promised him in this direction was only disrepute; he had had this one out with them before. Why hold these emotional stock-takings, he warned himself; why not just continue with commerce and leave well alone? He shouldn't have acted, he knew he shouldn't; but he did. He tapped Emma on the shoulder.

'I like you more than you like me,' he said.

'How do you know?' said Emma.

'I've missed you, very much,' he said. The remark was a dangerous one; it corrupted her responses, as he saw. But he went on, more and more, worse and worse. It was like sinking into a bog; you kept going on a bit further, thinking you could still get out, but of course you simply couldn't. He pointed out, judiciously, that it is the human function to express itself in contacts with others. He added that he did not find it easy to get on good terms with women, but he had from the very first found himself at ease with Emma. He quoted Nietzsche, but as Emma did not speak German she missed out on this bit. He said that man and woman were separate entities, and that the man was Pride, and the woman Virtue; it was the Woman's function to submit her Virtue to the Pride of the Man. He debated this motion from both sides for a while. He contended that love was comfort, the supreme malt extract, the perfect hot water bottle. He simply asked Emma to submit her Virtue to his Pride. If she did not, she would hamper his sexual development, do him psychological harm, corrupt his future sex life.

'Don't,' said Emma. But Louis's voice went insistently on; she could not see his face, but simply hear this rational, pained voice. She could not turn round. They sat like passengers in a bus, both facing the same way, while Louis went on with his Nietzsche. 'I need you, Emma,' he cried, standing up in wild excitement. '"*Du gicht zu Weibe? Vergess deine ...?*"' he added, falling into the river. Emma turned in terror. 'Louis, Louis,' she cried. He had quite disappeared from sight beneath the waters. Presently his head appeared; wisps of his hair draggled down his face; something of his excitement still remained. He cried out – was it more German? – and his head went under again. It seemed that he had not realized what had happened to him. 'You're in the river,' cried Emma, wondering whether he could hear her down there. She was weeping with fright. He came up again. 'Kick off your things,' she cried, throwing one of the canoe cushions at him; it just missed his head and straightaway sank, never to be seen again. Then his head was above water again, and this, thought poor, frightened Emma, scrupulously keeping count, this was the radical time, the last chance. She thrust a paddle at him and he grabbed the end, almost pulling her into the water. Gradually she worked the canoe so that it was beside him and he grabbed the prow. The rest was easy; she paddled backwards to the bank and leapt out, careless of the mud, to drag him out of the river. There seemed such a lot of him to pull out. But at last he was on the bank, and alive, and kicking, for 'Loosen my clothes!' he cried exotically. There were few left to loosen, and she did what she could. He sat up, and looked at her, and began, all at once, to cry. 'You mustn't,' said Emma, for this was the worst thing of the lot. 'I'm such a fool,' sobbed Louis, 'such a fool.' It was a proper payment for his *hubris*, he knew. And as she watched him she felt more desperately upset about him than she ever believed she could; he was, that was the truth, but it was so wrong that he should himself *know*. Presently he stopped crying and borrowed Emma's handkerchief and wiped his face and blew the river out of his nose. 'I think', he said, trying to be brave, 'you'd better give me artificial respiration.' Water gushed out of his lungs.

Luckily he had taken off his overcoat in order to paddle, and this was still in the canoe, quite dry. Emma wrapped him in this and paddled him shivering back to Stratford. Here Treece proved a tower of strength, and hurried him to the hospital, where they kept him, though he insisted he didn't want to miss the play. It was his big day, and he really didn't want to miss it. And Emma, at the theatre, watching poor Malvolio, so serious and resplendent in his virtue, duped and outwitted, thought of Louis and tried not to feel angry that his fate had got so aggravatingly mixed up with hers.

and a mass of dirty ironwork everywhere. It was an unpleasant building. He was put in a lift and then pushed out again and he found himself in a large open ward. A lot of men lay aimlessly in bed. Most of them were old and seedy. A youth with big teeth sat by his bed in a dressing-gown and played weakly on a guitar. Treece was lifted off the trolley and on to a bed near the door. Two nurses came and put screens around him and got him into striped pyjamas that were much too big for him. Then after a while a sturdy and efficient staff nurse appeared with a trolley and a small bundle wrapped in cotton-wool, and took out a syringe and some small bottles. She then stuck the syringe in his arm at the elbow and extracted a large quantity of blood. 'I thought they were going to give me some back,' said Treece. 'Haven't you made a mistake?'

'If you can run this hospital any better than we can . . .' said the nurse. She went away, and Treece reflected that he was really not the type to be in hospital, it was obvious. In two hours he had got himself universally detested. He saw another nurse and signalled her. 'What have I got and how long will I be here and can you get a message out for me?' he asked.

'How should I know?' asked the nurse, and went away again.

The staff nurse went by again. 'Please,' said Treece, trying a different tack. 'May I talk to you for a minute?'

'This isn't a tea-party,' said the nurse.

Treece lay still for a few hours. Someone brought him some hot milk, and later a meal. He moped. He worried about his evening class. He worried about the lectures he was missing. He did not think that anyone knew where he was. There were about thirty people in the ward, in beds ranged on each side down the wall. They stared at him with unbridled curiosity. Someone came round and asked him if he wanted to bet on the races that afternoon. There was a loudspeaker blaring forth the Light Programme. They kept playing 'I was a Big Man Yesterday', a tune that Treece particularly disliked.

'Eighoop, youth,' said the man in the next bed. 'Eighoop.'

'Who?' said Treece. 'Me?'

'Yes,' said the man. 'What are't tha in for?'

'I don't know,' said Treece. 'They didn't tell me.'

'I thowt tha looked ill when tha was browt in,' said the man. 'I've been left for dead twice.'

'I see,' said Treece.

At Treece's other side was an old man who now cried: 'Mester, grab a hold of this.' He took a urine bottle out from under the covers and passed it to Treece. 'I can't reach the floor.'

'Where shall I put it?' asked Treece.

'Down there on t'ground,' said the old man. Treece leaned out and two nurses sprang up from nowhere and pushed him back again. 'I thought you were on complete rest,' said the strong-willed staff nurse.

In the evening, before supper, the young doctor whom Treece had seen first came round. 'Don't open your mouth', whispered the man in the next bed, 'or he'll make tha have all thy teeth out.' When the doctor arrived at Treece, he said to the sister, who accompanied him: 'I never saw anything like it in all my puff; he marched in here and started talking about God and wouldn't admit he was ill at all.' The sister laughed. 'May I have a word with you?' asked Treece.

'What is it?'

'Could you simply tell me what's wrong with me, and let someone know where I am?'

'Well, I'm afraid I can't simply tell you what's wrong with you, and if I did you probably wouldn't understand, but what it amounts to is that you appear to have some sort of ulceration in the stomach or the duodenum and might have another hae-morrhage at any time. We're going to give you some tests and X-rays and get a specialist to look at you. If you tell the sister whom you want informed, she'll see to it. Has he had a blood-test?'

'Yes,' said the sister.

'I think we'll give him some blood then, as soon as possible.'

Something about the manner of both doctors and nurses puzzled Treece, but after a while he began to discern what it was. It became more and more apparent to him that apart from

235

himself all the persons in the ward were working class, and not expectant of deference. Moreover, they were given to asking just such questions as Treece had asked, as anyone would ask, but they were not able to understand the answers. The need to convert all that was said into fairly simple terms had created a special kind of relationship, such as that which exists between parents and children, or the sane and the insane, a talking down on one side and a deference on the other. In the world of illness all were lost except those who worked here. This situation, which was not unacceptable to his fellow patients, Treece found unbearable. He was a man who needed to know, and knowledge was what was denied; he could not cope when facts were concealed from him and where the issues could not be rationalized. He lay in bed and was miserable.

In the evening he asked the man next to him: 'Where's the toilet?'

'Down at the end on the right,' said the man.

Treece got up and walked unsteadily down the room and into the mean little toilet. Here at least he could be for a moment alone. He stayed there for a few minutes and then suddenly he heard a loud voice in the ward cry: 'And where is Mr Treece?'

'Who?'

'The fellow that came in this afternoon.'

'He's in the sluice.'

There were heavy footsteps. Treece pulled up his trousers. Then the door of the cubicle was flung open and the strong-willed staff nurse said: 'And what do you think you're doing, if it isn't a rude question?'

'Using the toilet,' said Treece.

'Don't you know you're on complete rest?'

'There are some things one *has* to do,' said Treece.

'You can do them in bed,' said the nurse.

'Well, I didn't know that,' said Treece.

A chair was fetched and he was wheeled up the ward, in public disgrace. The nurse lifted him into bed. 'If I catch you out of here again', she said, 'I'll put you in a crib bed that you can't get out of.'

'I'm sorry,' said Treece.

'You'd better be,' said the staff nurse, with a laugh.

'I thowt tha shudna ha' got up, but it weren't none of my business,' said the man in the next bed when the nurse had gone.

'Well, really,' said Treece, rather annoyed.

At ten o'clock the lights were put out and immediately people began to cough and spew up and down the ward. 'Fetch me a bottle,' said the old man on Treece's other side.

'Oh no,' said Treece. 'I'm not allowed to move.'

The old man got up and sat on the side of the bed and urinated on the floor. Treece felt sure he would get blamed for this as well, but the night nurse came and mopped up and told the old man not to do it again. 'It's the only way to get a bottle,' said the old man with a clucking laugh.

Someone got up and went to the toilet and then tried to get into Treece's bed by mistake. In the top bed someone was groaning hideously. Behind the screen the night nurse was telling the runner about her love life and reading aloud to her from the case history. 'He isn't a professor, is he?' cried the runner. 'He doesn't look much like one to me,' said the night nurse. This was true, thought Treece, for he didn't look much like one to himself any more.

Throughout the night transactions of all sorts continued – some got up and began to run up and down the ward in hysteria, someone died amid sobs and groans, the old man in the next bed kept shouting that he wanted to go home – and Treece got no sleep whatsoever. He was in a drowsy stupor the next morning at 5 a.m. when the nurse came and washed him and rubbed surgical spirit on his behind. The day continued much as the previous one had done. In the afternoon Treece had a group of visitors: Dr Carfax, Merrick, Viola Masefield. Merrick was complete with umbrella. They all looked an impressive sight. 'We told them that we were all doctors – didn't say what of,' said Viola with a smile. 'They thought the place had gone mad. They think you're the Prince of Wales or something.' Merrick said: 'Are they looking after you all right? Pretty rum crowd you've got in here, haven't you?'

'I wonder what happens to middle-class people when they're ill,' said Treece. 'There are none here.'

'Why don't you go in the pay-bed wing?' asked Merrick.

'I don't want to,' said Treece. 'It doesn't seem right that one should.'

'Honestly, Ian,' said Viola. 'You come in here with that umbrella as if this were the London Clinic or something.'

'This wouldn't suit me,' said Merrick.

'It suits me,' said Treece.

'Well, tell us, Stuart, what have you got?' asked Viola. 'Stigmata?'

'I think it's some sort of ulcer . . .' said Treece.

'Oh, ulcers. That's very good,' said Viola. 'Did you see in last Sunday's *Observer*, where it said that only successful . . . But need I go on? Everyone see last Sunday's *Observer*?' Heads nodded. 'Some time I must make some friends who don't read the *Observer*.'

'What else is there for us poor Lib.-Labs.?' said Merrick. 'The *Sunday Times*, I suppose, but it keeps having editorials beginning: "Mr Macmillan has been proved right again." '

'How do you feel?' asked Viola.

'Miserable,' said Treece. 'I feel that when they made me, they botched it.'

'Serves you right for eating the things you cooked,' said Viola. 'No one else would have dared.'

They sat for a minute or two, trying to be cheery, but no one could think of anything to say. Then Dr Carfax told the story of the time when he was in hospital and had his appendix out, and the day after the operation he was visited by a Chinese doctor, who, as Chinese are wont, did not pronounce his plurals: 'Have you had your bowel open?' he had asked Carfax. And 'My God!' Carfax had, so he said, cried out in alarm, 'You haven't taken them out *too*, have you?'

Then they went. 'Take care of yourself, Stuart dear,' said Viola. 'Is there anything you want?'

'Nothing at all,' said Treece.

'Well, be good, and don't get Complications. They're much worse than Symptoms. Good-bye.'

'Ta-ta,' cried the man in the next bed, eyeing Viola with a warmed look on his face. 'Ta-ta,' shouted the other patients as they all went out. 'That your missus?' asked the man in the next bed. 'No,' said Treece; 'she's not.'

4

Life in hospital is not the boring and peaceful experience that many imagine it to be. While nothing of great interest happens, and the mind does grow stale and concern with outside things subsides into selfishness, the sort of selfishness one has on shipboard, when all links with responsibility seem severed, something happens all the time. In fact, as Treece complained to his nurses, life in hospital was so arduous that it was a pity it had to happen to sick people; at least they should let them go home, now and then, for a rest. From 5 a.m. in the morning, when he was roused, Treece was subjected to an endless battery of attentions. During the day, when he tried to sleep, he was roused and told that the nights were for sleeping. At night, when he tried to sleep, people vomited by his ear, and nurses woke him up to give him sleeping tablets. He was permanently tired. Doctors and specialists prodded and poked him, almoners came to ask if he had a suit, Legion of Mary girls to ask if he was a Catholic, other patients to ask him to make their wills, fetch them a bottle, write to their relatives, shave off their whiskers, hold bowls while they were sick into them. There were nurses of all nationalities who needed things translating. Physiotherapists came to read his *Times* and night orderlies – nearly all pacifists with high I.Q.s, who wrote verse in the linen store when they were not busy – to read his *Manchester Guardian*.

A stand was erected by his bed, a needle gouged into his arm, and the blood-drip began. It dripped on inexorably for two days and nights. And as the days passed slowly on and his contingency to the world seemed to disappear, he found himself increasingly listless and depressive. It was a world almost wholly uncongenial. Deprived of his society he seemed nothing, so much did he depend on his society for his existence; now he was a lump of flesh only. Believing in civilized and respectful contacts, deep personal relationships, honesty and integrity of motive, recognition of the individuality of persons, he was lost in a world where all that mattered was the simple physical constitution, the preservation of life itself, at whatever torture to the personality. The staff here were very hard-working – but to them the personality issue was often an excrescence, and even to some a nuisance. As the staff nurse had told Treece, it wasn't a tea-party.

This situation was a problem for Treece alone. For it seemed as if his special human situation had somehow sapped him morally, in the plain sense of the word moral, which demands a sound and simple capacity for living life itself. Outside his own environment Treece's vital force emerged as a small thing, that was weak in front of the most eternal human test, whether he was to endure or to die; there is a further edge to alienation beyond which one ceases to have a real place in the world; and Treece had found himself more and more pushed towards the fringes of the society he lived in, into a peripheral and invalid existence.

What was the poor little liberal humanist to do? The world was fragmented and there was no Utopia in sight, and as a liberal he was a symptom of the fragmentation he abhorred. He would not have been anything other – it was a special fate. He coddled his fancy scruples, and they were everything to him. The great authoritarian structure of the Christian Church had tumbled under the impact of just such honest scruples; and the eye of God, which was the eye of structured society, no longer peered and penetrated into every nook and cranny. Life, Treece would claim, was more real when you went on from God, and go on you had to in order to live fully now. Once the principle of doubt had been admitted all was lost, as far as He was concerned. Whether you believed or not, men now fluttered foolishly like young birds tumbled out of the nest, at their highest point of freedom and more glorious than ever before, yet on the edge of an ungovernable disaster . . . or so it seemed to Treece. He could not be sure whether this was a figment of his own depressed mind or a discernible fact in the universe. The fact remained that he was a scrupulous liberal, too scrupulous to believe anything, willing to make his mind up only on the evidence; and in the end what he had was really nothing. Of course, he preferred it this way. If the choice was between compromise and destruction, then he was willing enough to destroy himself. In any case, whether he lived chastely or lecherously, believed or doubted, it made no difference. Because he lived late in the world, and was a civilized creature, he stabbed as few people in the back as possible and did as little harm as he could. But there was nothing he really wanted to *do*. And life was no longer, for people like him, a thing to trust so deeply, because there were other things he trusted more; what was proper became less and less what was viable. He had no goods or chattels or causes or faiths – or loved ones – to tie himself to now, when it was of use to be tied. The moral passions can drive one too hard, until, as with Gulliver, home from his travels, ordinary life is hardly to be borne.

And Treece, to whom illness had always seemed a cruel and unfair chance that attacked randomly its victims, was now forced into taking the things of sickness into his consciousness for the first time. And it was a cruel, defeating thing, a betrayal of the human possibility, a canker in the self, that he saw – a betrayal, he came to feel, that was *internal*. It seemed to him as he surveyed his weakly self that for this he had only himself to blame. It was a facet of his own soul. It was a savage test to have to take, this one, worse than any driving test, and it showed up one's weaknesses mercilessly.

5

After Treece had been in hospital for a few days, and Emma, surveying the notices that declared, 'Professor Treece is unable to teach today', wondered what had become of him, she had a telephone call from Viola Masefield. It was to tell her that Treece was in hospital – they had she said, caught up with him at last. She thought that Emma might like to know, if she hadn't heard, and might even like to visit him; this was possible the following evening. Admission was by card, absolutely free, and if Emma wanted to go she would post a card on to her.

At the hospital, the following evening, Emma said, 'I'm sorry you're ill.'

'I never thought I'd end up like this,' said Treece. 'Did you?'

'I did,' said Emma. 'To be honest.'

'I always had such promise,' said Treece. 'I was a man of promise until last week. But one has to stop and do something, I suppose, and I did. I was ill. I suppose one thinks one lives in a state of moral suspension, praise or blame deferred, for ever. It's only the others who are guilty. Until at last the challenge comes.'

'But how long have you been ill?'

'For months, I suppose.'

'When did you have the first haemorrhage?'

'Just after the poetry week-end, after I talked to you.'

'But why didn't you tell me?'

'Well,' said Treece. 'It wouldn't really have been fair would it? One can't use one's illnesses as a kind of moral lever, and if I had told you, that's what I would have done. I would have said, "Look, I need looking after. Won't you marry me?" I want to say that now. You see how much I need you. I have no one. And when one's like this – you need to be tied to something, to have something to bother about getting better for. I hate to be left alone. I feel so depressed. I think I have a fragmented *gestalt*. . . .'

'But, Stuart, this just isn't a real situation. It's a distortion. How can one make a pure choice at a time like this? You're right; it wouldn't be fair.'

'No; I knew it wouldn't be,' said Treece. 'But you know, sometimes, just now and then, I don't *want* to be fair. I can't say it's ever *got* me very much. Not that one seeks that: one isn't like that in order to be self-seeking. But they say: virtue has its own rewards, and I know it does, yet from time to time I feel like shouting out, just like an angry young man: Well, let's *see* some of them. You must admit that the rewards of virtue grow less and less as the present society goes on.'

'But isn't the proverb: virtue *is* its own reward?'

'Then it's too sanctimonious for me,' said Treece. 'If one

242

takes delight in virtue, then it ceases to be virtue; it becomes self-seeking. I haven't even got that.'

'I'm sorry, Stuart. I feel very cruel to you. I keep *doing* this. I'm a hideous creature to fall in with. But I must do what's right. I'm too good at making other people suffer. I suppose one day I shall have to pay for it. I don't know how I have the gall to feel, always, so superior. Sometimes I feel so remote from other people that I find it hard to believe that they really do exist in the way that I do, as subjects rather than objects. All these people here think I'm mad, look, talking like this.'

'Be careful,' said Treece. 'I have to live with them! *You* can go home.'

'Oh, Stuart,' said Emma. 'I've been terrible to you. Can one lead a good life in this world? I mean, without doing too much harm, and retiring too much out of it, so that people you are involved with suffer? I suppose I have an image of some perfect human condition that one day I shall reach by finding someone I wholly and fully love. But what about the people one meets up to then, and what about the things one does to them?'

'I suppose everyone thinks his kind of innocence the ideal innocence, and the inside chambers of oneself richer and finer than anyone else's. I can't blame you. But you are involved in the world, and your actions have consequences for other people, and if you don't recognize that, then that's the supreme kind of cruelty. Everyone shares everyone else's fate to some extent.'

'I think we have a lot in common,' said Emma. 'I certainly never thought to hear you say that.'

'Why not?' cried Treece. 'Haven't I always? No, perhaps not. Still, one can't go on being a professional young man all one's life, even nowadays when being young counts for so much. But one can't live as amorphously as this for ever. That's why people convert to Catholicism, or become party members, or marry. At least they have a sense of identity and cause and effect. But I've never been under the usual compulsions; I haven't really ever had to settle down; I've lived largely outside ordinary responsibilities, like having to worry about money or property or what will happen to one's children. I don't have to guard my actions. Then suddenly I see myself as some ordinary person sees me . . . like the people in here. I have no real relationships with anyone, though I have this broad and firm faith in human relationships. I contribute nothing at all to them, though. I look for love and can scarcely find it in me. Everything turns to ashes. I *am* ashes.'

'It's a cruel warning,' said Emma.

'For you? Of course, it's different when you're young,' said Treece. 'The young have terrible advantages: they have enthusiasms, vigour, power, new eyes; they're never ill and nothing can tie them down for a while.'

'I'm not that young,' said Emma.

'So . . . it's no good?'

'We'll see,' said Emma. 'Wait until you're out and we'll see.'

When Emma left the hospital she had an appointment with another invalid. Louis Bates had been in hospital at Stratford with pneumonia, and had really rather enjoyed it. He had been for once the centre of the world; international diplomacy had been nothing, compared with the movements of his fingers and toes. Coming back to University and to his work, he had found the self-conscious and highly personal state of mind he had developed in hospital slow to subside. Up to now events had existed simply to be reflected in his bed; this was the point of concentration for the whole of human experience. It was just like sex, as he imagined it, only longer-lasting.

When she reached his room, uncomfortable and foetid, Louis lay in his bed of convalescence, eating bread and jam. He moved some dirty pyjamas off a chair by the bed and she sat down. He showed her how, from his window, he could see a house across the road where another student lived. He keeps having his girl friend in, said Louis, and his bed is just under the window and you can see her legs kicking in the air. 'Actually you're smaller than I am,' added Louis. 'You'd probably have to stand on a chair.'

'It doesn't matter,' said Emma. 'So you watch?'

'What else can I do?' asked Louis. 'All that's left for me is artistic withdrawal. The truth about the artist is that he takes his tranquillity along with him everywhere he goes; he is recollecting even as he acts. His acts are of a different sort from other people's. I envy him, over there.'

'Why?' asked Emma.

'You know why. A man needs a nice woman.'

'Please, Louis, I thought we'd finished with all that.'

'I thought you'd bring that up,' said Louis. 'I wanted to apologize. You saved my life, too.'

'I didn't save your life,' said Emma.

'Yes, you did, and I shall never forget it.'

'Well, I shall,' said Emma.

'I shall never forgive myself for the way I behaved.'

'You will,' said Emma. 'Somehow.'

This was dishonest, Emma saw; he was trying to work her into some position in which they were firmly entangled, some vague emotional complex on which he could build, and she determined to resist with all her might. He began to speak of her as honest and virtuous, and this gave her her chance, and she did a stupid thing: she told him about her affair with Stuart Treece. It was an absurd cruelty, but then someone had to pay for the moral damage caused, and who could it be but Louis?

6

As the days wore on Treece found that the objectivity he had always possessed, the faculty he had for seeing himself as an actor in a play by some outsider, the faculty that looked down upon himself judiciously and thought of *other* ways to behave, began to fail under his current pressure. He ceased to be inquisitive object and began to be suffering subject. This was happening to him; the pain was his and soon it would be all of him. The experimental character of the whole incident, which had given it an interest for Treece and made it just bearable, now began to fade. He lay in bed, reading nothing; he fed; he moved his bowels. Moving the bowels was, so to speak, the breath of life for him, the real truth about existence, a dramatization of the emotional and intellectual processes that preserve us to go on living.

One night, about eleven, when the ward was dark, an emergency case was brought in. Doctors rushed about and telephoned for other doctors, and in the darkness Treece could hear a low, insistent voice behind the screens asking, over and over again, 'What did you take? What did you take?'

In the morning the would-be suicide behind the screens was visited by a policeman, and later by a psychiatrist from another hospital, a stout, sleek German who could be heard all over the ward.

'Why you take all these aspirins?' There was an inaudible reply, and the psychiatrist laughed. 'Toothache? I will promise you, you will not have toothache again for ten more years. You were anxious. You were depressed. Why? Was it about the world in general? About your own personal state? Did you want to kill yourself or just make a big demonstration? It says here you left a note. Did you know you would be found so quick? You must answer me, now, or I can do nothing at all for you. I am your friend.' The weak voice spoke again. 'You haven't any friends at *all*? I do not believe. Now, tell me, why did you not cut your throat? That would have been quicker, yes? Why not? I am afraid aspirins are not a good way. Did you know this? You must tell me these things. I am here to help you. Very well, I do not think this is a very difficult case. I think we understand him from what he does not say. Now, tell me, when you go down the street you hear these voices, yes? They are muttering obscenities, yes?'

'No,' cried the voice, audible for the first time. 'No voices.'

'But surely you hear some voices occasionally? I am a psychiatrist. I do not think I'm mistaken. . . .' 'You are,' said the voice.

The psychiatrist ended his horrifying bravura and went away; and later in the morning the screens about the new patient were removed. There, in a crib bed with iron bars at either side, with the rubber end of a stomach pump coming from his nose and plastered to the side of his face, was Louis Bates. Treece looked and looked again, and was sure. He asked a nurse and was confirmed. He tried to attract Bates's attention, but he was now sleeping. He was woken for his lunch, but would eat nothing and reverted to sleep again. In the afternoon Treece himself fell asleep for two hours, and when he was woken for his tea the top bed was empty and Louis Bates was gone. He called a nurse and asked where the patient had been taken. 'He's been moved to another hospital,' said the nurse. 'Which?' asked Treece. 'Don't ask so many questions,' said the nurse.

In the evening Emma came, and he told her about Bates. But she knew, and she knew something that Treece suspected but could not learn: that Bates had been moved to a mental hospital. He had been in such a hospital before, the sister had told them.

'It's terrible; it's all my fault,' said Emma, and she began to cry. 'Think of him locked away in there, for how long? Perhaps for ever.'

'We'll get him out,' said Treece confidently, though here what could he do? 'It might be better for him too in one respect; he may not have to stand trial.'

'Trial?' cried Emma. 'What for?'

'Attempted suicide.'

'Do they try people for that?'

'Yes, they do.'

'But that's shocking,' said Emma. 'Doesn't it shock you?' Treece said that it did. 'I don't understand it,' said Emma. 'This is a free country. Surely you can do what you like with your own life?'

'No, that's simply not true; you can't,' said Treece. 'I think it's legally assumed that every sane person must want to continue living, and therefore suicide is considered as an aberration, and one punishable by law.'

'It was all my fault,' said Emma tearfully.

'Why was it all your fault?'

'I made him do it. I went to see him. I told him what he was, how people saw him. I told him about us, you and me, what we did. I said he was other people's scapegoat, you know, a whipping-boy, the one they spanked when the prince was naughty so that wrong shouldn't go unpunished. I was absurd. I said all artists were like that. I said he should be pleased, not sorry. I said artists were the ones who felt the malice and

247

frenzy of the universe for all the rest of us, and that it was in a sense a favour as well as a cruelty. I told him perhaps he was lucky. He didn't have to live with his own crimes. He simply suffered for other people's. You know the poem: "See the scapegoat, happy beast, From every personal sin released." I told him that.' She put her head down on the bed and cried. 'And then I gave him some money. His clothes were ruined when he was in the river. I gave him twenty pounds and told him to buy a suit. I said it was the least the world could do for him, at least if the world made its artists suffer then there ought to be a levy. At least the whipping-boy got *paid*, and fed, and clothed.' She stopped and looked at Treece. 'I never thought he'd do *this*. You see, I couldn't love him; people couldn't. There were other women like me who thought this. I respected him, but not, you know, really love. And he had to know, really, or he would never have gone right. I said how much I respected him. I said it was only the uncommitted ones who could see the real tragedy and the real horror and the real excellence too. The others might hang on for a while, but they sell out in the end. And it's for them that the rebels sacrifice themselves.' She looked at Treece again and hoped he would absolve her. He listened and could not. It was his wound, as well, that the knife was being twisted in.

A bell rang and it was time for her to go. 'Take care of yourself,' said Treece. 'Don't *you* get in here; I'm running out of patience.'

'It's like Haydn's "Farewell" Symphony in reverse,' said Emma, wiping her eyes with a handkerchief.

'Come again,' said Treece.

'Very well,' said Emma.

'I feel guilty about him too,' said Treece. 'Guilty's all you can feel. I suppose all you can say for us is, at least we can feel guilty.'

She went away and he lay there in his bed, and felt as though this would be his condition for evermore, and that from this he would never, never escape.

*Some new Penguin books, mainly
by young writers are described
on the following pages*

CIDER WITH ROSIE
Laurie Lee

1682

Cider with Rosie puts on record the England we have traded for the petrol engine. Recalling life in a remote Cotswold village nearly forty years ago, Laurie Lee conveys the semi-peasant spirit of a thousand-years-old tradition.

'This poet, whose prose is quick and bright as a snake ... a gay, impatient, jaunty and in parts slightly mocking book; a prose poem that flashes and winks like a prism' – H. E. Bates in the *Sunday Times*

'He is like nobody else in the book world. The story of his childhood rings as true and as lingeringly as the bells of the village which he describes so vividly' – Richard Church in the *Evening Standard*

'A first-rate work of art' – Harold Nicolson in the *Observer*

Laurie Lee won the annual W. H. Smith £1,000 Literary Award with this book.

THE HIDING PLACE

Robert Shaw

1673

'Odd, off-beat, queerly haunting ... an exciting new talent' – Peter Green in the *Daily Telegraph*

There are echoes of the strange personal world of Franz Kafka in the pages of this remarkable novel. The central idea, and the detailed development of that idea, are so original and so masterly that attention is gripped from the start.

In a cellar in Bonn two British airmen, rescued from a lynching mob after parachuting down from their crippled Lancaster, are kept in chains by a half-mad German for years after the war has ended. The way in which they people their cell with fantasies and memories from the past, their manacled relationship with their gaoler, Hans Frick, the vital contrast between their characters – such is the material from which Robert Shaw constructs an extraordinary story in which the interest is always alive. The eventual solution is worked out with unexpected pathos and irony.

'The work of a real writer ... particularly good ... one of the most original novels of the year' – John Davenport in the *Observer*

A HIGH-PITCHED BUZZ
Roger Longrigg
1676

Roger Longrigg's first novel displays, as the *Scotsman* said, 'a devastatingly accurate ear for dialogue'. Against the background of a world he knows intimately – the bad-lands of Mayfair and the bandit-ridden territory of adver-tising – his story moves at a pace which is rare in a young writer. Amid a high-pitched buzz of bluff and chatter we watch the West End world go by in a pageant of fairly bright young men and shop-soiled girls, elbowing their way forward in what has been called the 'mouse-race'. Yet the central 'I' character holds us with his buoyant charm and, though he may appal us by his mishandling of true love, never quite forfeits our sympathy.

'A first novel that is intelligent, highly amusing, well shaped and something more than promising' – *Sphere*

'Brimming with talent' – *New Statesman*

'Sharply observed, unpretentious, and possessed of a positively terrier-like charm' – *Daily Telegraph*

THE TEACHERS

G. W. Target

1675

The Teachers aroused comment and controversy, on its
first publication, in both the religious and scholastic press.
This powerful novel exposes sadism and immorality
lurking behind the professional masks of the characters,
who are members of the staff of an imaginary London
primary school. With a technique which is reminiscent
of James Joyce, the author covers the events of one day
in the life of the school with consecutive accounts of the
movements of each teacher, recounted in the appropriate
language. It is no ordinary day : during the night one of
the classrooms has been wrecked and filthily defiled. In
their attempts to discover the culprits the teachers are
forced to examine the effects of their own conduct anew.

'The total effect has both a savage intensity and an
immense charity which makes it a book you cannot
forget' – *Guardian*

WITHIN AND WITHOUT
John Harvey
1672

'It has freshness and the real tone of the generation it's about' – *Spectator*

In his first novel John Harvey tells, in the first person, the story of a love affair and a stark betrayal. By its ruthless honesty the account catches some of the force of *Room at the Top*.

'This first novel is a remarkably true and fine description of young love' – George Millar in the *Daily Express*

'The love scenes have a sensuous accuracy rare in English fiction' – John Davenport in the *Observer*

'Beautifully observed, sparsely written, full of promise'
– *Evening Standard*

JACK WOULD BE A GENTLEMAN

Gillian Freeman

1671

' "D'yer think I'm bloody well made of money?" Jack Prosser stared angrily at his wife, then at his children and finally at the veneered television squatting on the television table.' And then a few days later: 'The pools man drew off one leather glove and wrung Jack's hand enthusiastically. "Not a bad sum, Mr Prosser. You've won fifty thousand pounds." '

In this way Gillian Freeman, whose understanding of the working class was so brilliantly demonstrated in *The Liberty Man*, plunges the Prossers into wealth. It is a situation we have all dreamed about. And here you can read how it worked out for Jack, the housepainter, for his discontented wife, and for their son and daughter.

'Quite out of the ordinary' – *Sunday Times*

'Miss Freeman writes with uncommon ease and emancipation' – *Guardian*

'Most sensitively and sympathetically done' – *Observer*

NOT FOR SALE IN THE U.S.A.